GNOME MA

When she looked down aga on the edge of some trees ma facing her, and seemed to actually be *looking* at her. It had *not* been there just a moment ago. Someone had to be up here with her, trying to freak her out.

"Who's out there? I'm serious, I'm going to call the cops unless you come out right now and cut it out!" She glanced over her shoulder...when she heard what sounded like something heavy rustling against grass. Right next to her. She slowly turned her head, keeping her eyes on the ground. There were boots, standing right in front of her. They were thick, pitted leather, with some sort of metal on the toes; something more like what Frankenstein's monster would wear than a person. Pure terror clutched her. Her breathing changed; short and stuttered. She started to raise her eyes, going from the boots up. Heavy trousers, ripped and spattered with mud and other...substances. A wide leather belt, kind of like what bodybuilders would wear, with an empty sheath as long as her forearm hanging off it. Poking underneath the belt was a tunic, the same disgusting fabric as the trousers. Finally, she saw the face, towering a full head over her. It looked like an old man, with mottled, out-of-proportion features. A full beard, soiled with bits of food and other fluids. What made her finally gasp were his eyes; they were like two chunks of coal stuck into his eyesockets, but she knew that they were staring right back at her. On top of the...thing's head was a red hat, and the end of it was dripping sticky, dark-red, clotted fluid down the side of the thing's face.

Staci couldn't even scream. Her mind was completely blank with terror. She watched with sick detachment as it raised an apelike, ropey and muscular arm above its head; a jagged and heavily nicked blade was nested in its meaty fist.

She was going to die. Her last thought as the knife came down was that she wouldn't have a chance to see Sean again.

SILENCE

A Novel of the
SERRAted Edge

MERCEDES LACKEY
CODY MARTIN

A Baen Books Original

Baen Publishing Enterprises
P.O. Box 1403
Riverdale, NY 10471
www.baen.com

ISBN: 978-1-4814-8240-0

Cover art by Larry Dixon

First paperback printing, April 2017

Library of Congress Control Number: 2015049954

Distributed by Simon & Schuster
1230 Avenue of the Americas
New York, NY 10020

Pages by Joy Freeman (www.pagesbyjoy.com)
Printed in the United States of America

To David Bowie:

Farewell Major Tom

CHAPTER ONE

The shabby front porch of the run-down little wood-sided house was already full of boxes stacked four high, but Staci's dad was bringing another load up from the rental van parked at the curb. At this rate, there might not be enough room to get in the front door.

He just can't get rid of me fast enough, she thought, her eyes stinging with the tears she refused to shed in front of him. She knew that he didn't mean to hurt her, not really. He had always been such a nice man . . . and that was the problem, she supposed. Her parents had been divorced for a number of years at this point; once her mother developed her "habits" there was no more to be done to keep the marriage together. So, Staci had elected to stay with her father in New York City; she would visit her mother during the summers when she had her life together enough to take care of Staci for two or three months, but she had seldom managed to keep up the good behavior for the full season. Staci was usually back in New York before the end of August, more often than not leaving her mother sleeping off her latest drunk.

"Dad, there's no room!" she said desperately. "Can't we wait until Mom gets home so we can—"

"I've got to get the van back to the rental before five o'clock," her father interrupted. He was trying to stay chipper, but it was all clearly forced. He didn't dare meet her eyes as he continued to unload. "If we don't get it back there before then, we'll get hit with late fees." This *we* did not include Staci, of course. *We* meant Dad and Brenda, and Brenda was the one who had arranged the rental in the first place.

Of course late fees would be unacceptable. Brenda, Staci's new stepmother, wouldn't approve.

Staci had wished for years for her father to find someone that he could be happy with. For a time, it was just him and her; when she was younger, she imagined just the two of them having adventures together forever. He had always been kind and patient with her, even doting at times. As Staci grew older, she started to notice the sad looks and the heavy sighs, always followed by a smile. She knew that he needed someone. Then, two years ago, he had started dating Brenda.

She had seemed so nice; she'd seemed interested in Staci, even going so far as to buy her clothing, movies and music she actually liked. She was pretty, blond, and very ambitious for Staci's dad's career, as opposed to what Staci remembered *her* mom being like—always complaining that Dad spent too much time at the firm, and "they never had fun anymore." "Fun" being going out to bars and drinking half the night, so far as Staci could tell. Staci had worried briefly about where Brenda's son Tommy was going to fit when the two started talking marriage—Tommy was a spoiled little shit, and she couldn't imagine him doing without his own room—but then she just assumed they'd move somewhere else. Somewhere bigger. After all, why not? In fact, she'd started to look *forward* to that, browsing through apartment listings for newer (much newer), brighter buildings. Places that had been renovated some time in *this* century. The whispered conversations about "rent-controlled diamonds" had just whizzed over her head.

Now, of course, she understood. Dad had inherited his rent-controlled apartment from *his* parents, and you couldn't lease a broom closet in New York City for what he was paying for the place she had called home all her life. All this had been carefully explained to her. Along with lines like "we can't possibly afford Tommy's school if we live here" and "you'll love living in Maine; you'll have so much more room!"

After the shock of what was coming had worn off, Staci had tried to talk, even plead with her father. But, he was such a nice man ... and Brenda had him wrapped around her little finger, completely. Lately, when he had tried to reassure her that this was for the best, it sounded like he was trying to convince himself a little bit, as well. *New wife, new family, new life. Out with the old ... me.*

Dad managed to wedge another stack of boxes onto the porch, though the wood planks underfoot groaned in protest. The view from the porch wasn't anything to inspire confidence in this "wonderful new life." This was a street of identical wooden houses, most of them painted in colors of faded gray or dirty white, most of them needing a coat of paint they obviously were not going to get. Dad had enthused about "genuine New England saltbox homes" but all Staci saw was the general air of decrepitude. The sidewalk was cracked, the street had potholes and lumps, and the grass, trees and shrubs all looked unkempt and ragged. Dad had used words like "rustic" and "old-fashioned" to describe the neighborhood on the drive in. Staci had a few different, less flattering words in mind. "Shantytown" sprang to mind....

Silence, Maine was too small to actually have a slum, but this part of town would have counted for being "on the wrong side of the tracks" if the place had actually had tracks running through it. Staci had never actually been here before; her mother had moved (abruptly, as she always did) around the first of this year. Now she had to wonder what had driven Mom to move *here* in the first place. If you were looking for a place to have a good time in—which was all Mom was ever interested in—this sure wasn't it. Aside from the crying of gulls, the only sounds in this neighborhood were the ones she and Dad were making.

"There we go, this is the last!" Dad said cheerfully, somehow managing to get the last stack of boxes onto the porch without blocking the door. "I've got to move if I'm going to get the van back in time!" He let go of the dolly, made an air kiss in the direction of her cheek, and practically ran back to the van. "Have fun settling in, kiddo!"

And before she could voice so much as a word of protest, he had started the van and was driving off down the street. She hadn't cried in front of her father; there had been no time, with everything moving so quickly. But she did cry now. There was no one to see her do it, besides. She collapsed on the sagging steps and sobbed into her hands until her eyes were sore and her nose plugged up. When she finally ran out of energy to even cry, she checked her watch. It wasn't even noon yet; her mother wasn't due home from her job for at least another five or six hours. Maybe more.

She pulled out her cell phone. At least she could get some sympathy from her friends—

But there were *no* bars on the phone. She stared at it in disbelief. How could there be *no* cell phone service?

Maybe the phone was broken. She tried calling a number, hitting one from her list at random.

Nothing. No ringtone. No dial tone. Not even an "out of service" signal. She broke down all over again.

Since there had been nothing else to do, she'd managed to get the boxes into the house by herself. She'd considered leaving them there, but Mom would be no help at all, she already knew that, and this was a pretty sketchy-looking neighborhood. So she managed to unlock the door with the key that Mom had sent her, and wrestle them all into what passed for a living room. There was plenty of space in there, anyway; there was nothing but an old TV that wasn't even an LCD screen, but an ugly tube thing, a saggy old sofa concealed by what looked like a threadbare bedspread, and a couple of mismatched, third-hand chairs. One was covered in a hideous blue-and-beige print, the other in faux leather, cracked and with tufts of something coming out at the corners. By that time she was starving, but a quick look in the fridge showed nothing but a lot of diet drink meals, some diet soda, a bottle of vodka, and a pepperoni pizza that was so dry that it had to be a week old.

Her father had shoved a bank envelope into the pocket of her jacket before they'd gotten out of the van. She hadn't looked at it yet. *I might as well head into town and try to find something to eat; I'll be on my own for dinner, anyways.* Her mother wasn't very big on home-cooked meals; Chinese takeout, delivery pizza, and frozen dinners were the norm whenever Staci had stayed with her in the past. This town wasn't *that* big, and she was used to walking. New Yorkers were; they walked to the subway, walked to the bus, walked to the *bodega* or another corner store, walked to local eateries and coffee shops, walked up and down stairs a lot; even her dad, a lawyer, didn't have his own car. That was, in no small part, because parking spots cost as much as apartments. She locked the door carefully behind herself, shoved her hands in her pockets, and went looking for whatever passed for a "downtown" here.

It was supposed to be the beginning of summer, but you wouldn't have been able to tell by the weather. It was overcast, chilly, and everything was damp from the barest drizzle of rain. A couple of times a minute, gusts of wind would tug at her hair and jacket, making her shiver and want to turn around and go back to the house, which at least was warm. But she had started out hungry and now was starving, and trying to make something edible out of that dead pizza wasn't going to happen. All of the trees were barely greening up and still shedding dead leaves, which were sticking to her boots as she trudged towards the center of town. She didn't see very many people out and about; who would want to do much of anything in this kind of weather?

I guess the likeliest place for downtown would be near the water? They hadn't passed through anything she recognized as a city center when they'd driven in here, but then, her dad had been following directions on the van's GPS, and they'd come in from the west. She squinted up at the sky, and guessed at "east" by the pale ball of the sun behind the dead gray clouds.

She walked for about ten blocks, and the only reason she realized she *was* downtown, was because what she had taken for houses had signs over their doors, big glass windows, and there were some old cars parked out front. Oh, and when she stopped and stared in partial disbelief, she saw there weren't even the sparse patches of grass that passed for a front lawn in her mom's neighborhood. Which wasn't unlike the neighborhood she had lived in back home, except that these were all house-sized and -shaped buildings, rather than being multistoried places that might have businesses on the ground floor but were all apartments above.

Maybe her mom didn't live in a sketchy neighborhood after all. These buildings were just as faded, and just as much in need of paint, as back there. Once, the colors might have been bright, especially the ones that had been painted barn-red, but not anymore.

She peered down the street, looking in vain for anything she recognized, but there wasn't even a McDonald's or a Starbucks. She hunched her shoulders against the wind and headed for a worn "Sinclair" sign, which looked like one that hadn't been changed since the '50s. But there should be a mini-mart at least, right?

Wrong. Four pumps, and a two-bay garage, with a pop machine and a candy-bar machine. Both looked like antiques. She shuddered to think how long it must have been since either were stocked, and what might be in them, and kept going. The signs were swaying in the wind, and without familiar logos on them, it was hard to tell what they were for until she was right on top of them. It was disorienting, actually. She'd never been in a place that had so little that was recognizable before. The last town Mom had landed in had been nothing *but* franchises and box-stores, with a liberal peppering of liquor stores and tattoo parlors in between.

She studied the signs as she passed under them. A hardware store, with dust-covered stuff in the window that looked as if it hadn't been changed in years. "Dry Goods?" What was that? There was fabric and sewing stuff in the window...but why wasn't it called a fabric or craft store? A post office. A lawyer, the windows painted black with gold lettering. "Package Goods" turned out to be a liquor store.

Finally, *finally*, "Giuseppe's Pizzeria." It was probably the same place the mummified pie in the fridge had come from. The cardboard sign in the door was turned to OPEN, and although she couldn't see inside thanks to the red-and-white checkerboard of paint on the bottom half of the window, the window itself looked clean and the sidewalk and cement step had been swept. The paint was faded, but at least it wasn't peeling and cracked. She pushed the door open; an actual *bell* got tripped and jingled as she went inside.

There were four little round-topped tables, with plastic tablecloths in red-and-white check on them, and uncomfortable-looking wooden chairs painted white around them. At the rear was a brown wood counter, with nobody behind it, but the sound of the bell must have alerted the owner, because he came in through a door with a curtain over it that was behind the counter, wiping his hands on a towel. He was a worn-looking man with gray threads in his hair, in a checked flannel shirt with an apron over it. Both looked second-hand, but they were clean, at least, as was the "dining room."

"What can I do for you?" he asked, in that accent that she associated with Maine from TV programs.

"I'm starving," she said. "What's fast to make?"

"Calzone," he replied, gesturing at the hand-painted price-board on the wall behind him. "Ten minutes." She searched in vain for something like salad or even pasta. Nothing. Calzone, pizza, garlic bread, and drinks were all that were offered. With a sigh, she dug the bank envelope out of her pocket and extracted a twenty. "Cheese and mushroom calzone, a cola, and a large pizza to go," she said. "Mushrooms, olives, peppers, tomatoes." That was going to be the closest she was going to get to anything healthy, it appeared. "Can I have the cola now?" The sugar would probably stop her stomach from growling.

"Coming right up, miss. Find a seat wherever you like while you wait."

Staci picked a table by the window; it was the most well-lit spot in the entire restaurant, even with the checker paint covering the lower part of the window. She kept trying with her cell phone to find a signal; nothing here either. At least the smells coming from the unseen kitchen were nice. After all these years of spending summers with Mom, Staci had a good nose for awful grease-bomb food. A survival tactic, as it were.

She was trying to access her Facebook newsfeed for the umpteenth time when she heard it. Something in the distance, moving closer. A deep, guttural *thrum* sound. As it came closer, it started to vibrate the windows slightly. Staci couldn't help herself; she stood up from her seat, almost knocking the chair over. She had to stand on her tiptoes in order to see over the paint on the windows. The rumble suddenly became louder . . . and a blinding light rounded the corner of the street, three blocks down. It took a few moments for her eyes to adjust; strange, given that the sky still seemed overcast. After a few moments, she saw what the limited sunlight was reflecting off of. It was chrome, and big, and loud. An exotic motorcycle, but perfectly maintained. She couldn't place what kind it was; her father had always read motorcycle and hot rod magazines, wishing for toys that he couldn't afford, so she had become fairly adept at recognizing makes and models. The only thing that she was sure of was that it was a cruiser, and it was beautiful.

The man riding it, however, was absolutely breath-taking. He looked to be anywhere from his late teens to his mid-twenties. He wasn't wearing a helmet; all the better, because it allowed his nearly shoulder-length blond hair to catch the wind. He had high, good cheekbones, and a strong if slightly pointed chin, lightly colored with a tasteful amount of stubble. He was tall, with a lean physique; even that much was apparent past the black biker jacket, low-cut white T-shirt, and blue jeans. Instead of a helmet, he was wearing a pair of dark goggles. Every part of him looked like he was cut from marble, a living artwork, fit to be on a Hollywood screen. When the man turned his head for a moment in her direction, she could've sworn that he was looking at her... with the goggles on it was impossible to tell, of course, but her heart stopped all the same.

A moment later, and he was past the window, and the pizza man was coming out from behind the counter with her calzone on a paper plate, with a second can of cola for her. He glanced out the window; the motorcycle's engine was still shaking the glass a little. "Hooligans," he grumbled. "Girls should stay away from guys like that. They're nothing but trouble and heartbreak."

She sat down as he returned to the kitchen. He didn't seem to need a reply, so she began eating the calzone. It wasn't the best she'd ever had, even with her hunger that would usually make cardboard appealing, but it was by no means the worst. She was about halfway done with it when the man came back with a plain, unprinted pizza box, and set it on the chair across from her.

Of all the places where her mom had landed, this had to be, by far, the worst. Unless there was something more, better, down by the waterfront... which didn't seem likely. The entire town seemed frozen in 1950. Not being able to get a cell phone signal was making her feel as if her right hand had been cut off—no, more as if she had been abandoned somewhere in some foreign country.

What am I going to do if my cell won't work? She hadn't seen anything like a cell tower. . . .

The town itself was bad enough. Not being able to even vent to her friends was much, much worse. Over the years, between her father and her friends, she thought that she could handle anything. Now... both were gone. What was she going to do?

Can I even get Internet? What am I going to do without Internet?

It was like Dad—or, rather, Brenda—had purposefully chosen this place to cut her off from everyone.

I've got to get back home, somehow. I'll be eighteen in two years, and they won't be able to stop me leaving. I can go anywhere I want!

For a moment she fantasized about getting back to New York, finding a job, maybe in a cute little boutique, getting her own place....

But then reality hit her with the last bite of her calzone which stuck for a moment in her throat. All that yammering about how important that rent-controlled apartment was... Brenda had hammered that home again and again, with stories about how the mailroom kids where she worked were jammed in six together in a one-room walkup. Staci had never held a job, ever. How could she get one on her own, much less one that would let her even make enough money to share a place with four or five other roommates? Her friends were all going to college soon enough. None of them were going to have to worry about staying in the city, getting jobs and paying through the nose just to live.

I'm going to be stuck here forever... By the time she was eighteen, Dad wouldn't have any more legal obligations to her—Brenda had made that crystal clear—so by that time, Brenda would probably have programmed him out of the idea of paying for any college. And Staci didn't have any idea what she'd do at college anyway. She had always done well enough in school; no real extracurricular activities, and she hadn't been a math-lete, but she had kept her grade average up so far. But there just wasn't anything she was particularly good at, or anything she really wanted to do. By now, she was supposed to be figuring out what the rest of her life would be like; what she would major in, what college she would go to; her entire life path. Except . . . nothing really appealed. And right now, it didn't look like anything mattered, either. If Brenda talked Dad out of supplying college money—and she would, Staci had no doubt of that at this point—just how would she even have enough for a couple classes at a community college, much less a real college? So why even bother to plan?

She had already paid the man, and he was out of sight in the kitchen anyway, so she picked up the pizza box and left. There was no sign of the boy or his motorcycle anywhere. For some reason everything seemed darker and more gloomy because of that. The street was back to being gray and bleak and unwelcoming. She trudged back to the house with her shoulders hunched against the wind, trying not to cry.

She threw the zombie pizza out and put the new one in the fridge, and explored the house. It was probably the biggest house Mom had ever lived in; downstairs there was the living room, a dining room, the kitchen, a pantry, and a bedroom with a bath that were obviously Mom's. Clothes strewn everywhere, bed unmade, sheets hung up at the window instead of curtains, makeup scattered all over the bathroom.

Upstairs there were four bedrooms with a bath, and a pull-down staircase into an attic. She picked the one room that had a bed and a couple of Goodwill chests of drawers in it. It had one window that looked east; you could see the ocean and docks, and from here, you could tell that the whole town was built on a hill that slanted down to the coast. The bed was pretty awful: white-painted cast iron, with a set of exposed springs and a lumpy mattress. Mom had left some mismatched sheets and blankets on top of it. With a sigh, she began bringing boxes upstairs and unpacking.

A lot of stuff she couldn't unpack; there was no place for anything to go but her clothes. She discovered that Brenda had packed up *everything*, including the curtains from her old bedroom. Which was pretty mean in principle, but welcome right now. At least she had something to put up on the windows to keep the sun and peeping toms out. She prowled the house looking for a sign of a cable. Nothing. No Internet router either. Just the TV, which had two dials, one with twelve channels, which must be VHF, and one with a lot of channels. And a radio. Her mother probably didn't have much home time to appreciate television; between her drunks and her hangovers, she was most likely out of it most of the time.

She turned on the radio, which got one channel, the rest being static. When she tuned into it, the station was playing "Hotel California," which seemed all too prophetic. *"You can check out any time you like, but you can never leave."*

She turned it off and tried the TV and got just one channel again. The show on was a woman showing how to make planters out of coffee cans. Some sort of public-access, she guessed. Staci turned it off, and turned the radio back on, just to have some sound in the house. Mom still was a no-show, which meant she was probably still working and knowing her, she'd segue from "working" to "drinking" and not come back until the bar closed, having completely forgotten Staci was supposed to be here today.

Staci heated up some of the pizza and ate that for supper, washing it down with one of the diet drinks. Then, since there didn't seem to be anything else to do, she watched a couple movies on her laptop, making the best of a bad bed with the throw pillows and cushions from her old room. Eventually she got tired enough that she closed the laptop up and fell asleep.

At some point she woke up, startled awake by the slamming of the front door, hearing her mom singing at the top of lungs. She thought about going downstairs and letting her mom know she was there—

Why bother? She won't notice me, or she won't remember in the morning.

So she rolled over, hugged a pillow tightly to herself, and cried herself to sleep.

CHAPTER TWO

The curtains weren't thick enough to block out the morning light. Staci's old room in New York had faced a building; this window faced due east. She woke up a lot earlier than she usually did on a Saturday, but she had gone to bed so much earlier than she usually did on Friday night that it didn't seem to matter. For a moment, she was disoriented. The bed was hard and creaked, not like her bed, and the walls were some faded flower wallpaper—and the smells were all wrong. Then she remembered, and wanted to cry. She was stuck in Nowheresville. She could hear someone stumbling around downstairs. Mom, of course.

She pulled on some clothing and got ready in the little bathroom. It actually was a bit better than the one back in the old apartment, which hadn't been updated since maybe the 1920s. This one had at least gotten new plumbing and a proper shower around the '50s. None of the upkeep of her old bathroom, though. After all, Mom couldn't afford a housecleaner twice weekly; she wasn't exactly the "homemaker" sort, either. *I guess I'm going to have to do all the cleaning too.* Ugh, and so *unfair.*

From the sound of things, her mom was rattling around in the kitchen. And sure enough, when Staci poked her nose in there, Mom was staring at the coffee maker as if she had never seen one before, still with a bed-head, wrapped up in a fuzzy magenta robe.

She turned at the sound of Staci's footsteps, and it was clear she was hung over. Her eyes were bloodshot, and not quite focusing, her forehead showed headache lines, her brows furrowed. And to clinch the diagnosis, there was a bottle of aspirin in one hand. She looked at Staci blankly for just a second, as if she didn't remember who her own daughter was.

Then her face cleared. "Oh hi, honey," she said. At least her speech wasn't slurred, so she was hung over, not still-drunk. "When did you get here?"

"Lunchtime yesterday," Staci said, as her mother put down the aspirin and rummaged in the fridge.

"Well, there's pizza and beer if you want breakfast." It took her a moment before Staci realized that her mother was serious. Rather than actually getting anything, her mother closed the fridge door and went back to filling and starting the coffee maker. "I was going to go back to bed; I'm on at four, and I worked a double yesterday, I'm beat."

Mom, you've flipped out. You just offered your sixteen-year-old daughter cold pizza and beer for breakfast. Staci had thought her mother couldn't get any worse the last time she'd visited, but . . . well, this was the first time she'd ever offered Staci booze when she was sober. She was, somehow, much, *much* worse than Staci had ever seen her before. Silence, evidently, was not good for her. . . .

Whatever happened to my real mom? she thought

in despair. Before the divorce, her mother had always seemed more of a free spirit than a wackaloon. She would always have a game to play, or a story to tell; about heroes and villains, creatures that could do impossible things and wondrous realms that those things inhabited. Stories with princesses named Staci who were able to save *themselves*, thank you very much, and who didn't *need* handsome princes to bail them out when the monsters came. But of course, there were handsome princes too, they just didn't get to do *all* the adventuring. There was no sign of that happy, spirited mom in this...thing...that was sitting at the kitchen table.

Staci wanted to cry again, but instead she settled for anger. "I'm going out. I'll find something in town."

"Okay, honey, have fun." Her mother flapped a hand at her and wandered back out. There was a Mason jar full of money in the middle of the table— the tip money from her mother's job. Staci grabbed a handful. *No way am I spending any more of my money,* she thought angrily. *Besides, if it's not here, she won't drink it.*

Today was just like yesterday: overcast, damp and chilly. She went back upstairs and pulled a hoodie on over the rest of her clothes before going out. Uphill seemed to be all houses, with a couple bigger buildings. At least one was obviously a church, complete with steeple with a cross on top—fairly rundown-looking all in all. Downhill had led to the pizza joint yesterday, so maybe there would be more stores in that direction.

The pizza joint was closed. The cardboard flip-sign on the door said it didn't open until one; she didn't feel like she could wait for it to open. She trudged down the cracked sidewalk, still not finding anything with food. Antique shops, Goodwill, Salvation Army, St. Vincent De Paul's...actually as far as she could tell, the antique stores had pretty much the same stuff as the three thrift stores, except the antique stores didn't have clothes. This was supposed to be a town with about 25,000 people in it. So far all she had seen were her mom, the pizza guy, a fleeting glimpse of a couple of people inside the storefronts and the motorcycle guy, passing through.

What a lousy, gross town. Even the people that live here don't want to be seen here.

She turned a corner at random. This, clearly, was not the scenic, quaint, fun little tourist town that her father had described for her. She'd been to one of those with Dad and Brenda in the fun days before Brenda had gotten what she wanted—a wedding ring. There had been neat boutiques, shops with interesting stuff in them, lots and lots of cafes, lots of real antique stores. Not like this. Dusty windows with merch in them that looked like it hadn't been changed in decades, and nothing she even wanted to *look* at, much less buy.

Staci started daydreaming about running away, going back to New York City or maybe even hitchhiking all the way west, see how California would work out... She was in the middle of wondering how she'd do in the California sun when she realized that she had no clue where she was anymore. All of the buildings had started to run together for her; everything was grimy and old...and she couldn't see any landmarks from the side street she was on, and the buildings were so close together, the street so narrow, that she couldn't see uphill or down, just the buildings around her.

Just when Staci was starting to panic, a man lurched out of the alleyway to her left, nearly knocking into her. She didn't quite scream, but she did squeak loudly, throwing her hands up to keep her balance. Strong hands grabbed her by the shoulders, and her mind went blank; she thought she was about to be mugged, or worse...when the man spoke.

"Hey, it's okay. Didn't mean to scare you, kid. Are you all right?" He let her go as soon as she had regained her balance and stepped back a pace or two, holding his hands out to the side in a non-threatening position. That was when she realized she'd seen him before.

It was the guy from yesterday who'd been riding that gorgeous motorcycle. Up close he was even hotter than he had been riding by—which wasn't always the case. Some guys kind of faded when they weren't on their bikes.

He definitely looked rough; not in a dirty way, but tough, what her dad would call "school of hard knocks," competent, sure of himself. He carried himself easily, and wasn't that menacing close up. What really got her were his eyes. For a moment she thought that they were fake. But only a moment, until she saw the light in them. They were almost literally perfect; no discoloration, no red lines; just two irises that were a shocking electric blue. And they were staring right at her. "Haven't seen you around here before." He added, "I'm Dylan."

Of course you are, she thought, a little dazzled. Then she collected herself. "I'm Anastasia Kerry, but my friends call me Staci. I just moved here yesterday. With my mom. She's a waitress at the Rusty Bucket."

"Okay, so you're Paula Kerry's gal." She felt a surge of dismay that he knew her mom's name, which meant he must know at least something about her, and—she flushed with embarrassment. Her mom never had a good reputation. He crossed his arms and leaned against the side of the alley he had surprised her from. "What're you doing in this part of town? Bucket closed a while ago." He had this little half-smile on his lips that kept on distracting her, making her trip over her own thoughts.

"I was looking for someplace to get breakfast," she confessed. *Is this where Mom works? Somewhere around here?*

He chuckled to himself. "You're definitely in the wrong place, then. Unless you've got a hankering for bait. Hardware store sells worms and some old shoe leather that they call 'beef jerky.'"

"What are you doing in this part of town? Besides scaring girls."

Dylan regarded her for a moment, that same smile on his face. "I parked my bike back there," he said, jerking a thumb over his shoulder. "Figured that I would take in the morning air on a walk." He looked up and down the street, pausing. "You know, I'm heading down towards the docks; that should be your best bet for finding some food. Want me to show you how to get there?"

The hottest guy I've seen all year, let alone here, is offering to walk me to breakfast . . . New York smarts would have said, "Ask him for directions, and let him wander off." But this wasn't New York. And he wasn't giving off a dangerous vibe even though he *looked* a little dangerous. Besides...how much trouble could he give her? You can't knock someone out and carry them off on a motorcycle without people noticing. This was a small town; people would notice anything unusual. "Sure," she said.

"There's a diner that opens for the fishermen," he told her, as they headed back from where she had come. "I don't even know if it's got a name. 'Diner' is all it says on the sign on top, and if you ask for 'the diner' that's where people will send you. It opens at 4 A.M. and closes at 2 in the afternoon. There's a fancy restaurant over by the Yacht Club, but they don't open until 3, and unless you happen to be the kid of someone that belongs to the Yacht Club, they'll never let you in wearing jeans." He glanced down at her slim-cuts and trainers. *Was he just checking me out?* "Us peasants have to learn to keep our place, y'know?"

Staci shook her head. "I—this isn't like New York. And every other place Mom lived at, I was never there long enough to matter." She felt her heart sinking. *So I'm going to have to go to school here, and...figure out the other kids here. Yacht Club? I mean*—In New York when you had money, you went to private school. Dad did all right but he didn't have that kind of money, or at least, he hadn't seen a reason to spend it on her schooling. Here...she was a complete outsider, from the Big City. She groaned internally, just thinking about what she would have to deal with when the school year started up.

"So tell me what New York was like," Dylan responded easily.

"Um. Louder. And brighter. And it actually had, you know, people." She bit her lip, determined to stare ahead instead of meeting his perfect eyes again. "People like my friends, everyone I've ever known. I just got here yesterday, and this place feels like a ghost town."

"Moving is never easy. Unless you're rich, of course. You'll find your place, though. Small towns like this can have their charms, if you give them a chance." She caught his grin from the corner of her vision, and instantly felt herself blush again. *Down, girl.*

"Have you been here long? Going to school, or...?" Staci let the question hang in the air. She chanced a look at Dylan; he walked so confidently, thumbs looped through his belt, chin thrust out and head up. He looked like someone straight from a movie set.

"No, not too long. I don't live in town at the moment. And I'm out of school, thank you very much. Just kind of doing my own thing, for now. I've got time, after all."

Now they were heading back towards the waterfront; the street was wider, and running downhill again. There were a couple of people out on the street, but they all seemed to be in a hurry to get what they needed to do done and get out. There were a couple of cars out too, parked in front of stores. They were all old models though, and looked as if they hadn't been washed since the last rain. Like the buildings, they looked faded and tired.

Another thing; there were wires everywhere. Old-fashioned telephone wires and electrical wires. Every other place Staci had lived, people had started putting wires underground, but not here. And most people she knew didn't even have landlines anymore, they only had cell phones. But here—big old telephone poles with wires connected everything. To her astonishment, there was even a public telephone box halfway down the street from where they were walking.

Reflexively, she pulled out her cell phone. Still no bars. She tried to think of what that was going to mean. *If I make any friends... I'm going to like, have to wait by the phone if I'm expecting them to call. I can't text! Oh my god... this is like the Dark Ages!*

Dylan didn't seem inclined to ask her any more questions, so she asked him one, to get her mind off the disaster her social life was about to become. "That's a nice bike you've got. What kind is it?"

He laughed, showing very white teeth. "It isn't. It's a custom job. I never saw any reason to limit myself to what some 'brand name' wants to offer me." He shrugged. "Besides, there are some places that you go to, a guy sees a brand name bike that he doesn't like, and he'll beat you or try to key your ride. People are funny, like that."

Her eyes widened at that. "What kind of places do you go, where people do that sort of stuff?"

Another shrug. "All sorts of places." He nodded. "Looks like we're here, kid."

They were *at* the waterfront; across the street from the diner on the corner were the docks. The diner itself—well, people who were all into retro would probably have gone nuts when they saw it, because it was a classic, streamlined, chrome-decorated diner, right out of the 1950s, like so much of this town seemed to be. But if it had ever boasted neon, the bulbs were long since burned out and taken off. Like everything else, it was showing its age, looking shabby and tired. And just as Dylan had said, it had a big white sign on top of it, with a faded blue outline around the edges and faded blue lettering that just said DINER. Staci took a couple of steps toward it, and realized that Dylan wasn't following her. She turned. He gave her a three-fingered salute and a half-smile. "See you later, kid," was all he said, and turned to walk away.

"Wait!"

Dylan stopped, only half turning to look at her.

"Um, thanks. For helping me find my way. To here. The diner."

"Think nothing of it." With that, he started to walk off again, closer to the docks.

She went up the three steps to the door, which had another one of those hanging cardboard OPEN signs on it. She pushed the door open.

There was a row of small booths on the street side, and a lunch counter. There was one tired-looking man in a faded plaid shirt and dungarees at the far end of the counter nursing a cup of coffee. He didn't even look up when the bell (another bell!) over the door jangled at her entrance. She didn't see a waitress, so she figured it was a seat yourself kind of setup.

She couldn't help herself; she leaned against the window, watching as Dylan walked down the street. Before he was at the end of the block, a police cruiser had rounded the corner and stopped next to him. An older police officer wearing a wide-brimmed ranger hat stepped out of the car; he looked pissed to Staci. He walked straight up to Dylan, and it looked like he was talking to the younger man angrily, pushing his finger into Dylan's chest several times to punctuate his words. Dylan looked...calm, but not at *all* happy. He didn't talk back to the police officer until the very end. Whatever he had said stopped the officer cold; the older man got back into his cruiser, calling something over his shoulder before slamming the door and driving away.

"What can I do for you?"

The voice startled her and she whipped her head around to see a girl about her age, or maybe a little older, in an honest-to-god waitress outfit, standing there with a pad and pencil in her hand. "Oh! Uh—" She fumbled for the menu. "Is it too late for breakfast?"

"It's never too late for breakfast. Don't order the sausage, it's gross. Or the fried potatoes, they're grease-bombs." The girl grinned at her. Staci blindly ordered what her dad would have called "a good solid breakfast"—toast, scrambled eggs, bacon, juice. As she finished, on impulse, she was going to ask the girl about Dylan, but when she glanced out the window again, he was gone.

When the girl brought her food, the man who had been nursing that cup of coffee had left, leaving them alone in the diner. "Can you take a minute to talk?" Staci asked, a little desperately. "I just moved here—and—"

"Sure thing." The waitress actually sat down across from her in the little booth. "Nobody cares what I do as long as there's no one here. My name's Beth Phillips. What's yours?"

"Staci. Staci Kerry." She crunched down a piece of bacon. "I just moved here. I'm staying with my mom."

"Okay, so you're Paula Kerry's daughter." The waitress—Beth—nodded knowingly. *Oh God, does*

everyone in town know about my mother? But
Beth's expression was one of sympathy, rather than
superiority. "I bet this place feels medieval to you."

"I can't find anything!" Staci almost-wailed. "Where's
the McDonald's? The Starbucks?"

"Forget that," Beth replied, flatly. "This town is
stuck in 1950. No big chains, no franchises, nothing
but stuff that was started by somebody's granddad and
is being run by the grandkid. This diner's probably
the newest thing in town." Reflexively, Staci reached
for her cell and pulled it out.

Still no bars.

"Oh, and if you want any reception, you'll have to
go to Makeout Hill." She pointed through the window
over Staci's shoulder; Staci turned in her seat and
strained her neck a little to see that Beth was pointing to a bluff high above the town that overlooked
the ocean. "It's a long walk. You'd better get a car.
Or a motorcycle or at least a bike, or make friends
with somebody that's got a car."

There hadn't been a car parked out in front of the
house when Staci had left . . . which probably meant
her mom didn't own one.

"Beth!" came a muffled shout from the back of
the diner.

"Finish your breakfast before it gets cold, I'll be
right back," the girl said, and stood up. "Coming, Ray!"

In a kind of numb haze, Staci finished the food,
nibbling on the last piece of toast when Beth returned,
carrying a pad of paper, a separate piece of whitish
paper and a red pen. "Here, this is a map of the
town," she said, spreading it out between them. It
turned out to be an old placemat, printed with a

map and the words *Welcome to Silence* in one corner. "Here's the diner," she said, marking it with a little red dot. "Here's the pizza joint." That got marked with a triangle. "Here's the drive-in, they open at four." She drew a tiny thing like a burger. "Here's the movie theater, here's the grocery store, this is the bookstore that doesn't kick kids out for browsing, this is the five-and-dime and they get decent magazines in anyway." These were marked with a movie reel, a bag, a book and a circle with the number five in it. "Everything else that matters is already printed on this, and it's not as if anything's changed in the forty years since they made these placemats."

Staci stared at her in shock. "Forty years?"

Beth shrugged. "What can I say? We only just started to get to the end of the print run last year. Nothing ever changes here. Okay, look. Here's the lumber mill, and here's the cannery, those are where most people around here work. Here's the school; grade school and high school right next to each other, so all anyone ever says is 'the school.' Here's the Yacht Club—like you and me will ever get invited there!" She snorted. "Here's the Hunt Club, which is mostly a bunch of old guys too cheap to go to a bar who got an old building where they can drink their own booze and smoke cigars without their wives around. This is the okay church—sometimes they do stuff for kids that doesn't suck. This is the not-okay church—they hate gays, hate feminists, hate blacks, hate Mexicans, hate—you get the picture. This is the boathouse where the stoners hang out." Marked with a little curl that could have been smoke. "Skaters hang at the high school parking lot. Jocks hang out here—the Municipal Gym. It's just a gym, no classes, no pool or anything."

Staci felt in shock, but Beth wasn't done. "This is where your ma works." She drew a tiny glass about a block from the pizza joint. "Anything else is in the phone book, and you should be able to figure out where it is on this map."

"Internet?" Staci said faintly.

Beth shook her head. "Dialup," she replied. "Fifty-two baud if you are really lucky, mostly it's not quite 24-baud. Except maybe the rich kids, I dunno, I'm not nearly important enough for any of them to talk to me. The Goths drive to the next town and the FreeSprings Mall, and use the free wifi there. There's no cable here, and I dunno why. I know for cell we're in some sort of dead spot; every year or two some cell company gets all excited about a whole town where no other cell company has come in, and they put up a tower and get frustrated because it won't work. Maybe the same goes for cable. I know when you use the phone around here, there's always a kind of weird background hum. The UFO crazies love it. Maybe that's why the Blackthornes have their place out of town on Gray Oak Hill; it might be out of the dead zone."

"The Blackthornes?" Maybe she ought to try and get to know these people . . . if they had net . . .

"Yacht Club people. More like *the* Yacht Club people. Ultra-rich. Own the cannery *and* the mill."

Well, so much for that idea. Nobody in the local silver-spoon contingent was going to have *anything* to do with the kid whose mom was the messed-up waitress for the local dive.

"Anyway, that's Silence. School doesn't have classes

in the summer, so you'll have to hook up with the kids that aren't working at the drive-in or something. Try to find a crowd to hang with, otherwise you'll die of boredom." Beth nodded as if she had experience of just that. "There's not a lot of jobs around here unless you want to work at the cannery or the mill or on a lobster boat. That's what the teachers all do in the summer, and most of the kids who are trying to make some money for a car. That's the only seasonal work. Not like tourists would ever come *here*."

"So, there's Goths, skaters, and jocks, rich kids, and that's all?" Staci asked, feeling a little desperate.

Make that a *lot* desperate.

"Well, there's some nerds. It's really *hard* to be a geek in a town where the net is dialup. They mostly stick to themselves, for obvious reasons. They mostly hang out at the bookstore." Beth put her finger on where it was on the map she had drawn. "The Blackthornes don't own that, but it's one of the few places they don't. They do own the drugstore. And the movie theater. And I think the drive-in. And the bar where your ma works, and the fisherman's bar and the lumberworker's bar."

"They own the whole town?" Staci said, aghast. "That's—like, *medieval!*"

"Told you." Beth leaned over the table, dropping her voice. "They've been here *forever*. Sean Blackthorne is a senior at the high school. They've got, like *prehistoric* money, they all look like movie stars and live like movie stars too. There's all *kinds* of stories about them, where they get their money, because the cannery and the mill can't be taking in as much as they spend. Some people say that they're in the mob, some people say they're a family of super spies or something equally stupid. I think it's simpler than that—I think they were smuggling booze in the Twenties and drugs after that. The stoners around here never seem to have any problem getting their stash, and the cops never hassle the stoners, which would make sense if the Blackthornes are the suppliers, since they pretty much own the cops."

Beth stopped to catch her breath, her eyes wide and a small smirk creasing her lips. "The little bit of excitement this burg has is the gossip about the Blackthornes; sorry about the run-on."

"Naw, it's okay," Staci replied, thinking to herself that the "mysterious" source of the Blackthorne money probably was no more mysterious than that it was all coming out of Wall Street. Having grown up mostly in New York City, and overhearing Dad's conversations with clients, she had at least a passing knowledge of stocks and investing; it seemed like magic for other people sometimes, and that always confused her. The only "mystery" about the Blackthornes to her would be—why live in *this* backwater burg, and why Sean Blackthorne wasn't going to a fancy prep school.

Then again, she'd glimpsed *crazy* money in New York, and maybe what kept the Blackthornes here was that here they were the local kings and could hold court in the Yacht Club, whereas in New York they'd be "just another millionaire" and couldn't get a table at Nobu.

Or maybe they really are running drugs, and are smart enough to stay where they have the cops paid off.

"Beth!" This time the owner of the voice came out from the kitchen and stood behind the counter, wiping his hands on his apron. "I need you to get the prep work done for the morning!"

"Yessir, Ray," Beth sighed. She stood up. "Nice to meet you, but it's back to the salt mines for now. See you later, Staci."

Beth vanished into the back, and since she was done with breakfast, Staci decided she might as well leave. She climbed the diner steps down to the street and stood there with Beth's map in her hands, looking up and down the street.

It was pretty obvious that Mom didn't have it together enough to keep groceries in the house. *If she couldn't manage to put stuff in the fridge when she knew I was coming...* And at the rate she was meeting people—or rather, not—there was no way she was going to make friends with anyone who had a car.

But there was a store down the hill with a sign with a bicycle on it. And Dad had given her a debit card.

And Beth had said that if she wanted to get any cell reception at all, she was going to have to go up to Makeout Hill. Plus...groceries.

She'd been thinking she'd be able to use that card to get herself stuff in cute little boutiques, and she *hated* to think about wasting that money on something as *blah* as a bike. A bike...*ugh*. But if she didn't...

She glanced up at Makeout Hill. It was a long way away. She thought about the yawning emptiness of the fridge. And she headed for the bike shop.

A half hour later, she was pedaling away from the grocery on a new bike with a cart, like some sort of hemp-wearing hippy or a second-wave hipster. She hated it...but at least she could get groceries once a week, then take it off and leave it at home. And at least now there would be *something* to eat in the house. It sucked that it was uphill all the way from the store, though, and she hadn't thought about how heavy all that stuff was going to be when she was buying it.

I am gonna give Dad the guilt trip of a lifetime over this.

She was actually sweaty and panting by the time she reached the house. Mom was already gone, and all but one slice of the pizza she'd bought had been eaten. *I guess it was a good thing I did the grocery thing then* . . . She put the stuff away, snarfed a snack cake, and went out to the living room to start hauling the last of her things upstairs.

CHAPTER THREE

Now that she was doing more exploring of the house, it was clear that none of the furniture was Mom's. It was all old...nothing seemed to be newer than the 1950s and a lot was like, Victorian old. Most of that was big, heavy pieces, too big to get out the door, like huge dressers and sideboards, and big beds. None of it had been taken care of well, most of it had been painted and repainted and repainted again, and where there were chips you could see six or seven layers of paint.

The bedroom she had picked out for herself had a couple of those big, heavy dressers, a wardrobe instead of a closet, and a white-painted iron bedstead, the kind that "shabby chic" people would kill to get their hands on. But it had a set of saggy bedsprings instead of a proper set of box springs, and the mattress was flat and hard. The cover was faded to a sort of unpleasant uniform yellow-gray. She still had aches from trying to sleep on it last night.

Maybe there's something better in the attic. She knew better than to ask Mom to get a new mattress.

It would be like asking a butterfly to do it. If she even remembered, which was doubtful, she'd just say there wasn't enough money, and why pay for something the landlord had already supplied?

There was an actual set of stairs up to the attic, and a kind of hinged, drop-down door to it. She listened hard before opening it, thinking about mice. And rats. And bugs. . . . As a New Yorker she was no stranger to cockroaches, but you could usually get rid of the things by fumigating the place every so often. She rather doubted anyone had *ever* fumigated this house, and who knew what kind of scary bugs or spiders were lurking up there?

On the other hand, if you had to get up high to get any cell phone coverage, maybe the attic was high enough she might be able to get a couple of bars. That thought finally made her push the door up.

During her unpacking, she had discovered some things missing—which explained why Brenda had been so eager to "help." All the jewelry she had inherited from her grandma was gone—three rings, a pair of diamond earrings and a diamond necklace. They were all that Staci had to remember her by. Only the cocktail ring was worth much money, but they were all *hers;* Gramma had wanted her to have them, to keep and to cherish, and Brenda had no right to any of it! A couple of her sexier dresses were gone too, including the cute beaded minidress she'd worn for New Year's Eve. And she knew darned well she and Brenda were the same size.

So if she could get some cell reception, bringing that up ought to be enough to get Dad to cough up something like a new mattress, and should be good enough for an increase on the allowance on that debit card.

The attic was *thick* with dust. It was pretty obvious that not only had Mom never been up here, neither had anyone else for a long time. The two windows, one at either end of the peaked roof, were lightly coated with cobwebs, but there didn't seem to be any active spiders or other bugs up here. She went to the nearer window to see if it could be opened.

After she beat the cobwebs away with what looked like a piece of old curtain, she did manage to pry it up. Gingerly, she eased herself out and perched on the window ledge, holding her phone up into the air, and got . . . one bar. Which was a heck of a lot better than no bars.

Dad was hopeless when it came to texts, so she opened her email app and furiously thumbed out a long, long email, beginning with the discovery that her stuff was missing. She didn't outright accuse Brenda, but she did say "the only person that 'helped me' was Brenda." Then she told him what the waitress had said about no cable, no Internet and no cell phone except on the hill—though she didn't call it "Makeout Hill"—and told him how Mom didn't have a car, she'd had to get groceries herself ("Just like always"), and how hard it had been to sleep on a mattress "from 1800." She told him she needed more money on her card ("if I'm going to have to keep buying groceries") a new mattress, and a motor scooter. Her first draft came off way too . . . mean. She revised it a couple of times; her dad could be sensitive, and the last thing she needed was to get him upset . . . only to have Brenda there to comfort him. She put in a lot more

about how Gramma had specifically put that jewelry
in the will for *her* to have and no one else. When she
thought it sounded reasonable, she tried sending it.

It took almost fifteen tries, and her waving the cell
frantically over her head, before it finally went out.
She sighed, stuck her phone back in her pocket, and
took a look at the neighborhood before she climbed
back in. It wasn't much better from this vantage, and
she still couldn't see any people. But maybe they
were all at work.

Then she climbed back inside the attic, though
she left the window open for now. It looked out over
the backyard—which was a weedy wilderness—but if
she found anything up here that was useful, it would
probably be a better idea to pitch it out the window
than to try hauling it down the stairs. Anything up
here would probably be full of pounds of dust. And
maybe dead bugs.

There were some locked trunks she was kind of itching to break into, just because they were locked. They
certainly weren't her mother's, and she had to find some
way to entertain herself. Maybe another day. There were
some open ones that were full of chewed-on cloth that
smelled like old mice. Ew. She guessed the cloth was
old blankets, linens and curtains, but there was nothing
there she was even remotely interested in trying to use.

Finally, in the far corner, she found a featherbed
wrapped up in yellowed plastic. She only knew it was
a featherbed because she'd slept on one before, when
she and Dad had gone up to Vermont to ski and stayed
at a little bed and breakfast place instead of one of
the lodges. That trip hadn't gone well so far as the
skiing was concerned; there hadn't been enough snow

and all of the beginner slopes were closed, so they'd gone back home after one night. The featherbed had been all right, though. Had to be more comfortable than that antique mattress, anyway.

After an initial struggle, she managed to stuff it out the window; it rolled down the roof and pitched into the unmowed grass, sending up a cloud of dust. She wondered if Mom was expecting her to do the mowing, the way Mom always seemed to expect her to do most of the housework. Well, unless a fairy turned up and materialized a brand new mower, *that* was just not going to happen.

Even if a mower *did* materialize . . . *I'm gonna have to be pretty bored before I go mowing a lawn for fun. But in this town, that might not be such a ridiculous possibility.*

She plodded down the stairs, after making sure her phone was still in her pocket. There had been something that looked like a wire tennis racquet in one corner; that would do for beating the hell out of the featherbed. She managed to get the thing draped over the fence and beat on it until her arms were sore, then dragged it back inside just as it was starting to get dark. You couldn't say "the sun was setting," since you couldn't see the sun through all the overcast.

When the bed was done—and it was somewhat more comfortable than just the mattress alone had been—she realized that she was starving and more tired than she ever remembered being in her entire life. It took an act of will to go down to the kitchen and heat up a frozen dinner. There hadn't been any brands she recognized in the store, but at least it wasn't gross and it didn't smell like dog food.

She had just about enough energy left to climb into bed and watch one of the DVDs she had brought before turning out the light. She didn't even hear when her mom came in.

There was no sign of Mom in the morning, other than her purse on the kitchen table and more small bills and coins in the jar. From experience, Staci knew that the highest probability was that her mom was drunk-asleep and would sleep until at least 5 P.M., since this was Sunday and a bar wouldn't be open. Hopefully, she was sleeping alone... the times Mom had brought guys home, they had all been creepy, and Staci had never stayed around when they were there any more than she had to. And if those guys spent more than one night, *she* always locked her bedroom door.

I hope this door has a lock.

She looked at the stuff in the fridge, but... *Hell. I am not making my own breakfast.* Especially since she wanted pancakes and they were a pain to make. She grabbed another handful of money from the jar, locked the house up behind herself, and got on her bike.

The nice waitress—Beth, that was her name—wasn't at the diner when she got there; it was an old lady this time, who wasn't *mean*, just tired-looking, and didn't seem even remotely curious about anything other than getting Staci's order. So she ate in a hurry, left an okay tip, and got back on her bike. Time to find out if the story about cell reception on Makeout Hill was a fairy tale.

It was a long, hard ride. The grade wasn't too steep, but the road itself was gravel once you left the pavement of the main streets, and it switched back and forth a lot. If you had wings, it probably wasn't all that big a trip, but by the road it must have been two miles, at least. She was too busy peddling up to the top—or stopping, getting off, and walking for a while when her legs got tired—to pay any attention to the view. It wasn't until she made it to the top that she caught her breath and looked around.

There was a huge old tree at the edge of what turned out to be a pretty steep drop right down to a little bit of beach at the edge of the water. The grass was all worn away between the road and the tree, proving that people did a lot of parking up here. Then the gravel road continued on into some woods. Staci didn't think she'd ever bother exploring that way. It wasn't that the woods were spooky, because they weren't. They just looked tired, and uninteresting. Pretty much the same as the town.

On the road side of the bluff, you got a good view of the entire town, which didn't look quite as shabby from here, although it certainly didn't look any more inviting than the woods. Staci dug the placemat-map out of her pocket and compared it to the view, and it was pretty clear the map had been drawn from this vantage. She picked out all the "landmarks" Beth had drawn for her, then, holding her breath, she pulled out her phone.

Three bars! And the phone started beeping as the texts came in.

She sat down in the roots of the tree—it wasn't bad, not uncomfortable at all—and began answering them. There was something close to the sensation of being a little high, like she'd had a couple of puffs of grass, as she *finally* got connected back to the real world. It was so euphoric that she took her time answering each one, even though under any other circumstance, she'd have done them with a "reply all."

She could have done just that, since she answered all of her friends pretty much the same way. *It's horrible here. The town is nasty and gross, stuck in 1950 and not in a good way. There's no cell, no net, and no cable. The only way I can get cell is to get to the top of this hill and it's like five miles to get there. Mom is worse than ever, I don't think I've seen her sober for a minute. She offered me beer for breakfast!* Then she decided to throw any pretense she had at pride right out the window. *Is there any way I could move in with you?* she asked. Or at least, she asked all the girls. There wasn't a single guy she knew that she'd be willing to shack up with, even if his parents were okay with that.

The reception was only 2G, which was like, Dark Ages, but she did manage to get Facebook to load, and she posted pretty much the same thing to her Facebook page, only without the begging to move in with someone. She didn't want Dad to see that. Not yet, anyway.

Then, finally, she got email to load, although it was *agonizingly* slow. It was pretty much the same as the texts, only longer. This time she did a group reply, which was just a longer and more elaborate version of her text replies. Since it was her friends...she got a little bitter about Brenda's sticky fingers. Several of them had their own problems with a parent's "new wife" or "new husband," so she figured she'd get some sympathy. She also got pretty bitter about Mom. *It looks like she hasn't cleaned since she moved in, so guess who she expects to be Cinderella?*

Then the return texts started to come in. All of her friends were supportive, commiserating with her and agreeing about how unfair it all was. But whenever it came to the question of if she could move in with any of them... most of them were silent. A few actually replied... maybe out of guilt. All of them had excuses for why it wouldn't work out, and how it wasn't possible right then. They all had plans for the summer, and their folks wouldn't go for it... and so on.

Finally, after getting text after discouraging text, she got to an email from Dad.

And guilt practically *dripped* from it.

Honey... Brenda and I went out last night, and while I'm no fashion expert, it wasn't hard to notice she was wearing your gram's ring and your New Year's dress. I waited until we got home, but after your email, I had to confront her on it. She said she'd taken them because they weren't "age appropriate" for you. I don't know, I suppose she could be right, but you're right too, that doesn't excuse stealing. I didn't say anything about the dress, but I couldn't let the jewelry thing pass, and I got it all back from her and locked it in the safe. And I'm going to make it up to you, because that just was rude and wrong of her, and there's no excuse. I'm sorry your mom is so... irresponsible. I'll be putting what I consider to be good child support on your debit card; you'll have to manage your own finances, but you're smart, and I know you can do that. If you get sick or hurt, you're still on my insurance, so that's okay. If you need anything more than that, get an email to me and I'll take care of it. I've already ordered you a mattress and bedding.

Well... it wasn't anything like the *You can come*

home now, we'll work something out that she had been hoping for. But it was better than nothing.

We'll see about a motor scooter when you prove to me you have a valid driver's license—not a learner's permit, a real license.

She sighed deeply. How was she supposed to get a license without a car?

Maybe the school has driver's ed?

Or maybe she could make friends with someone who had a car and he—or she—could teach her?

At least he hadn't outright said "no scooter, ever, no way." Which he sure *would* have if she'd asked for a motorcycle or a whole car. Though right now... a motorcycle like Dylan's... that would be way, way cooler than a scooter *or* a car.

I wonder if Dylan would teach me how to drive? The line of daydreaming that thought took her towards definitely helped to take the sting off of all of the earlier texts.

She spent the rest of the morning up on the hill until her phone ran out of power. She'd never had that happen before in such a short period of time—but then, she'd never done nonstop texting and emailing before without a phone charger nearby. Her thumbs were sore and she was hungry, so she tucked her phone back in her pocket and moved to the town side of the bluff, staring down at it.

The diner, the pizza joint, or the drive-in? She could see the roof of the drive-in from where she was standing. It was pretty obvious what it was, since she couldn't think of any other building that would have six covered walkways radiating from it like spokes on a wheel.

At least the drive-in would be new. And she might run into some of the local kids there, and get some sort of feel for them. Maybe she'd see Beth there? She climbed on the bike and headed back down into town, grateful that going downhill was a whole lot easier than coming up had been, but still dreading the return leg.

About halfway down, it occurred to her that she was going to look unbelievably lame, turning up at a drive-in with a bike. Who did that? Nobody, at least not in any of the movies she had ever seen.

Her fears about looking lame vanished once she got closer to the drive-in. It was certainly *not* like any of the ones she had seen in movies, or anywhere else, for that matter. Staci should have known better; it was exactly like the rest of this town. Worn out, run-down, and old as dirt, and riding up on a bike was probably no different than walking up.

The circular "hub" of the drive-in had inside seating, and a bike rack with two other bikes in it, so she obviously wasn't the only one who came here on a bike. And—*oh my God!*—it was actually called the "Burger Shack"! Clearly it had not been renamed since it was built. She locked her so-called "ride" into the rack, and went inside.

Once again, it was 1950s throwback time, but it would take someone who was really, really into the '50s to get excited about this place. There were vinyl-upholstered booths at the windows around the curve of the building, with a no-kidding jukebox at the far end of the dining area, and a curved lunch counter with circular stools along the inner wall. It was done up in turquoise, chrome, and black-and-white checkerboard—but the turquoise was all sun-faded, the vinyl of the seats was cracking and patched with tape, the chrome cloudy with age, the linoleum of the floor faded and worn, and the only things that looked new (or at least, not faded) were the black and white ceramic tiles of the trim. When she sat down at a booth and the carhop, who evidently serviced the inside and the outside, brought her the menu, it too looked to date from the '50s. It was a single plastic-coated sheet, the paper inside faded with age so that the colors of the food pictures were an unappetizing greenish and bluish, and the prices had been redone with little white stickers that had been stacked on top of each other over the years. It wasn't hard to choose, since the limited menu was "burgers and fries" with a "fish sandwich" and "grilled cheese" stuck over by themselves, like exiles. So that was the main difference between here and the diner; the diner served "meals" and not burgers, and the Burger Shack served burgers. The diner closed after lunch, the "Burger Shack" was evidently open until the *crazy* hour of 10 P.M.!

And after ten, they roll up the sidewalks and chase everyone home, she grumbled to herself, after ordering. She looked out the window at the kids in the two cars she could see from her vantage, then glanced at the two groups of four that were in booths and the two that were at the counter. They kind of all looked a lot alike . . . for a minute she couldn't put her finger on why, but then it hit her. They were all, every single person save for the drive-in staff, dressed pretty much alike. And not like her. Jeans, and not cool brands, more like the ones you got off the cheap rack at a big box-store. Faded plaid shirts, over T-shirts. Girls *and* guys.

Looks like a retro grunge-band convention. Did *every* kid in this town dress that way?

On reflection, she thought probably not. The Goths wouldn't be caught dead wearing grunge stuff, not even in a backwater place like this, and the rich kids *obviously* wouldn't be eating at the drive-in. But she was pretty sure she was catching them surreptitiously eyeballing her, and in her capris, henley and hoodie—none of them faded—she was standing out like a sore thumb.

And yet—after those first few glances, no one seemed at all curious about her. They all went back to their own, low-voiced conversations, talk that didn't seem to include any of the shrieks of laughter, broad gestures, or sudden rises in tone that you'd expect. In fact, there wasn't any real animation in their talk at all. It was as if they were too worn-out to get excited about anything. *I think I moved into a Stephen King novel.*

Then again, what was there to get excited about? *One* television station, *one* radio station, no cable. You had to get to the next town to get anything new, and how would you know about what was new in the first place? Magazines, maybe, but magazines would turn into a torment, showing you all kinds of things that you *couldn't have.* Maybe in the end it was just easier to give up and settle for what you could get?

It was strange to eat a burger and fries that clearly had never been formed by a machine, or cooked on an assembly line. The burger wasn't thin, like the ones she was used to; the patty was uneven, and there were charred spots on it, and the cheese wasn't evenly melted. The cheese didn't taste like burger cheese, it tasted like the cheese Brenda put out in chunks for parties. The chewy bun didn't help things. Some of the fries still had skin on them. The whole time she was there, the other kids kept...it was a weird sort of ignoring her. Not like they were snubbing her. More like they didn't know what to do about her, so they were ignoring her. She finished her food quickly, doing her best not to draw any more non-attention than she already was.

It was clear she was going to need to get some—what did Biology class call it? "Protective coloration." Maybe if she looked more like them, they'd talk to her.

Well, she was pretty sure there were some thrift stores between here and home. If she couldn't get grunge-chic there...

She got her bike, and headed back up the street. On the way, a sign caught her eye, and she realized it was the bookstore Beth had told her about, the one where the nerds hung out. *Hey...it might have wifi, if the nerds hang there. Or at least have a net-cafe...* It was worth a shot.

Another of the ubiquitous bells-over-the-door jangled as she pushed it open.

There was a cash register at the front, and a guy sitting on a stool behind it. Finally, here was someone who didn't look as if he was worn-out and worn-down. He was, she guessed, somewhere in his mid-thirties, maybe early forties. He had slightly long, wavy dark hair and a full beard; both had a few strands of gray in them, but not enough to be too noticeable. He had a sort of stern expression; more like "worried" stern than "I want you kids out of my store" stern. He was wearing a thin leather jacket, black, and a dark blue work shirt under it, with the collar open.

He looked up at her, nodded once, then went back to reading the heavy book he had in his hands. She turned her attention to the rest of the store.

There was a coffee bar at the back with some stools in front of it. The rest of the store was tables and chairs, and a couple of beaten up but comfortable-looking chairs and couches, mixed with bookshelves. More bookshelves lined the walls. It was warm in here, not a stuffy warm, but a comfortable warm. It smelled like paper, and coffee, and a little bit of leather. Right up by the counter with the cash register was a magazine rack, but she couldn't see what was on it from where she stood. The lighting was muted, but there were little green-shaded banker's lamps near the chairs for people to turn on if they wanted more light.

Sadly, there wasn't a computer to be seen. So... not a net-cafe. But there were other kids, kids who weren't like the ones at the Burger Shack, and who were watching her surreptitiously as they continued low-voiced conversations or read. There were a couple Goths—not tricked out in piercings and white-and-black makeup, but since they were the only people she'd seen so far who were dressed head-to-toe in black and had black-dyed hair and heavy silver jewelry, it was a good bet they were Goths. The rest at least weren't in the grunge uniform.

"Can I help you?" She started at the sound of a raised voice, and turned; it was the guy behind the counter, who had put down his book. Maybe he'd figured she'd stood there long enough, and he wanted to give her a little prod. But he didn't look unfriendly... and he didn't look all fake-friendly, either. "Do you need help finding something?"

"Uh, just looking around. Someone—a friend, I guess—told me about this place. Figured that I would check it out." She glanced around. "It's nice. First nice place I've seen in this entire town, actually."

"Would you be Paula Kerry's girl?" he asked. Staci felt her heart drop down into her stomach for a moment, before the man put one of his hands up. "It's a small town, so word travels fast. We don't often get many new faces around these parts, you know?"

"Yeah, I'm starting to get that," she said ruefully.

He extended a hand towards her. "My name's Tim. Welcome to my store, Miss...?"

"Staci." She tried not to sigh. He might take it as being bored, which she wasn't. At least not right now. "You look like the only person who might know; is there any way at all to get high-speed net around here?"

"'Fraid not." He shrugged, but it wasn't dismissive. "We're the land that time forgot. All we have is old copper phone cable, and count your blessings that we aren't still on party lines."

"Uh...what?" she asked.

He chuckled softly. "Before your time. Count your blessings, whipper-snapper. Anyway the best you can do is around 24-baud, dialup, from your home phone. Since Paula works at night, at least you'll have access to it while she's at work." He craned his neck a little. "Go on back to the table nearest the coffee bar and ask for Seth. He can help you get set up with a dialup modem and show you how to optimize your computer so you can at least read email."

For one moment, she had to fight back sudden and unexpected tears. This was the first person—the *only* person—who had pointed her towards *something* like her old life. Connections, at least. "Thank you," she managed. "I mean—really—thank you—"

He smiled. It did a lot to soften his stern expression. "No problem. Seth's a good kid and nothing makes him happier than being able to flex his geekdom." With that, Tim picked up his book again; it was a sturdy-looking hardcover. The artwork on the front caught her eye; it must have been science fiction, since it was a robot eagle, wreathed in golden and orange flames, doing a dive over a burning city. It looked like something that belonged on a thrash metal album cover instead of a book.

Staci made her way to the back, where the coffee bar was. It wasn't hard to pick out Seth; thick, hard-to-break glasses, shaggy brown hair, and a Firefly T-shirt. What did surprise her was that he was with three other people, and they were all talking and joking together. Not too loud, but it didn't seem like they were afraid that making any noise would end the world, like the people at the drive-in. They were clearly all friends.

One was one of the two Goth kids in the store; a girl about Staci's age with shoulder-length, straight black hair, dark red lipstick, and what she recognized as the self-satisfied smirk of someone that was used to being right. Or at least happy with being snarky.

The other two were snuggled up on a loveseat; a boy and girl, definitely an item. The boy had short blond hair; not a crew cut, just a little messy. The blue eyes and a good jawline completed the picture; he was kind of cute, actually. The girl had red hair done up in a French braid; from the amount of hair she had, it was probably down to the middle of her back when it was undone. She had what Dad used to call "classic Irish colleen" looks: pale skin, freckles, green eyes.

As she hovered a moment, hesitant about how she should try to break into the group and introduce herself, Tim solved the problem for her.

"Jedi Seth!" he called from the front, just loud enough for his voice to carry to the rear. "Got young Padawan Staci Kerry that needs your ubergeek Force Knowledge to get her something approximating inter-webs."

The entire group turned to look at her as one, and she felt like she was turning a lovely shade of purple.

CHAPTER FOUR

Seth looked up at the sound of his own name, then switched his gaze to Staci. "Oh hey," he said, with a trace of a smile. "Welcome to the place where the 'old school' is the 'only school.' I actually had to write physical letters to 'Captain Crunch' to get his arcane dialup secrets."

Staci looked at him, bewildered. "What does cereal have to do with computers?" she asked, feeling as if Seth had just left out the entire first half of a series and launched her straight into the middle.

"Oh, you will learn, young Padawan," he intoned, making a mystical pass with his left hand. "You will learn. . . ."

"Don't mind him," said the Goth chick, with a shake of her head. "He likes to pretend he's the reincarnation of Clifford Stoll, even though Clifford Stoll isn't dead yet."

"Who?" Staci asked, now completely lost.

Seth smacked the back of his hand into his forehead, theatrically. "There, now, you see? That is how completely the rest of the world has passed us by!"

The Goth girl snorted. "Like going to Crossroads Mall doesn't tell us that. Come sit down. We aren't all completely crazy. I'm Wanda. I'm only slightly insane."

The blond kid unwound himself from the girl he was sitting with, standing up with his arms wide. "Don't mind them; they'll be at this for hours if we let them." He held out his hand. "My name's Jake."

Staci shook it, gingerly. "I guess you guys already know who I am . . ." she said tentatively. It felt . . . weird. But then everything about this town felt weird.

"Like Tim said, you're Staci, right?" He let go of her hand, turning partially towards the rest of the group. "The odd couple is Seth and Wanda. Red over there is my girlfriend, Riley." Riley waved from the loveseat, smiling warmly. "If you want, you can sit with us, grab some coffee. You might need it once Seth builds up some steam talking about modems. Or *Star Trek*. Or *Star Wars*. Or *Doctor Who*, or—"

"Oh, like I'm the only one that carries on!" Seth was blushing slightly. Staci smiled sheepishly, moving towards the coffee bar while the group continued talking with each other. Once she had her cup of joe, she noticed that they had pulled another of the comfy chairs up, making space in their circle. She sat down, folding her legs under her in the chair, while she blew on her coffee to cool it.

"So, you're new to town, from New York right?" That was Riley; she was holding a truly gigantic cup in her lap; it looked like some sort of tea to Staci. "I'm guessing you didn't move here for the scenic ocean view."

"It's kind of a long, depressing story." Staci stared into her coffee, feeling her face flush. The others seemed to get the hint; Seth was the first to speak, breaking the silence before it could get uncomfortable.

"Tim said that you need some help getting hooked up to the net, right?" He cocked his head to one side. "In that cable doesn't exist, there's no possibility of cell-net, dialup is all you get. Are you on a laptop or a desktop?"

"Laptop," she said, a little more certain of her ground. There wasn't any accusation or hostility when any of them asked her questions. They actually seemed genuinely interested.

He nodded. "Good, pretty much all of them have a phone jack in them. So all we need to do is hook you up to a dialup service. Fortunately there actually *is* one that isn't a long-distance number from here; it's over in the next town. You got access to a credit or debit card?"

"Yes—"

Seth didn't wait for any explanations. "Awesome, that's usually the big stumbling block. Twelve-fifty a month, I'll come over whenever you want, set you up." He sighed theatrically . . . and to catch his breath. "Obviously, nobody ever has to worry about exceeding their download limit on dialup, so it'll never be more than that."

Since one of the first things she was going to do would be to email Dad that she was getting Stone Age net, well, this was a whole lot less than her cell per month, so she doubted he'd blink twice. She nodded.

"Don't start giving her the scenic tour of gimp-net until you're sitting down at the lappie, Seth," Wanda said, before Seth could start up again. "I don't suppose you're into RPGs?"

"Or console games?" Jake said hopefully. "Or better yet, both?"

"Uh—" She knew what console games were, though she'd never done anything but play Facebook games herself. But...RPGs? "I don't really have much experience with any of that. But, I'm willing to learn?"

"Good attitude," Wanda said approvingly. "Look, here's the deal. There's not a hell of a lot to do around here. You can get together and watch DVDs. The movie theater is a joke; by the time it gets anything, it's already out on DVD. If you're a skater, there's a parking lot...and whatever you can sneak to before the cops run you off. Have you seen the Burger Shack?" As Staci made a little grimace, Wanda nodded. "Yeah, you get it. So unless you happen to get touched by the Gilded Hand of Fate and the Blackthornes decide you get to be a hanger-on with the Elite crowd, there is not much left. Too cold to swim. Not enough wave to surf. Fishing around here is a job, not a sport. Nobody much who's our age can afford a car, and since most people work here in town, a lot of adults don't bother either. The school does nada for the kids, *nothing* in the summer because all the teachers have summer jobs at the cannery, and even in the school year they never have dances because there's no money for them, and we lose every football or basketball game we play."

Staci looked at her in disbelief. "That doesn't sound possible—it can't be that bad!"

"We're that bad," Riley assured her. "We get our own kicks, enough to make this place survivable. If you like fantasy or horror or sci-fi, you might like RPGs. They're kind of like improv plays."

"With dice-rolling," said Jake.

"And heck, if you don't like those, there's mystery RPGs, and historical RPGs, and steampunk RPGs, and military RPGs," Seth added, with enthusiasm. It was pretty clear now who was the "RPG expert" in this group. "Even superhero RPGs and an anime RPG. I'm pretty sure the rest of us would be open to trying those if that's what you like."

Well...she did like anime. "Maybe the last?" she said hesitantly.

"Great, I already have a copy of BESM still in the plastic," said Seth. "I'll scan and print up copies for everyone."

She sipped coffee and occasionally added something as the others talked. They seemed like a fairly close-knit group. Usually whenever Staci had encountered anyone like them in NYC, it had been hard to be accepted as one of them. Every group had its own initiations. But not this one. They had taken her in as one of their own almost immediately. Maybe they were all kindred; they were outcasts in their own town, and she was an outcast from out of town. Her initial nervousness eventually wore off the more she talked with them, until—and this was the biggest surprise of all for her—she felt good, for the first time since she had arrived in Silence.

Staci had actually lost track of time when Tim rang a bell that was at the cash register. The others looked up with a groan, but Tim shook his head. "You know the rules, folks. This is your half-hour warning. We don't need the cops hassling us again for you being out after curfew."

"Curfew?" Staci said, aghast. "There's a *curfew*?"

Jake shrugged his shoulders, grimacing. "Got enacted a few years ago. The cops have been pretty strict about it since it was actually a thing; bugging kids about being out too late is something for them to do besides sitting around bored, I guess."

"On game nights, depending on whose house it is, sometimes the 'rents let us all stay overnight," Riley added. "So there's that."

They all started to file out of the store after they had gathered up their belongings, each saying their goodbyes to Tim and each other.

"You going to get some sleep, Tim?" Seth was shrugging a heavy backpack onto his shoulder; Staci had seen earlier that it was packed with rulebooks for RPGs and board games.

"I only sleep every other leap year. Keeps me regular. Now git; I'll see all of you when I see you."

Staci was the last to leave the store, giving her thanks to Tim again for helping her out and just being nice in general. She was about to walk after Jake, Riley and Seth, heading for her bike, when she felt someone grabbing her elbow; Wanda, staying back behind the rest.

Jake turned around, looking for them. "You two coming?"

"We'll be a minute," said Wanda, answering for Staci. Jake shrugged, and continued on with the others. Wanda waited until he was out of earshot before she spoke again. "Look..." She scrunched up her face. "I don't know how much to say without making you think I'm crazier than you already do... but there's a lot that is *not right* about this town, and it's not just the Magical Cell Phone Hole we're living in. So... I'll just say this. Keep your eyes and mind open, and your mouth shut, and if things start adding up in a funky way for you, come talk to me, because it can't be any worse than the shit I'm already thinking. And watch your back. Seriously, watch your back, and don't let on that you're anything other than a drone or an airhead."

Before Staci could reply, Wanda started walking quickly, catching up to the group. Staci followed her; once she was back with the rest of them, Wanda was chatting normally again. She had seen something in the girl's face: real fear. Staci felt a very strong chill go up her spine. The rest of the walk was much like hanging out in the store; Staci said her goodbyes and traded contact information with everyone when it came time for her to split off for home. The rest of the way, she couldn't stop thinking about what Wanda had said. *Watch your back. Things aren't what they seem.* Somehow, as crappy as the house was (she couldn't think of it as "home" yet, if ever), she was glad to get inside those four walls.

With the phone charged up again, Staci decided that for the foreseeable future, she actually had a schedule of sorts. Breakfast at the diner, because the food was edible and Beth was nice, and sooner or later they could probably figure out when and where they could hang out. Then up to Makeout Hill for as long as her phone charge would last. Then lunch either at the Burger Shack or the diner, and then to the bookstore. But today, she had one detour: combing the thrift stores for something that would make her stand out less. Maybe Wanda was crazy...but she still wanted to get some of that protective camouflage.

Beth's advice about the thrift stores was useful, but the pickings were pretty thin. She was either going to have to do laundry loads every few days, or find another source for clothing. After going back to the house briefly to change—and getting a sleepy greeting from Mom, who was drinking coffee at the kitchen table—she headed back out to the Hill.

There was an addition she thought was kind of odd, since she had been pretty sure the thing hadn't been there the last time. Lodged in among some rocks near that big tree was one of the creepiest lawn gnomes she had ever seen. Seriously, seriously creepy—if she ever saw a person with *that* expression on his face, she would just know it was a serial killer . . . and the thing even had a nasty-looking knife stuck in its belt. How could she not have noticed the thing yesterday? Her first reaction was to try and pitch it over the cliff, but it was wedged in there so hard it might just as well have been cemented in there, and she couldn't even wiggle it. Finally she left it alone . . . but she had to go to the other side of the tree to sit, because it felt like the damn thing was staring at her.

Her phone was fully charged at least, and when she powered it on, it actually got three bars today.

But the results of getting a phone signal were . . . not what she had hoped for.

Okay, she hadn't expected to get a flood of her friends going "Oh wow, that sucks so hard, move in with meeee!" but she also hadn't expected fully half of them to unfriend her on Facebook either.

That . . . had been kind of a shock, actually, to look at her Friend List and realize it had gotten cut in half. She had actually sat there for a while, staring at the phone in her hand, feeling like someone had punched her right in the stomach.

The response from the rest had been pretty underwhelming. When they acknowledged her post at all, it had been on the other side of "I guess that must suck for you, now about *me*...." And then they would rattle on about shopping, or a movie, or a date. It made her feel all hollow inside. Like...they'd already written her out of their lives.

And no emails from anyone but Dad. It was a delivery notice for the new mattress and sheets and things.

The phone seemed to drain down even faster than before. It was dead right after she read that email, and with that creepy lawn gnome on the other side of the tree, waiting for her, she didn't even want to linger for a minute. On the way to the Burger Shack, she saw a couple more thrift stores and scored a couple more things.

When she got to the bookstore, Seth was there alone. "Hey!" he said brightly, as she walked in and said hello to Tim.

"Hey yourself..." She hesitated a moment. "Do you think there'll be time to get me—"

"Net?" he finished for her. "Sure, I have everything I need on my lappie. Let's go!"

Since he didn't have a bike, they walked back to the house. Mom was, thankfully, already gone for the day. "Are you hungry?" she asked, as he got his laptop out and plugged the phone jack into the back of it, then set himself up on the sofa.

"I'm always hungry!" he said cheerfully, as the laptop began to make some weird noises she'd never heard out of a laptop before.

"I'll fix you a sammich, and then I'll get my machine," she told him. She knew there was ham and cheese because she'd bought them and hidden them behind the pizza box. She brought him a soda and the sandwich; he thanked her absently, as he was doing...something... leaning over the keyboard and staring intently. She ran up, got her laptop, and came back down again.

"Okay!" he said, around a mouthful of sandwich, gesturing at the sofa. "Sit down, and get yourself signed up for the Stone Age." She sat, and he put the laptop in her lap. The screen was...curiously barren. *Really* basic information and fonts, and next to no graphics...but there was a form to fill out, including her debit card information, and she followed it, picking a username and a password. Seth inhaled the soda and sandwich while she typed, and when she was done, she passed the laptop over to him.

"Okay, the next thing is, I am going to be doing a lot of messing around with your lappie," he told her. "First, I have to turn a crap-ton of stuff off. Like, there is no way you're going to be able to download updates. So updates will have to wait until you get somewhere there is wifi and you have a couple of hours to kill. Or until I get them, which will be when I get somewhere there is wifi and have a couple hours to kill." He made a face.

"Is that a big deal?" she ventured.

He shook his head. "I'm going to give you an obscure browser in place of what you're using, and nobody really targets it for viruses." He pulled a thumb drive out of his pocket and began working. "Basically there is a lot of stuff that thinks you're on broadband and wants to be connected all the time, and turning it off is a pain and hard unless you know what you're looking for. Which I do."

It was strange, sitting there in the silent house, listening to someone tap on the keyboard. She couldn't remember ever not having music or something on. Or hearing people in the other apartments, maybe their TV or music, and street noises. It was really strange, hearing the house do random creaking noises, or a gust of wind rattling the glass in a window.

She got up and got Seth another soda, and leafed through a magazine she'd brought with her from the city. Finally, Seth was done.

"Here." He plopped the laptop in her lap, plugged the phone cord into the back. "Double-click this—" he pointed to a new icon that said "Dialup." "I've turned wifi off for now, otherwise your lappie will keep trying to find a connection."

"Yeah," she nodded. "I had to do that at home, otherwise it'd try to randomly connect to other peoples' servers, and ewww. You never knew who was spoofing to hack your accounts."

"Exactly!" he beamed at her, as if she had said something really clever. A box came up, and it was obvious where she was supposed to put what in for the new ISP. Her laptop immediately began to make all the weird noises his had, and she looked at him in alarm.

"No stress!" he told her. "The first was the dial tone, then the computer doing the dialing. Then the handshake signal—that's your computer talking to the router at the ISP. Then the signal where it verifies your account. Then—" There was a sound like static that cut off. "—That was the clear signal, and now you're in."

He walked her through the really, really basic things he had set up for her. Flash was off. Most graphics were off. Email was this . . . well, it looked like a page of text. Facebook was *barely* possible, in an even more primitive version than was on her phone. "You probably won't be able to shop," he told her. "Most online stores need higher graphics than the connection will support. So what you need to do is get phone numbers and order catalogs. But hey, this is better than nothing, right?" He looked at her so hopefully, that she had to agree with him, but . . . it was kind of like trying to watch a movie on a TV where only a fourth of the pixels were working. Yeah, you got the idea, but it wasn't . . . enjoyable.

But she thanked him as sincerely as she could, and the two of them went back to the bookstore. At least . . . she had people she could talk to now.

Three days later, she had given up on the trips to Makeout Hill. The texts from her friends had dwindled to a handful, and more of them had unfriended her. The only unsullied bright spot was the delivery of the mattress and goodies. Now, at least, her bedroom looked nice and she had a bed she could sleep on without ending up feeling like she'd slept on rocks. The featherbed had gone to rest on top of the equally bad mattress in one of the other three bedrooms upstairs.

Dad had sent her what had at first glance looked like a huge score, two enormous boxes of DVDs and CDs. But on closer inspection, they were all used, and three fourths of them were things she'd never watch or listen to. She had a pretty good idea that Dad had told Brenda to get movies and music, and

Brenda had cleaned out a thrift store or three. She'd cherry-picked what she wanted, and left the rest in the boxes downstairs, only to find the boxes gone today. She had a pretty good notion that Mom had taken them for herself or to try to pawn for more beer money. Well, okay, it wasn't as if it was anything she *wanted,* but now that she knew Mom had developed sticky fingers, she figured she'd better start locking her room when she wasn't home. Which was depressing. You weren't supposed to have to hide your stuff from your parents because your parents would *steal* it.

There were more of those creepy lawn gnomes around town, including one in the backyard of the house next door, and one in the front lawn of the house across the street. Where were they *coming* from anyway? And who would even want to buy one?

She was thinking about that as she browsed the bottom of a bookshelf at the back of Tim's store, waiting for the others to arrive. Somehow, even without the Internet, Tim managed to get some pretty good stuff in. *Maybe it's all just someone's idea of an epic prank.* It wasn't as if there was much to do here. Maybe someone had made the original, then made a mold so he could make lots of copies and was planting them around town to see who noticed and what they'd do. Kind of crazy, but bored people did crazy things sometimes.

The bell rang on the front door; Staci looked up, expecting to see her new friends. They had said they would be getting there around now. Instead . . . it was Dylan, still in his biker leathers. The way the sunlight streaming through the door hit his hair, it almost looked like he was wearing a halo. Once the door shut behind him, he turned to face Tim. Immediately, Tim's face hardened. His entire posture changed; it was almost like he was ready to attack, or defend himself. Meanwhile, Dylan appeared nonchalant; a bit of a smirk, leaning against the wall next to the register. The two men were talking quietly; even in the relative silence of the bookstore, Staci couldn't hear them. She didn't want to eavesdrop...but she couldn't help herself. Out of curiosity, she slowly walked forward, pretending to browse the shelves as she went.

"...I don't care why you're here. I just don't want any trouble."

Dylan cocked his head to the side. "Now, why do you think there's going to be any trouble?"

"You know exactly what I mean. I want no part of any of it. Understand?"

Just then, Staci bumped her knee into the edge of a small table, letting out a yelp of pain as she stumbled forward. Dylan and Tim both stopped talking to look at her.

After a tense couple of seconds, Tim spoke. "I had forgotten you were back there."

"I'm just waiting for the gang," she said, and started to move back towards the coffee bar. "I didn't interrupt anything, I hope..."

"Nothing important." Dylan looked at Tim for a moment. "I think we understand each other." As he turned and opened the door, he called over his shoulder. "Nice to see you again, Staci."

Staci thought that Tim looked like he wanted to say something more, but Dylan was already gone. Before the door had closed behind him, it swung open again; her friends had arrived, all of them greeting

Tim and talking amongst themselves as they made their way to Staci.

What was that *all about?* She could understand a cop hassling Dylan; so far, he was the only person she'd seen in this town that even looked remotely like someone who might be in a biker gang. But why would Tim go after him? And what was that about "not wanting any trouble"?

"That guy that was leaving when you came in—" she said tentatively to the others. "You guys know him?"

The other four looked at each other, then at her. Wanda was the one who answered. "He's been around here for a couple weeks. I mean, he kinda stands out like a sore thumb in all the grunge and plaid, right? But *I* never talked to him."

"He's never been in here before as far as I know," Seth added, and looked at the now-closed door. "I wonder what he wanted."

The group began settling in their usual chairs, Seth pulling out some printed-out character sheets and rulebooks; they were supposed to "roll up" some characters for that anime RPG today.

Staci tapped Seth on the shoulder. "I'll be right back, guys. Don't get too far ahead without me."

"Hurry back! I'll wait on explaining the rules... but it'll take awhile when we get started."

Staci walked up to the front of the store, stopping in front of the cash register. Tim still had the same look on his face from when he was talking to Dylan; it only softened when he looked at her.

"Who was that guy?" she asked, trying to sound casual. "You looked upset."

Tim just shrugged. "Some drifter. Didn't exactly

look as if he was going to be interested in books, and I don't need money badly enough to encourage him to loiter. Didn't he know you? He knew your name."

She paused before answering. "I literally ran into him my first morning here when I was looking for someplace to eat. Mom isn't exactly good about keeping food in the house. He showed me where to find the diner, that's all. But the way you were talking to him, I thought maybe you knew him."

"No, and I don't want to," Tim said shortly. "I know his type, and that's all I need to know. Anywhere a guy like that goes, there's always trouble." He looked as if he might say more about what kind of "trouble," but then decided to stop. "Look," he sighed. "I'm not your dad or your big brother, Staci, so I'm not going to try to tell you what to do. But you seem like a good kid. Be careful around that guy. It'll keep me from getting any more gray hairs than I already have. Okay?"

"Sure," she replied, and went back to the others. It was odd, though. Tim didn't seem to be the kind of guy who...well...*judged* people. Practically ordering Dylan out of his store seemed out of character.

But she put it out of her mind, once Seth started in on his game stuff. She'd never done anything like this before, and it took all of her attention to keep it all straight.

CHAPTER FIVE

It was a Thursday night, the bookstore was closed, and Staci was sitting in the living room with her laptop plugged into the phone line, reading the Facebook pages of the people who *used* to be her friends. She nearly jumped out of her skin when she heard the back door open, and someone come inside.

She was looking for something to use for a weapon when her mom peered into the living room. "Oh, hey," she said, vaguely waving in Staci's direction. "I guess you're settling in all right."

Staci bit back a million angry things that surged into her mind, and just said, "I guess. You're home early."

"Bar's pretty much empty so the boss sent me home," her mom replied, and made a face. "Big baseball game, so the usual crowd all went out to a sports bar to watch it. Then they'll come back tomorrow night and bitch all night about having to pay six bucks for a beer so they could watch the game. I'll let you interweb in peace. Night, honey."

Meaning, "I'm going to my room to drink myself to

sleep," Staci thought, acidly. *What the hell is* wrong *with this town?*

She could *kind* of see the kids giving up on trying to get anything to come here, but the adults, who *should* have been able to change things, seemed stuck in a case of permanent apathy. Even Tim didn't bother to care much about anything outside of his store. No, that wasn't quite right; he wasn't the same as the rest of the adults in town. There was a different reason for him being the way he was; Staci just couldn't put her finger on it.

Well, look at tonight. You would think that the owner of a local bar would be upset about losing his customers to a sports bar in the next town! And you would think he'd do something to get satellite in, even if you couldn't manage to get cable to work. It's not as if they were unaware that these things existed, after all—people went out of town to shop, or they caught games at bars and restaurants. But . . . no. The answer, the few times she'd asked an adult—like the lone guy who ran a computer-repair place—why no one tried to figure out why Silence couldn't support net or cell or cable, the answer was always "it can't be done" or "it's not worth the effort" and a shrug.

It was almost as if, once you left school, you got infected with some kind of zombie-apathy virus.

In disgust at seeing one more shopping post, she finally gave up on Facebook. She'd managed to send her dad a selfie today, when she'd gone up to Makeout Hill. She'd posed it very carefully, wearing the oldest and most faded of her thrift store finds. So there she was, no makeup, blond hair looking washed out in the overcast, a little thinner than she had been before (which she frankly thought was an improvement, and probably due to having to walk or bike everywhere), and looking more like an advertisement for helping street kids than the selfie on her Facebook page. She'd posed *that* one carefully too, wearing her best Juicy Couture outfit, makeup and jewelry that showed off her green eyes and good cheekbones, hair she had spent *hours* on. She'd told him she'd had to buy stuff to wear because she didn't fit in and anyway, everything she had for summer was too light to wear given how cold it was here.

Okay, it was manipulative, but Brenda was manipulating him too, and anyway, it looked like the selfie had paid off. The latest email from Dad said he was sending her an L.L. Bean card. So at least she could get stuff that wouldn't make her look like she was homeless.

If things weren't exactly looking up, at least they weren't quite sucking as much.

The sound of bottles clinking in the fridge made her decide she might as well take her lappie upstairs and watch a movie. *Not feeling like being Mom's drinking buddy,* she reflected cynically. Although, at least last year, when Mom had taken her as a drunken confidant, she hadn't also offered her beer. . . .

Friday found her early at the coffee bar, waiting for the others—who surprised her by coming in at five, rather than the seven she had expected. "Did you eat yet?" Wanda asked, as they all came in. She shook her head, expecting the answer to result in them all going over in a bunch to the Burger Shack.

"Good, then you might as well come along with us," replied Seth. "Second Friday of the month."

"Yeah, it is, what's that got to do with anything?" she asked, standing up, and slinging her purse over her shoulder.

"First Methodist does a BBQ for *teeeeeeeenz*," Wanda answered, drawing the word out sarcastically. "That means our folks don't bother feeding us. Fourth Friday is a movie night with hot dogs. Which means our folks don't bother feeding us."

After a moment of thought, Staci identified "First Methodist" as the "okay church that sometimes puts stuff on for kids," that Beth had told her about. "Okay," she replied, following them out the door. Free food was free food. It couldn't be worse than the Burger Shack.

As usual, the others were on foot, so she walked her bike along with them. The church in question was higher up on the slope that Silence was built on, and she was actually glad she wasn't going to have to pedal her bike up it. The road they were taking was almost as steep a grade as the one up Makeout Hill.

When they got to the church—which at first glance looked like something on a New England postcard, all white and complete with steeple, and only at second glance did you notice that the new paint had been slapped over the old without anyone scraping or priming the bad parts—the BBQ was already as close to "going strong" as anything she'd yet seen in Silence. There were six adults presiding over six old kettle grills, three giant aluminum tubs full of ice and sodas, and a table with a red and white checkered tablecloth holding paper plates, condiments and bags of chips. Someone's radio with blown-out speakers was tuned to Silence's only station, and there were twenty or thirty kids ranging in age from nine to late teens milling around with food.

Looks like the gang's 'rents aren't the only ones that don't bother feeding their kids.

This was the biggest number of people she had seen in one place, ever, in Silence. Even with the conversations and the music from the radio, the gathering seemed a little too quiet for that many people. Her group wove its way through the crowd until they had reached the tables with the food on them.

"Kind of dead, isn't it?" Staci noticed that most people were keeping to themselves; the only conversations that were happening were in small clusters of people. Everyone that she made eye contact with looked away shortly after, as if they were purposefully ignoring her.

"Are you kidding? This is a regular jumping time in good ol' Silence." Jake had piled three hot dogs on his plate, and was reaching for a fourth. "Almost better than watching grass grow."

It didn't take long for her group to make their way through the food line and pick a corner in some shade from the setting sun. They were probably the loudest group there, and constantly got looks from the adults and some of the other kids. And it wasn't as if they were being *seriously loud*. They were just talking normally.

As the sun went down, somebody turned on the exterior lights. There were a couple floods on the back of the church, and strings of old Christmas lights and the sort of bare-bulb things you used to see at used car lots before people realized having four big floodlights cost less to run than strings of bare bulbs.

I didn't know you could still get plain light bulbs . . .
Then again, this was Silence. *All 1950s, all the time.*
Except for the music which seemed to be stuck on
"All Eagles, all the time."

Staci ate mostly in silence, piping up for certain
parts of the conversation that the others were having.
By and large, she just listened.

"I don't care; Boba Fett is seriously underwhelming."

"Now that's a bunch of crap! He's an interstellar
bounty hunter. He's got weapons on every inch of his
person, and a badass ship. He's able to get the drop
on Han Solo, for crying out loud!"

"Actually, that was Vader—"

"Whatever. Point is, I hope we see more of him."

"He got knocked into the gut of a giant monster.
By a blind guy. *With a stick.* The most you'll be seeing of him is a pile of throwup with a dinged helmet
in the middle of it."

"Hey, read the Expanded Universe, Jake! You know
I got the books. Rule of Cool, man."

Staci was having a hard time keeping up with the
flow of the conversation, but she was getting better
than she had been when she first joined the group.
At least she actually knew what *Star Wars* was. Wanda
waited until the other three were fully involved in
science fiction minutiae before she scooted over to
where Staci was sitting.

"So, want the dope on the rest of the peeps here?"
Wanda asked, in a conspiratorial whisper.

"Sure," Staci whispered back, looking at her burger.
It was better than the Burger Shack, even if it was
a little burned.

"Okay, the adults don't really count, but they're the

minister, Reverend Franklin, his wife Eloise, Fred and
Thelma Krause, and Joe and Evelyn White. They're all
okay. Now, the six kids closest to us are the skaters.
Ken and Stan Jennis, Larry Green, Jerry Krause and
Tom Pendergras. You never see one of them alone,
it's like they are joined at the hip or something. The
jocks and their gfs, who are the Cheerleading Squad,
are just past them, and there's no point in telling you
who they are because you will *never* be invited into
their exalted company."

Staci giggled a little at that. "So the skaters are
okay with us and—"

"And to the Loyal and Exalted Society of Jocks and
Jockettes, we do not exist." Wanda rolled her eyes.
"You should remember I told you that our football
and basketball teams have never won anything in the
history of ever, right?"

"Yeah. Not sure what they have to be stuck-up
about," Staci agreed.

"Me either. The minute they graduate, they're gonna
go straight to work, and you know what the options are
around here. Not that too many people from Silence
ever go to college, but it's a cinch the jocks *never* do.
This is the best they'll ever get. Gotta hang on to what
little glory they can, I guess." Wanda sighed. "Seems
pretty pathetic to me, but they're Neanderthals, so,
uggah-wuggah, me strong, me alpha male."

"So . . . the guys with the white T-shirts—let me
guess, they're the science nerds?" Staci hazarded.

"Yes, and two of them are girls. Mary Krause, Bill
Schoeder, Bob Flint, Kyle Peterson, Maureen Silk.
They're cool. The only reason they aren't over here
with us is because they'd have to cross alpha-male

territory to get here." Wanda finished off by pointing out a few of the kids who were eating alone, one with her nose stuck in a book, a harried kid who was trying to keep his hyperactive brother from jumping off the steeple or imploding, and about twenty kids who were "from the bad part of town, if you can imagine that we have one" who were keeping to themselves, and a half a dozen kids too young for high school. "There's a lot of kids that don't come here, or only come here once in a while, because they're on night shift at a job, or they're too tired after being on the fishing boats all day," Wanda concluded. "Probably about two thirds of the kids going to high school have summer jobs. We're *desperate* to get car and gas money, as you can imagine."

"Yeah," Staci agreed.

"Then there's the Goths. Over there. In the shadows. Being mysterious. Sue 'Valentina' Griffin, Eric 'Vlad' White, Brittany 'Bella' Hailey, Rob 'Blade' Ketcham, and Kelsey 'I'm-a-mega-bitch-and-play-with-dead-things-because-it's-creepy' Johnson. I used to hang out with them, but then they started to get *way* too dark and mopey. Even for me, which is saying something. Jake, Riley, and Seth are a better fit, anyways."

"I was never into wearing uniforms," Staci replied, eyeing their all-black outfits, dyed black hair, identical black nail polish and black eyeliner.

Wanda nearly choked on her bite of hot dog.

That got the attention of the *Star Wars* geeks. "What?" asked Seth.

"Uniforms—" Wanda managed to get out, nodding at the Goth clique. Seth looked at her puzzled for a moment; Riley got it first, and smothered a fit of giggles behind both hands.

"Really," Jake said, when the light dawned for him. "And there is, seriously, only so much Morrissey and Nine Inch Nails you can listen to, am I right?"

And that was when the atmosphere changed, completely.

There was a...sound. Once you've heard the engine noise of a really expensive, really high-powered sports car, you never mistake that *sound* for anything else. The steel canyons of New York were good for that; Staci had heard, and consequently seen, a lot of high dollar cars. That was what Staci heard now, pulling up in the front of the church and stopping, and so did everyone else. All the conversations stopped dead. All heads turned; it was...weird. Even for Silence. Staci had never been in a situation where literally *everyone* stopped doing *everything* and waited for the appearance of—

He came around the corner of the church, and somehow, every bit of light seemed to be pulled towards him, as if he was creating his own spotlight. He paused for a moment, and cast his eyes over the crowd, giving the crowd more than enough time to take him in.

He looked to be in his late teens, he was blond and if you could be ruggedly handsome and angelic at the same time, he certainly fit both descriptions. Staci, as a New Yorker, knew how to pick out the subtle details that told you that someone's clothing was *expensive*, and his certainly was. It might just be a light gray leather jacket, a black T-shirt, and a pair of jeans and boots, but the way it fit him, it all *had* to be tailored.

"That," Wanda said, quietly enough that she didn't

break the silence, "is Sean Blackthorne, youngest of the Blackthornes, gracing us with his Presence."

Sean's eyes—a striking emerald green—passed over the crowd. He nodded to the jocks, waved a little to one of the adults, and then, locked gazes with Staci.

"None of them ever come to these things; I can't ever remember one of them coming here, at least," said Seth, his plate of food forgotten next to him.

The conversations started up again, now a little less muted than before, once Sean Blackthorne started to make his rounds. He flowed between all of the groups effortlessly, from the adults to the jocks to the math nerds to the Goths to the skaters. Staci couldn't keep her eyes off of him. Once or twice, it looked as if Wanda was going to say something about that—but then she shut her mouth.

Then, for the second time, Sean Blackthorne locked gazes with Staci. From across the entire gathering, he was staring directly at her. Not just a passing glance...but *staring at her.* All of the conversations fell to a quiet hush again, as more and more of the attendees turned to see what Sean was looking at. Staci felt her face flush, and did her best to focus on what remained of the food on her plate. *Oh god, oh god, oh god. Why is he looking at* me?

She felt a block of ice drop into her stomach when she noticed that an expensive pair of boots had just walked up to her. Slowly, she let her eyes drift upwards. Sean must've been six and a half feet tall, easily. A chin that looked like it was hewn from marble, a strong Roman nose, and eyes that had a peculiar—and almost entrancing—glint in them. His golden hair wasn't long, but it wasn't short either. It had that look to it that said someone who was paid an *awful* lot of money had cut it to look precisely halfway between tousled and tamed.

"Hi. I'm Sean Blackthorne. I don't recognize you, and I know just about everyone in this little town of ours. What's your name?"

"S-Staci," she stammered, looking up into his green, green eyes. "Staci Kerry."

Please, please, please don't let him say "Oh, you must be Paula Kerry's girl...." She did *not* want him to know she was the daughter of the drunk waitress at the Rusty Bucket.

"A pleasure, Staci." He smiled. It was a smile warm enough to make her knees feel a little weak. "I don't know if this is too forward, but I was wondering if you would accompany me back to my family's estate; a few of us are having a sort of impromptu get-together there, and my other date bailed on me."

She blinked, not sure what to say. On the one hand—*Oh my god, the hottest guy I have ever seen just asked me to his* estate *for a party!* On the other hand, wasn't this how every single rape-fantasy story *ever* started out? Or something like this? Not to mention about half the horror movies she had ever seen...

"Think about it," he urged, as if he was reading her mind. "The invitation is open-ended and I'll be here a while longer." Then he strolled over to the Jocks'n'Cheers, with an understanding smile cast over one shoulder.

"Holeee shit," Seth breathed. "That was Sean Blackthorne..."

"Inviting Staci to the Elite Meet and Eat, yeah," Riley replied, envy in her voice thick enough to spread. "Oh man. I am so jealous. I am *so* jealous." Then she looked down at herself with chagrin. "Not that I'm likely to pass as anything other than one of the maids."

Staci felt someone jiggling her elbow; it was Wanda. Her eyes were wide, but not with excitement; it was alarm. She didn't say anything, just kept her eyes locked with Staci's, shaking her head very slightly. *I didn't think she'd be the jealous type. How can I say no to him? This could be my chance to actually get noticed in this nowhere town, and have something to do.*

"You've got to go, Staci," said Seth, even if his voice dripped envy. "Seriously. I'm dying to find out what goes on at those parties. Actually, I am dying to find out if they somehow got broadband, and if the rest of us can figure out how."

"Get a gander at how the other half lives. And score some free chow! Don't forget us little people; bring back as many doggie bags as you can." Jake looked as if he was already daydreaming of lobster and steak.

Riley sighed. "Promise you'll take notes, or something. The only thing anyone has ever said about the Blackthorne mansion to me is that it's big and everything is expensive. Big duh there."

Wanda rolled her eyes. It was clear she had been outvoted. "Be careful. That's all I'm going to say." She stood up, dusted the grass off of her clothing, and beelined for the soda coolers.

With the encouragement of three of the four Musketeers, Staci wound up her courage and left the group. She hesitated for a moment, halfway between them and the gaggle of jocks and cheerleaders that Sean was currently talking to, when Sean turned his head a little and caught her eye again. Once more, she found herself mesmerized by his gaze as he made some comment, left the group and came towards her.

"Please tell me you decided to accept the invitation, not that you have a date with a good movie and some ice cream," he said with a smile. "I don't think my ego could stand it."

"I'd love to come," Staci said simply.

"Excellent. We were just about to head out." He offered the crook of his arm for her. "Shall we?" He allowed his gaze to drift over the various groups and made a tiny circling motion with his free hand. Roughly five other people detached themselves from their cliques and followed them down to the car.

Staci had expected a sports car from the sound of that engine. It wasn't. It was—well, she wasn't quite sure how to describe it. It was certainly as sleek as an expensive sports car, but it had the capacity of a limousine. It was easy enough to fit everyone else, though Staci got pride-of-place in the front passenger seat. She wished she knew more about cars; all she could tell for sure was that the inside was mostly glove-soft blood-red leather, with dark wood and black-chrome details.

Sean started the car. The engine roared to life, the sound of it suggesting that Staci had been right about this vehicle having the heart of a high-dollar sports car. Then he touched a control, and music started in the middle of a song. Pop, but played through some really amazing speakers, the music took on a lush quality she'd never heard before. The couple of jocks and their cheerleader girlfriends that were in the back talked amongst themselves; they all seemed excited to actually be going to *The Party*, and hardly even noticed that Staci was there. She didn't mind that, actually; it was a lot better to be overlooked than purposefully ignored.

Sean drove the car fast and hard, but not so hard that she felt even the least bit alarmed at the speed. Now and again he would glance over at her and smile slightly, as if to reassure her. She always smiled back.

She didn't recognize the road, but it was definitely climbing the slope on which Silence was built. Then, when it reached the crest, the road suddenly plunged into forest. There was nothing on either side of the road but darkness, and glimpses of reflected tree trunks standing so close together they almost made a sort of fence.

Then, when she was beginning to wonder just when they were going to *get* to the Blackthorne Estate, the car turned into a driveway she hadn't seen until they reached it, and as a pair of huge, solid gates opened up to let them in, she saw it, lit up in the near distance, like something out of a movie.

It was *much* bigger than she had expected. Not that she'd ever actually seen a mansion herself, except a couple in New York City that had been turned into museums or something. But this was enormous. Three stories tall, and it sprawled away on either side from a massive portico supported by six stone columns. All she could think of was that the electric bill to light the place must be the equivalent of most peoples' mortgages.

There was a circular drive (of *course* there was) that led under the portico. Sean stopped the car there; the kids in the back all piled out, as a servant opened the doors, first for them, then for her. Sean got out on his side and held out his hand to her to help her out. She flushed, wishing desperately that she was wearing something other than what she was. Like that cute little beaded dress that Brenda stole...

Rather than going into the mansion, however, Sean led the way around the side, giving her plenty of time to admire the gardener's handiwork and try not to gawp at the *size* of the place. Once they got to the back, it was pretty obvious that this was where the partying was happening.

There was a massive pool, of course, with not just one, but four huge Jacuzzis, and a sort of artificial stream, like Staci had seen in the brochures for fancy resorts that Brenda was always getting. The stream was big enough to have a bridge over it, and there were several people—some fully clothed—floating down it in brightly colored inner-tubes. There were four tent pavilions set up, one by the pool, one on an immense lawn between the pool and the mansion, one on an immense patio attached to the mansion, and one in the garden. They were all lit up with colored lights, and she could see big tables with stuff on them and servants standing behind them, and little tables and chairs inside the nearest. The pool had its own lighting, underwater, cycling through colors. The patio had its own lighting, designed to be bright enough you could see, but neither harsh nor glaring. The gardens had lights buried in the shrubbery, and the fountain in the garden was all lit up.

There was a second house beside the pool, easily bigger than the one she shared with her mom. "I live there," Sean said, with a nod at it. "It makes cleaning up after parties easier, and keeps the rest of my family from getting hassled. Just tell one of the servants if you want anything." He patted her hand and gently detached it from his elbow. "I have to make the rounds for a little bit, being as I'm the host and all, but I'll be back." He paused, and waved a hand at a lounge chair placed by itself a little away from the pool. "That's a comfortable seat. One of the servants will be around in a minute to see what you need."

Feeling utterly overwhelmed by so much luxury, she couldn't think of what to do except take his advice. The lounge was covered, not in the canvas she expected from outdoor furniture, but something soft and velvety. She tucked her legs up, and was just starting to look around when a man in a formal uniform approached her.

"And what may I get miss?" he asked, sounding like a butler in a series about rich English lords, only without the accent.

"I'm...not sure..." she stammered.

"Would miss prefer soda or a strong beverage?" he asked, his face absolutely blank, as she looked up at him. "Our bartenders can mix anything you like."

She cast a glance around. Everyone else seemed to be drinking beer or mixed drinks. And...most of them looked, at least to her, underage. Still... *yeah, I really need to get hammered when most of these people probably know my mom as one of the local lushes*... "Coke?" she asked.

"I'm sorry, miss," the servant said, actually *sounding* sorry. "The Blackthornes have a serious allergic reaction to caffeine. We have any other soda, however."

Caffeine allergy? She'd never heard of that before.

That must suck. Then she almost giggled as she thought of something. "I'll have a Shirley Temple," she said. "Thank you." She'd *look* like she was drinking, without actually drinking. And if she got tired of sweet stuff, there were always Virgin Marys.

"Certainly, miss, and I will bring miss an assortment of snacks, as well." The servant didn't wait for her reply to this, he just whisked himself off to the pavilion and before she'd had a chance to do more than try and find the kids from the BBQ among the other partiers, he was back with her drink and a plate of hot and cold snacks. He set both on a little table next to her, and whisked himself off again before she even had a chance to offer her thanks. She had never been waited on like this before; restaurant waiters in NYC weren't exactly rude, but they weren't waiting at your every beck and call, either, not when there were three dozen tables during lunchtime that all needed attention.

She was getting some veiled looks as she sat there by herself, nibbling and drinking. Eventually, Sean returned; one moment she was sipping her drink, looking at a wonderful fountain sculpture, and the next moment he was beside her.

"Finding everything to your liking?" He smiled down at her.

She decided that honesty was the best at this point. *I bet he's surrounded by phonies. So I'll be different.* "I don't fit in," she said. "But hey, I don't fit in Silence anyway. I'm a New York girl. I wouldn't even be here if my stepmother hadn't kicked me out so her little angel boy could have my room."

"I was asking about the party and the refreshments,

actually." He chuckled. He wasn't laughing at her, thank goodness. She was stumbling over herself for a moment to compliment him on everything; the food, the drinks, the service, how beautiful everything was.

"It's okay, Staci. But about what you were saying before . . . that . . . sucks," he said, shaking his head. "Seriously. I can't even imagine having . . . *everything*, right at your door, practically, then end up here, where there's nothing." Sean paused, thinking for a moment.

God, does he have to look gorgeous while he does that, too?

"How about this; let me introduce you around, help you to get to know a few people here. Would that be all right with you?"

"Sure—" she said, because, really, what else *could* she say and not end up looking like some kind of antisocial freak?

He held his hand out to her to help her up from her seat. She took his hand, and immediately noticed how strong it was; she wasn't expecting it, especially when he easily helped her up, hardly needing to bend over. His fingers were strong, but somehow had a delicate quality to them. No bitten off nails or torn up cuticles; not quite manicured, either, but close. "Let's get you properly introduced, now."

After that it was a whirlwind of faces and names, and Staci quickly lost track of who was who. She met the mayor's kids, a brother and sister, the chief of police's son—who was probably the most drunk person at the entire party—and a flood of others. While before they had looked at her with mild disdain, now that she was hanging off the elbow of Sean . . . they couldn't wait to get to know her. How she got to Silence, what it was like in New York City, if she went to Broadway plays or went clubbing all the time. Many of them expressed their sympathy for her living situation, and the way she had been dumped by her father and new stepmother. Some of it actually felt genuine. Of course, they also were all inviting her to their own get-togethers and along for their own plans; trips to the mall in the next town over, house parties, all of it, and how it would just be wonderful if she could join them.

There were others Sean introduced her to only briefly. People who were almost too drunk to stand. "It's what they like," he said apologetically, after one tried to kiss her, fell over his own feet, and miraculously landed in a lounge chair where he immediately passed out. "There's plenty of room to sleep it off here, anyway, so it's not as if I'm putting drunks on the road." He chuckled. "The servants are all trained in picking pockets. Anyone too drunk to drive won't find his keys until he's sober."

"Wow!" she said, impressed. "That's—"

"It's smart," he interrupted. "If I *didn't* take care of my guests, these parties would stop. Money doesn't shield you from everything, you know. And it's not as if there's much to do in Silence for some of them besides drink." He shrugged.

She looked at the food, at the pool, at the *house* . . . then again, if this was what you were used to, maybe you could get bored with it.

Well, she wasn't used to it. And aside from not knowing anyone, and so, often not knowing what people were talking about, this was probably the best party she had been to, ever. But after a while something made her look at her watch, and she realized with a sense of shock that it was after midnight. And once again, Sean seemed to somehow intuit what she was thinking.

"I bet it's getting late for you," he said. "And it's a long way back to town. Let me get you home."

He led her back around to the front of the mansion again, and that portico. She thought about being all alone with him in that car...wondered if he was going to try something... She had never had trouble putting off unwanted advances before, but everything about tonight seemed like it was from a completely different world.

But to her mingled relief and disappointment, he left her with the—was it a butler? a footman?—waiting at the front of the house. "Get Padrick to take Miss Staci home, would you, Harris?" he said, once again gently detaching her hand from his arm. "I'm the host, and at this stage in the party, it would not only be rude to leave, it might be stupid," he said with a rueful smile. "I'd find a television or all of the lounges in the pool, or something equally awkward. The chauffeur will take care of you. Just tell him where you need to go."

"Sean, thank you for everything. Tonight was...well, it was just great. I haven't seen or been to anything like this since I've come to Silence. But...well, I had one question."

"I just might have one answer. Shoot, Staci." He grinned, flashing those dazzling white teeth at her. *Damn if he isn't smooth.*

"Why me? I mean..." She let her voice fade, unable to articulate what she wanted to say. That she wasn't all that special. That she wasn't gorgeous—she'd seen gorgeous, there were *models* going to her old high school. She wasn't able to make conversation of the kind that had guys hanging off her words. She wasn't special, not in any way. She'd always considered herself *good,* but not *special,* because in New York, you could go see *special* walking around in Soho, or Dumbo, or the Village, any time you wanted to.

"It's not every day that we get anyone new coming to Silence. Especially cute girls." He paused for a moment, still smiling before shrugging. "I like to know everyone that I can. You never can tell when it'll be helpful, down the road. So, I figured I'd get to know you a little better tonight. Satisfied with my answer?"

She nodded, unsure whether she wanted to feel flattered or obscurely disappointed. And she never got a chance to sort things out further, because that was when a huge, blood-red limousine, complete with a uniformed chauffeur, pulled up.

"Here's your ride," he said brightly, and reached into a pocket, pulling out a little rectangular gold case. "And here's my number," he said, taking a card from it, and pressing it into her hand. Then he pulled out a tiny pencil from the case. "What's yours?"

She stammered, giving him her cell number first, by accident. "Oh wait, that's my cell—" she corrected, flushing.

"Which doesn't work here," he finished, with a nod of sympathy. She gave him her mom's number, and he duly wrote it down inside the case. "If for some reason I don't call you in a few days, *I want you to call me.* All right? I'm serious."

"Okay . . ."

"Cool. We'll hang out again soon, maybe get some coffee." There was a peal of laughter and shouts from the rest of the party. "That's my cue; better get back before anyone tries to climb on something. Good night, Staci." With a final wave, he started to walk back to the party.

Well, what else could she do but get in the limo, what with the driver standing there patiently holding the door open for her?

It was like being driven around in a luxury hotel room. There was even a bar. Since it had bottled water, she helped herself to a bottle. The bottles were glass, not plastic, and unlabeled; she had seen "artesian water" like this served in super-high-end restaurants. It was even chilled.

Just after they came out of the woods and were still at the top of the bluff, she remembered with dismay that she had left her bike at the church, and bit off an exclamation of annoyance.

The little speaker next to the bar activated with a faint hiss. "Yes, miss?" the chauffeur said.

She flushed. "Nothing. I'm just going to have to get my bike from the church tomorrow and it's a l—"

"Not at all, miss. Master Sean would be extremely put out if he found out we hadn't picked it up for you. First Methodist, I believe?"

"Uh—ye—"

"Very good, miss."

The limo rolled to an almost silent stop at the church, which was, of course, dark. The gang had warned her that everything would close up by eleven at the latest, and it was almost one, now. The chauffeur came around to her door and let her out. "I'll get the boot open, miss. If you'll tell me where—"

"No, no, it's all right," she said hastily. "I need to unlock it anyway."

"Very good, miss." He went to the back of the car. She hurried off towards the bike rack at the front of the church. It was sitting under a single yellow streetlamp, which was flickering intermittently. She bent down to unlock the chain; the lock was being stubborn, refusing to come open even after she put the right combination in. The light above her flickered a few more times...and then she noticed one of the creepy gnomes with the red, pointed caps, sitting right next to the light pole, facing directly at her.

Staci almost jumped out of her skin, falling onto her backside with a yelp of surprise and pain, her bike knocked over.

"Miss, are you all right?" The driver was calling from the car; he must have heard her or saw her fall over in one of his mirrors.

"Yeah, I'm fine...just got, um, startled." She stood up, rubbing her now sore backside with one hand. "Stupid, weird little troll," she muttered, kicking the gnome and sending it rolling off into some nearby bushes. Finally, she managed to unlock her bike, and trudged back to the limo with it in tow. *I really hate whoever is putting those freaky lawn decorations everywhere. Really, really hate.*

The driver had exited the limo by that point, and took her bike from her and loaded it into the trunk, which was big enough to hold three bikes. She got into the back as he held the door open for her, and picked up her bottle of water. As she did so, she cast a sour glance at the bushes she'd kicked the freaky little gnome into.

The light flickered again, and she thought she saw it—not lying flat, but standing up again. And . . . looking down the hill at the car, and her.

But the limo rolled away and the light flickered out again, too quickly for her to be sure of what she had seen.

Must be some shadows, or my mind playing tricks on me. It's been a doozy of a night.

CHAPTER SIX

As Staci unlocked the door to the house, she felt... eyes on the back of her neck. But when she turned a full circle, peering into the shadows, all she saw was another of those creepy lawn gnomes across the street. Shivering, she hastily got herself and her bike inside.

Mom was predictably nowhere in sight, though there was an empty bottle of vodka and another of orange juice in the trash, along with the zombie-pizza box. She kind of wished now she actually *had* gotten a doggie bag from Sean's party, crass as that was. The food had been really nice.

She left the bike in the living room. Given everything that had been happening, she didn't want to take a chance on losing her ride, and it was pretty obvious Mom wasn't going to care if she kept her bike in the house. She could probably have kept a horse in the house and Mom wouldn't care as long as it didn't break into the fridge and drink her booze.

When she got into bed, she had trouble falling asleep. She kept thinking about Sean... *Is he just being nice? Is it just that I'm the first new girl in*

*town for a while? Is this a whole trophy thing or
something?* Back at her old school, if a girl was good
enough to rank on the "hot" scale there was always
this jockeying to see who could nail her first. Depending on how she played that, well, there were a lot
of possible outcomes. Back home, she knew she was
pretty, but nothing like as gorgeous as some of the
other girls. But here...

I guess I could be hot on a Silence scale.

Then there was Sean himself. He was...well, perfect. Charming, cuter than hell, and rich; he didn't
seem to lord it over people, either. He looked equally
comfortable talking to any of the cliques, and always
had a smile ready. She could've gotten lost in his eyes
forever, and she wouldn't have cared. And for some
reason, he was interested in her.

With this and other thoughts running around in
her head, she tossed restlessly, and only fell asleep
after what seemed like hours.

By the next day all of that speculation seemed
utterly ridiculous. As she fixed herself some cold cereal
and milk, and looked around the shabby kitchen with
its ancient appliances, cracked and peeling paint, and
stained wallpaper, she swallowed down a lump of disappointment along with some orange juice. Because,
really, what could someone like Sean Blackthorne
have *possibly* seen in someone like her? She wasn't a
"lawyer's daughter" anymore, or at least, not in ways
that would count to the Blackthornes. She was the
daughter of a cheap waitress that worked at a dive bar
down near the docks. She hadn't even been wearing
her cute New York clothing; it had been what she'd

gotten from the thrift store. Even if he had been marginally interested in her, once he checked on her background (and she knew from the way things worked back home that people like the Blackthornes *always* checked; pedigrees mattered to the upper crust) he'd know everything about her, and know she was never going to be "the right people."

I bet the only reason he brought me up there last night was so his friends could scope me out, and once I was gone, they had something to make fun of, she thought bitterly. *I bet if I call the number he gave me, it'll be Dial-a-Prayer or Time-and-Temperature. Or something worse. Like, maybe one of his friends so they can record me making a fool of myself.*

So when she wheeled down to the bookstore, she was in a pretty dismal state of mind.

Tim seemed to pick up that she was depressed; he told her the first cup was on the house, and pointed her at some magazines he'd just gotten in. She managed to get up enough politeness to thank him, but buried herself in a huge cup of latte rather than reading.

Maybe when the others get here, that silly anime game they are going to start will get my mind off things. Because now, all she could think about was to go over and over and over the things she had said and done at the party, trying to pick everything apart and figure out how Sean's friends could have used any of it to mock her.

Seth was first through the door, and lit up when he spotted her. He waved to Tim as he quickly walked over to her, dropping his heavy backpack with a thud as he sat down. "Hey!" he said brightly. "So, what was the *food* like?"

His enthusiasm forced a smile out of her. "Really expensive finger food," she told him. "Upscale versions of a cook-out. So ... mini lobster rolls instead of hot dogs. Real bratwurst. Really expensive-beef hamburgers with bleu cheese and mushrooms. Baby veggies and avocado dip. Chips, but I think they were hand-cut and hand-fried, 'cause they were still warm. With sea salt, or pink volcanic salt, or salt and cracked black pepper."

Seth's face crinkled up, and he waved both hands at her. "Stop, I think I'm going to cry!"

Jake and Riley were the next to enter, with Wanda bringing up the rear. Everyone took their usual spots; Seth had gotten up to start on getting coffee for the group, save for Staci, who already had a mug.

"So, you didn't turn into a pumpkin at the end of the night, right? You've gotta dish." As Seth handed her a steaming mug, Riley nodded her thanks, blowing on it as she waited for Staci to spill all the details.

She stalled for time by dwelling on the details of the mansion, the pool, the garden, and the party, figuring that was what Riley wanted to hear anyway. "I didn't go inside the mansion or the pool house," she finished. "The drapes were open at the living room of the pool house, so I *could* see inside ... it looked like a picture in a home design magazine, if you crossed fifties-retro with darker colors. There was a *huge* LCD-screen TV though." She sighed. "It probably had cable, or satellite; it looked like it was playing music videos, but you couldn't hear anything over the sound system around the pool."

Cable and satellite; they seemed a million miles out of reach at this point.

"Anyway, I said I had to go home, and he sent me home in the limo," she finished.

"That's *all?* That's *it?*" Riley asked.

"Oh, there was probably plenty after she left," Wanda said cynically.

"Come on, Wanda. You just wish he had picked you instead." Seth elbowed her lightly. Her return elbow was a little less than light. "Hey!"

"Hey what?" Wanda snorted. "I bet by the time she got there, half of people were so polluted they won't remember she was there. And by the time she left, all the rest were so polluted they've forgotten. You know what's sad?"

"I'll bite," Jake replied, lightly.

"To think of all that great food being wasted on people who won't remember eating it, don't appreciate it, and are probably throwing it up at this very moment." Wanda actually looked a little . . . happy? . . . when she said that last.

"Well, someone has a job making it, at least," Riley observed. "So I guess that's good."

"Whatever," Wanda said. "I just think it's borderline creepy; party with a lot of underage drinking, spiriting a girl away—specifically away from her friends—to be alone with you at said party? There are news stories that start that way."

"I don't want to think about that," said Seth. "Ew. Besides, nothing happened, and Prince Charming sent her home untouched in the coach with white horses. Your ability at prediction, Wanda, is right up there with Miss Cleo."

Who's Miss Cleo? Staci wondered. But Seth was still talking.

"Anyway, have you all got character sheets made out? Staci, I did yours like I promised; I figured you'd want to play a Magical Girl. Schoolgirl sailor suit is optional. Tentacles are off the menu."

By this point her spirits had revived. "They had tempura-battered calamari," she teased.

"*Stop!*" Seth moaned.

Although she'd been skeptical, the first game session had been fun. She'd watched enough anime to know what was expected of a Magical Girl—although apparently her character was not yet aware she *was* a Magical Girl. That was fine, a lot of anime started that way too, so she knew what was expected of a Magical Girl who didn't know yet. Even Tim had smiled at some of the antics that Seth got them all up to. The guy had one heck of an imagination—and, she suspected, had seen *way* more girl-centered anime than he was ever going to admit to watching. *I bet he has the* entire Sailor Moon *collection. And* Princess Tutu.

She did *not* call Sean, now absolutely certain he had given her some sort of a prank number as a joke. The more she thought about it, the more it made sense. *He probably gave me the number of one of his friends, actually,* she was thinking, as she went down to the curb the next morning to bring in the mail—which Mom had, predictably, forgotten to do. That L.L. Bean catalog should be coming any day now, and she was getting to the end of her thrift-store clothes. She wasn't sure how much of her wardrobe was going to survive a round in the ancient washing machine in the basement.

In a rare display of good luck, the catalog *was* there. So were several others, which she might be able to exercise her bank card on. She was just closing up the mailbox when the sound of a car horn lightly tapped made her turn and look up the street. Not that she thought it was for her, but this would be the first car other than Sean's limo that she had actually seen driving on this street.

This was a gorgeous little sports car; not the big, powerful thing that Sean had been driving when he picked everyone up at the church BBQ, but a cute little two-seater. Bright red. The yellow badge on the nose, visible against the red even at this distance, told her it was a Ferrari.

That can't be— But the car pulled up next to her, and the driver leaned towards her, and it *was* Sean. The passenger-side window rolled down silently. "Hey," Sean said, with a smile.

"Hey yourself," she replied, smiling back, but determined not to act excited about this. Because . . . well, because she was just not going to count on this being as good as it looked. "How'd you know where I live? I kind of doubt you were just cruising by this street."

"Limo dropped you off here, remember?" He arched an eyebrow at her, still smiling.

"Oh, right." *Duh, you ditz. I'm going to die from embarrassment. It'll make for one hell of a tombstone inscription.*

"You have plans for this afternoon and evening?" he continued.

Well, it wasn't a game night for a game she was involved in. It was a *Shadowrun* game that the others were already deep into; "cyberpunk fantasy" is what Seth called it. Staci figured that she would watch a few games, but didn't feel like juggling a ton of characters the way that Seth and the others seemed to do. And she'd already warned them she just might stay home and watch a movie instead. "No, nothing," she replied quickly. Too quickly? She seemed to be second-guessing everything she said to him.

"Good, leave a note for your mother and go get a bathing suit and maybe a change of clothes," he replied. "I'll keep you from being bored today."

She didn't hesitate. She ran up to the house and inside while Sean waited in the car; this time she changed into one of her cute New York outfits. She was *not* going to make the mistake of turning up in front of his friends looking like Little Orphan Annie again. She didn't need to camouflage herself to keep from being stared at this time. Then she stuffed another outfit into a gym bag along with the new bathing suit she'd never had a chance to use, and ran back down, half convinced he'd have left.

But he hadn't.

With her bag at her feet, and cradled in the red leather of the passenger's seat, she marveled as Sean drove the sports car at what had to be an illegal speed back up the bluff; once there, it was obvious their destination was, yet again, the Blackthorne Estate. This time he didn't leave the car at the front; he drove it around to the side, down another private road, and to a garage that was the size of several houses put together. He left it parked in the front of one of the doors with the keys in it, came around to the passenger side, and the next thing she knew, they were walking between the mansion and the garage, approaching the pool and the pool house from the opposite side as last time.

There were about a dozen people there already.

The music was a lot quieter, and no one seemed to be drunk. Already she was feeling her spirits buoyed.

"I figured I would give you a chance to actually swim, and see the politer side of my parties," Sean said, with a smile, as the group of people disporting themselves in and beside the water all turned to face them. "Staci, this is part of the Blackthorne clan—the younger part. Clan, this is Staci Kelley."

They were all, *all,* movie-gorgeous. Most of them, like Sean, were blond, although there were a couple whose hair was so black it had blue highlights. Most of them had green eyes. The guys weren't ripped; they were lean and graceful. Any one of the girls could have walked into any model agency in New York and gotten a contract without a portfolio.

Sean began introducing her. They all seemed to have Irish-ish names. Meaghan, Brigit, Patrick (though it sounded like Padrigh), Ian, Caelen, Finn, Siobhan, Niamh, Liam, Connor, Niall, Aengus. Four girls, eight guys. Normally fourteen people would feel like a crowd, but the pool area was so spacious, it was more as if they were all rattling around in an Olympic stadium.

She was *really* glad she had changed before she left; the guys were all in opened guayabera shirts and Speedos, or a designer version of Speedos, but the girls were wearing little cover-ups over their suits that wouldn't have been amiss at a dance, back home. *If I'd been doing the faded flannel number, I think I'd just melt into a puddle of embarrassment.*

"Sean, *acushla,* I'm starving. Can we eat?" asked one of the girls—one of the dark-haired Blackthornes. Niamh?

"Sure, ring for it, no point in waiting," Sean said,

laughing. "Can't have you wasting away in front of us now, can I?"

She didn't catch how they "rang for it," but a moment later three uniformed servants came out of the mansion pushing carts with silver-domed dishes on top of them, and a fourth pushing what looked for all the world like a street vendor's ice-cream cart. That turned out to be a refrigerated thing with soda and beer in it. The beer was not in cans, it was in a little keg with a tap, and with it were aluminum steins to drink from.

Not cook-out food this time, but picnic food. Gourmet sandwiches and cold but crisp fried chicken of the sort that had never even caught a glimpse of the Colonel. Staci got something that she had thought was tuna salad that turned out at the first bite to be lobster salad. The sandwich was chunks of lobster and a little of something that crunched that she couldn't identify, with a spicy mayo.

She ate quickly, and asked where she could change. "Go ahead and use the cabana," Sean said, waving at the pool-side house. "You'll see the bathroom as soon as you're in the door."

She grabbed her bag and tried to hurry without looking as if she was hurrying. Part of it was not wanting to miss any of the conversation or the chance to ogle Sean some more . . . and part of it was fear that they would start in with making fun of her behind her back. And she was really glad that her suit was something she'd gotten from Saks last year at the end-of-summer clearance, since it was actually going to measure up to what the other four girls were wearing: a red two-piece, not a slutty thing with a thong, but not something that would make her look like a prude, either, complete with a matching cover-up.

When she was satisfied that her look was put together, she walked quickly without looking like it back to the pool. It seemed like the conversation had taken a different turn from local gossip and the like.

She knew immediately that there was something going on between Finn and Sean, just by the way that the others were standing, subtly arranging themselves into two factions. Everyone's faces were neutral, except for Sean, Finn, and a girl that Staci recognized as Meaghan; all three of them were smiling, but their eyes were...different. Mean, a little predatory. Staci quietly inserted herself behind Sean, doing her best not to disrupt the talking.

Finn was as blond as Sean, but had a scar bisecting one eyebrow. And unlike the other girls here, Meaghan had *really* long hair, down to her knees, pulled back in a tail.

"...you haven't exactly been pushing yourself for the firm, my lad," Finn was saying. "You know what I've been up to, because you've had the benefit of all the new *clients.*"

Sean shook his head. "It's risky, and you know it. The old reliable way, we have everything under control at all times, and a steady flow of income. Your way...one slip, and those clients will vanish like snow in summer, and if we've started to depend on them, what then?"

Finn shrugged. "No risk, no reward. I don't see anything to admire in sticking to a rut. Might be the old man will feel the same."

"Or it might be he's waiting for you to fall in the shark tank," Sean countered.

"He won't be around forever, and he knows it. He's looking for someone to look to the future; the only way

to do that is for someone to help the firm expand."
He theatrically examined his fingernails. "Noncing
around town like a movie star certainly isn't doing it."

"Blackthorne didn't get where he is by being a
coward," Meaghan purred, *"or by taking foolish risks."*

"Thankfully, none of us are cowards. But I'm having strong doubts about how many of us were raised
to be fools." Sean turned to face Staci; he looked
surprised, but in a good way.

"Leaving us already, Sean my boy? C'mon, stick
around. You know it's only polite to share your toys.
Even if they are *second-hand."*

Staci felt her cheeks burning, and she had the
overwhelming urge to smack Finn. But Sean's eyes
flashed darkly and he spoke before she could move.

"That just proves what a poor judge you are, of
anything, Finn Blackthorne," he replied. "You can't
tell a diamond from a bit of glass. But I can. And
that is why the old man will always favor me, and
my choices." And he took Staci's hand, holding it up
for Finn to see for a moment. "Let me give you a
tour of the house, Staci. Some of my cousins need
to brush up on their manners before we allow them
in polite company again."

He didn't wait for her answer, but then, he really
didn't need to. She was only too happy to get away
from Finn . . . and Meaghan. He didn't rush towards
the mansion, he sauntered, as if he owned the place
and he could have Finn thrown out at any moment.
Behind her, she felt Finn seething, and Meaghan's
amusement.

"What was that all about?" she asked, in a whisper,
once they were far enough away not to be overheard.

"Nothing you need to worry about," Sean replied lightly. "My cousin is under the impression that *he* is my father's golden boy at the moment. What he doesn't know is that father likes giving people plenty of rope so he can sell tickets when they hang themselves."

By this time they were at the French doors leading from the terrace to the mansion. Sean opened one side, dropping her hand to do so, and bowed her in.

They were in a long, shallow room that on the garden side was floor-to-ceiling windows. There were tons of plants in huge pots that looked like they were marble, and each pot had an entire tree in it, plus some smaller plants. There were white wicker chairs, lounges, and tables scattered over the expanse, and the floors were marble tile. "The loggia," said Sean. "You know how winter can be up here. Keeps you from going insane with cabin fever when you can sit out here."

Staci couldn't imagine even getting a bit of cabin fever; the entire mansion was *huge*, unlike the shack she was currently living in. You could have fit three houses that size just in this room.

Sean led her to the left, in through another pair of French doors. This room had a lot of windows too, and was set up with one big table. The furniture was dark wood, and the walls were wood-paneled, with big mirrors on them. "The breakfast loggia," said Sean, and she tried not to look startled. A room the size of her whole house just for *breakfast*?

"The pantry is through there—" He waved at a door at the end. "The gallery is through here. Do you give a crap about art, weapons, heads of dead animals and pictures of old, dead people?"

Only if you do, she wanted to breathe, but instead she shrugged noncommittally. He chuckled. "Well," he said, his tone faintly mocking, "I might as well let you know all the dark family history." He waved her through the door nearest them and she found herself in . . .

. . . it looked like the exhibit hall of a museum, but the museum of a collector who might not entirely have been sane, and certainly was bloodthirsty.

Up near the ceiling were the promised "heads of dead animals"—and lots of them. Deer—or deerlike animals—with antlers that were bigger than anything she had ever seen in her life. Big cats. Bears. Wolves. All of them *huge*. They must have been ancient, because she didn't think there was anything that got that big anymore. They had been mounted so that they managed to stare *down* on whoever was standing on the floor below them. Their eyes glittered in the half-light.

Beneath the heads were pictures, but not, as she had expected, portraits. No, these were battle scenes, or pictures of the conquerors surveying the battlefield, and as Sean had promised, there were a lot of dead people in them, and the artists hadn't exactly been squeamish about portraying them, either. Some looked historical. Some were clearly fantastic in nature, since they showed riding animals and packs of . . . things . . . that weren't real.

Between the pictures were row upon row of weapons. Swords. Axes. Bows and arrows. Spears. Things she couldn't even recognize. All of them were wicked-looking, yet gorgeous, and must have been serious works of art.

In the middle was a statue, twice life-sized, of an ancient warrior atop a heap of bodies. Arranged around the walls on tables were various objects that...part of her thought they *couldn't* be made of gold and silver, but with everything else in front of her, what else *could* they be? Cups and vases, boxes and chests, necklaces that must have weighed pounds...

"And there, is the *paterfamilias*," said Sean, gesturing to the lone portrait at the end of the room. "The Blackthorne of Blackthorne himself, Bradan Blackthorne, my father."

It was a life-sized portrait of a man who looked startlingly like Sean himself, and incongruously, he was the only person portrayed in a modern suit. His eyes and cheekbones were more severe than Sean's, and he definitely had a colder look to him. "You will note that there is no portrait of my grandfather," Sean continued, though that hadn't even occurred to her. "He and Bradan didn't get along."

"But your father inherited everything—" Staci ventured.

Sean chuckled. "To the victor go the spoils," he replied. "Fortunately, Bradan and I get along reasonably well, considering the combative nature of our family. But enough of that. Shall we continue the tour?"

The tour took them to the dining room—another room big enough to hold four houses and a place that would have made any self-respecting Goth weep with desire, what with the ornately carved dark wood banquet table, matching chairs, *matching mantelpiece*, matching sideboards, and red velvet wallpaper. From there they crossed the entrance hall, all dark marble threaded with white and gold, with a spiral staircase leading to the second floor, and entered the drawing room, which, if the dining room had made a

Goth weep, would have made her insane because she couldn't have it—red velvet upholstery, a thick carpet so soft you couldn't even hear their footfalls, red velvet drapes, dark brown wood-paneled walls, black marble fireplace *literally* big enough to roast a whole cow in, and red crystal and silver trinkets and lamps everywhere. From the drawing room, Sean led her to the card room, which had card tables, a billiard table *and* a pool table and, incongruously, videogame machines and a huge LCD TV. To the left was a room he called "the study," which had dark leather chairs, a desk, and a load of books. Then they crossed the drawing room again to the library, which had floor-to-ceiling bookshelves, plus freestanding shelves and dark leather couches and chairs.

"And that concludes the tour of anything interesting," he said, as she looked out of the library windows at the garden, and saw that the cousins were swimming or lounging. "Kitchens and other uninteresting but useful things are downstairs in the half-basement. Servants all have their own hallways and staircases; father is extremely old-school that way, he prefers not to see them. Bedrooms are all upstairs. Speaking of which, would you like to stay the weekend? We've got tons of room, the cousins either don't stay or have their own wing, or use the cabana with me." Before she could object, he smiled. "I'm sure we've got weekend wardrobe for you. We keep things on hand. Plenty of father's guests don't even bother to pack when they visit. I'll make it right with your mother."

"Are—" she began.

"I'll do it right now." He pulled a cell phone out of his pocket, and all she could think was, *Oh, of course the damn things work up here. Even if this house is in the dead zone he probably has a satellite phone.* "Ah, Ms. Kelley? Yes, this is Sean Blackthorne." He laughed. "Yes, *the* Sean Blackthorne. I'm having a house party and I wondered if you would permit your charming daughter Staci to stay the weekend for it." He paused, listening. Staci felt the hairs on the back of her neck stand up. It felt like there was something off with the way that Sean was talking to her mother. He was being his usual charming self, and his voice flowed like milk over chocolate. But . . . she couldn't shake the feeling that he was *making* her mother agree with him. She shook her head, feeling her face blush again. *Of course he's persuasive. He's the complete package, girl: rich, smart, and smooth. He's probably been practicing how to talk anyone into anything since he could speak. Especially if he's going to inherit the family business, whatever the "firm" is.*

He handed the phone to her. "Go ahead, Staci. I don't want you to think I'm trying to pull something over on you."

She took the phone. The first thing she heard was her mother's voice, and it sounded breathless. "Staci, don't mess this up. The Blackthornes own the whole damn town. Of course you can stay, just don't do anything stupid, all right?"

She almost rolled her eyes in disgust. Of course, that would be the very first thing her mom would think of: the Blackthornes owned the town so don't mess things up—for *her.* No "Be careful," not even a "Have fun." *You're a great mother, Mom.*

"It'll be great, thanks, Mom," was all she said, and handed the phone back to Sean.

CHAPTER SEVEN

After the tour, Sean brought her back to the pool and his cousins. Finn and Meaghan had disappeared, and the others didn't say much. They weren't mean or even unpleasant—the opposite, in fact. She spent the afternoon sunbathing and swimming in their company; the afternoon seemed to pass really quickly, in fact, and before she knew it, the sun was setting. A uniformed maid just appeared at her elbow, and suggested she "might want to go to her room and change before dinner."

Intrigued, and full of a dreamy lassitude, she followed the maid up to the second floor, where she found herself in possession of . . . well the only time she had ever seen a setup like this, it was in a TV program about "high-roller" suites in Las Vegas. It was a drop-dead gorgeous room, all black and gold, with its own bathroom that had its very own Jacuzzi and a fancy shower with more heads and attachments than she had ever seen before. The maid opened a closet, to display a small but fantastic wardrobe of clothes, more than enough to see her through the weekend even if she changed three times a day.

109

There was even a little beaded dress even cuter than the one that Brenda had appropriated. On a whim, Staci chose that to wear.

When she went back downstairs to the dining room, she was glad she had. Everyone else was wearing "dinner" outfits. Even the guys were in suits, though they weren't wearing ties, and had their shirts open at the neck. Finn and Meaghan were back, but they were seated at the far end of the table from her, too far away for her to hear anything they said.

It all felt like a dream. When dinner was done, they all went to the card room for movies and drinks. She stuck to soft drinks...or at least, she thought she had. Maybe all the swimming had tired her out, because after about one movie, she felt a little... vague...and excused herself. She barely remembered getting a quick shower and falling into bed, because the next thing she knew, it was morning, and another maid was bringing in breakfast on a tray.

Sean spent most of the morning with her after she came downstairs; she didn't say much, but she didn't have to. He knew an *amazing* amount about all kinds of things, and she liked listening to his voice. Whenever he spoke, everyone was enthralled; it was like he was holding court. In the afternoon, he excused himself. "I need to take care of some...family business," he said, with a wry smile. "Just have to make sure Finn hasn't eroded my position." But there was the pool, and the sun, and she didn't feel at all deprived.

So this is how they live, every day...it's like a permanent vacation at a resort. Things could not be more different from the way she lived down the hill in Silence.

The afternoon just ... passed, so quickly that once again, she hardly noticed. There was a brand new little dinner dress in the closet, a red one this time, and Finn was noticeably absent from dinner, though Sean seemed to have a satisfied little smirk the entire time. Instead of movies, they all watched Sean and three of the other guys play some sort of fantasy video game. It was ... both amazing and incredibly bloody. She wondered how anyone had ever gotten it into stores.

Then again ... maybe this was the sort of thing only rich people ever saw.

The third day was Saturday, and by afternoon, there was a party going around the pool. She recognized some of the people from the last one, but there were a couple new kids, who Sean introduced as friends from elsewhere. They almost looked like Blackthornes; they were incredibly well-dressed and good-looking. This time she saw what happened when the party wound down; about half of the kids from Silence were drunk off their asses, and servants helped them to other guest rooms—except for the two who passed out in lounges next to the pool. She vaguely recalled thinking, as she went to bed, that at least Sean was a lot more careful to keep his guests from getting into trouble than even her father was. Dad had let some of his party guests drive home drunk, more than once.

It was all like some sort of amazing dream. But, like all dreams, she discovered she had to wake up. And wake up, she did, on the fourth day when the maid brought breakfast and a note from Sean.

Well, that "family business" is going to take me a few more days, Staci, and I did tell your mother this was only a weekend party. We can't have her worrying.

Enjoy your breakfast, and the limo will take you back home when you are ready. We'll hook up again in a couple days. Cheers, Sean.

At first she was disappointed that Sean hadn't been able to see her off himself, but she realized that whatever business he was attending to had to be urgent. The entire weekend had been so thoroughly wonderful, she was having trouble imagining going back to her normal routine in Silence. How could you stand walking in the mud after you've played in the clouds?

But there was no chance she'd be able to call her mom and get an extension. She hadn't seen a single phone except Sean's cell in this house, and hers was still getting no reception. With a heavy sigh, she ate that delicious breakfast, changed into the—now cleaned and hung up in the closet—outfit she had worn here, packed her little bag with her cleaned bathing suit and cover-up, and plodded down the circular staircase to the front door.

Like magic, the limo, and the chauffeur, were waiting for her.

The entire trip back sank her deeper and deeper into the gloom that was normal in Silence. She saw all of the same, used-up and dead-eyed people, all of the shabbiness. It felt horrible, knowing that this was where she really belonged. It was almost like a physical blow, being torn from Sean and all of the beauty of the mansion. She almost wanted to curl up on the limo seat and cry instead of getting out when they reached her house, but instead gathered up her belongings and trudged to the front door as the limo sped off.

Once Staci was inside, she saw that her mother

wasn't home; the usual suspects still occupied the fridge—zombie-pizza and whatever she had bought— and the tip money jar was empty. She couldn't stand the idea of being in the house alone, waiting and thinking about Sean. She knew she wasn't going to get a call of deliverance from him any time today or tomorrow, but at least she had the hope of his promise in the note to "hook up with her again in a couple days."

She checked her phone; no bars but a mostly full charge. Might as well go up the Hill. At least she could make some Facebook posts about the weekend party. Discreetly, of course, since she didn't want to make the Blackthornes think she was a blabbermouth. Rich people didn't like that. But it would be nice to throw something back in the faces of her not-so-friendly friends.

The creepy lawn gnome was gone. It *had* to be some kind of local, lame joke. Then again, depending how into hassling the local kids the cops were, it was probably safer and easier to tote garden statues around than it was to tag things with paint. She still wanted to find whoever was leaving those awful things around and give them the kick to the shin that they deserved.

She settled down, sitting on one of the flat parts near the top of the Hill. After the agonizingly slow connection was finally made, she started going through her tweets and statuses. There weren't nearly as many as before. Strangely, she was beginning to be fine with that; it just showed her who really gave a damn about her, if anything. She noticed that there were several texts from Riley, Seth, and even Wanda; they were all concerned and wondering where she was, especially Wanda. Staci texted them back, saying that she was fine, and that she'd see them at the bookstore to update them. She would probably run into them there before they received the texts, anyways, but it didn't hurt to be safe.

Staci looked up at the sky; it looked like it was going to be another completely overcast day. Funny, how everything had seemed so sunny and bright at the mansion. There were even what looked like a few big thunderhead clouds forming in the distance, out over the sea.

When she looked down again, she saw the gnome, just on the edge of some trees maybe sixty feet away. It was facing her, and seemed to actually be *looking* at her. It had *not* been there just a moment ago. Someone had to be up here with her, trying to freak her out.

"Who's out there? I'm serious, I'm going to call the cops unless you come out right now and cut it out!" She glanced over her shoulder...when she heard what sounded like something heavy rustling against grass. Right next to her. She slowly turned her head, keeping her eyes on the ground. There were boots, standing right in front of her. They were thick, pitted leather, with some sort of metal on the toes; something more like what Frankenstein's monster would wear than a person. Pure terror clutched her. Her breathing changed; short and stuttered. She started to raise her eyes, going from the boots up. Heavy trousers, ripped and spattered with mud and other...substances. A wide leather belt, kind of like what bodybuilders would wear, with an empty sheath as long as her forearm hanging off it. Poking

underneath the belt was a tunic, the same disgusting fabric as the trousers. Finally, she saw the face,
towering a full head over her. It looked like an old
man, with mottled, out-of-proportion features. A full
beard, soiled with bits of food and other fluids. What
made her finally gasp were his eyes; they were like
two chunks of coal stuck into his eyesockets, but she
knew that they were staring right back at her. On top
of the . . . thing's head was a red hat, and the end of
it was dripping sticky, dark-red, clotted fluid down
the side of the thing's face.

Staci couldn't even scream. Her mind was completely
blank with terror. She watched with sick detachment
as it raised an apelike, ropey and muscular arm above
its head; a jagged and heavily nicked blade was nested
in its meaty fist.

She was going to die. Her last thought as the knife
came down was that she wouldn't have a chance to
see Sean again.

A brilliant explosion right in the center of the
creature's face caused Staci to fall backwards. Her
lungs found air again, and she screamed this time.
She landed right on her rear, fell back and hit her
head, and saw stars. She blinked furiously, trying to
clear her vision as she crawled backwards. The creature wasn't looking at her anymore; it didn't have the
knife, either, but a long staff with a blade attached
at the end. It swung the staff around wildly, as if it
was confused and looking for where whatever hit it
had come from.

There was movement on Staci's left; what looked
like a shaft made of light sprang from out of nowhere,
streaking towards the creature. It hit, and another

mini-explosion blinded her; this time it was centered on the creature's chest, causing it to stagger. Two more shafts of light, seconds apart and from different directions, flew from thin air. The creature was driven to its knees this time, still swinging its head side to side to look for its attacker. Staci heard someone running from behind her; she curled up into a little ball, hoping that whoever it was, was a rescuer, and not someone else there to kill her.

In a shower of loose grass over her head, someone leapt over her. The person—and it was a person, not another monster—landed in front of her. He was holding a sword in one hand; it occurred to Staci that it was too shiny, with how overcast the sky was. In the other...was a sort of disc, made out of light. The person held it in front of himself like a shield. The creature was back on its feet again, but it was clearly hurting; its breathing was labored, and it was holding its spear-thing unsteadily.

The person and the creature stood still, watching each other. Then the person charged forward, sword above his head and shield out. The creature swung its spear in a vicious diagonal swipe. The person—Staci could tell it was a man by the way he moved—ducked under the attack, slashing his sword at the creature's midsection as he ran past it, leaving a streak of red on the creature's tunic. They traded several more blows; the man taking the hits on his shield, while replying with more cuts to the torso and extremities of the creature. In a final, desperate gambit, the creature charged the man, the spear held out in front of it. They crashed together, and Staci yelped in fright; it looked like the creature had run the man through with the spear. A tense moment later, the man took a step backwards. The creature's arms were locked under his shield arm, the spear's shaft against his side. With a backhanded stroke, he lopped the head off of the creature, releasing its arms a moment later.

The dead creature's body collapsed to the ground. Almost immediately it—along with the clothing and its weapons—started to dissolve into a foul-smelling muck. Staci struggled to stand up. She felt like she was going to pass out, and the world was spinning faster than she could handle.

"Who are you?" She managed to whisper, still dizzy.

The man turned around to face her, the shield dissipating into strands of light that absorbed through the man's arm. He wore a leather jacket and jeans, and motorcycle boots.

It was Dylan.

The first thing that Staci did was drop down to her knees and puke her guts out. She was afraid that she was going to black out and land face-first in her own sick, but eventually she was able to gulp enough air down to steady herself. When she looked up, Dylan was still standing there; instead of a sword, he was holding out a handkerchief.

"Here, take this. Take a minute to get your wits about you. I'm about to drop a bomb on you, girl, and you'll want to be all there for it."

She took the handkerchief and swallowed around the nasty taste in her mouth. Dylan helped her to her feet, and they moved away from the puddle of muck and what she'd left on the ground. As soon as they were out of smell-reach she sat down again. "Oh my god, what *was* that thing?" she moaned. "It looked like a lawn gnome from *hell.*"

"Yeah, the glamour they use is pretty effective; most people don't even notice them, no matter where they show up. Helps the little bastards do whatever dirty job they've contracted for." Dylan shook his head, then looked back to her. "It was a Red Cap, by the way. Nasty suckers; they're fast, move quietly, and are deadly strong. A lot of them take on jobs as bounty hunters for that very reason. That one," he said, pointing at the vaguely person-shaped black sludge on the grass, "seemed to want to shuffle you off from this mortal coil."

She shook her head, still confused. "But what's a Red Cap anyway? And why was it trying to kill me?"

He leaned back against a tree, and crossed his arms over his chest. The breeze—which was blowing from them to the puddle—ruffled his hair. "Red Caps are one of the many types of Fae creatures out in the world. Oh, right. Do you remember how I said that I was going to drop a bomb on you? Well, here it is; magic is real, kiddo. Some of it just tried to kill you."

She stared at him. Surely she had just imagined him saying those words. "What do you mean, 'magic'? Was that guy a delusional lunatic? Did he think he was some kind of fantasy videogame monster? Is that what you mean?"

Dylan chuckled, as if she was being particularly dense, and he was amused by it. "I mean, magic. Literal, defying the laws of nature and science, magic. Now, there's still laws that go along with magic, but it's not like anything you know about. For the most part. And that thing wasn't crazy; cranky and greedy, more like. Definitely a monster, though, and not just pretending to be one." He cocked his head to the side. "I get that this is a lot to take in, especially for a mortal. But you'll have to trust me on this. You're in a world of shit, Staci."

"I'm . . . is this a drug trip or something?" she asked desperately. Because, of course, it couldn't be *real*. There was no such thing as magic. And why would anything want to kill her? But . . . how would anyone have gotten something hallucinogenic into her way up here? Sprayed it out of the tree? A ninja dart? That *almost* was crazier than . . . magic . . . ,

"It'd be a lot simpler if you were just high out of your gourd. But I'm 'fraid that everything is exactly as it seems. Magic exists, so do monsters, and all sorts of crap you haven't heard of. Most of it isn't very nice." Dylan recrossed his arms, looking contemplative. "You're a skeptic . . . but only kind of, I think. All right; how would you like me to prove to you that you're not tripping, and that I'm on the level?"

"Sure?" she managed, because she was thinking, *while he's pretending to be Harry Potter, maybe I can get to my bike and find the cops* . . . She'd *thought* he was an okay guy, but now . . . now she wasn't so sure. Maybe *he'd* somehow—sprayed the air with something to make her hallucinate? Maybe this was some sort of special effect thing he'd rigged to scare her?

And that's even crazier than . . . what he's been saying! Because that Red Cap thing hadn't been a special effect, it had nearly killed her, and again, how could anyone have gotten drugs into her up on this windy Hill? Both scenarios were impossible, but the second was a lot more impossible than the first.

"Let me think. Ha! I've got just the thing." He turned to the small dirt path that led to the crest of the Hill, put his fingers in his mouth, and whistled. A moment later, there was a familiar rumble; the sound of a well-maintained motorcycle. The same motorcycle that Staci had seen Dylan riding when she first saw him quickly came into view . . . with no one riding it. It drove up to them at a frightening speed, skidding to a halt right next to the pair in a cloud of dust. "Staci, I'd like you to meet Metalhead. Metalhead, Staci. This hunk of junk is my trusty elvensteed, as it were."

She felt her mouth dropping open. She looked for tracks, wires, an *antenna,* even, that would have shown the thing was being driven by someone out of sight. . . .

"All right—" she said, feeling angry. "Who's driving that thing? *Come out!* You think I've never heard of RC cars and shit?"

"Hear that, Metalhead? She thinks that you'd actually let me *drive* you. As if I had that kind of say in our relationship. Metalhead isn't being driven by anyone but himself, Staci, he's—"

There was a loud crash and an explosion of fireworks, followed by an ear-splitting metal guitar solo. Where the motorcycle had been, there was now a . . . horse? It was huge, and heavily muscled. Its skin was silvery-white, more like gunmetal than silk. Its mane was . . . weird, brushy and short, like a mohawk, and its tail had been braided into a kind of club. At the shoulder, chest, and thigh, there were plates of armor, each covered in spikes and intricate designs. To top it all off, there were more pyrotechnic fireworks going off behind the horse and to either side of it; the entire scene looked like the cover of a heavy metal album.

Staci blinked, and the guitar solo ended. The horse was back to looking like a motorcycle again.

"—a huge show-off. Sorry about that; Metalhead likes to ham it up for pretty girls when he gets the chance." Dylan casually strode up to the motorcycle, patting his hand on the gas tank. "Fireworks this time? Really?" He turned his attention back to Staci.

"What...is...that..." she gasped. "And...why... how..."

"Like I said, elvensteed. Where I'm from, they only look like horses; any kind of horse, really. But up here, they can look however the hell they want. Metalhead there pretty much refuses to be anything but a chopper, nowadays; suits me just fine. If you've got enough gumption, you can coax one into letting you ride it, be your friend. Oh, you also have to be an elf. Kind of a snag, that."

"An...elf." She stared at him.

"Not of the Tolkien or cookie or Christmas variety, but, yeah, an elf."

"If you're an elf," she said, her anger rising, though she was not sure why, "Then why don't you look like Legolas? Where's your bow and all of that shit? Huh?"

"Would you be giving Marlon Brando shit for not looking like Brad Pitt? An apple is an apple is an apple; just depends on how you look at it." He swept back his hair with his right hand, displaying his ear. His left hand waved over it...and suddenly the ear had become pointed. "Kind of conspicuous, isn't it? Plus, it makes it a real pain to deal with sunglasses. Or hats. And don't get me started on bike helmets." He waved his left hand again, and the ear went back to looking human. "Anyway that's not the point. Magic is real, so are monsters and things that go bump in the night. And so are elves. Deal with it. The point is, someone sent that Red Cap to kill you, Staci. Whoever it is, he's probably going to try again."

Her insides went to ice. Some rational part of her mind held on to reality, however. "But why?" she wailed. "And why do *you* care?"

"To answer you in reverse order, I care because I don't like seeing assholes having their way with the world. So, I've made it my job to see to it that they don't, basically. I'm kind of a roving troubleshooter; jerks pop up, I knock 'em back down. As for your first question, I aim to find out why someone, some *Fae*, would want to kill you. That's going to take a little detective work and, of course, your help."

A million questions were racing through her mind now. Like, how had he known she was in trouble? But the one she blurted was, "You mean there are other elves? In Silence?" Because . . . that just made no sense at all. How would they hide?

"That's the only way I can figure that a Red Cap got hired to take you out. No one else topside that I can figure out as having the scratch to pay for a hit like that." He scratched his head a little. "Not to pay for the Red Cap; they like murdering, it's what they do. Then they dip their hats in their victim's blood to keep the red color."

With horror, she remembered how the cap had been dripping thick, clotted . . .

"But covering it up afterwards—that would be the trick. That's why elves don't meddle with humans. It's a lot of work to cover it up, make sure the rest of us don't find out about it." He tilted his head to look at her slantwise. "So, just who did you make an enemy of here? That'd be the place to start. I kind of doubt it's your stepmom. Our kind don't live in big cities for—well, it's complicated, there are a lot of reasons."

A little part of her wished it *could* be Brenda. That would make her the perfect Wicked Stepmother. "Are you sure?" she asked, wistfully. "I mean, aren't there other . . . things . . . that'd be able to pay off one of those . . . things? Like a witch or something?"

"Naw, there's not much of that around here. They run in the same circles, sure, but I wouldn't call it likely. It's not like you've been punting black cats or anything. Has anyone recently seemed to have taken a dislike to you? Any grudges, stuff like that? Anyone been giving you the evil eye? That's a thing, too, by the way."

"I . . . dunno," she said doubtfully. "There's been awful lawn gnomes everywhere I looked ever since I came here."

"Hm. Might be that someone had an eye on you, since you showed up. Or the Red Cap was scoping you out for a quick fix, then got hired to take you out after he already had you picked." He gave her a penetrating look. "Are you sure there wasn't someone who's been giving you a funny feeling? It's not the bookstore dude, he's okay. A pussy, but okay."

Staci started to feel indignant over Dylan calling Tim that; she remembered the exchange they had had at the bookstore, and how off it had all been. Then, all at once, it came into her head. Finn. Maybe his girlfriend, but definitely Finn. "I got invited to a weekend party at the Blackthornes," she said hesitantly, not sure what his reaction was going to be to *that*.

It was disappointingly neutral. "So...getting invited to parties is unusual for you? What's the connection to some big ugly trying to kill you?"

"Well...the party was kind of...strange. Mostly strange in a really good way, but...Sean just kind of invited me out of nowhere, and I don't think... I mean, my dad's a lawyer, but we don't get invited to the parties of people who have, like, mansions." She was trying to fumble her way to some sort of explanation. "I know the Blackthornes own the whole town and everything, but there was a lot of stuff that should have been up there, like computers and Internet and business stuff, that wasn't. And..." she remembered that "gallery," with all the weird weapons and the *huge* animal heads, so big as to be fantastic. But what if they had been? Fantastic, that is. "And there was stuff that didn't seem real. Dylan, could the *Blackthornes* be more elves? The whole family looks *really* alike! And they have this art gallery full of weapons that look out of a D and D book."

He shrugged. "It's a good place to start, if nothing else. So, which one did you say invited you to this party? 'S' something?"

"Sean. He's like, the heir or something. And he was really, really nice, but his cousin, Finn..." She shivered a little remembering the taunts and hostile looks. Could that have meant way more than she had thought? "He was mean and nasty. Sean took my side and told him off, but I could tell Finn didn't like me."

Dylan didn't say anything for a long time, instead looking down at the town. After what seemed like hours, he finally turned to her and spoke. "Staci, I normally wouldn't do this, but I have to ask you a

favor. More than a favor, really. I need your help. It's
going to be dangerous, for you and for me. You're
going to need to learn fast, and stay on your toes,
otherwise we're both screwed. But right now, getting
your help is my best chance to save this town, and
everyone in it." He stepped closer to her, his fists
on his hips. "If you don't want to get involved, I'll
understand. I'll try my best to keep you safe. What
do you say?"

"What?" Okay, this had just gone from weird to
insane. This was like something that would happen
in a movie, not like real life....

And a giant lawn gnome just tried to murder you.

Yes—but—since when did cute, mostly strange guys
just come up to her and ask her to help save the
town? That was nuts! It was—it was like something
Seth would come up with for one of his games!

*Hello. Giant lawn gnome. Murder. Plus elves, and
magic motorcycles.*

Okay...but she wasn't going to just blindly promise someone something without knowing what it was
going to involve.

"Maybe," she said cautiously. "You have to tell me
what I'm getting into first. 'Cause this isn't a game or
a movie and I'm not gonna do something just 'cause
it's in the script."

He nodded, as if he had expected her to say something like that. "No, it certainly isn't a game. And I
wouldn't expect you to just go full-in for nothing. So,
I'll tell you something that you really ought to know
about yourself...something that'll help you. Are you
ready? I sure as hell hope you are."

"Ooookay," she said cautiously. This just kept getting

weirder, when she thought it had already gone past weird. What could he tell her about herself? He didn't even *know* her!

His mouth was set in a little, grim, "I'm not joking about this," sort of expression. "I think I know why you've piqued the interest of whatever baddie is out there." He paused. "You've got some elven blood in you, girl."

"*What?*" Of all the crazy things she expected him to say, this wasn't one.

He nodded. "Diluted as the beer that they serve in the excuse of a bar in this town, but you've got the blood all the same. Mortals with elven blood aren't all that common, so when one pops up, everyone that can sense that sort of thing takes notice."

She sat back on her heels, feeling... not exactly stunned, but coming on top of everything else, it was almost too much. Just like the moment in an anime when the schoolgirl finds out she's really a Magical Girl, right? *And that's when her life goes to hell...*

But this wasn't an anime. This was reality. A reality that, frankly, was turning out to be a zillion miles away from the reality that held New York, lawyers, stepmothers that stole your jewelry, and moms that drank too much.

And the first question she blurted out was absolutely stupid. "Does that mean I can do magic?" And she felt stupid as soon as it was out of her mouth, because, of course, if she *could*, then she'd have been doing it before now, right?

Dylan smiled, but not in a way that said he was laughing at her. "We'll get to that soon enough, tiger. For now, let's just focus on keeping your head attached to your shoulders. You help me, I'll help you learn some of the tools of the trade. Deal?"

"... I dunno. I still don't know what it is you want me to do," she said, suddenly getting back part of her caution. "Dad always said to never sign a contract without reading it."

"Wise man. You said that this Finn character doesn't like you? And he's related somehow to this Sean guy, who seems hot to trot for you? Then just keep doing what you're doing. Hang out with Sean, keep an eye on Finn. Learn what you can, keep your eyes open. Right now we've only got one suspect. There's a whole lot of stuff going down, if you couldn't tell; the hit on you was just a piece of it. I want to crack the whole coconut open, see what's squirming around inside."

Well, that seemed easy enough. "Okay," she temporized. "I mean, as long as Sean still likes me after this weekend." Because there was always the chance that the "family business" had been made up just so he could get away from her without disinviting her, and once she was off the estate, she'd never get asked again. "Like, I don't know if I passed the Blackthorne Test or anything this weekend, so I might never see him again except off in the distance." She actually felt a lump in her throat as she said that. Everything had been so *perfect* up there, and everything was so gray and gross and *worse* than ordinary down here.

"If he's elven, or any of his kin are—which I can't imagine they're not—then I doubt he's going to lose interest in you. When he does call, let me know." He grinned. "*My* cell phone's got some...extra stuff. Magic. The blank spot around here doesn't affect it. Your phone will be able to call mine, even down in town."

As he reached in his pocket and pulled out a little card, like a business card, but with just a phone number on it, she couldn't help thinking, *His phone works too. Like Sean's...*

"Here, let me see your phone." Staci fumbled around in her pockets until she was able to produce the cell. Dylan held it lightly in his left hand, focusing intently on it. With his right hand, he started to trace designs in the air; Staci could see a weird afterglow wherever his fingers went, almost like the contrails from jets high overhead. The phone actually started to float up from the palm of his left hand...before it set back down, the designs in the air fading. "There. You'll be able to get ahold of me, even when you're in town."

"So, I can text and get Internet, too?" She felt her hope rising; finally, she wouldn't have to drag her bike up the Hill every time she wanted to check her email. No more sore calves, no more muddy shoes. No more ambushes by freaky gnome characters.

"Sorry, I'm just a basic, garden-variety magician, not a miracle worker. Think of it more like a connection between our phones, now. But just our phones; no one will be able to listen in, or figure out who you're talking or texting to." He paused for a moment, then started fishing around in one of his motorcycle jacket pockets. "There's something else you should have."

He handed her a phone charm; one of those things on a thin, wirelike lanyard that you could attach to your phone. She used to have a lot of them, but they'd fallen apart and left her with only the lanyards, so right now her phone was bare. She peered at it; it was a tiny, octagonal, silver charm with what looked like a tree on it, with the words "Fairgrove Industries" in fancy script around the edge. "What's this?" she asked.

"Think of it like an emergency locator beacon. If anything untoward—magically speaking—starts to happen to you, it'll let me know, and I'll come running. With Metalhead over there, I can get most places pretty damn fast. And . . . you wanted to do magic, right?"

She nodded, vigorously. He grinned.

"You aren't up to anything but baby steps, but I can show you the first trick every kid learns to do. Just hold that charm in the palm of your hand." He held one hand cupped upwards, and she imitated him. "Now just point at it, and kind of stir your finger around it, imagine you're stirring power into it. You'll start to feel something building up in your chest, and when it feels like you can't hold it in anymore, say *beura.*"

"What's it mean?" she asked, doing as he told her. And, strangely, she *did* feel something, a tightening in her chest, as she circled her finger clockwise about the charm. And the tension built up *really* fast. When it got to the point where she could hardly breathe, she choked out, *"Beura!"*

Then tension released like an arrow. And the little charm erupted into a tiny ball of light, almost too bright to look at, in the palm of her hand.

"Fallen star," said Dylan.

CHAPTER EIGHT

After he showed her how to put the light out, and made sure she could bring it back up again, Dylan explained everything to her. How his job was to make sure that others of his kind—other elves, that is—toed the line, didn't try to hurt humans. He was a private investigator in a way; following clues, solving mysteries, that kind of thing. It was all terribly exciting for Staci. Especially when he told her why he needed her.

"Whoever is pulling the strings around here, they've taken notice of me. I've got kind of a reputation, besides; anyone that has their fingers into something dirty is on the lookout for me, nowadays. That's why I've got the cops in this town breathing down my neck; whoever is *really* in charge is hoping that getting the fuzz to lean on me will get me to back off, find something easier to go after. But that's not my style." He grinned when he said that; it reminded her of how the heroes in movies always grinned when they got hit with a challenge. "It's also where you come in. You can go where I can't; no one will ever suspect you of snooping around. You can get close to the Blackthornes, find out what's going on there with that Finn character. You're already neck deep in this, besides."

"What's going on—is this why things are so rotten here? Why no one ever seems to get a break, why everything is like, stuck in 1950, only depressing, and why..." She stopped, before she said *why you can't get cell and net and cable*, because that all seemed awfully petty.

"Very astute of you. That's what brought me here; a lot of, I guess the easiest way to describe it would be 'magical vibes.' Someone is purposefully keeping this place depressing, keeping everyone here downtrodden. I don't know why. Not yet." He looked over her head for a moment. "I checked out the idea that it might be a side effect to something bigger and nastier going on, but it's not. This is purposeful, not accidental. And right now, the only place I *haven't* been able to check out is the Blackthorne Estate." He must have read her expression, because he shrugged. "Walls, dogs, armed guards, cameras, that sort of thing. Normal precautions that rich people take to keep intruders out. If I were more of a magician, I might be able to get around security like that, but I'm not."

I guess I can see that... It was a little disappointing— an elf, having trouble getting past a guard with a dog?—but on the other hand, being less superhuman made him more like her. Not quite such a big deal. Especially not if he needed her help.

"Anyway, if you're all right now, I should make tracks." He looked down at the town again. "I'm late for a meeting as it is."

A meeting with what? she wanted to ask, but she was pretty sure he wouldn't tell her.

"I figure it suffices to say, you shouldn't let anyone know about this. I hate secrecy, but it's a necessity for this gig. It's safer for you, and safer for me." He stepped up to Staci, taking her hands into his. "I'm counting on you. I know it's a lot of responsibility, but I think you can handle it. Okay?"

She flushed, feeling happy and warm inside. She trusted Dylan; well, he'd just rescued her from nearly being chopped into bits, that was a good reason to trust someone! And now he had asked her to help *him*, he trusted *her*, and he trusted that she could handle herself. No one had ever trusted her with more than a credit card, before. She had had responsibilities before: laundry, taking out the garbage, little everyday stuff like that. But this...this was beyond. This was *special*.

"I'll do it," she said firmly. He squeezed her hands, then let go.

"All right then. Just do what you'd do as if none of this had ever happened. The best thing you can do is to act normally. Hang out with your friends, continue your routine. Whenever you get the chance to go up to the Blackthorne Estate, though, accept. Make whatever excuses you have to, but go." He stared into her eyes as if he was trying to make sure she obeyed him. "Blow off your friends, do whatever it takes."

"I know how important this is to you. I can take care of it. I'm not a kid, you know." She laughed to take the sting off what she'd just said. She didn't want to get him mad... "Besides, I think pretty much anybody that lives here would cut off limbs for the chance to go to one of those parties, you know? It'd look weird if I *didn't* want to go."

"Cool." The motorcycle rolled up next to him without him doing anything, engine thrumming enthusiastically. "That's my hint I need to get back to work. I'll be in touch. You keep yourself safe, okay? And keep your eyes open, Staci. This doesn't work without you."

"Okay—" she began, but he didn't wait for any more of a response. Or maybe that was Metalhead's doing, because the engine roared, the tires spun so that the bike pivoted in a half-circle, and the next thing she knew they were disappearing down the road.

After all that, getting groceries was a distinct let-down. Especially after comparing what was offered in the store with what she'd feasted on up at the estate. Since it was pretty obvious that Mom didn't intend to pay for food if she didn't have to, Staci decided she was going to buy only what *she* wanted, and if Mom didn't like it, well, tough.

By the time everything had gotten put away, it was a little later than she usually met the gang, so she was pretty sure they would all be waiting at the bookstore when she got there.

She was right.

"Where the frakking *hell* have you been?"

Jake was the first one to stand up. Riley and Seth both kept their seats, but shared the same look of concern. Wanda was the one that actually marched up to the front of the store, took Staci by the arm, and dragged her to the back before Tim could even utter a word.

"I hate to sound like a frickin' parent, but we've been worried sick about you! Where have you been?"

Jake, Riley, and Seth all looked worried; Wanda just looked pissed off.

"Sean Blackthorne invited me to a weekend party," she said, feeling a sullen anger that she tried hard to suppress. "He even called up my mom to make sure it was okay with her. He didn't have any Internet up there, and there wasn't a phone in my room and I didn't exactly feel like being pushy and asking for one so I could call you guys, when I figured you'd call Mom and find out where I was. I tried to leave a message for every one of you when I was checking Facebook up on Makeout Hill not too long ago, you know. And then, because Mom hadn't left anything worth eating in the house, I had to do a grocery run." She flopped down in a chair. "I got here as soon as I could." After that she launched into a flurry of details about the party: the food, the music, the house itself. And especially about Sean Blackthorne.

Riley and Seth went from worried to envious by the time she was done; Jake looked like he was still kind of on the fence between envious and upset. Wanda still looked pissed off.

"You know, we were really worried," Jake said. He almost looked bashful. "I mean, your mother isn't the most reliable person out there, as far as knowing where you are...or talking to. And...well, shit, we were just worried."

Wanda cut in. "To hell with that, I filed a police report. You disappear for days, and no one knows where you are? Hell, yeah, I went to the cops, for all the good they are in this shit-kicker town."

"C'mon, Wanda. She's fine, she had a good time. Her mother knew where she was...so it's okay, right?" Seth was clearly uncomfortable with the direction Wanda was trying to take the discussion. He kept rubbing his arms, trying not to look either Wanda or Staci in the eye.

Riley cut in before Wanda could start off on another tirade. "So—*weekend party?* We've *heard* about those, but no one we know ever went to one! Did you see inside the house? What happened? What do people do all weekend? Was it like—crazy, riot, no parents, or what?"

Wanda settled back to seethe in silence as Staci gratefully took the change of conversation and ran with it. "The only people that got crazy were some of the town kids that came up Saturday night," she said. "Mostly it was me and a lot of Blackthorne cousins, and we sat around the pool, and they all look like supermodels, I swear."

"When you've got all the money in the world, what doesn't look good is easy to fix," Riley said, with just a *hint* of acid. "So don't get intimidated because you're not a product of better living through chemistry and surgery."

"This is still so much bullshit." Wanda had her arms crossed, her coffee mug forgotten, looking off at one of the bookshelves.

Jake came down off the fence. "Oh, come off it, Wanda. Staci is a big girl; she can take care of herself. *Her mother said she could go.* Sean Blackthorne called her mother himself. Nothing bad happened, other than this town preventing us from living like civilized people with regular texting capabilities. If she had been able to text us from the word go, we wouldn't have had any reason to worry. Hell, we would have been begging to tag along." He settled down in the loveseat with Riley. "You need to stop looking for the train wreck in every situation."

"Yeah, sure. Begging to tag along." Wanda huffed,

then slapped the arms of her chair. "Whatever. I can't hear any more of this. I'll catch you all later." Without another word, she gathered up her backpack and marched out of the bookstore, letting the door slam behind her.

Riley rolled her eyes. "*Awk*-ward," she said. She and Jake exchanged a look, then nailed Seth with one. He sighed exaggeratedly. "All right, I'll handle her," he said. Then he turned back to Staci. "So...what do the rich people do on the weekend?"

She spent the next half hour spilling the rest of the details about the party; the food, the music, the house. Even the weird parts like the trophy room. Seth *really* liked the trophy room. And he was purple with envy about the video game setup, though he couldn't identify the game they were playing. "It might be something you can only get in Asia," he observed. "They can get a lot more graphic there." She had to check herself, though; she almost let slip a few times about...well, magic. And Dylan.

Ever since he had rescued her earlier, she was having a hard time not thinking about him. He was an honest-to-goodness elf; real and in the flesh. And so was Sean! Or at least, that was what Dylan had hinted. It was all so surreal, and if she hadn't had that phone charm to tell her it really had happened, she'd have been sure it had been some sort of...maybe a nightmare she'd had, falling asleep on the Hill. But it was real; it had happened. Dylan was gorgeous in a rough way, but he was also a little dangerous. She had only met him a couple of times in town, and he had sprung so much crazy stuff on her...but he seemed to be trying to help her, trying to help the town. Then there was Sean; he was a dream. He was probably an elf, too, and ridiculously hot. But there was something seriously wrong with Finn. Could it be that Sean just didn't know what was going on? Her own human family was dysfunctional enough that it wasn't a stretch of the imagination to believe that elves were just as screwed up. Hadn't Finn kind of threatened Sean? That "family business"—could that have been about Finn?

So she had only half her mind on what the others were saying, although at least she kept it together enough that her answers to them made sense.

With the curfew looming, they all finished the last of their drinks and began packing up to head out the door. Staci, of course, didn't really have anything to pack up, but she took her time, cleaning up the cups, tidying the coffee bar, waiting for the others to get out ahead of her so she could ask Tim about Dylan. Dylan had implied he actually *knew* Tim somehow, and Tim had sure seemed to know him. Discreetly, she allowed the others to shuffle out of the shop ahead of her; Seth and Jake were arguing about a British television show, and Riley was trying her best to moderate. They each in turn said their goodbyes to Tim, who was finishing his own coffee and setting a book down as they left. When she was sure the door was closed, Staci came to a stop in front of the counter.

"Hey, Staci. Did you all have fun tonight?"

"Yeah, it was fine. Wanda storming out kind of put a damper on things for a bit."

"She's just worried about you. Wanda doesn't really open up to a lot of people, and you four kids are all she's got. I think she's afraid that you're going to get lured away by the glitterati up at the Blackthorne Estate." Tim smiled wryly. "It's hard to compete with private pools, lobster rolls and home theaters when all you can offer is a tabletop game and popcorn."

Staci felt a little bit guilty; after all, hadn't *she* been feeling like the one deserted with three quarters of her "friends" back in New York abandoning her and the rest offering a couple of tweets of sympathy, then going back to talking about themselves? "Well, I can't see any reason why I can't have *two* sets of friends," she countered. "And maybe Sean will start inviting them, too."

"I leave that up for you all to figure out; I'm just a humble bookstore owner." Tim suddenly seemed to lose interest in the conversation. Staci decided not to let him off the hook just yet.

"You've been here for a while, what do *you* know about the Blackthornes?" she asked, figuring she could probably segue that into asking about Dylan, too.

"About the same as everyone else. The Blackthornes are Silence originals, rich as God, and pretty much synonymous with the same around here as far as city politics goes." Tim shrugged. "When I started this store, I figured the best way for everyone to be happy was if I kept my head down and didn't make waves. So I don't mess around in politics and it seems to work out."

That looked to be about as close as she was going to get to an opening, so she took it. "So I guess that biker guy, Dylan, is messing around in politics?"

Something subtle changed in Tim's expression. "I wouldn't know, and I don't particularly care to. Guys like that are usually trouble." He leaned forward, crossing his arms on the countertop. "Why do you ask?"

"I've run into him a couple of times, and he seemed like an okay guy," she replied, pretending to be casual about it. "But I saw you arguing with him, and I wondered why."

Tim was silent, studying Staci. Just when he opened his mouth to speak, the door swung open again. It was Riley.

"Hey! We thought you were right behind us for, like, three whole blocks. Seth and Jake were really into their *Doctor Who* discussion, and . . . well, you know how they get. You coming?"

Tim looked pointedly at the clock. "You don't have much time till curfew," he said, and turned away. "See you lot tomorrow."

Damn. Staci hardly remembered the entire trip home, from walking with the group to getting her bike and walking through the front door. Her head was still full of questions; about Dylan, Tim, the Red Caps . . . about *magic!* Tim knew something, knew a lot more than he was going to tell her, and she was sure about that. He'd been way too quick to evade. So what did he know . . . and why not tell her?

Wait though, Dylan told me to keep the magic stuff secret. Tim doesn't know Dylan told me. So maybe all this is about magic. She kept trying to figure things out while she got ready for bed, but instead of getting neatly sorted out, she just got more and more questions. She thought she'd lie in bed trying to at least figure out what she knew and what she didn't know, but she must have been a lot more tired than she'd thought, because she fell dead asleep and when she woke up, it was Monday.

✧　　✧　　✧

Monday meant doing the laundry, since the L.L. Bean order hadn't arrived yet, and her limited wardrobe was all dirty except for one black T-shirt and a pair of pink capris. She thought she'd save her New York clothes for parties at the Blackthorne place. Assuming she got invited back. Which, the more she thought about it, the less likely it seemed.

She stared at the wash going around and around the ancient machine in the basement, feeling the general depression that Silence was steeped in sink into her soul.

Who was she fooling? Of course Sean wasn't going to see her again. She was no one; elf blood or not. What did that even mean, besides that she could make a bauble light up? *Flashlights do the same thing, all with the press of a button.* She wasn't gorgeous. She didn't have any talents, aside from running into everything or tripping over her own feet. She wasn't super-smart. She was a good listener, but somebody like Sean could *pay* for someone to listen to him out of pocket change, without any risk of that someone "getting the wrong ideas." Not only was she not going to see Sean again, at least not in that way, but she was also going to let Dylan down. Why would he want to talk to her if she couldn't help him?

As she was sinking deeper into gloom, she heard someone knocking at the back door. For one second, her heart leapt. Then logic hit. *Sean Blackthorne? At the* back *door? Get real.*

She was tempted to ignore it—for all she knew, it was some scuzzy friend of her mom's, looking for Mom, or a handout, or...ewww...*let's not go there.* But the knocking came again, so she trudged up the stairs to see who it was. After all, she didn't have to let whoever it was in.

But when she got to the kitchen and peered around the head of the stairs at the glass panes of the back door—it was Wanda. Her friend was looking off to the side, arms crossed over her chest—that was all Staci could see.

For just a minute, Staci was still tempted to pretend she wasn't home. But Wanda had come all the way over here on her own, and Staci doubted it was for the opportunity of pitching another bitch. So she came out into the kitchen, deliberately making footfall sounds, and Wanda turned around, spotted her and waved at her through the glass. She waved back and came to unlock the door.

"Hey," Staci said.

"Hey, Staci." Wanda looked extremely uncomfortable; she was fidgeting and wouldn't meet Staci's eyes for more than a second. "Um, can I come in?"

"Sure. I'm in the middle of laundry, though. The machine that came with the house is from the Stone Age so—"

"Great." Wanda didn't wait for Staci to finish, breezing past her and into the house.

Okay, sure, come down to the creepy basement with me then. Staci headed for the basement stairs, not waiting to see if Wanda followed. Good thing too, because the stupid washing machine was starting to rock. She stopped it, moved the soggy clothes around, and started it again.

"All right, listen. I just wanted to say that I'm sorry about last night. I didn't mean to snap at you, or barge out like that." She waited a few heartbeats, looking at the ground between her feet. "I'm not very good at this sort of crap, you know?"

"I don't think this town lets anyone get good at anything," Staci said, after a moment. She waved her hands in the air a little...helplessly. "It's...it's like the place doesn't want anyone to have *anything* good." She took a deep breath. "But if you're going to get all bent out of shape because Prince Blackthorne invites me to parties and I don't run and tell you...I dunno, doesn't that seem kind of *black hole of need* to you?"

"Yeah, you're right, you're right...but it's not like that! I mean, you've seen this town, you've seen how it tears people down and no one seems to do anything... but you don't really know yet. You haven't been here long enough. To see people, who start out hopeful and full of dreams and everything...and watch those same people turn into the walking dead. It's not just small-town blues; there's something seriously wrong here." Wanda finally looked up; she looked wretched, barely held back tears in her eyes. "I told you to be careful because of *that*. Because of this town. People don't leave...but sometimes they just don't show up anymore. Okay?"

A chill went down her back. Wasn't that why Dylan had said he was here? She bit her tongue before she blurted out something about that. "Okay," she agreed. "You know what? I've got an idea that's about as prehistoric as this washing machine. What about if I go get an old answering machine and hook it up to the phone, and if I get an invite, I'll just leave a message for you guys on it?"

Wanda let out a half-choked laugh/sob. "My god, it's like we're in the Eighties again. Which wouldn't be so bad; the music would be better." She wiped her eyes with the back of her hand. "Sure, that sounds good. Again, I'm sorry for being such a spaz." She sighed heavily. "Well, you need any help folding laundry?"

"Sure. Then we can check the junk shops for answering machines. Ones that need batteries so even if the power goes out, you won't have an aneurism on me." She hugged Wanda's shoulders, relieved that everything had worked out all right. *Because when Sean doesn't call again, I'm gonna be better off with friends who at least get worried about me.*

After breakfast two days later, Staci decided that it might not be a bad idea to see what she could research about elves. Wouldn't she be that much more helpful, if she knew what she was actually dealing with? Sure, elves were kind of a secret . . . but *she* had found out about them. There had to be some useful information written down somewhere, by someone that had interacted with them; she couldn't be the only one. Unfortunately . . . the always-reliable-until-now Internet was not going to be possible.

At least . . . not *here*. But maybe there was Internet at the public library? And even if there wasn't, there should be *something* in the way of books that had things about elves in them?

After consulting the map and the phone book, Staci got on her bike and pedaled to another unprepossessing and rundown building a block away from the high school. It looked like something out of a model kit; a cement and brick square, two stories tall, with "Andrew Carnegie Public Library" chiseled in the stone lintel over the door. She locked her bike to the empty bike rack and went inside.

There was a single, tired-looking old lady sitting behind a desk that looked as old as the building at the front. "Can I help you, miss?" she asked, her voice wispy in the dusty silence.

"Do you have Internet terminals?" Staci asked hopefully.

The old lady shook her head. "I'm sorry, miss. We don't." She waved at a bank of . . . well, Staci wasn't sure *what* they were. They looked like wooden filing cabinets, except the drawers were too small to hold documents. "We haven't modernized at all, I'm afraid. No money for it, nor any interest. You're the first person we've had in here in a week. You'll have to look up what you want in the card catalogue."

"The . . . what?" Staci blinked in confusion.

An hour or so later, after personal instruction in how to use the card catalogue and the Dewey Decimal System, the librarian left her alone while she "put the returns away." Another hour, and several trips to the bookshelves later, and Staci had a small stack of books beside her where she had set herself up on the second floor, in something that the librarian called a "study carrel," another completely weird term she'd never heard before. It turned out to be a desk, with a bookshelf above the working surface and wings to either side to block what you were doing from the person in the next carrel.

She'd outright rejected the stuff from the kid's section; the usual fairy-tale books, including a line of them in every color she could imagine. That hadn't left her with much, and at least half of *that* was gaming books of the sort that the gang toted around; these copies were earlier editions, from the

'70s and '80s with the signs of heavy use on the corners and binding.

Three hours later, she closed the last of them, feeling frustrated and brain-tired, with not much in the way of notes to show for her work. So much of it was ancient mythology, and almost none of it appeared to, one, be consistent, or two, match what she had personally *seen* about elves. There certainly wasn't anything about elvensteeds that also happened to turn into frickin' motorcycles.

She decided to give up and go home for now. Maybe one of her orders would have arrived by now. The clerk hardly noticed her leaving; she was absorbed in a book of her own, apparently happy to collect a paycheck with as little effort given as possible.

Staci was upstairs, putting away the L.L. Bean order that had *finally* arrived, when the phone rang. The sound was startlingly loud in the quiet house, and she jumped. When it rang a second time, she ran down the stairs, figuring it was one of the gang telling her . . . something. *Sheesh, it's like I'm in a '50s musical or something*, she thought, as she reached for the handset. At least the phone wasn't rotary . . . though the answering machine next to it was a kind of jarring note.

"Yeah?" she said—*not* identifying herself, because her dad had drummed into her *never* to give your name until you knew who was calling.

"Hello, Staci? It's Sean Blackthorne."

Now her heart started pounding. She took a deep breath. *Okay. Don't squee. Don't act like it's a big deal. Be cool.* "Oh, hi, Sean! I hope that family busi-ness went all right. And thanks for the invitation the other night, I never got a chance to tell you what a good time I had."

"Not a problem. That's sort of why I was calling you; we're having a little bit of a lighter get-together tonight. I was wondering if you would want to attend?"

She clutched the handset. "Mom's at work . . . so I can't ask her if I can stay late." Mom had been *very* adamant about that. *If you're not run over, bleeding to death, or the house isn't on fire, you do not call me at work.* She supposed that, in a town with no Internet, where the phone was all you had, a bar was going to be pretty hard on people using its business phone for personal reasons. "If it's not too late, I'd really like that."

"Shouldn't run all that late. Again, this is a more intimate sort of gathering. Can I send a car for you around . . . let's say, seven?"

"That would be *awesome!*" she said with enthusiasm. And after he had hung up, she clung to the handset for a moment until the *blat—blat—blat* coming from it made her hang up.

It was only five. Plenty of time to decide what to wear. And plenty of time to call the others and let them know she wouldn't be at the bookstore tonight.

Her cell phone in the back pocket of her jeans suddenly reminded her that Dylan had asked her to call him if she got another invite. But . . . he hadn't specified whether it was supposed to be *before* or *after.*

She hesitated a moment, then shrugged. After. She didn't really have anything to tell him right now, so why bother? Better to wait until she had something to report back with, if anything.

So call at least one of the gang, then get on to the really important part. Deciding what to wear.

CHAPTER NINE

Wanda wasn't home, but someone female said she'd leave a message. Seth wanted her to bring back a doggie bag; she reminded him that would be pretty low-rent. He agreed, but definitely sounded like he was disappointed. Riley wanted a blow-by-blow fashion show; that was easy enough to promise. Jake just said, "Have fun."

She left a note for her mom—*reminding* her that she'd been ordered not to call—and ran up to change. She was waiting at the curb when the car turned up; after thinking about it, she decided that she would rather keep her makeup intact and not swim, than have to spend half an hour in the bathroom after swimming and miss something. The car, chauffeur, and the ride to the mansion were all much the same as the last time. Staci kept her eyes peeled during the trip for any more freaky lawn gnomes, but didn't see a single one. For some reason, that seemed more unnerving than if she had seen any.

But once the car crossed the wall onto the Black-thorne Estate, she relaxed. Even if Finn was the one who had sicced the Red Cap onto her, he would never dare let them on the Estate. That much she was sure of.

Tonight the mix seemed to be about half Blackthornes and half townies. It was easy enough to tell the two apart, or it would have been even if the Blackthornes hadn't looked so much alike. Even though the townies were all shopping from the same catalogs Staci had been, they still weren't dressed like the Blackthornes, whose outfits were likely never shown in catalogs at all. And the townies all looked awkward and... unfinished somehow... next to the graceful Blackthornes. There were about thirty guests altogether, and the action was at the patio, rather than poolside, where there was a buffet set up with sandwiches, an entire dessert buffet, and a bar. Music and dancing seemed to be the entertainment tonight.

She was glad she had opted for another of her outfits from home. Even though the fashion was nothing like as *haute* as the stuff the Blackthorne girls were wearing, it was also distinctly *not* Silence's version of "couture."

Sean was in the middle of a group of people, all of them hanging on his every word. As soon as Staci was visible, however, he stopped talking, smiled, and left the group without another word, walking towards her. She did her best to smile demurely, only glancing at him for a moment before taking in the rest of the party.

"I'm glad you made it, and not a moment too soon. I thought I was going to die of boredom back there," he said, jerking a thumb over his shoulder. "You look great."

She blushed and was glad she had picked her little silk "Juliet" dress to wear. It was one of those things that had turned up at a vintage fashion place, somehow mismarked to a price she could actually afford, and dated to the late '60s, she thought. It didn't have a label at all, so it could have come from one of a hundred boutiques around New York back then, or even been seamstress-made for some rich girl after the Zeffirelli movie came out. Sean was clearly not planning on swimming; not wearing that outfit—a tan linen blazer, a cream silk shirt open at the neck, and cream linen trousers. He looked like he'd stepped out of a fashion magazine.

It was great up here; just cool enough that she was comfortable in the long sleeves of her dress. Somehow it was nice here, where it was clammy and cold down in town. Maybe it was because Silence was right on the ocean, but up here, you got dry breezes.

"I could say the same of you," she replied playfully, "except I bet you never look anything other than fantastic."

"Oh, you'd be surprised. Keeping the relations in line can be . . . exhausting work. Apt to leave one looking pretty haggard." He looked around for a moment. "As always, if you want anything, feel free to ask. On that note, would you like anything to drink or eat? I figured we could talk for a bit."

She was actually starving, since she hadn't eaten anything since lunch. But she didn't want to look gauche, so she wasn't going to act like she was ready to eat anything. "Sure, if you're hungry," she said.

He waved a finger at one of the servants behind the buffet table, and the man quickly brought two plates of sandwiches and fixings. Right behind him was a girl from the bar, who handed Staci a clear, fizzy drink and Sean a beer. Sean gestured at a little table; the servant put the plates and napkins down on it, and they took seats. Staci cautiously sipped her drink, but it seemed to just be ginger ale.

The two of them sat, eating quietly while the music and bits of conversation went on around them. No one quite stared at them, but plenty of people who thought they were being discreet were watching them. Sometimes one of the townies—but none of the other Blackthornes—would wander close by, clearly wanting to speak with Sean. But he would always wave them off, not even bothering to look in their direction. No one protested. The entire time that they were eating, Sean stared directly into Staci's eyes. Nowhere else, not even at his food. It was, in a word, intense.

When they were both finished, Sean snapped his fingers; more servants came out, clearing away the plates and empty drinks, leaving the table clear save for a fresh bottle of upscale beer for him and another ginger ale for her.

"The last few times we've seen each other," Sean began, "we haven't had much of a chance to talk to one another. I'd like to know more about you." He took a slug of his beer, his eyes still locked with hers.

"Gosh, there's not that much to tell," she temporized.

"All the same, I'd like to know. I'm sure it's more interesting than anything that these . . . people could offer to say." He flicked his chin out at the other guests. "And I know everything there is to know about my cousins."

She really hadn't intended to talk about herself.

All the dating guides said you were supposed to get the guy to talk, because talking about yourself made you seem narcissistic. But somehow, he managed to coax out the shorthand of what passed for her life story—which got a bit more elaborate and a lot more bitter when she got to the Brenda part.

"...so that's how I ended up coming here," she finished. "It's..."

How to put this in a way that doesn't sound like I'm trashing the town?

"...different," she said, making a little face. "I really miss stuff like cell phones working."

"Even though it may not seem like it now, Silence has its charms. I'm sure it'll grow on you, in time." Sean finished his beer, signaling for another. "What sort of things do you like to do for fun?"

"Pretty much what anyone does in the city—" she began, when she spotted Finn over Sean's shoulder, and froze for a minute. Finn locked eyes with her for a moment...and smirked. Sean noticed her expression, finally breaking eye contact with her to turn in his seat. Finn's eyes flicked over in Sean's direction, and then he laughed heartily, throwing his head back before turning to some of the guests that were near him. When Sean turned back around, Staci felt as if she was jolted by a shock when she saw his expression. There was a moment of fury, of utter rage. It wasn't like Sean was snarling or anything, but it had the same effect; he looked almost feral, primal, and it was all the more terrible because of his beauty.

Just like that, it all vanished. He shook his head, sighing, and ruffled his hair with his free hand. "Like I said, keeping a handle on this herd can run a man ragged. You know, Finn is actually jealous of me. For talking with you, that is."

Well, that wasn't the impression *she* had gotten, but she wasn't going to contradict him. "Do you need to go be the host for a while?" she asked, wistfully, wishing he would say "no" but pretty certain he was going to say "yes."

Sean looked over his shoulder in Finn's direction once more, then sighed again. "Unfortunately, I think I'll have to. Would you accompany me? That way you can tear me away after a while, give me an excuse to break off from the rabble."

She felt herself brighten when he invited her to come with him. "Sure!" she said, standing up and taking her drink with her. She was pretty sure she was not going to think of anything to say, so having the drink would give her something to do.

Sean wandered over to a group of five townies who were congregated just on the edge of the garden. The light from the patio lamps didn't come too far—a deliberate choice, she was sure—so the garden was mostly just a collection of shapes and shadows behind them. The group turned out to be two jocks, two cheerleaders and a girl jock—the "star," if there could be such a thing at a school that seldom won games, of the volleyball team. Sean's approach made them all brighten up, and the first flurry of conversation was mostly from them, sucking up.

She didn't mind, since the sideways looks she was getting from them were not *what's she doing here*, but more along the lines of *lucky, I'm envious*. So at least as far as the townies were concerned, maybe her mom was the local drunk bar-waitress, but *she* was accepted as fitting with the elite crowd. Probably because Sean clearly wanted her here, and what Sean wanted, Sean obviously got.

As before, they all hung on Sean's every word; he talked about her, for quite a bit actually, and everyone nodded along and offered their platitudes just like at the first party. The entire time, a small, nagging voice at the back of Staci's mind kept telling her; *remember why you're here.* As fun as this was for her, it was still supposed to be work. She had something important to do; she was helping Dylan to save Silence. But why couldn't she have a good time while she was doing it?

All the same, she kept her eye on Finn. He was making the rounds, much as Sean was, though he seemed to encourage the townies to drink or otherwise overindulge. She didn't actually *see* anyone doing drugs but... a couple of the townies really looked baked. Even though he had the same good looks as Sean, Finn wasn't nearly as polished, or smooth. He came off more like a Hollywood child star, all grown up and diving towards burn-out. Too big, too loud, and trying too hard.

After a while, the conversation shifted away from Sean talking up Staci towards other topics: summer break, everyone's plans, who was dating who, the usual. Staci did her part, hanging off of Sean's elbow and pulling him away to another group of townies whenever he started to look bored. But she always kept her eye on Finn, in between sips from her drink. Finally, something happened. One of the jock couples on the edge of the patio staggered their way towards the garden. What really caught her attention was Finn; he was watching the couple, and his eyes looked...hungry. Cold and calculating, almost shark-like. Once the pair had disappeared into the garden, Finn disengaged himself from the conversation he was in...and followed.

Well...this might just be what Dylan was talking about! She held down her excitement, and excused herself with a little laugh. "Too much ginger ale..." she said, letting her words trail off, and headed towards the house, since that was more in the direction of the garden than the pool house was.

She soon had the pavilions—cabanas?—between her and Sean and his group, and as soon as she was out of their immediate line of sight, she followed in the direction she had seen Finn go.

It was a little easier to see once she was out of the brighter light, though the garden plantings were still pretty much just lumps of foliage, either low lumps or tall, carefully sculpted lumps. She tried hard to remember what the garden had looked like in daylight, but it was all just a bit vague. The garden hadn't had Sean in it, so she hadn't paid a lot of attention to it. But wasn't there...a hedge?

Sure enough, a few moments later, something tall and solid-ish loomed up in front of her. The hedge. Except it had an opening in it.

A *maze?* It could be...she'd seen hedge mazes in movies—*Labyrinth* used to be one of her favorites as a little kid, when Dad would pretend to be Jared, the Goblin King.

The only light in the maze came from the moon, which was thankfully almost full tonight. Still, Staci had a hard time seeing; the shadows played with her depth perception. Then it occurred to her that even though her phone was useless to call or text anyone with, it could still double as a semi-decent flashlight. She slowly made her way through the maze, getting completely lost after the first half-dozen turns. Her cell phone didn't throw out much light, and the corridors of hedge, despite the walls being dotted with sculptures and busts and fountains, all looked the same.

When she'd been in there *much* too long, and still hadn't seen anyone else or the way out, Staci knew she was completely turned around, and was starting to panic. She could still faintly hear the music from the party off in the distance, but couldn't tell how far she had gone. To top it all off, her phone began to die. *Aw, come on! I just charged this before the party.* She slapped the side of the phone in the vain hope that it would somehow start working again. The light from the screen flickered a few times, then went out completely. She became very aware of how dark it was in the maze, even with the moonlight. A chill seemed to fill the air, and she found her teeth chattering. *Okay, officially not fun anymore. Time to head back.* She stumbled around the maze, her hands out in front of her as if she were blind. Every time she tried to head back towards the music and the laughter of the party, it seemed as if she found a dead end or was forced to move further away.

Staci was close to tears. Completely lost, utterly freaked out, and alone in the dark.

And then, as something dangling from the cell phone brushed her hand, she remembered. The charm!

She cupped it in her hand, and concentrated, circling her finger clockwise over the top of it, feeling the tension building and building in her chest until she felt as if she couldn't hold it in anymore. *"Beura!"* she said—though it came out as a choked whisper.

And brighter than the brightest LED flashlight she had ever seen, the charm exploded with white light. Quickly, she raised it up over her head, blinking to clear her eyes from the afterimage, waiting to be able to see again.

There was—something—just ahead of her.

She blinked harder, willing her eyes to clear.

It was something...human-shaped...

Then as she raised the charm a little higher, the light fell fully on it.

There was a woman there. And she was...gorgeous. Her golden hair fell down to her ankles, and she was wearing a long green dress that clung to her as if it had been painted on. It was held in close to her waist by something that was part corset, part belt, all in gold, and there was a gold headband around her head, centered by a green stone that matched her green, green eyes. She was standing next to what looked like a gigantic kettle, of a very dull gold. For a moment, Staci felt as if she had stumbled into a scene from *Lord of the Rings*.

But then, the woman smiled, and all resemblance to the fantasy film vanished. The smile was—cruel. And there seemed to be the body of a young man at the woman's feet.

And as she dipped one finger into the cauldron and pulled it out, still smiling at Staci, the finger dripped a horribly familiar red.

The woman uttered a low chuckle, and licked the blood from her finger.

Staci gasped, almost dropping her phone. She lowered it to her chest, clasping her hand around the charm, which was still glowing brightly. *Oh crap, oh crap. What did Dylan say about turning it off?* Slowly, the light from the charm faded from between her fingers. She had ducked behind the edge of the hedge wall. Every fiber in her wanted nothing more than to run screaming, to get back to the party and the light and Sean. But there was a tiny voice in the back of her mind that told her to be brave, to peek around the corner and see what she could see. She listened to that voice; slowly, she edged up to the wall, crouching down and leaning over until only the left side of her face was out from behind it.

The woman was still there, stirring the kettle with her finger. Another figure had joined her, though.

It was Finn. Only . . . it wasn't.

The first thing she saw was pointed ears, like Dylan's, poking through his hair. Then as her eyes adjusted to the moonlight, she realized she could see the woman and Finn much better than she should have been able to—there was a sort of haze of light around both of them, a sort of sickly yellow. And Finn wasn't wearing the open-necked crew shirt, blazer and trousers he'd worn at the party; instead, it *looked* to Staci as if he was all in black and gray leather, but not like biker leathers. More like fantasy-movie leather. Thigh-high laced boots, very tight leather pants, and something that, if she'd had to put a name to it, she would have called a *tunic* that was laced up the arms and down the chest.

Staci had to strain to hear, but she could barely make out the two of them talking.

" . . . and so I trust that everything is to your satisfaction?" That was Finn. He was looking even more smug than usual; Staci hadn't thought that that was possible.

"Indeed it is. Though . . . I was expecting more than this *snack*." The woman gestured to the jock on the ground. It was hard to tell for sure, but Staci thought that he wasn't breathing. "There was not much substance to him. Creativity, imagination . . . I need the flame, rather than the feeble spark."

"Just a down payment, securing your services in the future. Side with me, and this town will be an open buffet; no more scraps, no more hiding. I know where your 'flames' reside, and I know how to get them for you. Do we have an accord?"

The woman smiled, licked her finger again, and made a gesture. The cauldron vanished. "Just see to it that you can keep that side of the bargain. You would not wish to cross me, I do pledge you."

"Nor you me. We're finished here. I need to get back, before my absence is noticed as being anything other than innocent."

Staci realized at that point she was going to have to get out, and fast. Finn would notice if she wasn't at the party . . . Sean might, too, but Finn was the important one. She clutched the phone, and her charm, desperately, and didn't so much think as *feel* how badly she needed to find her way out of the maze . . .

That same tension was building up inside her. When it became . . . impossible to hold in, she half-sobbed in the thinnest of whispers, "Please . . . get me *out* of here!"

And then she felt a burning spot on her fingers and looked down at her hand.

She saw a glow of light through her fingers where the cell charm was. But . . . it was in the shape of an arrowhead. Pointing back the way she had come.

She didn't even stop to wonder if it was possible,

she just ran, turning when the arrow turned, until all at once she emerged from the maze into the garden.

She looked down at her hand again. The light went to a vague blur through her fingers, then faded. She put the phone back in her bag, and took several long, deep breaths. *You didn't see anything*, she told herself firmly. *It was probably just some role-players. Finn likes games like that, I bet* . . . If she told herself that enough times, she hoped she could convince herself enough to get calmed down and look and act normal.

When she thought she was as ready as she was ever likely to be, she made her way back to the rest of the party. Sean had migrated to another group of guests, and turned around to face her when she was near.

"Hey, there you are. I was starting to get a little worried." Sean reached out, pulling her closer by the crook of her arm.

"Big mansion. I—I got turned around in there, even after the tour the other night. Sorry." She laughed a little. "Would you believe I had to find the guest suite you put me up in before I could find a loo?" She liked using the word "loo" instead of bathroom. It was British, and it just sounded more . . . sophisticated. And now that she was back with Sean . . . her panic in the maze seemed utterly laughable. And *of course* she must have run into Finn's role-players rather than anything more sinister! Seriously? Murdering someone in the middle of a party? Someone who was *going* to be missed? That wouldn't fly even in the *worst* teen-slasher horror movie, much less in the real world. She felt herself relaxing as Sean gently squeezed her arm.

"Think you have time for a movie before I have to send you home in a pumpkin?" he asked playfully.

"Sure!" That sounded fantastic. Whatever movie it was, she really didn't care. Sean wanted her to be with him for at least an hour and a half, without his attention divided, and her heart was racing at the thought.

Sean took her by the hand, then led her and the rest of the guests—those that weren't passed out drunk or just as good as—to the game room. There were plenty of comfortable leather seats; Sean directed her to one large enough for the both of them. They both settled into the seat, with Staci snuggling up next to Sean's chest after he threw an arm around her shoulders. Once everyone else was seated, Sean hit the remote, bringing up the menu on the DVD player. The movie was a heavily anticipated teen romance; Staci had heard that it was coming out in the fall, but somehow the Blackthornes already had a copy.

Halfway through the film, after the misunderstood but ultimately lovable female protagonist had finally shared her feelings with her beloved, the school heart-throb that was unattainable for everyone—especially her—Staci felt herself tearing up. She reached into her shoulder bag, trying to retrieve the package of tissues that she kept in there just in case. As she was fumbling through the bag, her hand brushed the charm on her cell phone—and it felt as if her entire body had been plunged into an ice bath. A fog seemed to clear from her mind. She remembered the hedge maze, the woman with the cauldron, the body of the jock, and especially Finn. *It wasn't role-players, it wasn't something fake. It was all* real.

Sean must have felt her tensing up, because he started rubbing her shoulder, looking down to see what was the matter. Quickly, she smiled, retrieving

the tissues from her bag and getting one out to dab
her eyes with. She couldn't let him know what she'd
seen, or *he* might be in danger from Finn. She had
to protect him. "I'm just a sucker for this kind of
movie," she whispered.

He smiled at her. "I thought you might be. You're
an incredible romantic, and you haven't let anything
take that away from you. Never let that fire go out,
Staci. It's what makes you so alive." While she liked
hearing Sean say those things to her, she couldn't
help but think about what Finn had said in the maze
about fire and sparks. It kept her feeling on edge for
the rest of the movie.

She kept looking for . . . something . . . all the way
back home in the limo. It was really creepy, expecting to see things lurking in the shadows, waiting to
pounce, and had her on edge the entire time. But
there was nothing there, nothing at all. She could
hardly believe it. Had that . . . whatever she was . . . not
told Finn that Staci had *seen* her? And why would
she not have told him?

By the time the limo reached the house, Staci had
calmed down some. She knew that she needed to keep
a level head. Just get inside, avoid Mom, call Dylan
and tell him what she had seen. But the house was all
lit up when the limo pulled up, and she knew, from
past experience, that avoiding Mom was not going to
be easy . . . or maybe even possible at all.

She could hear the stereo blasting from the porch
as she tried the door. As she had figured, it was
unlocked, and when she walked into the living room,
it was clear she was walking into a party zone.

Even if it was only a party for two.

Or . . . maybe one and a half.

There were beer bottles everywhere, a couple of empty bottles of harder stuff on their sides on the coffee table, half-empty bags of snacks, potato chips on the floor, and Mom was sprawled on the couch while an unshaven guy in dirty jeans, wife-beater and open plaid shirt, who looked like he had probably lived his whole life in a trailer park, danced drunkenly in the middle of the floor.

"Hi honey!" Mom slurred. "Thi-this's Pete." She waved vaguely at the dirtbag. "He's m'boyfrien'." Then her head lolled back and she passed out.

"Hey," Staci said indifferently, trying to edge past to the staircase.

"My name's Patrick." The man didn't stop dancing, but did incline his head to ogle at Staci. "You must be the daughter." He stumbled forward into her path, tripping over his own feet and landing on his hands and knees. As he was crawling, he found a still half-full bottle of vodka, bringing it up as he swayed to his feet. "Want a drink, girlie? Still plenty here."

"No," she said, and took the chance that if he lunged at her, she was faster than he was, and ran for the stairs.

"Aw, c'mon, no reas'n not t'try a *leetle* taste, huh?"

She didn't answer him. Because this always ended the same, when her mom brought home a boyfriend. From the time she was twelve, it ended with clumsy come-ons at best, and at worst? The demand that since *Mom* was passed out, Staci automatically owed the dirtbag sex.

"Hey!" This time he grabbed her arm, hard. "Yer momma never taught you how to treat guests?" She could smell the horrible stink of the cheap booze on his breath mixed with stale body odor, and his eyes were completely bloodshot. Even through the drunk, she could see that he was pissed off, and was getting ready to *do* something about that.

She grabbed the bottle out of his hand and hit him with it. It didn't break when she hit him, the way it did in the movies, but it sure broke when it hit the floor. He yelped and staggered back, inadvertently letting her go. She turned and ran up the stairs to her room, locking the door behind her.

She more than half expected to hear him come falling up the stairs, now doubly angry, but instead, she heard shouting. Her mom's voice, then his, then her mom. Between the (thankfully!) thick door, and the fact that they were both drunk as skunks, she couldn't understand what either of them were saying—

Right up until her mom got very clear indeed. "—my daughter! Right in front of me, you pig! Get out! *Out!* I never wanna see you again!" She ran to the window of her bedroom, just in time to hear the front door slam open.

The man, Patrick, stumbled off of the porch, now shirtless and wearing only his wife-beater and jeans. He turned around, flicking off the house. "Bitches! Just a couple of lousy bitches!" Staci nearly started crying; she had been through this before, and had become inured—for the most part—to a lot of "almosts" when it came to her mom's boyfriends. But it was never easy. And every time it happened, she was afraid that *this time* the guy would be a little less stoned, a little stronger, a little quicker. Afraid that *this time* he might come back, with friends, or a gun.

He continued for a few more minutes, dropping f-bombs right and left, and then, suddenly, stopped.

Staci half expected to see someone next door or across the street coming out of their house to yell at him, but the houses all around remained dark and quiet, although . . . the shadows seemed to be deepening. She had an odd feeling in the pit of her stomach; like she was expecting, anticipating something, but she didn't know what it was.

He peered into the shadows around the house next door, acting as if someone *was* speaking to him, although Staci couldn't hear a thing. Then he nodded, at first tentatively, then enthusiastically.

Still nodding, he staggered off next door, walking into shadows that were so black, she couldn't make out anything in them. Not even him.

A chill went up her back as she waited for him to come back out again—because if past history was anything to go by, he wasn't done yet. But he didn't. And the night was utterly silent.

Probably has a friend living next door, she told herself, as that icy unease crept over her. *Probably let him in to sleep it off.*

Her whole body shivered for a moment, then she shook her head. After a few deep breaths, she went back to her shoulder bag and pulled out the cell phone. It'd be better to call Dylan now, while everything was still fresh . . . and also to keep her from thinking too much about what had just happened.

Dylan picked up after the first ring.

"Staci. It's kind of late . . . is everything okay?"

For some reason, she couldn't hold back any longer; once she heard his voice, his concern, everything came rushing out at once. "No!" she said, choking on a sob. "My mom's drunk boyfriend tried to rape me!"

"Are you hurt? Is he still there? Listen, I'm coming over right now. Are you somewhere safe?"

"I'm okay, I locked myself in my room, but he's still next door!" she wept. "I don't—I don't—"

"Okay, sit tight. Keep the door locked. I'm on the way." The connection cut, leaving Staci to slide down to the floor, dead phone in her hand, staring over the windowsill. Waiting.

Even if she didn't really know what she was waiting for.

CHAPTER TEN

Staci almost jumped when she heard the motorcycle's—
well, elvensteed's—engine rounding the corner to her
block. She didn't waste any time; she unlocked her
door, pelted down the stairs, and slammed open the
front door. From the corner of her eye she saw that
her mother had passed out again, and didn't even stir
at the noise. When she was on the porch, she saw
Dylan. His face was stern, his lips pulled tight as he
scanned around the yard, searching for . . . something.

"I got here as fast as I could. Are you okay?" His
features softened when he turned to face her.

"I went to Sean's party like you said I should and
when I got back, Mom had this dirtbag here and they
were both drunk and—" she began blurting.

"Whoa, whoa, you said he had just gone next door.
Let's get out of here, in case he comes back out.
Hop on."

Staci hesitated for a moment, glancing over her
shoulder at the house. Then she walked up to the
bike, throwing her leg over the bike behind Dylan.

"You'll want to hold on really tight. Metalhead likes

166

to go fast. Just lean with me when I lean . . . and try
not to fall off."

"What about helmets—" Before she could finish
her question, the motorcycle roared to life, sending a
plume of dust and gravel spitting out behind the rear
tire. Staci saw the entire world tilt backwards as the
front wheel came off the ground for a few seconds,
before planting back down on asphalt. With the wind
in her eyes and Dylan's jacketed shoulders in her
way, it was difficult to see much besides the houses
and lawns on the side of the road streaking by in the
night. It felt like they were going ridiculously fast,
taking corners without even braking. And sure, she
and Sean had been going a lot faster in his sports car,
but that had been a *car*, with a whole *body* around
them, and four wheels. And seat belts! And air bags!

Despite the speed, the wind and everything that
had just happened earlier in the night, both at the
Blackthorne Estate and at her mother's house . . .
Staci felt safe with her arms wrapped around Dylan.
She couldn't understand why. The vibrations from
the engine, the way the world seemed to melt away
from them . . . it all made her feel free and shielded,
rather than in danger. She tucked her head against
Dylan's back, closing her eyes and losing herself in
that moment.

What seemed like hours later, but what could have
only been a few minutes' worth of riding, they arrived
at Makeout Hill. Dylan waited for her to let go of him
and dismount the motorcycle before he swung off of
it, patting the elvensteed on the gas tank approvingly.

"All right, I figure that we're pretty safe here.
Now . . . are you okay? Tell me what happened."

Staci crossed her arms tight against her chest, all the good feelings from the ride draining away. "Okay... Mom's got...a drinking problem, *and* a boyfriend problem, which are kind of the same problem if you know what I mean. And this happens every single time I come to stay with her. I got back from Sean's party, and she was drunk and almost passed out, and she had this dirtbag guy with her who was drunk but not passed out yet. And since she was too drunk to have sex with him, he decided he was going to have it with me instead. It's not the first time this has happened but"—tears started streaming down her face—"but this time he was more sober than the others have been, and stronger, and even after I hit him with a bottle, he kept coming up the stairs after me. Mom kind of woke up then and they had a fight and she threw him out. But...this time, I can't call Dad and go home, because no matter what I say, my stepmother is going to convince him I'm lying, or I'm a slut, or that I'm exaggerating. I'm *stuck* here, Dylan! There's gonna be a next time! And the next time if it's still the same guy, he knows me now, maybe he'll get Mom falling down drunk on purpose and..." She started sobbing. "And if it isn't *him,* it'll be someone else and there's no place for me to go for help! Who's gonna believe me? I'm the daughter of the alcoholic slut that works at the Rusty Bucket!"

Dylan waited for a moment before reaching out, touching her shoulder. "I believe you, Staci. And I don't care who your mother is, or isn't. I'm not going to let you face this alone, or let this happen again. You did a brave thing, standing up for yourself. Luckily, the guy was at least somewhat drunk, and you were able to think quickly on your feet. Next time, though, that might not be the case." He let his hand drop to his side, then brought it up to stroke the end of his chin. "Listen, I think I can show you something that might help. In case anyone gets...fresh like that again. But...this is an 'emergency use only' sort of thing, got it? If you go doing this to the wrong person for no good reason, it could turn out very badly. Do you understand?" He reached into his back jean pocket, producing a handkerchief that he then offered to her. "Dry your eyes, kiddo. Don't worry, it's clean, as the old joke goes."

She cried for a little longer into his handkerchief, but it was more out of relief than fear, now. The fear of exactly this sort of incident had been lurking in the back of her mind ever since she'd been told she was being shipped off to her mother permanently. She'd *tried* to tell Dad about this, but she could never get him alone, and Brenda would always cut her off with "I'm sure you're just exaggerating things" while Dad nodded, as if she couldn't tell a guy trying to be friendly with his girlfriend's daughter from a guy who figured every female in the house owed him sex! And she'd been afraid that if Dad and Brenda were that dismissive, what stranger would ever believe her?

But *Dylan* believed her.

Finally she got some control over herself, wiped her eyes and nose a final time, and awkwardly offered him the handkerchief back. He laughed and waved it away. "All right. You wanted to know how to do magic? I'm going to show you something new. Give me your left hand—'cause if a guy grabs for you, he's almost always going to grab for your right."

Curious now, she did as he asked. He traced a complicated little diagram in her palm, and as he did so, it glowed for a moment. "Now," he said, "remember how you gathered up power and put it into the cell phone charm? When someone threatens you, you gather up power, put it in the palm of your hand, and when it feels ready, you smack him in the forehead with it, like this—"

He lightly smacked the palm of his hand against her forehead, like she'd seen faith healers do on TV.

"—and you yell, *reodh!*"

"Reh-oth," she repeated, obediently. "What's it mean?"

He grinned. "Literally—freeze. It'll coldcock whoever you do that to. I also recommend kicking them as hard as you can between the legs. It's instructive, if nothing else. Now, try building that power up and letting it go." He looked around. "Hit the tree, I guess, since I don't see any douche boyfriends around. There's nothing there to stun."

She did as he asked, and felt her eyes widening as the design in her hand got brighter and brighter, until at last she felt as if her chest was too tight to breathe. Then she shouted, *"Reodh!"* and smacked the trunk of the tree with her hand. There was a flash of light under her palm, and she felt all that power just *drop* out of her in a way that left her breathless for a moment.

"That'll do it," Dylan said approvingly. "Couldn't have done it better myself, actually. You've got a knack, girl."

"This will really knock someone out?" she asked.

"If you get them right on the forehead, it sure

will. Anywhere else, it'll smart like a son of a bitch on fire, and definitely make the transgressor think twice. Wouldn't hurt to learn a few self-defense moves, too. But that's something we can talk about later." He folded his arms in front of his chest. "So, earlier you said you had gone to the party. What happened?"

"Well, not much for a while. But then Finn showed up..." With a feeling of nausea, she told him everything she could remember about following the drunks into the maze, seeing what she thought was a body at the feet of the gorgeous woman with the cauldron of "...blood. It looked like blood. And she looked at me, and I could swear she saw me, but when I hid and Finn came and talked to her, she didn't tell him I was there."

Dylan chewed on his lower lip. "That's nasty stuff there. That woman? One of the Leannan Sidhe. Finn's playing with fire. They promise the world to whoever they're dealing with, and they can deliver...but it almost always ends with death. That cauldron of hers, and the blood in it...that's where she gets her power, how she gives that power to others."

"But why—"

"—didn't she nark on you to Finn? You're insignificant to her. The Leannan Sidhe only care about men. You might just as well have been a leaf on the wind to her."

"The guy," she ventured in a small voice. "Was he...dead?"

"Probably not yet. She inspires her victims first. That's so they can build up and discharge whatever creativity they have. But once that's gone—" he snapped his fingers. "—generally they go nuts, or kill themselves.

Plenty of Irish poets can attest to that. Given that the poor schmuck was a jock, I don't imagine there's a lot of creativity in him. He'll do one thing, then—*piff.*"

"Piff?" she said, in a small voice.

"Yeah. He'll probably kill himself, when he does his single creation and then all the life drains out of his world. Not much worth it, in my opinion."

"So . . . what are you going to do?" Staci didn't even know the guy, not really, but . . . that was so unfair! It was worse than what Silence was already doing to people—things might suck but at least people still had their lives, and *some* good times! And the guy hadn't done anything to Finn in the first place!

"I'm going to find the Leannan Sidhe and kill it. Save the boy if I can." The matter-of-fact way that Dylan had said that left little doubt in Staci's mind that he intended to do exactly that.

"But—how—" She shook her head. "I mean—can't you just talk to her, or something?"

Dylan's eyes went wide for a moment, then he burst out laughing. It took him a moment to recover enough to get out a sentence. "Sure, I could talk to her. But it wouldn't do much. Fae like her live off of death, like parasites. Well, not technically; it's the 'vitality' of those she seduces that she feeds off of, from their blood. But they end up dead because of it. No, talking with her would only give her more time to think about how she would try to kill me. Besides, that boy doesn't have time for me to trade gossip with his would-be killer."

"But . . ." She stopped, realizing she didn't have anything to actually say. Well, other than, *You realize you sound like a cold-blooded killer, don't you?* Which wasn't going to save that guy. And might make Dylan mad at her and stop helping her and Sean. But it gave her an uneasy feeling in her stomach, to hear him just *say* that, without a second thought.

"So, are you feeling well enough to go home?"

That got her mind back on her own situation. "As long as douche bag isn't around..." Then she considered the palm of her left hand. "I guess, even if he *is* around."

"I'll stick around after I drop you off, make sure the coast is clear. If he does come back around, call the cops first. If that doesn't work, you've got my number. And Metalhead here is *fast*."

She sighed. "Okay then. Let's go."

The next day was a blur for Staci. She woke up, made herself presentable and went downstairs, ignoring the mess in the living room. Her mother was nowhere to be seen; she probably stumbled into bed or fell asleep in her bathtub again. After making a quick breakfast of toast and scrambled eggs, she got on her bike and rode into town. Nothing looked any different from any other day...but Staci couldn't help but look at everything in a new light. There was so much more behind the everyday mundane than she could have imagined; a lot of it was dark, and dangerous. Some of it had tried to kill her. Then there was Sean...*and* Dylan. She was finding that she worried about certain things less than she had before; her old friends, what she was going to wear, how she was going to fit in. How she was going to keep from going crazy in a place with...nothing modern, really. Without things she used to think she was going to *die* without, like cell phone service and Internet. All of that seemed unimportant now.

She got to the bookstore, greeting Tim on her way in. He had started treating her differently, in subtle ways, ever since she had tried to ask him questions that one night. He wasn't unfriendly... but he was definitely more guarded, a little withdrawn when he talked with her. She sensed that she had moved from one category into another for him. What those were, she couldn't say. Time would tell. After getting a cup of coffee and settling in at the back with everyone, she started dishing on the party at the Blackthorne Estate. The rest of the gang was the same as always; Sean asked her about the food at the party, Riley about the fashion, Jake about the video games or any supercars she might have seen, and Wanda just wanted to hear about how much the upper crust had made asses of themselves. This time, Staci figured there was no harm in obliging her a little. "The only people that got drunk this time were the townies," she said, and made a face. "But I have to say, maybe I don't know much about Ghost Recon, but they suck at it. Seriously. I bet you guys could take them." She thought a little more. "You know, it's kind of funny. Now that I think about it, the Blackthornes don't seem to have a lot of imagination, either. Everything in the house or what everyone was wearing is gorgeous, but... it's all like they're copying something else."

She had suddenly remembered where she'd seen most of last night's outfits, at least, the ones on the girls. *Vogue International*, the issue she'd picked up right here a week ago. There'd been two copies, because Tim had said he'd make sure she got one.

Both were gone now. *Here I was so intimidated by them!* she thought. *And all it was, was money. Well, okay, I guess I'm intimidated by the money too, but if I had that kind of money, I could do better than just buy everything on a list and wear it just like in the picture.*

"I guess if you've got enough money, you can pay someone else to think for you," Wanda said snidely, echoing her thoughts. "So, okay, let's get this show on the road. I am jonesing for some dice-bouncing."

The next few hours passed relatively quickly; Staci was really starting to pick up role-playing and the game mechanics. She enjoyed getting into character, and fighting monsters or chasing clues. It was almost like what she was doing now, helping Dylan and saving the town. In fact, the only real difference was that in the game, the monsters were obvious. In real life . . . not so much.

When she got home, she opened the door to find her mom stalking up and down the living room with the phone in her hand, yelling. " . . . Shit, Melinda, you were right, you were right all along, I am such an *idiot!* I was stupid enough to loan that dirtbag money, and just like you said, first he sneaks off last night, and now he's a no-show, he's not answering his phone, and all of his so-called friends are acting like he's—"

She broke off her rant to stare at Staci as if she didn't recognize her own daughter at first. " . . . you're home early," she said finally.

"I'm home at curfew, like I always am," Staci pointed out, acidly. "Why aren't you at work?"

"Slow night; they sent me home." She stared at

Staci a little longer, but this time as if she was trying to remember something. "Okay, honey, this is private, do you mind?"

Since Staci had stopped at the pizza joint on the way back and gotten herself a calzone and soda, it wasn't as if she needed to be downstairs. She shrugged, said nothing, and went up to her room. But inside... she was wondering. Last night, the scum-butt had vanished into the shadows and hadn't come out again. Today... he was gone. And it hadn't been the habit of her mom's boyfriends to disappear after only a single "loan." Usually they stuck around until they'd milked her of a couple of months' worth.

And last night... Dylan had said he'd "stick around" after he dropped her off.

And he'd pretty much confessed to being a stone-cold killer. Unless Fae didn't count? But wasn't he Fae?

Okay, last night she'd wanted to *hurt* that bastard. But... she hadn't actually wanted to kill him.

She didn't have a lot of appetite after that, but she ate her calzone, trying not to feel too queasy about it.

Staci needed to leave soon; she had promised to meet with Dylan that night, back on Makeout Hill. When she had first made the promise, she had looked forward to the meeting. But now... she didn't know what she should think, or how she should feel...

Staci slipped out easily enough; Mom was in her room, and Mom's solution to just about every problem was at the bottom of a bottle. She didn't have to wait very long until she heard the sound of Metalhead's engine in the distance. Dylan pulled up right next to her at the crest of the Hill; immediately, Staci could tell something was wrong. After he swung off of the elvensteed, she was able to get a better look at him. Cuts, scrapes, and bruises showed on his face and hands, and he was walking with a slight limp.

"Hey there, Staci. How's kicks?" Dylan grinned, then immediately winced.

"Dylan!" She ran to him, but then stood awkwardly right in front of him, not knowing how to react. "What happened? Are you all right?"

"Thanks for not running up and hugging me. Ribs are a little on the creaky side." He pointed to a patch of grass past her, walking over to it and sitting down gingerly. "Well, the jock is okay. He's not going to remember much, which is all for the best, really. The Leannan Sidhe . . . she wasn't much of a talker. And she had some friends."

"I should never have said anything—" Staci blurted. "If I'd just kept my mouth shut—"

"If you'd just kept your mouth shut, that boy would be dead." He leveled a stare at her. "Listen, Staci. You didn't do anything wrong. If you hadn't told me about what you had seen, that kid would be dead. I know I wouldn't want something like that on my conscience. Anyways, I'm fine." He winced again as he sighed. "For the most part."

"But you were hurt!"

"Part of the job sometimes. It's not all so bad, though; I know some tricks that'll have me back in tiptop shape soon enough. The important thing to remember is that somebody got saved. *And* Finn doesn't have the support of a Leannan Sidhe and her sisters anymore. That'll be a nice-sized monkey wrench in whatever his plans are."

"Is there anything I can do to help you?" she asked anxiously. "I mean, I guess you don't—can't go to a doctor, but is there something I can do? I think there's an all-night pharmacy open—I *know* there's one in the next town."

"Actually, yeah, there is. Over on Metalhead, the left saddlebag. There's a jar with some waxy-looking stuff in it. If you could grab that, please?"

Staci jumped up and ran for the motorcycle; the correct saddlebag obligingly unlocked and flipped open as she got there, and the top of a jar poked up. "Thanks, Metalhead," she said, feeling very weird to be talking to a motorcycle, as she grabbed the jar. "You're awesome." The elvensteed revved his approval.

"Don't tell him that, his ego already needs its own house." Dylan chuckled as she ran back to him. She knelt down next to him and handed him the jar, which was made of pottery rather than glass, and had a cork stopper. He opened it, handed it back to her, and started taking off his jacket and shirt. "I need you to put that on my back."

Before she did, she dug out her cell phone and concentrated on the charm, making it glow. "Hey do—" Dylan began, then shrugged. "Oh well. Don't freak out on me, it looks worse than it is."

In fact, his back looked horrible—black and blue and greenish. She bit back an exclamation. "I'm afraid to touch you now!"

"It'll be all right. Besides," he said, flicking his chin at Metalhead, "he can't reach behind my shoulder blades."

She dug some of the waxy stuff out of the jar with her fingers. It had a curious scent she couldn't identify. A little like pine, but not that, a little like eucalyptus, but not that either. The scent had a bitter undertone to it. But it didn't make her fingers burn or tingle or go numb or anything so she gingerly started to apply it to Dylan's massive bruises, trying not to put any pressure on his skin. She couldn't help but notice that underneath the swelling and bruising, he was, well, *built*.

Awk-ward . . . This was the part in a movie or TV episode where things would get hot. Except they were *right* out in public, and anyone could drive up here at any time. In fact, given that this was *Makeout Hill*, she was kind of surprised there wasn't anyone here when they got there. Bad enough she was out here after curfew, with a guy the cops in Silence already didn't like, but . . .

"What do you *do?*" she asked. "When you aren't rescuing girls from monsters and jocks from evil witches? Do elves have jobs or anything?"

"Actually, I used to have a pretty normal gig. Well, normal for my kind. I was a motorcycle test driver for Fairgrove Industries. Racing bikes, mostly. They're based outside of Athens, Georgia. The company is a mix of elves like me and mortal magicians. Pretty cool stuff, really. It was a lot of fun." There was a moody rev from the elvensteed. "Not like riding Metalhead, of course; nothing could compare to you, old chum."

"'Used to?' Did you get laid off or fired or something?" Somehow she could see that. *Somehow? He's the original Bad Boy.*

"No, nothing like that. I quit, to be quite honest. Caused a bit of a stir, too, from what I've been told." She waited to see if he would tell her why, but when he didn't, she decided he probably wasn't going to tell her. Unless she asked, of course . . .

"Why did you leave? It sounds like it would have been a dream job for someone like you."

"Philosophical differences." He sighed, flexing his back a little bit. "I thought that my kind should be doing more to combat the Fae out in the world that were operating quietly, doing their dirty deeds under the radar. The company disagreed. Balance and keeping the peace were more important than saving lives." Dylan went very quiet at that, and tensed up.

She decided to change the subject a little. "So what do you live on? Air and sunshine?" She made a face. She was halfway down his back now. The bruising was really bad here. Wasn't this where they punched people if they were trying to hit the kidneys? "I figure Metalhead doesn't need gas, and he can probably eat flowers or something, but you?"

He laughed at that. "Oh, we have ways. It's called *kenning.* It's a magic spell, I can duplicate pretty much anything I care to, as long as I've seen and handled it. And don't start in on duplicating your stupid paper money and serial numbers, we figured that part out a long time ago. When I need money, I duplicate a couple of gold chains or rings and sell them at a pawn shop." He looked back over his shoulder at her, smirking. "Nobody's ever surprised to see a biker pawning gold jewelry."

"I guess...so where do you live?"

He waggled a finger at her. "Ask me no secrets, I'll tell you no lies. But I can tell you that camping is very comfortable if you're elven."

She blinked in the light from her cell charm, considering that. If all he needed to do was see and handle something...well, he could probably have the

most comfortable camp on the planet just by visiting
a sporting goods store.

When she'd thought about him, she'd vaguely
pictured him living in seedy motel rooms, the kind
you saw drug dealers and hookers using on TV. It
sounded like he was doing all right instead, which
kind of vaguely annoyed her, though she couldn't
have said why.

She realized at that point that she'd finished putting the stuff on his back and already the bruises
did seem to be fading. He pulled his shirt on almost
immediately, somewhat to her disappointment. "That's
great, Staci, thanks." He took the jar from her, putting
the cork back in and setting it down before shrugging
his jacket back on. "Any other questions?"

"Do I keep doing what I'm doing?" she asked.
"Because . . . I dunno, I think I'm okay with that, but
I don't want to run into any more monsters."

"I think you should keep doing what you're doing,
yes. You've already helped to save one life . . . maybe
more than that; who knows what Finn could have done
with that Fae backing him? Nothing good, that much
I'm certain of. As for running into monsters . . ." Dylan
shrugged. "I can't promise that. I also can't make you
help me, only ask. You've been doing great so far; I
would have never been able to get as far as I have
with this without your help."

She let out her breath in a sigh. "Okay then. I can
do that, I think. I'll just be more careful." She smiled
a little. "No more running into mazes alone when I
don't know what's in there."

"Remember, if you ever get into trouble, I'm always
available."

She started to put her cell phone away, after dimming the charm—and that was when she remembered the rest of it. "Dylan! After I left the maze, I was trying to tell myself that I'd imagined everything—you know, so I could look calm? Except that the further I got back towards the rest, the more I actually started to believe it, until by the time I got back to Sean, I thought all I'd seen was a bunch of Finn's friends playing some kind of game." She took a deep breath and continued. "It was kind of like a haze. We went into the club room to watch a movie, and it wasn't until I accidentally touched my cell charm that it kind of disappeared, and I remembered everything again."

Dylan sat up straighter and turned around to face her. "That, dear Staci, was a spell. Designed to cover someone's tracks when they've been up to something; I'll give you one guess who it was. Your boy Finn is playing fast and loose, operating out in the open like he is. The spell was probably an afterthought, a just-in-case sort of thing. It's a good thing you have that charm; it warded you, knocked you out of the mindspace where you wouldn't think about anything that didn't fit in your ordinary world."

"He's not *my* boy Finn," she said sharply. "I didn't like him before you told me he was working with this Leannan Sidhe thing that *kills* people."

He made a conciliatory gesture. "Poor choice of words. I apologize. He's bad news. We're going to have to find a way for me to get closer to him. We'll need to find out what he's ultimately planning. You said that there's a bit of a power play going on now between him and the other one, Sean?"

She nodded. "Sean. He's supposed to be the heir,

but he said that Finn is trying to prove that *he* is the better choice. Could that be how?"

But Dylan shook his head. "No way of telling. Truth is, we divide ourselves between *Seleighe* and *Unseleighe Sidhe*, but there are a lot more shades of gray than that divide allows. There are *Seleighe*—my kind—that aren't too particular about where their power comes from, as long as it isn't *overtly* from dubious sources. They won't dirty their hands with death and misery themselves but they aren't all that careful with their...toys." He smiled sadly. "You might look up the ballad of *Tam Lin* some time. The Queen takes a mortal lover, but she really doesn't care that he has a girl of his own pining for him. And once she tired of him...well..." He shrugged. "Cautionary tale. Creatures that can live for thousands of years tend to think of creatures that can't as disposable and interchangeable."

He gave her a long, hard look when he said that. And for a moment, she felt a chill. Not the chill of fear, but something more subtle...more like being out on a lonely highway in a growing fog...the chill of uncertainty, maybe.

But then he smiled, pulled on his jacket, and got to his feet, offering her his hand to get up. "And that's enough depression for one night. You did a great job, Staci. You helped save someone's life tonight. And we'll get to the bottom of this."

She got to her feet with his help, and watched him as he mounted Metalhead, and tucked the jar away. With a wave, he was gone.

Now I just hope I can bike home without the cops catching me out after curfew. Of course they would probably just give her a warning. And she could say she was starving and there was nothing in the house so she had been going to that dockside place. When the cops heard who her mom was, they'd probably believe there wasn't anything to eat.

Whoever would have thought Mom would be useful in any way, she thought cynically, and began the ride back down the Hill to the house she would never think of as "home."

CHAPTER ELEVEN

The next few days went by in relative peace. No more monsters, no more abducted townies . . . also no more word from Dylan. Or Sean. That she hadn't heard from Sean worried her a little. Her insecurities all jumped up and took their turn spinning around in her mind, about how she wasn't worth his time, that there was no way he really cared about her, of course he wasn't going to call back, and so on. She knew why Dylan was interested in her, why he talked to her; he was here on a case, to take down bad Fae like Finn, and she was the best source of information he had, even though she had just moved into town. Sean was still a mystery, one that caused her no small amount of heartache. Staci was afraid that each time she saw him would be the last one, and every day that she didn't hear from him just seemed to confirm that.

She tried to just enjoy the company of her now not-so-new friends, and it *was* fun . . . she managed to get distracted by the two games she was in, the anime game, and a post-apocalypse game Jake decided to GM ("to give Seth a rest," he said). But whenever she was alone, all her insecurities just got between her and everything else. She even had to stop and restart movies, because she'd lose track of the plot and have to go back.

Finally, Friday afternoon, right after she got back from grocery shopping on her bike—a task made even more depressing by the fact that she figured she was going to be down here in town all weekend—the phone rang.

One thing that had been preying on her mind—besides Sean—was her mom's drinking, and more importantly, whether or not her boss had noticed it. It wouldn't have been the first time Mom had gotten fired for being a lush. So when the phone rang, just before Mom's shift at the Rusty Bucket and while Mom was actually in the shower getting ready, the first thing that went through her mind was, *It's Mom's boss. He's going to tell her not to come in, and to pick up her last check.*

What they'd do then for rent... she had no idea. This was the first time, ever, she'd had to worry about that. There had always been Dad to fall back on. If they got kicked out... if Mom couldn't find another job... would they be homeless? Was there a homeless shelter here? Could she move in with Wanda or Riley?

So she picked up the phone—there was no caller ID in Silence, of course—and answered it with a sense of dread. "Hello?"

"Hi, Staci. It's Sean. How are you doing?"

Her heart leapt and started racing. And she throttled down quickly on her automatic reaction, which was to cry, *Where have you been? Why haven't you called me?* Because guys hated that. Guys hated girls that were too "needy." So she ran through a dozen possible responses and finally came up with one she thought acceptable. "Bored," she said truthfully. "And cold. Does it *ever* get warm down here?"

She heard him laugh into the receiver. "For about three weeks, then it's back to the charming gloom and fog of Silence. I was calling to see if you were free tomorrow night? And if you were, if you wanted to come up for a party. You could bring your friends along, too."

She blinked, half in shock, half in amazement. "Of course! But...I mean, I *know* they'll all want to come, but why are you asking them up? I didn't think you..." What to say? *Not, "I didn't think you even noticed them,"* or *"They're not exactly in your circle..."* "...were interested in the same things. They're all gamer geeks, and not really your kind of game..." Then truth prompted her to add, "...though Seth and Jake and Wanda have *talked* about playing video games and I guess they're good at them."

"They're also smart. And they have to have good taste to have you as a friend. If you like them, I think it'd be interesting to get to know them as well. Does that sound okay?" He paused for a moment. "If you don't want them to come along, that's fine; it can just be you. Which would you prefer?"

They'd never forgive me... "I'd *love* to have them along!" she said immediately. "Seth will go out of his mind!"

"Great! Well, I'll send a car to your place at eight tomorrow night. That should give you plenty of time to tell them. I'll see you tomorrow, Staci; I'm looking forward to meeting all of your friends."

"Thank you Sean!" she said. "Thank you *so* much!"

"Think nothing of it, Staci. See you tomorrow." With that he broke the connection.

She dialed Seth immediately. She was pretty sure everyone was home, but Seth would want to be the first to know.

Now if they can just keep their feet out of their mouths, and get along with everyone else... maybe everyone is going to get a good summer.

Staci was happy to see that Jake and Seth had made an effort at dressing. Obviously none of them were going to be able to match Sean's family, but at least the guys weren't slopping around in old work pants and plaid shirts. She'd taken no chances with Wanda and Riley. She'd dragged both of them up to her room and put out some of her New York outfits on the bed. The boys wisely chose to stay downstairs, debating the finer points of the *Lord of the Rings*. "Look, what you guys wear to Tim's is fine for Tim's, but if you don't want to look like dorks at this party, you need to step up a notch."

Riley was more than happy with Staci's selection, but Wanda was having none of it.

She huffed and looked offended. "He invited us to be who we are, not to be a carbon copy of the Trust Fund Brigade. I've been done with uniforms for a while."

But this time Staci wasn't going to give in. "All you know is the townies. You've never met *any* of the Blackthornes. How do you know you won't like them? For all you know, you'd be like sisters or something. But if you look like a dork, you'll never get a chance to find out." She did some rearranging of the stuff on the bed, and dove into her closet for the plaid skirt from her New York school uniform, and some of the requisite black-on-black-on-black stuff of *every* New Yorker's wardrobe. Including something she thought might clinch the deal; a black silk *haori* jacket from the used kimono store.

"If the Silver Spoon Squad wouldn't even give me a chance because of how I *normally* dress, then what does that say about them? I don't see a reason why I ought to change." Wanda crossed her arms in front of her chest, eyebrow raised and waiting.

But Staci had been figuring that would be Wanda's attitude, so she had planned her reply in advance. "So, you would think it's perfectly cool to go to France, refuse to learn a word of French, and insist everyone speak English? You'd refuse to eat at a French bistro, and insist on eating at McDonalds?"

"Well, no, but that's different—"

"No," Staci said firmly. "It's not. Look, Wanda, when that guy said, the *rich are different,* he just wasn't trying to be clever. They *are.* Sean makes a real effort to get people up to his place and try and be the ambassador, get it? And they can't help dressing like the Trust Fund, this is how people dress in their 'country.' But if you show up looking like you don't give a shit, and acting like you don't give a shit, what does that say about *you?* It says you're a—a bigot. Somebody that just turned up so you can turn up your nose at *them.*"

"Fine, fine! I'll put on one of these outfits if it'll get you off my back. But I do this under protest!" She stuck her tongue out, and then started eyeing the silk *haori* coat.

"You wanna go Goth-loli with that, or cyber-geisha?" Staci asked, coaxingly. "Or that would work as a Lara-Croftish kinda thing with the skinny black pants."

"Can you picture *me* as Goth-loli?" Wanda scoffed. "But...have you got..."

"Try this—" Staci said with authority, and before too long, Wanda was looking...well...*hip*. In fact, she wouldn't have been out of place in the circles where Staci was used to bumping into the kids from private and prep schools. The skinny black rayon pants, the *haori*, over a black bamboo T-shirt with a Japanese *mon* on the front...and instead of an *obi*, a shiny bike chain with a matching bracelet that Staci had found in a thrift store.

"Damn, girl, you clean up *good*," Riley said in awe, as Wanda looked at herself critically in Staci's mirror. Riley had another of Staci's vintage finds, an actual Betsy Johnson from the late Sixties. This time Staci had gone Eighties—not disco Eighties, but Alexander McQueen Eighties, a black vintage tuxedo/harem jumpsuit. Her one real gift had always been a nose for the thrift shops that got the good stuff in...and didn't know how to price it. She'd been able to hold her own with the girls who had thousands of dollars to spend on clothes. In fact, that little beaded number that Brenda had stolen was one of her finds.

"This isn't *that* bad, I'll admit. I didn't know you had such an eye for this kind of stuff, Staci."

Since she knew that was the best she was going to get from Wanda, she just grinned. "You think because my father's a lawyer I had a ton of money?" she asked. "The only reason I'm buying out of catalogs right now is because the thrift shops here *suck rocks*. If I could sew..." She sighed. "But we didn't have room for a sewing machine."

"I can teach you to sew." Riley and Staci both looked at Wanda. "What? This town doesn't exactly have a lot to cater to Goths. Taught myself, picked up a few tricks here and there. I've got an old Singer Model 320 that I can show you on, if you want."

"With accessories?" Staci asked, breathlessly.

"A boatload. My great aunt was a professional seamstress. Everything from the zipper attachment to the ruffler." Wanda looked inordinately pleased with herself and she should be. You couldn't buy one of those vintage Singers for *anything* in New York. Staci had coveted one forever. You could even sew *leather* on them!

"If you would...I know *so* many makeover tricks..." Staci began, when Riley laughed.

"Later, you two. Let's get down to the curb before the guys think we fell down a rabbit hole."

The "car" was the limo, and the driver on the other side of the darkened thick glass was utterly indifferent to anything they were doing in the back, so the gang got to explore the interior and the amenities to their hearts' content.

"This is *insane*, Staci! You didn't tell us that it'd be a limo. This is some real-deal Hollywood stuff." Seth marveled at the different adjustments for the seats, from heat, to air conditioning, to lighting, and especially the massage option.

"We don't even need to go to a party; we could have one in the back of this thing. It's completely hooked up for gaming." Jake had helped himself to some of the refreshments already, and was now engrossed by the flatscreen monitor and the game systems that were installed.

"I guess when the airport is over a hundred miles away you need something to keep you busy," Staci laughed.

"No doubt." Wanda did her best to seem unimpressed, but Staci could tell that she was still wowed by the luxury. And somehow, that made Staci happy; she was getting a chance to *share* this with her friends. She wanted them to be happy for her, but she also wanted them to enjoy the same things that she had, these past couple of weeks.

When they arrived, the house was just like Staci remembered it; beautiful, extravagant, the only bright spot in dull, drab Silence. Servants escorted her and the rest of the gang to the house and out to the back patio, where the party was already in full swing. Seth had already spotted the buffet tables, and it was clear that that was going to be his first stop. Riley was gawking at all of the clothes that the Blackthorne girls were wearing, envy plainly written on her face—but the Blackthorne girls were looking back at Riley with approval. Jake, meanwhile, was eyeing the impressive home entertainment system that had been set up, with a projector and an extensive library of video games. Wanda, again being herself, tried her level best to appear disinterested in everything around her.

The crowd parted magically, and Sean appeared, heading straight for them. "Staci!" he called, with a big smile, and reached out to hug her and peck her on the cheek. "Now, you don't have to introduce me to your friends. You've told me so much about them,

I feel I know them already." He reached out and shook Seth's and Jake's hands. "You would be Seth, and Jake. I want you to get yourselves some food and drink, and there are two controllers waiting just for you over there at the game station."

Actually, she couldn't remember talking to Sean about her friends in any great detail, but she must have at some point for him to know what he knew.

Then he took Riley's hands in both his. "And the lovely Riley! The gamer girl! There is a controller waiting for you, too, and I cannot *wait* to watch you kick my cousins' asses. I've been telling them for a year now that girls who game are always better than men. Calmer under pressure, and better reflexes."

Riley flushed, but looked pleased, though tongue tied. Sean let go of her hands and let her follow the boys to the buffet.

"And you are Wanda." Sean made no move to take *her* hands, which was probably just as well. "My cousin Morrigan has been plaguing me for a month to get you up here. She wants to talk your ear off about . . . well, I'm just a guy, I have no idea what she's going on about, but I know you will." He waved in the direction of the pool. "Mori!" he called. "Wanda's here!"

A raven-haired girl dressed in a black, Victorian-style gown complete with a tiny bustle separated herself from a little group poolside and hurried over. "Oh . . . migod," she said happily. "I have *so* been wanting to meet you! I thought I was the only Goth *in this whole city!*"

Wanda held up a hand. "Before we can talk . . . Siouxsie and the Banshees?"

"Yes. Their fourth album especially—"

"Celtic Frost?"

"'*A Dying God Coming Into Human Flesh*' is my anthem."

"Okay. Final question. Voltaire?"

Mori absolutely sparkled. "*Sooo* funny! And I looove '*Goodnight Demon Slayer*,' it's adorable!"

Wanda sighed. "Okay, we can talk. Come with me, and I'll teach you everything you need to know, whether you want to know it or not." Staci was certain she actually saw Wanda *grin* as she threw an arm over the Blackthorne cousin, leading her away.

Staci let out her breath. "Oh...wow. That went well!"

"I'm actually surprised. Happily so," Sean said, grinning toothily at Staci. "Shall we?"

He offered her his arm, and she took it. He whisked her around the party, from group to group. Sean was as charming as ever, introducing her to everyone, making conversation and including her in everything. She saw that her friends were getting along just fine, as well. Seth and Jake were absolutely devastating everyone else at some first-person-shooter game, taking on all comers with smug satisfaction. Riley was holding her own in that department as well, but regularly took breaks to talk fashion and Silence gossip with both Blackthorne and townie girls. Wanda was in her own little world with Morrigan, off away from the rest of the party, heads together, over a pile of magazines, talking as intensely as a couple of scientists over an experiment.

It was all...perfect. Even her one fear, that the Blackthornes or the townies or both might encourage her friends to get drunk...maybe in order to make fun of them ... never materialized. In fact, once she even heard one of the waiters say to Jake, "Not that one, sir, that's gin and tonic, not ginger ale. Here you go."

"You know, Staci ... your friends are as much fun to have here as you are," Sean said. "Well ... *almost*. As much fun for my cousins, I should say. Would you mind if we found somewhere a little more private to talk? The noise of the party is a little much, sometimes."

Since that was pretty much exactly what she was hoping for, she nodded. "Of course, if you think you don't need to play host so much." *Don't look needy, girl! Don't blow this.*

"They'll survive without me." He took her by the hand. "Follow me." Sean led her along, past the pool and out of the range of the music.

He was at his most casual tonight: khakis and a simple chocolate-brown short-sleeved, V-neck sweater—a sweater which she knew, from casually brushing against him, was silk. He also had on some sort of after-shave or cologne that had an unusual, woody smell to it, with a hint of musk.

Sean waited until they could barely hear the din of the party before he stopped. It was dark on this part of the property; they were behind the pool house, well onto the rear lawn where there was only moonlight. Staci could see the expanse of the hedge maze off to the left, and vaguely shuddered at the memory of what she had seen there. Finally, Sean stopped walking, turning to face her and taking both of her hands in his.

"Staci ... I want you to know that you're really special to me." He sighed, chuckling to himself. She had the sense that he wasn't amused, but rather sad in his mirth. "I can't really talk to any of the others about this. Not even my own family, really. All of them, especially Finn, are looking for any opening that they can get. Weakness isn't well tolerated amongst my family."

She squeezed his hands. "I'm so sorry, Sean . . . my family . . . well, they're pretty dysfunctional too. I can't say I know what you're going through, but I can sure understand. And you can always talk to me, I want you to know that."

Sean pulled away from her, breaking the grasp. "How could you understand? *Really?* Do people only care about you because of your name? Do they only see you for your money, or what you can do for them? Do they hate you for what you have, and what they don't? As if it's *your fault?*"

She took his hands back in hers and looked deeply into his eyes. "Sean, my dad threw me out because he loves my stepmother more than me. He *threw me under the bus*. He knows what my mom is . . . what *everyone* in this town knows she is! She's the drunk slut who'll sleep with anything in pants and it's a wonder she hasn't managed to lose her job at the Rusty Bucket like she's lost every other job she ever had! Every time the phone rings, I'm scared it will be her boss telling her not to come in! And my father *cares so little for me* that *that* is what he sent me to live with! Everyone in this town who knows her, knows all that. And even her *boyfriend* thinks I'm just like her, and if she's not available, I am! Yes, I can understand being despised! Maybe not the same as you, but . . . equally!"

Sean searched her eyes for a few moments, then

looked down in shame. "I'm sorry, Staci. I got caught up in my own bullshit for a minute. It's tough, always being on guard and having to pick your words." He looked up, meeting her eyes again. "You wouldn't believe the pressure. Everyone is focused on success, achievement. It seems like a lot of other things get forgotten in the mad rush for a bottom line. My father values success above everything else. He'll cut me off in a heartbeat if I can't perform. And my stepmother is worse. I don't have any stepbrother or sisters, but that wouldn't stop her from encouraging him to slough me off if she ever thought that I wouldn't continue to help supply her with the lifestyle she's become accustomed to. So you see"—he smiled crookedly—"we aren't that different after all. Our parents are equally focused on their own selfish desires, regardless of what happens to their children."

Before she could think of more than how odd it was that Sean was involved in the family business, and that he would talk about his father cutting him off if he couldn't perform, when he was *still in high school*, Meaghan approached them. Not from the party side, but from the garden, out of the shadows. Staci was startled by the other girl's sudden appearance; Sean, though surprised, seemed more angry than anything else.

"Meaghan. I was having a private conversation with Staci. What do you want?" Very subtly, Sean had pushed Staci back and to the right of him, so that he was slightly between her and his cousin.

Meaghan tossed her hair back and smiled at Staci. It wasn't a nice smile. It was the sort of smile that Staci had seen—

—on Brenda, when she looks at Dad!

"I was just coming to see how you and your special town-friend are doing, Sean. The rest of your guests are missing you. Would you like me to take her to—"

"*No!*" Sean took a step forward towards Meaghan, until he was almost nose to nose with her. For the briefest moment, Staci thought that he was going to hit his cousin, right then and there. "You don't have any business being around her, especially when *I* am talking with her. I'll go back to the party when I feel like it." He seemed to catch himself for a moment, glancing over his shoulder at Staci before leveling Meaghan with a stare. "You need to leave. Now." His tone didn't leave any room for argument.

Strangely, Meaghan didn't seem in the least put out. She ran her fingers through her long hair and smiled again, a smile that this time looked supremely self-satisfied. "Why, of course, Sean. I was only trying to be helpful. But if you don't want my help, that's all right with me." Before Sean could retort she turned on her Jimmy Choo stiletto heels and stalked back to the party with her hips swaying.

"Sean, I'm sorry about that . . . I see what you mean about them—" Just as she reached for his arm, Sean whirled on her. She had seen his face that angry before, once, when he was talking with Finn. It scared the hell out of her, especially now that it was directed at her. The expression lasted for only a flash; then he was back to looking apologetic and bashful.

"No, I'm sorry, Staci. My family brings out the worst in me, sometimes."

The conversation seemed to turn into . . . little nothings. Not long after that, Sean escorted her back to the party. The rest of the gang were cleaning up on a Team Deathmatch round on the game system, save for Wanda, who was still educating Morrigan on the finer points of Goth fashion. The remainder of the evening continued on like that; Sean whirling her from one conversation to the next, everyone stuffing themselves at the buffet table, and generally having fun. But Staci couldn't shake a tickle at the back of her mind, and what strangely felt like a knot of ice deep in her gut.

The way Sean looked at me after Meaghan found us... It gave her chills, and not the good kind. He had been *very* quick to shut Meaghan down at the very idea of separating the two of them... he actually looked like he was ready to become violent, at that. She didn't know exactly how she felt about that. On the one hand, it was... well, it was the sort of thing you saw in movies, where the guy would do anything to protect his girl. But on the other hand...

He's under a lot of pressure. And it was clear that Meaghan was trying to push his buttons. Of course he's going to be short and snap a little bit after something like that.

...but...

Just as she was beginning to give in to her unease, Sean took her a little aside from the rest during a lull. "Staci, I've been thinking about what you said earlier. About your mother, I mean, and I can at least do a little something to make your life easier." He took her hand in his, and held it gently. "And this will be no problem, and it won't make any problems for me. Father has me managing all the entertainment venues we own down in Silence, and one of them is your mother's bar. I'm going to have a word with her boss."

He held up his hand. "Nothing to worry about—but he has alcoholics in his family, and he knows how to handle them. He'll make sure your mother doesn't drink on the job, and that if she shows up under the weather, he'll start making her come in early enough that he can get her sobered up before she starts her shift. And he won't fire her. I hope that will help you feel a little more secure."

All of her doubts evaporated. How could she even *think* Sean might be overly aggressive when all this time he'd been thinking about this? "Sean... I don't know what to say. Thank you—"

"Think nothing of it. I know you'd help me like that if you could."

Again, Staci was torn. While she needed all the help she could get with her mother...

She shook her head. *No. Don't sabotage yourself when you finally find a guy that's worth it! Don't look this gift horse in the mouth, girl.*

When things started to wind down with the party, Seth, Jake, and Riley found Staci and Sean by the pool. Seth and Jake both looked absolutely stuffed and tired; Riley just looked tired. "Wow. I didn't know a video game tournament was like a marathon," Staci said, looking from one to another of them.

"You'd be surprised at the stamina it takes to kick that much butt." Riley stretched, cracking her back. "Luckily, I have practice."

"Hey, we held our own!"

"Well, you did okay, Seth. I was barely keeping along, though. Riley knows all of my moves," said Jake, grinning. "Hey, where's Wanda? It's about time we got back."

"Your queen is here. No need to panic." Wanda strolled up, yawning. "I am going to sleep like a rock. It's exhausting to be this awesome."

Seth stared at her with his mouth dropping open. "All you did was talk all night about clothes and music!"

"Like I said. Awesome."

Sean bathed them all in a gracious smile. "I take it we passed your tests, then?" he said teasingly.

It was Riley who said the right thing. "We're awfully glad we came, and it was wonderful of you to invite us, Sean," she replied.

"Then you will have to consider yourselves invited whenever Staci is—" Sean began.

It was Jake who held up a hand. "Not that we don't appreciate it, because we do, but . . . our parents are a lot stricter than Staci's mother is. There's no way we can do entire weekends."

Sean looked disappointed, and sighed a little as if with resignation. "I can certainly understand that, but it is a shame. I was looking forward to a real all-night gaming session, but I will just have to content myself with watching you wax my cousins over the course of a couple of hours. Some other time, maybe. Perhaps with enough urging on my part, your parents will relent. I'll call up a car to take you all home. Until next time!"

The mood in the limo on the way back down was generally contented and happy. Riley actually fell asleep with her head on Jake's shoulder. Jake and Seth were drinking the designer water as if they were dehydrated, and talking over particular moments of triumph in the games they'd played. Wanda kept to herself, but did have a slight smile on her face as she listened to the guys.

Staci was—just happy. It seemed that her friends had scored well with Sean, which meant she was no longer going to have to choose between time with him and time with them.

And Sean was going to help her with Mom . . . or at least, make sure that Mom didn't screw up everything like she always did. Hopefully that would give her one less thing to worry about at home. Things finally seemed like they were looking up.

This had to be one of the best evenings she had ever had in her entire life.

CHAPTER TWELVE

As always, when the weekend magic at the Blackthorne Estate was over, Staci felt...depressed was the only word for it. The contrast between *up there* and *down here* was just so enormous, and it was in a way that wasn't entirely to do with money. *Down here* was always dull, the days always seemed to drag, there never seemed to be any sunshine. Everything was bland and uninteresting, except, of course, for her characters' lives in the gang's games. And...that wasn't real life. It was so bland you couldn't even say "Real life is horrible" because, except for when Mom's boyfriend came after her...it wasn't. It was just blah.

Mom's boyfriend hadn't reappeared...so Mom was out the two hundred bucks she had loaned him. She used that as an excuse for why the tip jar was now empty when Staci went to get groceries. *At least I have my credit card.* Mom could just starve, as far as Staci was concerned. She was buying salad stuff, whole wheat bread and things that required actual cooking, or things she knew Mom hated, like tuna fish. Unfortunately, the grocery store was pretty...

well...stuck in the Fifties, like all of Silence, and it didn't have things like hummus and pita, which Mom would never touch but Staci found very comforting. And when she wanted comfort food or was too lazy to cook, she went to the Burger Shack, the diner, or the pizza place and never ordered more than she could eat by herself.

This morning...with Mom sleeping off the weekend, the memories of the party where *everyone* had had fun, and the emptiness of the fridge staring at her, felt like a morning she was going to need comfort food. A great big plate of hash brown potatoes, scrambled eggs, and bacon was called for. After getting showered and dressed, she gathered up her shoulder bag and bicycle, pedaling for town and the diner.

Since she was "late" by the standards of the fishermen and dockworkers who usually ate here, the diner was empty, and Beth Phillips was doing busywork behind the counter. Rather than take a booth, Staci hopped up on a stool as Beth greeted her with a big grin.

"Hey, stranger! How have you been? Silence treating you okay?"

"Silence? Not so much." Staci made a face, and ordered quickly. "But there are some bright spots."

"One second while I finish this stuff up. Then dish. I never seem to have free time to do much around town, so I want details." The other girl finished her prep work before plopping down on a stool next to Staci, pushing a large glass of orange juice in front of her. "On the house, but keep it between us."

"Naw, my dad is paying for this. He can damn well afford it after dumping me here." Staci smiled a little. "And a twenty percent tip, too. So...like I said, Silence sucks, but it turns out some of the people don't. You—" she tipped the glass at Beth. "Some kids I met at the bookstore. Seth, Jake, Wanda and Riley." She figured she would start with the "small stuff" first.

"I think I know them. They seem like a good bunch, if a bit on the nerdy side. It's good that you found a group to hang out with, though! Everyone needs someone to hang with in this town, since there's nothing else to really do, aside from watching paint dry. What else have you been up to?"

"Well...Sean Blackthorne's been inviting me up there for parties," Staci said coyly.

Beth's eyes grew wide. "No joke? *The* Sean Blackthorne? Of *the* Blackthornes?"

Staci had to grin at that. "Yeah...I'm...kinda shocked. He turned up at the church hot dog thing, and next thing I know, he's invited me up there. I'm still not sure why."

She described everything that had happened—without the Leannan Sidhe or the Red Cap, of course, because the last thing she needed Beth to think was that she was crazy—as Beth hung on her every word. "And this weekend he invited the rest of the gang up there."

"That's insane! None of the upper crust ever takes an interest in anyone besides some of the jocks or the other popular kids." Beth looked at her sidelong. "Sooo...have you made out with him yet?"

Staci wasn't even going to pretend to be shocked. Seriously? She wasn't ten. It wasn't as if she hadn't made out with guys before this. "No, and actually, I'm not sure why he hasn't put any moves on me. I don't think he's gay. Maybe it's 'cause he doesn't want to take the risk with a lawyer's daughter?"

"He obviously likes you, though. I mean, the limo rides, the parties...I've *never* heard of anything like that happening, not with him. Sean Blackthorne is the one and only, the unattainable. I'm not going to lie, I envy you, girl. Me and every other female with a pulse in Silence."

She blushed. "Oh stop it. It's not like there's anything going on. I keep telling myself as soon as the novelty wears off he'll drop me like a dead Tweet." She looked earnestly at Beth. "I mean, that has to be all it is, right? The novelty?"

"I couldn't say. He's being *awfully* nice to you if it's just because you're new and shiny." Beth frowned for a moment. "What's the rest of his family like?"

Staci had to roll her eyes a little at that. "*Weird.* Well, okay only a couple of them are weird. There's this Morrigan chick who is seriously Goth, and she and Wanda were like besties after ten seconds. And there's some gamer guys, so, you know." She shrugged. "The difference between Blackthorne gamer guys and regular gamer guys is the price of the toys. Otherwise, it's eight straight hours of thumb exercise and then a break for food. Okay, the difference is the Blackthornes have twenty-six flavors of artisan popcorn and lobster rolls, and regular gamer guys have Cheezy Puffs and pizza that hasn't quite turned into a board yet."

"So...who's creeping you out?" Beth prodded. "Because something—or maybe someone—is."

How much can I tell her without giving too much away? There was Finn. He was clearly trying to hurt people, and was just awful in person besides. But...

then there were a few times when she had seen Sean angry. There was something there that she couldn't put her finger on, and the fact that she didn't know what it was bothered her.

"Well, there's a couple of cousins. Finn and Meaghan. They're ... I dunno. It's really hard to put a finger on it." She thought a moment longer; what could she say? "Okay. Finn. He's got this whole Cain-and-Abel thing going with Sean, and you know what? I think that could be literally. Meaghan. I get this *Game of Thrones* vibe from her, like she's maybe one red dress away from being Cersei. And yeah, maybe literally."

She saw the incomprehension on Beth's face at the second. "Right. No HBO in Silence. Ah, how about ... Lady Macbeth? And she's trying to get Finn to do the stabby part for her. Anyway, I thought my family was dysfunctional, I think at least part of the Blackthornes take that to a whole new level."

"So ... there's some kind of power struggle? What does that concern you, other than making boy-toy Sean unhappy?" Beth wriggled her eyebrows for that last part.

"Because where there is a power struggle, people are always looking for pawns or weapons. I don't want to be either one." That felt right.

"That actually brings up my next question. What *do* you want?"

"You would ask that." She sighed. "I haven't figured that part out yet. It's complicated. I *really* like Sean, but he hasn't put any moves on me, and I still haven't figured out where that's going, or if it's going at all. And there's another guy. Who *also* hasn't put any moves on me."

"The plot thickens! Who is this other guy, then? Someone from the bookstore . . . Seth?"

"No . . . it's a guy I don't think lives here." *I don't think camping counts as living here.* "I don't even know if you've seen him around. His name's Dylan, and he rides this amazing motorcycle. . . ."

"Oh . . . *that* guy. I've seen him around town. He's been hassled by the cops a couple of times, looks kind of dangerous, right? Also . . . like you could iron your laundry on his abs. What about him? Do you know him or something?" Beth propped her chin on her hands and waited, avidly.

"I met him my first morning here. He's the one that showed me how to get to the diner. I'd have starved otherwise." Had that been an accidental meeting? With everything that had happened since, with the Red Cap, with Sean and Finn . . . now she wasn't so sure. Would Dylan have seen that "elf ancestor" stuff on her and made a point of meeting her? "And I keep running into him. When Mom's boyfriend came after me the other night, he even came riding to my rescue." That was safe enough.

"Okay . . . so, what's the deal? Do you like him, too? You said he came to your rescue—I won't pry, I can tell that's something kind of serious—but how do you feel about him?" Beth had lost that *okay, time to dish* look and had gotten more earnest. Staci liked her more and more each time she saw her.

She's one of the good ones. "That's just it. I don't know. It's like with Sean, I can't tell what either of them think, and I'm not going to, you know, get my hopes up until I've got some clues about it. If one or the other would actually *do* something, I'd have a better idea.

I'm not exactly a mind reader. For all I know, they both think of me as a little sister or something equally lame." *But maybe the reason Sean hasn't done anything is to protect me. If Finn thought he was really interested in me...that might be bad. And I still don't know what Dylan thinks. But maybe he's trying to keep his distance for some other reason? Or maybe he's one of those guys that doesn't even want a hint of commitment?* "I guess I'll have to be patient and wait and see what happens."

"Hey, in the meantime...you're going to *Blackthorne* parties! Which is about a million times better and more exciting than anything going on around here!" Beth sighed with envy.

"You certainly have a point there," Staci agreed. She was about to say more when Ray called from the back. "Beth! Order up! And I need the salad cut up for lunch!"

"Back to the salt mines. If you ever have an extra invite for one of those parties, let me know. Anyways, I'll be right back with your order." She turned to the kitchen. "Coming, Ray!"

Beth returned with Staci's heaping plate of food; it was more than Staci remembered getting the last time. "Ray thinks you're too thin, and he knows about your mom," Beth whispered. "I think he figures you never eat because she never cooks—according to him, moms are supposed to be the ones doing the cooking. Ray can be an asshole, most of the time, but he's got a soft spot other than the one on his head."

"Hey, come by the bookstore tonight and we'll hang," Staci replied. "The Nerd Squad are pretty cool and it'll give me someone to talk to if they start in on gaming stats."

They probably wouldn't, though. They'd probably talk about the party, and that would give someone else for Beth to ask questions of. Someone who didn't know about the *other* side of the Blackthornes...and Dylan.

Staci was mulling over whether she should try to talk to Tim again as she pedaled down the street on her bicycle. He definitely knew more than he had let on to her, even if he didn't want to talk about it. She was pretty sure that she could trust him...at least with some of the details about what she had been through. And it might help her to get some better perspective on Sean and Dylan, hell, about elves in general, maybe.

She was so lost in thought that she almost didn't notice until it was too late that there were three people just ahead of her, standing in the middle of the narrow street. She clutched the handbrake, bringing the bike to a screeching halt barely ten feet away from the people. They were young, around her age or a little older. All of them were boys, and dressed similarly; a sort of small-town version of "gangsta," with sports jerseys under jackets, baggy pants with wallet chains, and tan work boots. Warning bells immediately went off in Staci's head. She started to turn her bike around, when she heard more boots-on-asphalt behind her; two more boys had come from a side alley and positioned themselves behind her, blocking off the way she had come.

"Nice bike you've got there."

Do they just want the bike? They can have *the bike!* She couldn't remember; were you supposed to talk to thugs who looked like they were going to come at you, or just run?

"I *said*, 'nice bike.' What, your momma didn't teach you any manners, girl?"

She couldn't see any weapons on the ones in front of her, but that didn't mean anything. In New York, she'd *know* they had guns. Every street punk in New York had a gun. But here? *I haven't seen a gun store. And I wouldn't think the cops would have just talked to Dylan if they'd thought he was packing. But these guys could have knives, easy.*

The one in the middle was the one doing the talking. He looked like the oldest of the bunch; probably out of high school, but not by much. He glanced nervously from side to side, and she could tell he was building up courage to do *something*, pumping himself up to keep his image up in front of his gang. Finally, it happened. The leader took a step towards her, his hand reaching for the handlebars. She knew that if they took hold of her, she was screwed, totally at their mercy. Instead, she did the first thing she could think of.

Staci ditched the bike, running to her left. She almost got tangled up on the bike as it crashed to the ground, but she was able to right herself and keep running. She could hear shouting behind her; it had taken a second for the thugs to process what had happened and start pursuing her. Her only chance now was to get away from them, get indoors somehow, get around people. Everything was a blur to her as she ran, clutching her shoulder bag close so that it wouldn't get caught on anything or move around, slowing her down. The alley she was running in was narrow, with parts of it cluttered with shipping pallets, barrels, or bits of trash. The buildings on either side were really run-down; on the left, corrugated metal, weathered to a dusty silver, with streaks of rust down some of the corrugations. To her right, wood, once painted white, now flaking, the wood underneath sunbeaten to a dull gray. It was incredibly noisy; from inside both buildings it sounded as if poorly maintained machinery was running dangerously fast, clattering, and rattling. There was a smell of diesel exhaust, oil, the ocean, and over everything, fish. There wasn't a single sign of another human being, even though *someone* had to be working in those buildings. Any of the doors she tried were locked, some of them chained shut. She could have screamed, shouted for someone, but she doubted that anyone would be able to hear her over the din. She couldn't afford to stay still, either; the thugs were still behind her...and catching up.

She couldn't tell where she was, as she darted into a space between two buildings, a space with a wood floor. She had to be close to the docks, but where?

She stopped herself just in time, teetering on the edge brink of the walkway. Below her—at least a story below her!—was the water. There were a couple of boats tied up to her right, about fifty feet away, but they were empty. There was no way to get to them, anyway, and no way to get to the docks on the other side.

The thugs came to a skidding halt behind her, just as out of breath as she was. They immediately spread out in a semicircle around her, cutting her off from running down either side of the walkway.

The leader was in the middle, hands on his knees, panting as he looked at her. "You, you really need to be taught a lesson," he said, still catching his breath.

With a flick of his chin towards Staci, the two thugs on the end of the semicircle to either side of her closed in. For a split second, Staci's mind shut down. She thought she was going to die, or get raped, and there was nothing that she could do to stop it. It was going to be like with the Red Cap, or if she hadn't taken hold of the bottle that she had used to bash her mother's for-now boyfriend with when he tried for her.

Then she remembered what Dylan had taught her, the self-defense moves she had practiced for a short time with him. She tried to calm down, control her breathing, but all of her breaths were shallow with her heart feeling like it was thumping in and out of her chest. She vaguely noticed her vision going dark around the corners, narrowing down to what she was focusing on. Her hands were shaking, and her entire body felt cold. But that wasn't important. What was important, was the guy nearest to her, closing in on her.

In a fit of desperation, she threw her shoulder bag at the face of the guy on her right, shouting, "Here, leave me alone!" By the time she turned back to the one on her left, he had reached her, clamping his hands on her shoulders. Screaming, she lifted both of her hands up as high as she could, then brought her elbows down on his arms, breaking his hold. Before he could grab her again, she socked him blindly; the punch caught the punk in the throat, causing him to stumble backwards and land on his ass, clutching his throat.

Holy shit! It worked—

Then someone grabbed her from behind.

She wasn't even thinking now, just moving. She brought her foot down *hard* on his instep, grateful she was wearing her kicky boots with the Cuban heels, and not, say, her trainers. She actually *felt* his bones break.

So did he.

He screamed like a girl, and let go, flailing wildly. With one foot broken, he had lost his balance, and in the next second he fell off the end of the walkway, still screaming. She heard a splash, but her attention wasn't on him.

"Don't look at me, you morons, grab her, damnit!" One of the thugs moved to respond; so did the leader, while the last one just stood there, not willing to commit. The thug that did move, however, came at her head-on in a full sprint. He had picked up a pipe somewhere along the way, and was carrying it over his head in both hands. She knew that when he hit her, it was going to probably be in her head or shoulders. Panicking, Staci threw her arms up in front of her face, shutting her eyes, and thinking about how she had done nothing to deserve this. In that moment, she felt overcome with anger bordering on rage, and screamed at the thug.

"Don't hit me!" She started at the sound of her own voice. It was...loud. Not like, screaming loud, but like echo-chamber loud. With a snarl in it.

And a glowing dome of light suddenly *exploded* out of her, covering her like a cupcake dome, ending about an arm's length away.

But when the pipe hit it, the dome didn't act like a glass cupcake dome. It acted like it was made of cement.

The pipe hit it, and bounced right back into the thug's face, breaking his nose, splattering blood everywhere as he staggered back about three steps before keeling over backwards.

Did I do that? Staci looked down at her hands, uncomprehending for a moment.

The leader stopped short for a second, dumbfounded. His confusion didn't last long, however; with a bellow of rage, he pressed forward, grabbing Staci and backhanding her. She felt her nose and lip begin to bleed, and the entire left side of her face began to throb immediately. Staci fixed her eyes on the leader; his mouth was curled in a half-snarl, half-grin. He thought he had her cowed, thought that he finally had the upper hand. That only pissed Staci off even more. She *hated* assholes like this guy. People who thought that because they could beat people up, that they should. That might makes right. That because they had it shitty, they should make it that way for everyone else. Staci felt something building up inside of her, until it felt like it was bursting through her skin, her pores.

Staci smacked her open palm against the leader's face, and shouted, *"Reodh!"*

There was a burst of light from her hand, and she felt for a moment as if every bit of energy had just *drained* out of her, and she was going to faint. In fact, her vision went gray for a moment, before it cleared, and she swayed back a step.

But the leader of the muggers was not so lucky. He stiffened like a board, his eyes rolled up into his head, and he fell straight back, exactly like a tree being cut down. The back of his head hit the wooden walkway with a sharp *crack*. Still pissed off, she took a couple of short steps and then kicked him as hard as she could in the crotch, just like Dylan suggested.

By this time, most of the other thugs had recovered—all but the one that was in the water, anyway. Shouting to each other, they all started running...not towards Staci, but away from her, scrambling out and down the alley. Looking behind her, she didn't even see the thug that had fallen; he must have decided to bail on his buddies. Or maybe he drowned; she didn't really care. For a few moments, she considered gathering her purse, running as fast as she could back to her bicycle, and then finding the nearest cop and telling him everything that had just happened. Some small part of her, however, told her to stay.

The leader of the thugs started to come to; he was groaning, clutching his face and his crotch as he writhed on the ground. Staci still felt the sting on her face from where he had hit her, and the trickles of blood from her nose and the cut on her lip. She walked up next to the thug. On the ground, in pain, he looked far less intimidating; a kid playing at being a gangster, a bad man instead of the real McCoy. *The cheap, little, dirty...*

Staci jabbed the toe of her shoes into his ribs. "Why did you attack me, you little *jerkwad*?"

"I don—nothin'!" he gasped, and she kicked him again in the side. "*Shit!* Stoppit ya little psycho-bitch!"

"Then *tell*"—kick—"*me*"—kick—"*why*"—

"Shit, shit, shit, *okay!*" The thug was curled up on his side, trying vainly to protect himself, but all he was getting was bruises in new places. Maybe even a broken rib. She was kicking *hard*. She stopped for a moment, and he looked up at her through fingers trying to protect his face. "It was the cops!"

She took a pace back. "What?"

"It was a cop. The juvie one. Krupke. He told us t'find you an' rough you up. Said your ma was the slut at the Rusty Bucket and you'd prolly put ou—"

Enraged, she gave him another kick, and this time there was a little flash of light when she connected and she *did* hear a bone snap . . . and again she felt energy drain out of her. He screamed, clutched his side with one hand, and fumbled in his pocket with the other. She got ready to stomp on his hand in case he had a knife, but what he brought out was a handful of glittering gold chains. "Here!" the punk gasped. "He paid us with this! Take it! Just—stop kicking me!"

She bent down and snatched the jewelry from his hand. Then she stalked over to where her purse was lying and stuffed the chains inside it, turning to glare at him. "Follow me—or come after me again—and you'll wish you hadn't," she snarled, and stalked down the wooden walkway. "And my bike better still be there!" she added as an afterthought.

When she got out of sight, though, she ran. Now that it was all over . . . she was sick, and scared, and all she wanted to do was get home and lock the door.

Thankfully, her bicycle was still where she had left it. Evidently, the thugs had been too preoccupied with chasing her to do anything with it, so it only had a couple of scratches from when she had dropped it and ran. The entire ride home was a blur to her; moments of panic, checking over her shoulder to make sure she wasn't being followed, having to stop when she started to shake from fear and shock, almost getting sick when she remembered the sound of the thugs' bones breaking—and her being the one that made those bones break.

When she finally got home, she left her bike on the front porch and marched through the living room and straight upstairs to her room, slamming the door behind her and locking it. If her mother had been home, she didn't notice or care. Then she fell down on her bed, curling up and fighting back the tears. She had never been in a fight before. She'd never hurt anyone before, especially in such a physical way. She felt sick; she felt as though she couldn't breathe. More than anything, she felt terrified. How could... that person, the person who had done all that... be inside her?

And the punk had said it had been a *cop* who had paid his gang to attack her! If the *cops* were after her, how could she possibly be safe in this town?

Was that the same cop that was hassling Dylan the first time I saw him?

She started to cry, helplessly. *I'm only a kid! No one is going to believe me, especially not if the cops are in on this! What am I going to do? Why are they doing this to me? Who is doing this to me?*

Suddenly, the memory of the punk holding out that handful of gold chains struck her and dried up her tears. She reached over the side of the bed and dragged up her purse. The tangle of gold was still on top; she pulled it out and stared at it. She knew good jewelry and this was good stuff, heavy gold chains, several thousand dollars worth.

And in her mind she could hear Dylan. *"It's called kenning. It's a magic spell, I can duplicate pretty much anything I care to, as long as I've seen and handled it. And don't start in on duplicating your stupid paper money and serial numbers; we figured*

that part out a long time ago. When I need money,
I duplicate a couple of gold chains or rings and sell
them at a pawn shop."

An elf had sponsored this attack. An elf had paid
for it. Who else in this town would have heavy gold
chains with an antique look to them? Silence was the
sort of place where anything like that had ended up
in a bank vault or a pawn shop a long, long time ago.
And certainly no one would be using gold like this to
pay off a street punk gang. Staci was absolutely sure
of it in that moment. But that surety only brought
more questions . . . and more fear.

CHAPTER THIRTEEN

She might have thought it was all a nightmare when she woke up the next morning, except for two things. The bruises on her arms, and the fistful of gold chains still in her purse. Strangely, the bruises on her arms were not nearly as bad as they had been last night— and the damage to her face had already healed.

Last night she hadn't been able to think. But now she wasn't full of adrenaline and panic. She reached past the chains to her cell phone, and called Dylan. Dylan would know what this meant...and maybe he'd know who did this.

He answered on the third ring, sounding sleepy. "Hey, Staci...it's kinda early..."

She glanced at the clock, and felt a sense of shock. Six A.M. She was *never* awake this early. "I know, but something bad happened last night. I need to talk to you right now!"

"Okay, okay. Not over the phone. It's not...safe. Meet you on the Hill."

Then he hung up and she stared at the phone in her hand. *Not safe? What does* that *mean?* Then she shook her head. It didn't matter. She was wide awake and he had just said he'd meet her. That *did* matter.

In a few minutes she was dressed and out the front door, picking up her bike and racing towards Makeout Hill. All the fear that she had shut away yesterday was coming back to her now in full force. Initially, this entire deal seemed like it would be cool. She would get to play the spy in the pretend movie in her mind, going to exclusive parties, hanging off of the arm of the hottest guy in the room, and trading secrets to save the world—well, at least Silence. But yesterday was all too much. People—*and monsters, let's not forget the creepy gnomes-turned-hulking-monsters-with-huge-knives*—were *after* her. The cops were in on it; she felt certain that Finn had to have at least some of them in his pocket. And she was just a kid; how was she supposed to deal with this? She should have been worrying about what to wear, what the latest gossip was, which of her favorite musicians was coming out with a new album. *Not* whether she was going to live through to the next day.

All that fear just put more strength in her legs, and she was at the top of the Hill in record time, hardly out of breath at all. And Dylan wasn't there.

He still wasn't there five minutes later, by which time she had punched his contact three times, and gotten no answer.

She was frantic ten minutes later, when she finally heard the sound of Metalhead approaching. By this point, she wasn't sure whether she wanted to punch him in the nose or cry on his shoulder. She settled for running up to him as he skidded to a halt, yelling, "Where have you been?" as he pulled off his helmet.

He frowned. "Listen! I got here as fast as I could. I was out and away from town, and Metalhead can't fly. There's some things even elvensteeds can't do. What's going on?"

She began babbling, just spilling everything out in no real order, talking as fast as if she was on drugs or something. After only a couple of minutes he held up a hand.

"Whoa. Stop. You're not making any sense, kiddo." He looked around, then back to Staci. "Listen, sit down, catch your breath. I'm going to get something for us real quick. I'm not going anywhere, just over to a saddlebag on Metalhead," he said, noticing the panic in her eyes at "I'm going."

She sat down on a wide root, although she felt so wound up she was ready to jump to her feet at any moment. To try and steady herself she clutched at the top of her purse, reminding herself that if Dylan showed any doubt of her story, she had the evidence right there.

He came back with something wrapped up in cloth, and two perfectly ordinary water bottles. "Here," he said, handing the bundle to her. "There's two in there, I get one. I haven't even had breakfast yet."

She unwrapped something that looked like...two giant turnovers, except they were shaped like half-moons, and weren't flaky. Or calzones, except they weren't pizza dough. It was more like pie crust. She poked one with a fingernail, dubiously. "What are these?"

"Cornish pasties," said Dylan, taking one and biting into it, ravenously.

Well, that didn't answer her question, but they looked good, so she bit into hers. The crust was a pie crust, and the inside was chopped meat, potatoes, onions, and something she couldn't identify. It was *good*. In fact, it was just what she needed; it brought her back to the moment, helped her to ride the fear down.

"So," Dylan said around a mouthful of pasty. "From the beginning, what happened last night?"

She opened one of the water bottles and took a drink, and a breath. More slowly now, but with no less urgency, she began describing what had happened. Getting ambushed. Getting attacked. Fighting back, and *that,* she described in detail.

"You actually manifested a *shield*?" Dylan looked as if he was going to drop his pasty for a moment. "You . . . you shouldn't even be *able* to do that yet, with no training. That's . . . interesting."

"I had *plenty* of motivation!" she said. "He was coming at me with a *pipe!*"

"No doubt. Motivation is only part of it, though. What you did was something a novice *shouldn't* be able to do, off the cuff, with no training. It'd be like you jumping up on a balance beam for the first time and doing a perfect acrobatic routine." He looked . . . perplexed. Well, at least he believed her.

"Maybe I'm a Jedi," she retorted, not entirely joking.

"Maybe . . ." Dylan looked at her queerly for a moment more, then went back to eating his pasty. "Continue on, young Padawan."

"When I got the last one on the ground, I was really, really pissed off. I started yelling at him to tell me why he and his gang-bangers had come after me. And he did . . ." She gulped. "He said one of the cops had told them to. And he'd paid them off with *this*—" She dug in her purse and brought out the handful of gold chains, holding them out to him. "It's elves, right? Or *an* elf. I don't know who else would pay off a gang to do a hit in gold chains!"

"If a cop gave them to the punks, could be stolen chains he picked out of evidence, or confiscated as stolen property from a pawnshop or something. Here," he said, putting down the remains of his pasty and holding out a hand after wiping it on his jeans. "Let me have a look." Staci handed Dylan the chains, and his eyes immediately grew wide. "No doubt about it; magic made these. Definitely elven in origin, too." He handed the chains back to her. "Whoever is in control of the cops, they're elven. And they want you taken out."

Her mind went very still. And all she could do, was wail, "But what do I *do?*"

"Well, if someone wants you out of the picture, it means that you're a threat to them. It means that what we're doing? It's *working.* I'm still here for you, Staci. We can make this work. You're clearly a lot stronger than I thought; with some more training, we can make you into a true badass. If you want, that is." He reached out, taking hold of one of her hands. "Things are dangerous right now; they have been from the beginning. But you have to ask yourself if you want to see this thing through to the end or not. I can't make that decision for you."

She thought about that. Really *thought* about it. *I've got nowhere else to go,* she told herself. And it was true, of course. She couldn't go back home; Dad hadn't accepted her anguished pleas to stay before and he certainly wouldn't now that the only anguished plea she could make was by text or email. He would *never believe her* if she told him about the cops being after her. And if she told him something mundane, that he *might* believe, like the fact that mom's boyfriends were trying to molest her, he'd—or, more properly, Brenda—would say she was exaggerating and demand proof that she didn't have.

So her choice was not whether to stay or not. There was no choice in that. She was stuck here. Her choice was whether to let whoever this was run over her and leave her as road-pizza, or fight.

Which when it came right down to it, wasn't much of a "choice" at all. Because she knew how this sort of thing went. If, for whatever reason, "they" couldn't get to you, they'd come after your friends, your family, or both. So yeah, there was a thought. *Go after Mom, throw her in jail, and then let Social Services come get me. And I get put into Child Protective Services, or even into juvie hall as a stop-gap, because allegedly they can't get hold of Dad, and then . . . something bad happens to me.* Dad being a lawyer and all, she knew all about how kids fell through the cracks all the time, and then the cracks squeezed shut on them. Sure, saving the world sounded great in a movie . . . but saving yourself was a lot more important.

At least if I fight, Dylan's going to give me something to fight with.

"I'll stick with it," she said.

Dylan grinned. "I was hoping you'd say that. I really meant it when I said that I didn't think I could do this without you, Staci." He gave her hand a squeeze. "Together, I think we have a fighting chance to save Silence."

She held his hand as long as he let her . . . and he

didn't seem in any hurry to let go. "You said something about training?" she said.

"Indeed I did. The lighting up the phone charm? Kid's stuff. From what you've said about manifesting that shield, and finding your way out of that maze, I think you're ready for something more advanced. Stuff like that whammy I taught you. If you've got people trying to put you in their sights, the more offensive punch you're packing, the better." Now he gave her hand another squeeze and let it go. "And much as I hate to leave you, since you woke me up so early, there's something I need to do." He stood up, then offered her his hand to help her up. She took it. He held it long enough for the two of them to walk over to her bike. "Remember. I'm only a call away. Okay?"

"Okay . . ." she replied, but he dropped her hand and walked quickly over to Metalhead. He turned and waved to her, and in a moment, he was gone.

When she got back to the house, she wandered around restlessly for a while before deciding to do laundry. She had just gotten done putting the load in the dryer and was halfway up the basement stairs when the phone rang. She ran the rest of the way up and into the kitchen where the phone was; Mom hardly ever got calls, which meant that this was probably for her. Slightly out of breath, Staci picked up the receiver. "Hello?"

"Staci, I'm glad I caught you." With a shock of delight, she recognized Sean's voice. It was such a jolt of happiness that for a moment it drove all her anxiety out of her mind. "I'm having another house party. It's going to be a long-weekend one. A week really. Wednesday to Wednesday. If I make it right with your mother, can you come up for the whole week?"

"Of course! I mean, yes, once you talk with her. I'm sure she'll say it's okay." If nothing else, Staci could think of a number of things she could say to her mother to convince her to let her go. *Like the fact that her most recent deadbeat boyfriend went full-on creep and tried to get handsy with me. Whatever neurons are still firing in her brain, maybe some of them still register guilt.* "Is there anything I should bring?"

"Only what you want to. I'm going to have some 'theme' nights, and I'll make sure you have what you need for that. What do you think about a '50s night on Friday, maybe a horror movie night for Saturday, and we can have your friends up for those?" Sean's voice took on a warm tone. "We'll have a full house for the week. Not just my cousins, but associates of my father. I think you would charm them."

Staci was glad that Sean couldn't see her blushing over the phone. "That all sounds wonderful. What time should I be ready? If my mother okays it, that is." *And I don't think anyone is going to* dare *try anything to get me when I'm up at the estate.*

"Wednesday afternoon, I'll send the car at around one. It's Monday, that should give us plenty of time for me to convince your mother, and you to tell your friends. Give your mother my number when she is free and tell her to call me. I will be my most persuasive. I'm looking forward to this, Staci. I'm glad you said yes."

"I'm *really* glad you asked me. I'll see you Wednesday, Sean!" With that, she hung up the phone. She felt lighter than air for a few moments, before she remembered everything that had happened yesterday, and her talk with Dylan. She was still happy, even if it was tempered with lingering fear over last night's attack, and feelings of the responsibility she had now. *I've got to call Dylan, let him know about this. He'll want to know, and he might get worried if I just go dark for a full week.*

Just in case Mom woke up, she went up to her room and stared at the clock in shock—it was only ten A.M.! So much had happened this morning, and she had woken up so early, it felt as if it should be much later.

She punched Dylan's contact on her cell phone. *I hope he answers. I hope he doesn't think it's me freaking out again, that I'm all needy and clingy. I hope—*

"Staci? Is everything all right?" He'd picked up on the first ring. She let out a sigh of relief.

"Sean just called. He's having something he calls a 'house party' that's starting on Wednesday and lasting a whole week. He wants me to come up there and stay for all of it." She waited, a little breathlessly, for his answer.

"Go," Dylan said immediately, without any hesitation. "And don't just hope you'll hear something this time, get proactive. Do a little snooping. I am sure you can find some excuses for it. Get into the maze by daylight and see if you can discover anything. Just be careful, no matter what you do. If you get into any trouble that you can't handle, contact me, and I'll come get you. Okay?"

"I'll be fine, and I'll be careful," she said. It felt good that he was trusting her to investigate on her own. And she was beginning to wonder . . . because

Sean and Dylan seemed to be about the same age, if Dylan wasn't trying to help Sean get out of some kind of trouble? It wasn't the right time to ask, in any case. But by helping *Dylan*, she was probably helping *Sean*.

Maybe that is another reason why Sean's asking me up there. He *thinks I can help him.* Now that thought made her feel really, really good. She hoped it was true—both that Sean thought she could help him, and that she actually *could* help him.

Well, now all she had to do was wait for Mom to wake up. *I'll make her breakfast pancakes, then give her the number and tell her to call Sean. Between a carb coma and her hangover, she'd probably agree to let me hitchhike across Europe with a witchcraft cult; getting her to let me go to her boss's boss's party should be a snap.*

Mom was a pushover. In fact . . . right after she got off the phone with Sean, she was ready to shove Staci out the door right then and there. Staci would have considered this suspicious, except that Mom had looked guilty about it. Not the "I know I am doing a stupid thing to my daughter" sort of guilty, but an "I know I am going to get something out of this" sort of guilty. With maybe a touch of "thank god I can get rid of her for a week" guilt. Staci had thought that her opinion of her mother couldn't get any lower before today. She was wrong.

Well, whatever it was that Sean had said to her, Mom made sure she was ready and at the curb on Wednesday, with a bag in hand. Meanwhile, Staci had made sure that the rest of her friends were informed and on board with showing up on Friday and Saturday nights; even Wanda seemed to have some enthusiasm, this time. Staci thought it was too bad *they* couldn't stay overnight too, but it didn't appear that Sean had included them in that part of the invitation. When the limousine arrived, it was all that Staci could do to keep her breathing even. Every time she was taken up to the Blackthorne Estate, it seemed like she was being whisked away to another world, far away from the common and boring one of her life in Silence.

The driver was as polite as ever, opening her door for her and shutting it behind her before speeding off. Well, "speeding" was something of a misnomer, because he took his time, this time, giving her plenty of opportunities to watch the "scenery" of Silence pass by outside the limo windows. From in here... well, the panorama looked like a depressing art film.

She helped herself to some of the crystal clear water; even the *water* tasted better than anything she could find in Silence. Finally, when she was starting to consider tapping on the partition and asking the driver to speed up, they were on that mysterious road through the forest, and then, turning into the long driveway to the Blackthorne Estate.

Sean didn't meet her; instead, there was a woman in a maid's outfit waiting at the front door, who took her bag from her. "I'll just show you to your room, miss," the woman said politely. "The Master asked me to have you join some of his early guests by the pool. Master Bradan, that is, not Master Sean."

Master Bradan? *That's Sean's father...* Well, Sean *had* said that he wanted her to meet some of his father's... what had he called them... "associates."

But he hadn't said anything about his father being here for the party.

Okay, okay, maybe that was because he didn't want to make it sound like "visit to meet my parents" relationship stuff, she told herself. Which made sense, they weren't even *dating,* much less at the "meet my folks" stage. Nevertheless, she decided to change into one of her vintage couture finds, rather than stay in "New York casual." It sounded like this was going to be a more formal gathering than that. She chose a vintage 1960s silk Dior jumpsuit; it was both sexy and covered everything but a little cleavage and her arms.

When she got to the pool, she knew her instincts had been right to change. There was a string quartet playing classical music out there, a scattering of three-piece suits among the designer "leisure" outfits, and she strongly suspected that had anything like a hot dog been found in those covered dishes on the buffet tables, there would be at least one mortified heart attack.

As she approached, one of the elegant men turned to her, smiling broadly; it was Sean, looking dashing as ever. He was standing among a group of older men, all of them—including Sean—holding glasses full of an amber liquid that she assumed was Scotch. Sean quickly walked up to her, embracing her gently so as not to spill his own glass.

"Thank goodness you're here. I thought I was about to be bored to death by those doddering old farts," he whispered into her ear. Then he asked, loud enough for the group behind him to hear, while holding his arm out, "Staci, would you like to meet my father and some of our friends?"

She was...well, petrified was not the right word. She'd met plenty of men who had quite a bit of power at the various fundraisers and whatnot that her father had taken her to. Not that they ever paid any attention to *her,* or even to her father, but she'd certainly brushed elbows with them.

Now, however, they were bending their gaze to her; she was not some insignificant lawyer's daughter. She was someone who...was worthy of introduction. So she wasn't *petrified,* but she became hyperconscious of every move she made, and every word she might say. She would have to put her best foot forward for this; first impressions were everything with people like this, and she couldn't afford any mistakes.

"First, my father, Bradan Blackthorne." Sean's father could have been his twin. That is, if their birth had been separated by thirty years, and the eldest had none of the mirthful laughter in his eyes as the younger one had. If nothing else, Staci now knew that Sean had good genes; his father was dignified and handsome, age having given a slight amount of haughtiness to the boyish features that Sean also carried. He nodded to Staci, bowing slightly at the waist as he held out his right hand, which she accepted.

"Charmed, my dear," the elder Blackthorne said, taking her hand and kissing the back of it. "You're even lovelier than my son had led me to expect. And he is usually prone to exaggeration about the women in his life, so this is a welcome surprise."

Staci could see Sean bristle at that last quip from his father; he did a good job of hiding it, however, and she suspected that no one else had noticed. Feeling awkward, she moved carefully, vigilant in making sure she didn't do *anything* that could be interpreted as ungraceful. Men like this one kept company socially with no-kidding movie and theater stars. She needed to live up to that sort of standard, at least temporarily.

"It's good to finally meet you, sir," she said, still feeling the heat on her cheeks.

"Here, let me introduce you to the rest of the circle." Sean stepped forward, his arm in hers carrying her forward with only a little encouragement. "From the left, we have Ryan Dubghail, Lynch Collins, Nolan Gearalit, and Stewart Casey. All longtime friends of my father's, even before I was born. They help to keep the business running along smoothly, in between games of golf or hitting on secretaries." A polite chuckle ran through the group, several of the men raising their glasses before sipping from them.

"You'll be able to appreciate the finer things in life once you have more responsibility on your shoulders, young Blackthorne." The man who spoke was the one that Sean had introduced as Lynch Collins. The two Blackthorne men were tall and well-built by any standard, but he was a giant; easily a head taller than any other man at the party, with a barrel chest and wide shoulders. He looked like a legendary hero come to life . . . save for the coldness in his blue eyes. After he spoke he speared Staci with his gaze, and she felt those eyes boring through her.

"The boy still needs to earn that responsibility before he can enjoy the fruits that come of it, of the hard work that it takes to keep a family going." Staci remembered the name of the man speaking now: Stewart Casey. He was tall and thin, with long dark hair that was pulled back into a neat ponytail.

"It's not something taken lightly. Parties such as this, bought and paid for with the wealth of his forebears, do nothing to secure his position. Do they, boy?" Stewart turned to look at Sean, a hint of challenge in his voice.

"Come now. What is youth if not for spending in enjoyment?" Nolan Gearalit was a bear of a man; not as tall as Lynch, but certainly as strong-looking in his squat frame. His full beard outlined a bemused smile that never seemed to leave his face, and his eyes were quick to dance from one person to the next whenever he spoke. For now, however, they seemed fixed on Staci and Sean.

"Father has always expressed the need for a balanced life," Sean said smoothly. *"Work hard, play hard,* is what he's said. As long as the "work' comes first, that is."

"And what work are you doing, boy?" Stewart leaned forward, raising his drink before taking a loud slurp of it conspicuously close to Sean's face.

"What a Blackthorne has always done, sir," Sean replied, without even a hint of deference. "Tending the harvest. It should be a particularly good one this year."

"What benefits the Blackthornes benefits us all," said Lynch, nodding to Sean's father. Even though his words were warm enough, Staci couldn't shake the feeling that the man had nothing but ice in his veins, cool clockwork for his brain.

That these men were powerful was a given. That they were very definitely cut from a different cloth than the powerful businessmen and politicians she had seen in the past...well, that was also a given. Sean and his father were certainly elves; most, if not all, of the "cousins" were certainly elves. But there was no telling what these men might be. Wizards? Psychics? Something even stranger? She just didn't know what was possible. All that she *did* know was that magic or psychic powers would probably make succeeding in business much easier than mere money and talent alone.

Being able to conjure up pure gold when you need it wouldn't hurt either. What did investment losses matter when you could do that?

There was only one thing she was certain of: they were not involved in conventional politics. This coterie of the powerful looked like men who were not at all interested in anything outside of their spheres of influence—whatever those were. And she had the feeling that anyone who tried to shine any light on what those spheres of influence were would find himself in more trouble than he could handle.

The only one that didn't talk was the man that Sean had introduced as Ryan Dubghail. He was as thoroughly unremarkable as her own father, with sandy colored hair and gray eyes. Still somewhat handsome for an older man, he paled in comparison to Sean or his father, or even Lynch and Stewart. What made him stand apart was the way he hung on every word that everyone was saying, without looking terribly interested in it. Staci had picked up on that sort of body language, from all of her experience with her stepmother; this was someone always looking for some advantage to capitalize upon in either conversation or something that someone might let slip.

"Enough of that, you old dogs. My son will do the family proud, I'm sure." Bradan's tone was easy enough, but from the way his eyes met those of the other men, Staci could tell that he wouldn't brook any further discussion of the point. He turned to Staci and Sean, smiling again. This time there was some emotion in his smile. It looked like . . . approval? "I'm sure you two have much better things to do than listen to us go on about business. Go, have fun, enjoy the party. Sean," he said, "we'll talk later, once you're free."

Sean smiled back. Not a big smile, but not one of those tight little "this is not really a smile" things she'd seen on his face when introducing her to the group. "Thank you, Father. I hope your guests will enjoy their entertainment as well. I personally made sure it was going to be the sort of thing they prefer."

Then he took Staci by the elbow and steered her towards the pool and the buffet. "Thank God that's over," he said in an undertone. "It's easier swimming with sharks. And I've swum with sharks."

She wondered if he meant that literally. . . .

Actually, he probably did.

CHAPTER FOURTEEN

Despite knowing the quality of parties that Sean threw, she was still taken aback with the opulence and service every time. He introduced her to a few more people, some more "friends of friends," and occasionally had to stop to talk with a gaggle of his cousins, but for the most part he did his best to spend time with her and her alone. The next few hours were a blur of music, food, and staring into Sean's eyes as they talked. He showered her with compliments at every turn, making her blush despite her best efforts not to. Whenever she needed anything, a servant was immediately at their side to attend to her every wish. It was magical. *Everyone should live like this*, she found herself thinking more than once. She felt *good*, and that went a long way towards keeping her mind off Dylan and her ulterior motive for being at the party. Besides, there was a whole week this time, seven whole days in which she would probably find herself temporarily abandoned while Sean tended to "business"—whatever that was—and played courtier to his father. Time enough to snoop around when she was alone.

Tonight, she wanted just for herself. Was that too much to ask? Of course not. Ever since she had arrived here, *she* had had to be the responsible one. *She* was making sure there was food in the fridge, and that Mom paid the bills on time. *She* did the house-cleaning, the laundry. Heck, *she* had gotten together with Sean, who had pretty much safeguarded Mom's job! All after being thrown in the deep end from the only life she knew in New York City. She deserved something for herself, and this was it.

So she enjoyed the fantasy of being part of a fabu-lous party right out of a movie. She wasn't the star of the movie of course, that was Sean. But she was part of it, and she liked being part of it.

When about half of the partygoers had drifted off . . . to bed, she presumed . . . she found herself fighting back yawns, to her chagrin. And to her even deeper chagrin, Sean caught her at it. But he just smiled. "I was looking for an excuse to call it a night," he said, and pointedly looked around the poolside, which at this point was all but vacant. The only actual group of people still awake were Sean's father and his cronies. He stood up, and offered her his hand to get her to her feet. "Let's both get some rest. I hear that lounging by the pool is a very exhausting activity; we'll need our energy. I'll see you in the morning, Staci," he said, giving her a kiss on the cheek and turning to walk to his poolside "bachelor pad."

Well, a kiss on the cheek was better than no kiss at all. . . . She glanced at the group still standing, con-versing and drinking together, but they didn't seem to notice that Sean had left. She made her way to her room, yawning the entire time, and fell into bed.

✦　　　✦　　　✦

Staci was having a surreal dream when she started to wake up. Through the haze of her sleepiness, she could only remember the barest details of the dream; Sean and Dylan were both in it, as were her friends. It all seemed shrouded in mist, though. She would see Dylan's face, turning away from her with a half-smile, and then Sean's, fading away. Her friends all looked worried, even terrified, but vanished just as quickly. Even Tim was there, looking stern and staring down at her. She knew that there was something beneath it all, but the sense of the dream retreated from her as she came back to consciousness.

Her eyes drifted open, and she could see a dark shape in the chair by the window across from the foot of her bed, silhouetted against the dim light coming through the curtains. It took her a few moments... until she realized it was a person. Then her eyes shot open fully. Panic ran through her entire body like a bolt of lightning as she focused on the person, until she recognized who it was.

Sean sat there, staring back at her.

"What are you—" she squeaked, mouth dry and throat tight, still frightened by the unexpected intrusion.

"Staci, I'm sorry, I didn't mean to wake you." He smiled, and suddenly all her fear just washed out of her. Of course there was nothing wrong. This was *Sean!* He would never hurt her! "I came to see if you wanted to come down to breakfast with me, and you were so pretty lying there, like Sleeping Beauty, I just sat down to watch you for a moment."

Self-consciously, she pulled the covers up a little further, and put her hand to her head. "What, with bed-hair?" she replied, trying to sound funny. She squinted at the light from the windows. It seemed *awfully* dim. "What time is it, anyway?"

"About five-thirty," he replied. "I'm a lark, I always have breakfast before everyone else does. Even Father, workaholic that he is, waits until eight. It gets kind of lonely."

"I'll meet you down there, okay? I need a couple of minutes at least to get presentable, throw something on other than a nightie."

"Of course! I'm glad you're awake enough. I'll see you there." He smiled again, and although she was both afraid and hopeful that he would approach her, he went straight out the door, and closed it softly behind him.

As soon as he was gone, she jumped out of bed, grabbed the first approximately reasonable thing she saw in the closet and retreated to the bathroom, locking the door behind her. And then she chided herself for being silly. What did she have to fear from Sean? He had been nothing but gentlemanly towards her the entire time she had known him. He hadn't tried to ply her with alcohol—though plenty was available—or otherwise force her into anything she didn't want to do. He was everything he seemed to be, expect for the elf thing. Wasn't he? Still, she kept the door locked, some tiny voice in the back of her mind winning that much from her.

This wasn't one of her own outfits, which she was obscurely grateful for. With Sean's father lurking around the edges of the weekend, she wanted to look...well...*Blackthornely*. It was silk, she could tell that immediately: finely pleated palazzo pants and a matching sleeveless tunic in a soft turquoise. She took extra care with her makeup, and all but ran down the stairs to the huge dining room. Staci paused for a few moments before rounding the final corner of a wall that opened up into the dining room, catching her breath and putting her best smile on.

Sean was sitting alone at one end of the empty table, with a woman in a maid outfit at his elbow. He waved Staci to the seat beside him. "The buffet will be when everyone else is up," he said, as Staci looked at the empty tables in curiosity. "Just tell the girl what you want; she'll bring it up for us."

Staci suddenly felt tongue-tied. "I think—I'm still too foggy to think—" she said.

He chuckled, and turned to the maid. "Steak and eggs for both of us. My usual side dishes. Chamomile tea and pomegranate juice."

For a moment Staci wondered why no coffee...it was going to be hard to get her brain started without it. Then she remembered: the Blackthornes, and presumably a lot of the cousins, were allergic to caffeine. *Oh well. Caffeine deprivation is a small price to pay for a week of all this...*

Breakfast was heavenly. She didn't think that she was going to feel quite up to something as hearty as steak and eggs until she took the first few bites. Every item was done to perfection, and somehow exactly the way that she preferred. Staci wondered how much of that was magic or just good service. Staci and Sean passed the meal quietly eating, enjoying each other's company and the food without need of small talk; there would probably be plenty of time for that later.

After they had finished the meal and the dishes were cleared away by the servants, the two of them sat for a spell, finishing their drinks, until Sean suggested that they take a walk on the grounds since the weather was pleasant. Staci agreed to the idea enthusiastically; if nothing else, it was more time alone with Sean, and away from the possibility of Finn interrupting them. She hadn't seen Finn since she had arrived at the estate, and hadn't pressed Sean for any information on him; part of her didn't want to show that she was afraid of his cousin, but she also just didn't want to know, as if the mere mention of his name would summon him to them. And to tell the truth, she not only was not sure if Sean could protect her from Finn, she was not sure if Sean could protect *himself* from Finn. Now would not be the time to find out, not when everything was so perfect.

As they walked, Sean firmly took her arm and placed it under his. Staci stiffened for a moment, but quickly relaxed. The sun was still low in the sky, and the air was cool and slightly moist. Here and there she saw gardeners tending to the lawn or potted plants around the pool. After walking for a few minutes, Staci noticed that Sean was leading her towards the hedge maze. Memories of the night when she had followed Finn there came unbidden to her mind, and she felt a well of coldness build in her stomach for a moment. *It'll be okay. Sean is here. If anything happens, you can just use the moves and tricks that Dylan showed you. Relax, girl,* she told herself. Staci willed herself to calm down, and it started to slowly work. The maze wasn't nearly as frightening in the daylight; just like everything else on the estate, it looked magical, as if it was from a princess fairy tale instead of something from a nightmare.

Sean took her through the maze, showing her plaques and statues that she hadn't noticed the first time she had gone through it. At one point they became separated for a few moments ... until Sean jumped from around a corner, shouting "Boo!" and causing her to yelp. But he was laughing, and a minute—and a few mock punches into his arm—later, so was she. When they got to the middle of the maze—something she hadn't managed to do on that scary night—she found that the center was occupied by an amazing gazebo. She would have expected wrought iron, but this was wood, all carved into what looked like lacework. It wasn't painted; the wood itself was a strange silvery color and lacquered to a glasslike finish. Actually, it looked as if the wood had been coated in ice. It was breathtaking. "Oh wow, it looks like it would break in a high wind! Aren't you guys scared the first storm will take it down?"

"Here, take a look at this." He pulled her along, taking her hand and placing it against one of the upright braces. The surface felt ... natural, but at the same time much more firm than it should have been. The material of the gazebo was extremely dense, whatever it was; a few experimental raps from her knuckles didn't give the usual knocking sound that wood did, but a flatter, almost muted *whud*. "It would take quite a bit more than a storm to come close to harming this. It's been in my family for ... many, many years. Before either I or my father were born. The wood comes from a kind of tree that is incredibly rare. But of course"—he laughed—"that didn't matter back in those days. If people with money came across a tree that was rare, that was just all the more reason to cut it down and make something out of it."

Sean started to lead Staci away. Something made her look over her shoulder towards the gazebo one last time; a funny feeling running up her spine and down her arms. As she was turning away, she caught a glimpse of something in the corner of her vision. It looked as if the gazebo floor was covered in symbols...and blood. There was a dark figure standing in the middle, clutching something; a person, also covered in blood. Staci drew in a sharp intake of breath, ready to scream as her head snapped around. Whatever she had seen, it was gone now; the gazebo was as pristine as it had been moments ago, no sign of blood or menacing figures. She quickly quashed her fear when it became apparent that Sean had noticed her reaction. "Thought I saw a bee on my shoulder," she said, trying to brush it off. Sean looked at her strangely for a moment, then smiled, and put his hand over hers on her shoulder. Immediately she felt reassured. Of course she hadn't seen anything! It was just her own overactive imagination, fueled by that night when she'd been so frightened here. She let him take her hand and lead her out of the maze again.

When they came out, she suddenly realized that the sun was high overhead, she was *ravenous,* and there were lots of people poolside. How long had they been in there? She glanced at her watch. *Noon? Already?*

"Time seems to do funny things in the maze," Sean laughed, seeing the expression on her face. "I think it's because there is so much artwork and so many interesting things in there that you just lose track of it. Time, that is. Look, they're serving lunch, and Father and his friends are off somewhere so we won't have them lurking like vultures over us."

The afternoon went by in a blur of music, pool games, food, and lounging. For a change, this evening, the whole group dressed for dinner, and gathered around that enormous table for a full formal meal with the senior Blackthorne and *his* guests. Staci was grateful that she'd been to a couple of dinners like this with her father—pre-Brenda, of course—and knew how to use all the silverware in the right order. She hardly tasted the food, though, she was so acutely aware of Bradan Blackthorne's watchful eye on her. It was an acute relief when dinner was over and Bradan announced that he and his friends would be retiring to "the lounge" for the rest of the evening. "You all enjoy yourselves," were his final words, tempered with a kind of...sardonic look.

The partying was just a bit more subdued, probably because of the knowledge that "the lounge" had windows that overlooked the gardens and pool. Finally everyone went to the pool house to watch Sean and three of the cousins kick ass on another one of their fantastic video games. Which was yet another one that Staci couldn't identify. It seemed to involve horse-riding and hunting something, using packs of scary-looking hound-things. She got sleepy early, probably because of the *really* early morning. Sean gave up his seat on the couch and his controller to give her a kiss goodnight. A real kiss this time, though it wasn't what she would have called a "passionate" one. Still, that let her float back to her room, and fall asleep with a smile on her face.

Friday went much the same as Thursday had. Staci and Sean had breakfast together, went for a walk for conversation and taking in the beauty of the grounds, then lunch and more socializing with the rest of the family. After lunch and spending time by the pool with Sean, she had retired to her room to get ready for the party that evening; her friends were finally going to be coming up, and she wanted everything to be perfect when she saw them. They all arrived together in a car that Sean had sent for them, and everyone was all smiles and hugs; even Wanda, in her own semi-sarcastic way.

Sean had promised "costumes" for all of them; she checked her closet and found exactly that, only not tacky polyester stuff. And lest there be any mistake, each one was in a garment bag that had their names on them. Jake was a "greaser"—chinos, white T-shirt, black leather jacket with a bike gang patch on the back and black motorcycle boots. Riley matched him with tight pink capri pants, a pink T-shirt and a matching black leather jacket and boots. Before she checked Seth's bag, she had been afraid the costume was going to be a jock—but it wasn't! In fact, it wasn't a high-school type costume at all...it was a typical '50s scifi scientist, complete with lab coat and goggles! Wanda—again, she was afraid that Wanda was going to get something she would *never* agree to wearing, but Wanda was a beatnik: tight black capris, little black ballet slippers, tight black turtleneck sweater and a beret. Since beatniks were basically '50s Goths, Staci figured Wanda would like that just fine.

And as for her...her costume half-filled the little closet. And when she opened the garment bag it turned out to be a strapless full-length pink prom dress, with about a hundred petticoats. It looked like something Audrey Hepburn would have worn. But instead of being scratchy it was all soft as anything she had ever felt, because it was all silk.

And there was a note: *Staci, let your friends know they can keep these costumes. You too. I'm sure you can find a use for them!*

Her first instinct was to tell Sean that it was too generous of a gift, but she checked herself. This was how he showed that he cared; he could certainly afford it, if nothing else. And really, what else could he *do* with a handful of '50s costumes? She rather doubted any of the cousins or friends would wear something that anyone else had worn before them.

Staci, Riley, and Wanda all dressed and prepared together; Staci filled the other two girls in on what she had been doing for the past two days, for the most part, while they did their makeup and made sure each others' hair was behaving correctly. Once they were all ready, they met the boys out in the hallway; Jake and Seth were busy arguing about the portrayal of faster-than-light travel in films as opposed to in books, but both of them fell silent when they saw the girls.

"Hubba hubba!" Jake wrapped his arms around Riley and planted a kiss on her lips, causing her to giggle and playfully slap him a few times.

Seth blushed bright red, looking at the floor for a moment. "Black really is your color, Wanda. I mean, you look nice."

Wanda looked taken aback for a moment, then blushed. Staci had never seen her blush before. But Wanda didn't let that stop her from making a wise-crack. "And you actually look *intelligent*! But I'd rather have Jake fix my car."

Jake popped two thumbs up in imitation of the Fonz. "Ehhhh!" he said. "Just hand me your carburetor, baby! I'll rev you up."

Riley elbowed him. "You aren't touching anybody's carburetor but mine!"

They all laughed, and headed for the pool, where, somehow, in the time it had taken to change, *someone* had put together a complete "themed" setup. There was a "malt shop" arrangement instead of a buffet, with a counter with stools and a couple of stand-alone booths and tables, a jukebox and a dance floor. And off to the side, a "drive-in" with a screen and half-cars, just phony front ends and bench seats.

Staci was getting used to this, but her friends' eyes all got big. "How—" said Riley, finally.

Wanda was the first to recover. "Lots of money and lots of servants can do anything," she said dryly. "If some rich dude can completely make Lothlorien for his wedding, this is like, child's play." Staci found herself wondering again how much magic had to do with what she was seeing. It amazed and frightened her at the same time how much there was to the world that she was only now beginning to learn about.

Sean met them shortly after they got to the party proper, greeting each of them in turn and complimenting everyone—especially the girls, and most especially Staci—on their costumes and appearance. She couldn't help but notice that he was in a '50s tux—the match for her prom dress. The food, while fitting in the theme, was still clearly gourmet and expertly prepared. The servants were similarly in costume; the women were dressed as carhops complete with skates, and the men as mechanics in vintage coveralls. Both sets of costumes had the servant's name printed over the breast.

Once everyone was properly greeted and shown the attractions for the evening, Jake and Seth, naturally, descended on the food like a pair of starved wolves. Riley and Wanda, after sharing an eye roll, followed with a measure of restraint. Sean and Staci picked up the rear, her on his arm again, talking as they went through the line with their plates. The evening only got better from there; after they had finished eating, they each had turns dancing to what came out of the jukebox...which, no surprise, had a much, much better speaker system than the original could have ever boasted. Classic pop hits, R&B, some blues, and more than a few Elvis hits; Seth turned out to be a not half-bad dancer, despite what Staci would have thought. Even Wanda seemed impressed, though she did her best to hide it.

Thoroughly danced out, Sean saw to it that everyone got milk shakes or soda floats before taking them around and introducing the gang to different cousins or hangers-on. Wanda paired off with the Blackthorne cousin she had met her first night at the estate, but didn't stray too far from the group, trading looks with Seth every now and again. *I really hope that something happens between those two; they would work well together, if they gave it even half a chance.* The night went on; more conversation, more compliments, the occasional nibble on a morsel brought by a skating carhop or a mechanic. The partygoers started to calm and the party's tone became more relaxed and slow-paced; after a final slow dance that Staci shared with Sean, with Riley and Jake also in their own little world as they swayed to the music, everyone settled into the half-cars to watch a double feature. Both were '50s horror classics: the original *The Blob* and *I Was a Teenage Werewolf*. Of course, Wanda knew everything about both films; Staci was pleased to see that she was sitting with Seth in one of the half-cars, quietly expounding on the films as they watched.

Staci felt happy. It was nice and cool out, but she was warm enough snuggled up next to Sean, his arms wrapped around her shoulders as they watched the double feature. When the final credits rolled, it was apparent that everyone was ready to crash for the night. Sean escorted everyone that was staying to their rooms; he had made arrangements so that each one of the gang had a separate room. Staci did her best to suppress a smile as she watched her friends' eyes go wide at the richly appointed accommodations before wishing each of them goodnight. She lingered a little in Riley's room. Riley closed the door behind herself, Staci and Wanda, then did a running leap into the enormous bed, landing with a laugh. "This is amazing!" she said, rolling over and spread-eagling herself over the expanse.

"I dunno why he didn't put all three of us in the same room," Wanda observed, looking around at all the space.

Staci shrugged. "Maybe because he figured we'd prefer privacy over a slumber party," she suggested. "They certainly have enough rooms to spare; I doubt they have ever completely filled the house before."

She and Wanda left Riley exploring her own little mini-bar and refreshment center and went to Wanda's room. It was virtually identical to Riley's except for the color (browns and creams instead of lilac and green) and the art on the walls. "I'm almost relieved," Wanda said, after looking around. "If this had been done up in black and red, I think I might have run away screaming."

Staci blinked at her. "Why?" she asked, puzzled.

"Because...okay, the '50s costume made for me... I can get that. You figure a Goth Girl is going to like being a Beat Girl, and it was all stretch stuff, so not hard to fit. But if they'd tailored a whole *room* to me? That pegs the creepy meter." Wanda strolled into the room and threw her beret on the bed. "This... looks like a swanky hotel room. I'm okay with that."

"I'm glad it meets with your approval," Staci said dryly. "I'll see you in the morning. Follow your nose to the dining room, they're laying out a buffet."

She didn't wait to hear Wanda's answer, but Wanda really didn't have one; like Riley, she was busy exploring. Staci went back to her own room, smiling a little. This was going to be a great weekend.

Staci had another dream that night. The gazebo in the middle of the hedge maze seemed to be a central part of the dream; she kept running through the maze, trying to get away from something, but every time she turned a corner she was back in the center with the gazebo. There was some sort of faint light coming from behind it...or from the structure itself, she couldn't tell. Everything seemed to go dark around the edges of it, and she felt as if she were being sucked into a black hole, unable to turn away or escape. Staci felt a scream rising in her throat, but before she could let it out...she woke up in bed, sheets twisted around her. She must have been thrashing in her sleep.

I've never *had nightmares this bad before. What's happening to me? Is it the magic, or all of the monsters that seem to want me dead?* And why should she have dreamed about that gazebo? It was a decorative building and a beautiful one at that. She did her best to try to forget the dream as she got out of bed and started to get cleaned up for breakfast; the clock on the nightstand said that it was nearly six, so Sean would surely be up by now. No matter what she tried to think about, however, the image of the strange gazebo kept coming back to her. It had seemed so beautiful the other day...save for the glimpse of horror that she had caught at the edge of her vision, turning the beauty into something sinister.

Once she had brushed her teeth, taken a shower, made sure her hair was presentable, and thrown on one of her New York outfits—not a vintage thing, just a nice summery top and skinny jeans, something that was completely out of place in Silence—she figured that she was ready to gather up the troops. As she made sure her top was smoothed down, she couldn't help but think about the last time she'd worn it—just about this time last year, and it had been so hot in New York that people were searching for *any* spot of cool they could find, and the roar of air conditioners had been audible even above the traffic noise. Here...if she wore this outfit down in Silence, she'd half freeze to death.

She knocked on Wanda's door first. "You up?" she called softly.

A few moments later Staci heard movement in

the room. The door cracked open, and Wanda was there; her eyes were half-lidded, her hair a mess, and she didn't have any makeup on. "Gimme a minute. I never sleep this hard. Must be one of those space-age wonderbeds or something. If there isn't coffee somewhere, I won't be held responsible for my actions." With that the door slammed shut; for a second Staci considered opening the door and making sure Wanda wasn't plopping back down in bed, but then she heard the faucet running in the connected bathroom. The same scene played out for Riley, Jake, and Seth; each of them was completely out of it, groggy and in full-on sleep inertia. *We didn't party* that *hard last night. It's not like any of us were drinking, either. Weird.*

Or maybe it was just simpler than that. Staci remembered all too well trying—emphasis on trying—to sleep on the miserable excuse for a mattress that was all she could find when she first moved in with her mom. None of her friends had access to Dad's credit card, maybe they had nothing but mattresses that were as old as their parents were...and she'd bet not one of them had ever slept on a really good bed before. That was probably all there was to it. Maybe that was what was causing her dreams; being unaccustomed to a really nice mattress. Staci shrugged it off; breakfast and seeing Sean again were more important, so she went downstairs.

Sean was alone in the dining room, but the buffet had been set up. As always, it was impressive, just like a brunch buffet at a really fancy restaurant, complete with a servant making custom omelettes, one making fresh pancakes, waffles and french toast, and one carving a whole ham. She had a hard time deciding, but eventually settled on ham quiche, some fresh fruit and a waffle with whipped cream and strawberries. By the time she was done making her selections, Wanda and the others appeared, followed by Finn, Morrigan, and a couple of the other cousins. Staci mentally shivered at the sight of Finn, but did her best to not let anything on. Wanda and the others looked awake now; the others, especially Seth and Jake, perked up when they saw the food, but Wanda looked as if she ought to have a storm cloud over her head. While the rest picked out something to eat, Wanda had an urgent, whispered conversation with the servant in charge of omelette-making. He went out and came back with a big teapot, which he gave to her. She sighed, and took it, left it at the spot she'd chosen as her seat, and got herself food. Meanwhile Finn and Morrigan parked themselves at the far end of the table; the rest of the cousins—and the ones who kept arriving, including Sean's father and the rest of the adults, dispersed themselves over the intervening space. It was really odd; Finn kept staring at Wanda with a little half-smile on his face, saying nothing. Wanda either didn't notice or pretended not to. Either way, she wasn't nearly as talkative as the others, quietly eating and sipping a large mug of what she had poured out of the pot, and Sean said was strong green chai. It wasn't coffee, but since Wanda hadn't assaulted anyone, it must have met with her approval.

The conversations were muted, for the most part. Everyone relaxed and enjoyed the food and company. But strangely, as Wanda became more and more human, Finn lost his smirk, which slowly turned into a slightly petulant expression. Finally he spoke up.

"This morning I had to look twice to realize I was here at Blackthorne, and not in the dining room of the Hyatt, there are so many strangers here." It *could* have been a joke, except that Finn's inflection made it sound, ever so slightly, like an accusation. Staci felt as much as saw Sean tensing, getting ready to take issue with Finn, when his father spoke.

"I, for one, am glad that we have some new blood here. Keeps things fresh. And, besides, Finn," Bradan said, "I've noticed that it's been a long time since you have brought anyone new to our table. And no one as interesting as Staci. And her friends, of course." He inclined his head first to Staci and Sean, then to the rest of the gang before fixing Finn with a stare. "I think you're finished eating. You're excused."

Finn stared back for a tense moment, before grinning and putting his napkin over his plate. "You're right. I am quite finished." He stood up quickly, almost knocking his chair back, and left the room, sending servants scurrying out of his path.

That briefly put a stop to conversation. Then one of the female cousins laughed. Morrigan glared at her, but that didn't stop her. "Welcome to *Family Feud*," she said merrily to Staci and her friends. "With this many of us in a room at the same time, it was bound to break out sooner or later. Just ignore Finn. He doesn't think anyone who doesn't polish his shoes with their tongue is worthy of life."

Bradan was smiling, and said, with only a *tiny* touch of rebuke, "Now, Brigit, that is scarcely fair."

"True, sir. He prefers the tongues to operate somewhat higher than the shoes." Brigit smirked.

Bradan actually laughed out loud at that. "Brigit,

either someone is going to murder you in your sleep, or you'll go far."

She smirked even harder. "Hey, at least it will be entertaining, sir."

The rest of breakfast was incident-free. Once everyone had their fill of the delicious food, Sean announced a special treat for everyone; since the preparations for the party that evening were going to cause a bit of noise and commotion around the pool, he had arranged for a trip to one of the nicer beaches in the area, with plenty of refreshments of course. "It will be an old-fashioned New England clambake," he said cheerfully. "Something that has, sadly, long been absent around Silence."

"That's because you'd freeze your patooties on the beaches around Silence," Seth observed. "Nobody sane here ever goes to the beach."

Bradan excused himself, but wished everyone to have fun and enjoy themselves; "Work, of course. It seems that it's never done, sometimes."

"Go run up and get what you need, there will be cars waiting out front," Sean told them. "We'll meet you there."

Staci did just that; she'd warned the others to bring suits. She stuffed hers into the beach bag she found waiting on her newly made bed, and ran down again.

This time she wasn't the first; the boys had gotten there already, and were climbing into a limo—this time one of a line of four that were waiting for passengers. Thankfully, it seemed that Finn was not going to join them. Apparently his exchange with Bradan over breakfast had been enough to cow him—for now, at least.

The limos rolled through the forest on what appeared

to be a private road, until, suddenly, the sun broke through the ever-present clouds and shone down on... a cliff-side parking lot, which the limos lined up on. Clutching her beach bag, Staci got out of the car with the others, and went to the edge of the lot.

There was a zigzag staircase made of white-painted wood making its way down the cliff and ending at a perfect beach—a half-moon of sheltered white sand, currently bedecked with portable cabanas, changing pavilions, and even, prosaically, a pair of port-o-potties. There were servants—at least Staci guessed they were servants—moving among the tents, setting out stacks of towels, unfolding lounge chairs, digging the pit for the clambake, getting out food and drinks.

"Holy crap," Jake said, "How did they get all of this out here? If it wasn't the Blackthornes, I'd suspect magic!"

The others laughed. Staci did too... but she had to wonder, how much of it *was* money, and how much magic? So far, what she'd seen and done herself had all been small... she supposed you could count making gold chains out of nothing "small." *Could* you do something like—create or transport all this stuff by magic?

Then she realized she didn't care, and it didn't matter. Because it wasn't as if she could find out by herself, and if you *could* do that sort of thing, Dylan would almost certainly already know.

"What, someone brought a bag of holding?" Staci said mockingly, and punched his arm lightly. "Come on, let's get down there and enjoy the first sun I've seen since I got here!"

CHAPTER FIFTEEN

By the time the cars were ready to take them back to the Blackthorne Estate, it was past dark. They had campfires burning, had had a *second* clambake, this one with lobsters, and were munching on a high-end version of s'mores, with exotic chocolates and handmade marshmallows. To be honest, Staci would just have soon stayed here. It was still actually warm on this beach, and aside from the ritzy food, this was the most normal things had been since she arrived at Silence.

But it was clear that the rest of the guests, her gang included, wanted to get back to the estate to find out just what the Blackthorne idea of a "horror movie night" was. So they all changed out of their swimming gear, climbed back up the cliff to the waiting limos, and piled in.

This time Sean came in the same car as the rest of the gang.

"Are we doing costumes again?" was the first thing that Seth wanted to know when they all settled down comfortably. It was pretty clear to Staci that he'd loved his '50s Scientist getup.

Sean smiled. "Only if you want to," he said. "Some of the other guests are very into...cosplay?"

Wanda nodded. "Cosplay's the right word."

"Some of the cousins don't see the point. So some people will be in something like the costumes we were wearing last night, some will be in casual attire, and some will be...well...you'll see." He smiled even larger. "Strangely enough, Father and his guests are *extremely* fond of...cosplay. So even if you see them, I am certain enough to place a bet on it that you will never recognize them. There *are* a selection of costumes hung up in a storage closet that we'll open up for everyone, since there are more people from Silence coming up tonight. Feel free to costume or not."

With that, everyone retired to the house to freshen up and, if they wanted, to get changed into costume. Seth was practically skipping the entire way up to his room. Staci and Wanda decided that they were just going to dress normally; Riley and Jake decided to pick out a pair of the provided costumes, so that Seth wouldn't be the only one dressing up again. This time, Seth changed up his costume a little bit; black PVC gloves over a white lab coat, goggles of course, and white rain boots. He was going for a *Dr. Horrible* vibe, he said, with enthusiastic recommendations that Staci borrow the DVD he had of the character. Riley was able to put together an Ellen Ripley cosplay, while Jake modified a Vietnam soldier costume so that it more closely resembled "Dutch" from *Predator*; his Arnie accent wasn't half bad, though he did sputter a few times trying to get it just right. Wanda just got into her overnight bag and brought out more of her Goth gear: black yoga pants, black spike heels, and a black poet's shirt with big puffy sleeves and a black beaded belt holding it in at the waist. Staci got out her vintage black silk jumpsuit again; this time she wore it over a dark green silk turtleneck with a dark green fringed "pirate" sash. She already knew that when she did that, it looked like an entirely different outfit.

When everyone was ready, they made their way downstairs and to the backyard. The house staff had to have some sort of SFX experience among them; the effect of all of the decorations was breathtaking. The entire area had been transformed; the swimming pool had fake moss-covered stones and reeds around its perimeter, giving it the appearance of a natural pool. Most of the underwater lights had been turned off, with only a couple of dim, green lights left that gave no hint to the depth or the shape. Mist emanated from the surface, seeping out onto the rest of the yard. The trees had been done up with spider webs, and strange lights would occasionally shine through the branches; it looked like a UFO abduction was happening in the distance. The rest of the lighting was muted, casting long shadows onto everyone; some torches were set up here and there for extra light. The outdoor theatre had been made up to look like a graveyard, complete with chairs made of pillows that looked like mounds of moss and leaves, and backrest-headstones; the head-stones actually had guests' names on them, with either disturbing or comical inscriptions. Finally, there were speakers cleverly hidden everywhere; spooky sounds played over them, the finishing touches on the creepy horror movie ambiance complete. Nor were the effects confined to the pool area; out in the larger gardens and the maze, mist billowed, strange lights came and went, and there were more sounds, some of them . . . unsettling. Absolutely every bit of it looked real. Not one piece was out of place, or looked artificial.

Seth just stared. "Whoa."

"Seth, you have a knack for understatement," Wanda drawled.

There were several buffet tables set up, as usual. All of the servants were dressed up as either mummies or zombies this time, shuffling around with trays of drinks and food. There were townies milling about, eating, drinking and talking. Sean spotted the gang, freeing himself from a group of his cousins; several were in costume, but most were not. Of the costumes that Staci spotted, most were on the female cousins. One was a Victorian woman in full mourning, complete with a head-to-toe veil. One was in an Italian Renaissance gown in a garnet-red velvet; she carried a golden, jewel-studded goblet that looked real. Two more were in medieval gowns. Staci didn't know what time periods they were from, but one was dark blue and high-waisted with a broad gold belt, and long, pendulous sleeves lined with gold and a fancy headdress; the other was a tight-fitting cream-colored gown with a kind of loose sleeveless gown over it half blue and half red, the sides open to almost her knees, showing the gown underneath. She wore a simple gold circlet on her head.

That one Staci recognized, it was Niamh, who sidled over to her. "I'm Queen Isabella, also known as the She-Wolf of France," she giggled. "When Isabella got competition from one of her husband's *special friends*, she had him tried for treason and killed by being impaled on a red-hot poker, so the murder wouldn't leave any outside marks. And Caelen is Countess Elizabeth Bathory of Hungary."

"Isn't she the one that's supposed to be like a female Dracula?" Staci said, thinking she remembered a movie about that—vaguely.

"Oh, Bathory was *much* better," Niamh whispered. "She not only drank virgin's blood, she bathed in it to stay young."

"Trying to scare my girl, Niamh? It'd be better to wait until after the movies, when everyone is good and jumpy." Sean walked calmly up to them, towering over everyone and interspersing himself between Niamh and Staci, putting an arm around Staci's waist.

"I just thought she'd enjoy a little *history* with the cosplay," Niamh pouted. "It's not as if we were being so lazy as to dress up as Eddie and Bella. Caelen and I put a lot of work and thought into our outfits! You *could* say," she continued, her eyes shining oddly, "that we know those time periods so well, it's almost as if we lived then."

Staci did her best to just laugh along with Sean and the others.

For the next hour, everyone made their rounds of the party, sampling the food and drinks—strictly non-alcoholic for Staci and her friends, though she did see several of the townies partaking, and heavily at that—talking with the cousins and some of the other guests, and enjoying the production value of the decorations. Seth, Jake, and Riley got to be as nerdy as they could, talking trivia about old horror movies. Wanda was a little more reserved, staying near Staci and the Goth Blackthorne cousin, Mori. Sean whisked Staci to and fro between the different groups, making her feel included in every conversation and having nothing but good things to say about her. Thankfully, neither Finn nor Meaghan were anywhere to be seen; apparently Bradan's chastisement had caused the pair to go off somewhere to lick their wounds.

After everyone had a chance to eat and mingle, Sean called the partygoers over to the theatre. It was going to be a triple feature tonight: first, *Evil Dead*, followed by the original *Hellraiser*, then one that Staci hadn't heard of before, *The Descent*. From the way Seth and Jake were talking about it, it was supposed to be gory and scary as all hell. The gang took their assigned seats, with Jake and Riley paired up, Seth and Wanda next to each other, and Staci in a loveseat with Sean. Or perhaps it should have been called a "double tomb" since that was what it looked like.

Evil Dead, even though it was made before she was born, still managed to scare her plenty of times. She found herself clutching against Sean's chest more than once. She didn't even touch her popcorn during the second half of the film. When the screen finally went black and the credits started to roll, Jake, Seth and Riley were all whooping and clapping, along with a few of the other cousins. They had seen the movie before, of course, and didn't get as freaked out as Staci did.

"That was intense," she said, blowing out the breath that she had been holding in anticipation of another scare.

"Can't beat the classics, sometimes." Sean peeled himself out from under Staci, standing up and facing the crowd. "I think it's time for a little break in the action. Say, half an hour? Everyone can stretch and get something more to nibble on or drink. Then we'll dive into *Hellraiser.*" A few people started stretching in their seats, but most of them got up and made their way to the buffet tables. The gang did the same, Seth leading the way.

But then a servant, incongruously *not* in costume, intercepted Sean. The servant whispered something in Sean's ear that made him frown. He turned to Staci.

"Something's come up that Father can't handle. I need to deal with it. Nothing *terrible,* but it is urgent. You'll be all right until I get back?"

She wanted to say she would go with him, or that she really didn't want to be left alone, but that would sound awfully clingy. Plus...she *had* promised Dylan to do some more snooping, and so far she'd been sticking so much with Sean that she couldn't. This might be the right opportunity. For instance, she was feeling more and more certain that the gazebo at the heart of the maze wasn't what it seemed to be. Now that she knew how to get to the center and out again, this would be the perfect time to have a closer look at it.

So she smiled and said, "Of course!" And as soon as he was out of sight inside the house, she made her way as obliquely as possible to the entrance of the maze. The rest of the partygoers were otherwise occupied; her gang was distracted by the food, so they wouldn't be any trouble. If they noticed she wasn't there, they'd probably assume that she had gone off somewhere with Sean for a little "private time."

Entering the hedge maze, Staci was wary. She kept her hand inside of her shoulder bag, clutching the cell phone charm that Dylan had given her.

She didn't want to be taken by surprise if she could help it; one run-in with a Red Cap was enough for a lifetime, but she was ready to defend herself if it came down to it. The sounds of the party grew faint the deeper that she went into the maze, but the mist from the pool had drifted over the ground here, too, and added to the spooky atmosphere. It didn't take her long to retrace her steps from when she and Sean walked through the maze; she arrived at the small clearing with the gazebo. It still looked beautiful in the pale moonlight, but also ... sinister. As she got closer, she felt the hair standing up on her arms, and her breathing became shallow.

Because ... when she looked *through* the gazebo, she didn't see the other side of the clearing, and the hedges on that side.

Instead, it was as if the arches of the gazebo framed the entrance to another world. It was a world of moon and forest, trees with bone-white limbs dripping dark moss, a world with no stars in the sky, and between the floor of the gazebo and the edge of the forest stretched an expanse of silver sand.

Despite the fear that made her shake, she felt drawn to that place. She didn't want to go there, but somehow, she could not keep herself from putting one foot slowly in front of the other, until she was mounting the three shallow steps, then crossing the floor—

Then she felt for a moment as if she had been struck by lightning.

The shock drove her off the floor of the gazebo, stumbling, then falling onto the sand on her hands and knees. It should have been soft, like the sand of the beach this afternoon, but it felt . . . harsh, as if every grain was made of sharp edges. She got to her feet and turned around.

It should have been the gazebo that was standing there behind her. But instead, there was an arch of bones, intricately fitted together to form a sort of macabre lacework. And framed by the bone was the clearing of the maze and the hedges she had just come through.

Before she could even think of stepping back through the gazebo-portal, she heard a blood-chilling howl. The howl was *close*. She whirled around to where she thought it had come from, and felt all the blood drain from her face. A pack of gigantic dogs, their shoulders easily coming up to her head, were charging towards her. There was no way she could make it back to the gazebo before they reached her; their path was going to cut right past the gazebo. Staci didn't think; instead, she ran for all she was worth.

She could hear the dull thud of the dogs' paws hitting the dirt, hear them panting and barking right behind her. Still she ran. Ahead of her, she saw a young man; his clothing was ripped and he was bleeding from several places. She recognized him as one of the townies who had been at the party earlier. He was looking around frantically, and his eyes bugged out of his skull when he caught sight of Staci and the pack at her heels.

"Run!"

The young man didn't need the encouragement; he was already back on his feet and sprinting by the time she caught up to him.

"Oh god, we're going to die! Shit, we're going to die!"

He was limping, and Staci could tell that his wounds were slowing him down; she was getting ahead of him, and there was no way he could go on for much longer. *He's not going to make it. I can't carry him, and if I tried we'd get overrun by those...whatever they are. But I've got to help him!* Staci swallowed her own fear, grabbing the boy by the shoulder and forcing both of them to skid to a stop.

"We've got to keep running, you crazy bitch!" He tried to wrench his shoulder free from her grip, but she had a handful of material from his shirt in her fist.

"We won't make it! I'm going to try something, but stand behind me!" Frantically, she dug in her purse until her fingers found her cell phone. She withdrew it from the bag, and just in time. The dogs had caught up with them, pulling up short and growling. *They want us to run. They want us to be afraid, to chase us...* Staci started to focus on her emotions, her feelings and memories; all the pain, the fear, the terror. She let it build in her chest until she thought it was explode, her hands shaking with the effort. One of the dogs in the middle had grown tired of waiting, and launched itself straight for her, jaws snapping and spittle flying. She couldn't hold the energy any longer, and thrust her cell phone out, charm in her palm.

"Fuck off!" she screamed at the top of her lungs. It was the first thing that she could think to say; her mind had scrambled for the magic word she used for the light charm, or even the defensive "whammy" that Dylan had taught her. But, in her panic, she couldn't remember either one.

The energy that had been building up inside of her released in that moment. The light from her charm went off like a small bomb, with a deafening thundercrack and a flash bright enough to cause spots in her vision. The dog that had been coming at her was in mid-leap when she released her magical energy; now, it was smoking on the grass in front of her, whimpering and trying to crawl away from her. The other monstrous dogs were all either on their backs or sides, baying and clawing at the ground, obviously dazed. Staci made a split-second decision.

"Come on, we've got to go! This is our only shot!" She pulled on the boy's shoulder, trying to urge him to run back through the pack of dogs with her, towards the gazebo.

"No! No, no, no!" He pushed her back, the fabric of his shirt finally tearing away. He gave one final horrified look at the dogs, then began running—in the opposite direction of where the gazebo was.

"Wait!" Staci yelled after him, but it was already too late. The dogs would be up again in seconds, and if she chased after him, she wouldn't be able to get enough energy to stun the dogs again; she didn't even know where that magical blast had come from in the first place. She didn't have any choice; she took a deep breath, then ran through the pack of gigantic dogs. One swiped a paw at her, but she was able to easily evade the confused and befuddled attack. The dogs were definitely starting to come to, shaking off the shock and pain from her magic. Staci couldn't afford to look back, running with everything she had left back in the direction of the gazebo.

Please say I'm not lost, please say I'm not lost . . .

She heard howls and barks behind her. There weren't as many as before, and she soon understood why; there was a very human scream off in the distance behind her, and it very suddenly cut off. She couldn't afford to think about the young man she had found; the part of the pack that was after her was gaining. Her lungs were on fire, and her legs felt like limp spaghetti. She didn't think she was going to make it until she saw the gazebo in the distance. The sight gave her a little extra drive, a little more energy. She was almost there when one of the dogs caught up to her . . . and then she was at the gazebo.

She stumbled and fell across the bone threshold, felt a second terrible shock, and landed on her hands and knees.

Not on sand, but on that strange, pale substance the gazebo was made of.

Dazed, she still looked back over her shoulder for the dogs, ready to run again. If they should chase her through the portal, whatever it was, they could still catch her before she could get to help!

But all she saw behind her were the hedges of the other side of the clearing. Whatever passage to whatever strange world had been there . . .

It was gone.

It took Staci a few moments to calm down and catch her breath. Dylan would want to hear about *this,* for sure . . . but she had to make sure she actually was able to get to him with the information in the first place. That meant not giving herself away, not to anyone, since there was no way of telling whose side who was on right now. So she waited until she thought she had everything under control, straightened out her clothes and hair, and walked as calmly as she could out of the maze.

Or rather, she was calm right up until the moment, one turn from the end, that she almost literally ran into . . . someone. Someone tall, and dressed as the head guy from the Black Riders in *Lord of the Rings*. The Liche King? Something like that.

She yipped and jumped back a step, and he turned. "Ah, hello, Staci. I cannot tell you how happy I am that Sean has brought you into our circle. I think we are going to enjoy having you with us very much, and for a long time."

She recognized the voice as that of Bradan Blackthorne, Sean's father. She swallowed hard, and looked up at the . . . dark, fathomless space under the tattered hood. "I'm really honored that you think so, sir. I need to get back to the party. I was just taking a walk while Sean handled something."

"Of course you were." The voice sounded amused, and moved aside. "Please, rejoin your friends."

She scuttled past, trying not to look as if she was in a hurry, and with relief, came out onto the garden paths again. Something was itching in the back of her mind about the exchange, and she felt her skin begin to crawl at the memory of looking up into the darkness of Bradan's costume hood. She didn't have time to think about it at the moment; she needed to get back to the party before she was missed. If someone noticed her absence and thought it was unusual, it would raise questions about where she had *actually* been.

What were those monster dogs? That poor, poor boy . . .

There was some sculpted shrubbery—tall stuff, actually, taller than Bradan with the costume on—that was between her and the flower beds of the garden. Mist curled in the pathways between the shrubs, and it had gotten awfully chilly. As chilly as it had been on—in—that place the gazebo took her to. She was passing one of the biggest shrubs, when she heard Sean's voice from the other side.

"...you were given a single task. And that was to *watch* her!" Sean sounded angrier than she had ever heard him before, even though his voice was kept low. There was something in his voice now that made her blood go cold; fighting against her every instinct to keep walking and pretend she didn't hear anything, she crept closer to where she heard him talking, trying to be as silent as possible. "She is *mine*. If any harm comes to her, I will use everything in my power to make you suffer the worst and most lasting pain imaginable. Do you understand me, Hunter?"

She found a tiny gap in the hedge, and peered through. Sean's back was to her. Towering over him was an enormous, heavily muscled man, like Andre the Giant from *Princess Bride*. He was dressed all in black leather, but not like motorcycle leathers, more like what you'd think to see on people at a Renaissance Faire. His face was hideously scarred, his hair was pulled back tightly into a braid or a ponytail, and he was carrying a bow and arrows. His head was bowed slightly, and his posture was submissive.

"I do, Master. I have my beasts looking for her at this very moment. My hounds never fail me. She will be found."

Staci's breathing stopped, caught in her throat. *Hounds? Were those dogs in that other...place, were they after me specifically?* The thought horrified her, that she might have been partially responsible for the boy dying, at least in some small way. Whether or not they were the same ones that Sean and the Hunter character were talking about, she didn't want them to find her here, snooping. As quietly as she could, she snuck away, making her way back to the party. Everything was as it had been when she went investigating; it seemed unreal, that these people were all laughing and having fun when one of them had just been brutally murdered not too far from where she stood. *No, that's not right. Wherever that place was . . . it's a far way away from here.* She gathered herself, putting on her best smile before walking back to the buffet tables, where the rest of the gang was.

"That was a short pee break," Wanda smirked. "You took less time than Seth."

"Hey!" Seth protested.

I . . . what? Staci reached for a soda so she could turn her wrist and covertly check her watch, and was shocked to discover she'd been gone less than five minutes. It had seemed like thirty, at least!

"I had to get back in time for the next movie," she said, feeling breathless and cold. And just that moment, Sean came up behind her and slipped an arm around her. She managed not to jump and squeak.

"You're going to love this one," Sean promised. "Well, maybe not *love*, exactly, but it is a fantastic movie, and very well done. Definitely stands out from the others."

They made their way back to their seats with gourmet popcorn and sodas, as the big screen began a countdown to warn everyone still at the buffet that the movie was about to start. She settled down into her seat with

Sean, and did her best to relax, but she couldn't stop her shoulders from tensing up. Sean pulled her closer as the movie started to roll.

It was brutal from the very beginning; extremely graphic violence punctuated the film every few minutes, and the characters' fear seemed to filter through to the audience. There were more than a few screams whenever a monster jumped out of the shadows, or someone suffered an incredibly brutal death. Every time that happened, all that Staci could imagine was the boy she met after she had walked through the gazebo. All of the fake blood became his blood, the screams and cries his, the looks of terror on the actors' faces were pale visions of his. She jumped constantly, shaking at certain points from the adrenaline and fear coursing through her. Sean was smiling for the entire film, keeping his arm wrapped around her and rubbing her shoulder or arm whenever she freaked out over a scene in the film.

When the credits finally rolled, there was clapping again, but it was much more muted. Most of the crowd were smiling at the "thrills" they had experienced watching the film, but Staci felt completely played out. Not just from the emotions the film raised in her, but from the running, the magic, and the trauma she had gone through before even sitting down to watch. As soon as she was able, she excused herself, citing that she was merely sleepy when she felt utterly wiped. Everyone said their goodbyes and goodnights to her, though she caught Wanda casting an odd glance at her several times during the process.

Once it was Sean's turn, he seemed to be absolutely glowing, his smile wide and showing teeth. "I'm very glad that you were here with me tonight, Staci. I love spending time with you, and now your friends, too. I can see why you hang out with them. I can honestly say tonight wouldn't have been the same without you." He leaned down, bringing his lips to hers. The initial thrill that she felt quickly dissipated, and she felt even more run down. He was a good kisser, but she pulled away before it went on too long.

"Goodnight, Sean. I'll see you in the morning."

With that, she dragged herself back to the mansion and into her room. She didn't even bother to change or clean up her makeup before she flopped onto the bed, fast asleep.

CHAPTER SIXTEEN

Staci slept late; a lot later than she had intended to. She had had more nightmares; she was back on the other side of the gazebo. This time, instead of finding her way back, she got lost, and the boy screamed endlessly for her to save him as she was being chased. She wished all of last night was just a nightmare, but no such luck. It was Wanda who came to wake her up rather than the other way around. And once she got down to breakfast, she felt as if she could devour the entire buffet.

The morning passed uneventfully, with the gang and about half of the cousins either playing in or spectating a water-polo game—a unique version that was a lot like tag-team wrestling, in that any of the players could "tag out" any of the spectators if they were dangling their legs in the water poolside. Wanda and Staci sat that out in one of the Jacuzzis; Wanda because she said that she'd lose her Goth card if she was caught playing anything with the word "polo" in it, and Staci because she was still feeling drained.

Lunch was the most amazing buffet of sandwich-makings that Staci had ever seen, and once again, she felt so hungry it was almost as if she hadn't stuffed herself at breakfast. After lunch was more poolside lounging, swimming, and soaking in one of the Jacuzzis for some, while some of the rest of the cousins played some vicious tennis on the two tennis courts. Finn and Meaghan were two of the latter lot; they were playing mixed doubles and put just about everyone out without scoring.

But in late afternoon, it was time for the gang to go back home. They were all very grateful for being invited this time (not even Wanda was the least bit sarcastic), thanking Sean for the wonderful weekend and looking forward to seeing him—and in Seth's case, the buffet lines—again. When the goodbyes and thank yous were all said, Wanda hung back from the group a little bit, giving Staci a long hug.

"Talk to you when we're back in town," she whispered into Staci's ear, low enough that for a second Staci thought she had imagined it, until Wanda nodded her head as she rejoined the others. *Something is going on with her. She couldn't have seen anything like what I saw last night, not with the glamour stuff. Right?* Staci had been sure to grab hold of her magical cell phone charm every now and again, playing at checking the time on her phone, just to make sure she wasn't under the same sort of mind-fog spell she had been the first time she came here.

Then they were in the limo and heading back to grim, bleak Silence. And she was still here, for another three days, the princess in the enchanted castle.

Except the castle has monsters in the forest. . . .

But there was no sign of the monsters at dinner— which was another formal dinner, with all the fancy silverware and Bradan Blackthorne and *his* guests in attendance. Conversation was subdued—Finn didn't speak at all except to ask a servant for something. And yet it wasn't a *depressed* sort of subdued. It was much more as if everyone at the table was anticipating something, something they wanted, and thinking about it too hard to make any effort at talking.

All save for Sean, who looked like the proverbial cat that had caught the canary. Normally, when Finn was around, he was on edge; not tonight. He ate heartily, but looked as if he was already sated, and merely eating out of habit or simple sensuous enjoyment of the food.

After drinks and some light conversation around the table, the younger cousins retired to Sean's poolside "palace" (and now that she thought about it, it really was palatial) and his living room. His living room was bigger than the entire house she lived in with her mom—all three floors, basement included. Though she had been spending days at the estate, she still found herself getting overwhelmed by the size and luxury that the Blackthornes were utterly accustomed to. She stayed close to Sean, which seemed to suit him just fine. The rest of the cousins quickly booted up the projector and a game system; it looked like they were in some sort of four-player, split-screen cooperative game.

She'd seen this before, the last time she was up here. It was some sort of medieval fantasy game, but one she had never heard of before—and Seth and Jake knew about a *lot* of games. It seemed to involve hunting something, using mounts that . . . well, they weren't *horses,* though they were vaguely horse-shaped. And packs of huge, black, mastifflike dogs. She never really saw what was being hunted; by the time the hunters and dogs cleared away from their prey, it was already de-rezzed and dissolved. There seemed to be several sorts of territory to hunt in, but they were all confusing. Impenetrable forest, that you had to find the paths through, with things in there that would ambush you. Swamp, with weeds as high as the riders' heads, and if you got off the path you were sucked to your doom. Mountainous desert, with quicksand *and* ambushes. Frozen wasteland, where you had to traverse crevices, frozen valleys and mountain paths, and you got ambushes, avalanches, and the possibility the path would break off beneath you and hurtle you a million feet to death. And caves. Caves with *all* of those perils. So it wasn't as if the hunters had it all their own way.

Still. Sean's cousins were really, really good at this game. Sean himself didn't seem interested in playing; instead he sat with her, watching the game and talking. It was all pleasant enough, save for how the dogs in the game reminded her of last night. She was still feeling drained, though, and soon excused herself to go to bed early. Sean escorted her back to her room, this time ending the evening right at her door with a very long, very soulful kiss, holding her so closely it felt as if he was holding her up. Maybe he was; she was so tired even her knees felt weak. It wasn't long after shutting the door that she had brushed her teeth, changed into the silk nightie provided for her, and drifted off to a hopefully dreamless sleep.

Staci was having another dream, but this one was formless and terrifying instead of vivid and terrifying. Not much of an improvement in her mind. She was thankful when she woke up, but couldn't shake the feeling that something had caused her to wake up. She checked the clock on her nightstand; it was almost a quarter past midnight, so she hadn't been asleep for very long. She was about to lie back down and try to sleep again when she heard a noise; maybe somewhere outside of the mansion.

No, it wasn't *a* noise; it was one, louder noise that had carried over the sounds of . . . well, it sounded like thudding, like feet on grass, and some snorting, and some watery sounds. The louder sound had been something like a squeal and something like a bleat, and something like a bark. Like an animal, but not like any animal she had ever heard before. A very big part of her wanted to hide under her covers and ignore it . . . but she had to look, to find out what it was. Carefully, she swung her feet over the edge of the bed, gingerly putting her weight on the floorboards. She felt ridiculous, creeping along the floor like a robber out of a cartoon as she made her way to the window. She was about to give up, and chalk it all up to her imagining things in a dark house . . . when she heard the noise again. She slowly pulled the edge of the curtains with her right hand, peering out of the exposed corner of the window.

What she saw made her blood freeze in her veins.

The "Hunter" she had seen last night was there on the lawn by the pool. There were others that looked almost identical to him, though he was the tallest of the lot. They were milling around, looking anxious. Most of them were astride equally giant horses of some type; all were jet black, and mean-looking, pawing at the ground with monstrous hooves. That was horrible enough, the sight of the Hunter, the others, and the mounts. What truly scared her were the dogs; they looked like mastiffs, only bigger. Several of them were lapping water from the pool; the underwater lights illuminated the water, and wherever the dogs were drinking from . . . the water looked pink.

Those are the dogs from last night . . . and that's blood *coming off of their mouths.*

A group of four riders came from around a bend of the hedge maze. They were clad in similar leather garments as the Hunter, but weren't nearly as tall or solidly muscled. At a guess, they were elves; some of the Blackthorne cousins, or maybe Bradan's "guests." She couldn't see who it was clearly from the window. What she could see, however, was that each of them and their mounts had been spattered with blood, and quite a bit of it. She leaned in closer to the window, daring to lift the curtain a little bit higher. If she could just get a look at one of the riders . . .

Suddenly, the Hunter from last night looked directly at her window. She stifled a yelp, letting the curtain drop and quickly ducking down beneath the edge of the windowsill. *Please say he didn't see me, please say he didn't see me . . .*

Staci took a chance, using a single finger to lift up the barest edge of the curtain; the Hunter wasn't looking at her window anymore. But one scare was enough for her; just in case, she wanted to be back in bed if anyone came up to investigate. She had to remember that, even as wonderful and pleasant as things were with Sean, she was still in "enemy" territory here. As quietly as she could manage, she slipped into bed. Before she could form a thought about what had just happened, she was asleep again.

She woke up. It was gray, gray dawn again, and once more, there was someone in the chair by the window. But this time she wasn't afraid. She knew it was Sean, and she knew he would always make sure she was all right.

Last night . . . the horses, the Hunters . . . must have been a nightmare, caused by watching too much of that video game.

She must have moved, because the silhouette of Sean's head moved. "Are you all right?" he said. "I was coming to see if you were awake and wanted breakfast and I heard you cry out. But when I came in here, I saw you were asleep."

"Just a really, really weird nightmare," she replied. "Nothing even happened, really, it was just nasty." And even now, it was fading. She could scarcely remember *why* it had been so terrifying, much less what had happened. "I'm starving," she said, "I'm glad you woke me up, I might have eaten my pillow in my sleep."

Sean got up from his chair, and she could hear the smile in his voice even if she couldn't see him smiling. "Then I'll get out so you can get dressed. I'll see you downstairs. About half the guests are gone, so the next couple days will be quieter."

The next two days were a blur of more leisure and fine dining. She spent almost all of her waking hours with Sean; the more she was around him, the less and less she worried about what she had seen on horror movie night, or the night after. She'd take care of it when she got back down to Silence, but right now it didn't seem nearly as important as looking into Sean's eyes. She found him in her bedroom again on the last morning that she would be staying at the estate; it was comforting, knowing he was there, watching and protecting her. She still felt tired, more than a little drained, but didn't care; probably just getting lazy and easing into actually relaxing for a change.

When she left at noon on Wednesday, she cast a single wistful glance back at the estate. Sean had seen her to the limo, giving her a final kiss and thanking her for everything over the week, saying how her being there had made the entire week for him. She glowed with every compliment, and wanted to stay, but of course she would have had to get permission all over again from Mom. And anyway, he said that they would have plenty of time together soon enough. With that, she was driven back to dreary, dead Silence. She felt as if she was going into exile; she didn't belong in Silence, she belonged up here, in the sun with Sean.

It was with some irritation that she remembered that she had promised the gang to meet them at the bookstore that evening. She really didn't want to, but a promise was a promise. *More blah blah blah about games, I guess. Not that I can blame them too much; the games are the only excitement they have going for them.* How sad was it, when the only thing worth doing in a town was getting together in a shabby old bookstore and playing fantasy games? Anywhere else, and she could *so* see all four of them doing amazing things. Jake and Riley could be going on real dates, to real clubs and things, like a real couple. Wanda would probably be at a magnet school doing art. And Seth—well Seth would be up to his eyes in computer equipment, and *he'd* probably already be in college with tech firms eyeballing him and salivating.

She put her clothing away—no need to do laundry

for herself, the maids had laundered everything except the outfit she was wearing, and damned if she was going to do Mom's. Mom had to do *something* for herself, and if she wanted clean clothes to wear, she could wash them herself. Then she got on the dialup and checked—as best she could—her Facebook page. Even though she'd been away from the net for a whole week, there were only three posts and none of them were even asking about her. She'd have slammed the lid of the laptop shut *hard* in a surge of anger, if she hadn't felt too dull to really get any anger going.

Whatever.

She retrieved her bicycle and started the long pedal down to the bookstore, still remembering the feeling of the sun on her face and Sean's hand in hers.

The minute she stepped through the door to the bookstore...something happened. It felt just like she'd had a cold—that foggy, not-quite-focused feeling—and now it was lifting. She realized just how exhausted she had been feeling. *Still* was feeling, although at least she was thinking more clearly. She nodded to Tim, who had looked up as she came in, and was about to ask which coffees had been brewed today, when he spoke first.

"Hi there, Staci. I—" He stopped short for a moment, his eyes going wide before narrowing as he looked at her. There was something in his gaze, but it was gone before Staci could figure out what *it* had been; his eyes crinkled into a smile as he cleared his throat. "Sorry about that. Missed you around the shop, this last week. The rest of your crew seemed to have had a good time, though."

"Well, it's the Blackthorne Estate. They've got more money than anyone I've ever met and they don't seem to mind spending it on parties," Staci replied, feeling a bit . . . awkward.

"Right. Well. Coffee is on the house today. You look like you could use some java. Your friends are already in the back waiting for you."

She could feel Tim's eyes on her back as she walked past the counter towards the rear of the bookstore. *What's gotten into him?*

Just as Tim had said, the rest of the group were already camped out in their usual space in the back. Staci said her hellos as she made her way to the coffee machine; the smell of freshly brewed coffee was already working to perk her up, and she was starting to feel like coming into the shop wasn't such a waste of time after all. She fixed herself a large mug, turning to sit in her usual spot. She expected the gang to be embroiled in some discussion about a video game or movie, as per usual.

But Seth and Wanda were already deep in an agitated conversation, and Jake and Riley were sitting as tightly together as you could get, holding hands, and looking worried.

"Their car is gone," Seth was saying, as if he was answering some question Wanda had answered. "It's not like they just got beamed up to the Mothership or something. *Their car is gone.* So maybe they went for a joyride after the party and, I dunno, they're wrecked, somewhere."

"Wait, whoa, I just got here," Staci interrupted. "Whose car is gone? What's the big deal?"

Everyone turned to look at her, and she could see

that this wasn't some argument about nerd minutiae. Riley looked worried, and Jake, though determined to try to comfort her, looked the same. Seth seemed to be fighting a losing battle with Wanda, who appeared to be equal parts upset and scared. Wanda was the first one to talk to Staci.

"There are some kids missing. Three of them. They were all at the party the other night, the one we were at—"

"Which doesn't *mean* anything!" Seth blurted out. "They might've just gotten drunk and drove over to the next town, or gone on a road trip. Or wrecked. Or, heck, maybe they decided they'd had enough of this stinking town and just decided to leave. We don't know, so there's no reason to jump to conclusions without any more information."

"You don't find it the tiniest bit strange that all three of them up and go at the same time? Or that the cops haven't even talked to the Blackthornes? I didn't know them, but that doesn't change the fact that they're *gone*, and some of the last people to see them haven't been questioned a bit."

"It's only three people—"

"No, it isn't. It's only three people *this week*. Other people have gone missing, too. People just refuse to talk about it. Why are you trying to rationalize this so much? It's not like you're going out with one of the Blackthornes." Wanda caught herself too late, looking at Staci and then at her feet. "Staci, I'm sorry. I didn't mean it like that. It's just . . . it's really strange, whatever is happening."

Staci felt a wave of anger wash over her, but bit back the snappy comeback she was going to use on

Wanda. Instead, she just blew out the breath she had been holding in a sigh, and shook her head. "Can we just talk about something else, please? This is a job for the police, anyway, isn't it? Especially if they're kids like us. It's not as if we were the Scooby Doo gang or something, solving mysteries."

Riley nodded, leaning forward to grab her own mug of tea. "Staci's right. Let's just focus on something a little less messed up; it's not as if we knew those kids all that well, just to say hi to, if they even felt like saying hi back, which, you know good and well, they pretty much didn't."

But although Jake and Seth tried gamely to get the conversation on other things, conversation just fell flat. After an hour and a half of fiddling with some character sheets and a few abortive attempts to get a game going; finally, Riley sighed, and said she had to get back home to do the dishes. Jake said he'd go with her, and Seth added he'd walk home with them both. That left Wanda and Staci sitting there staring at each other.

Staci had been steadily sipping her coffee during the entire awkward hour and a half the group had been together, and was thinking that it was time to head home, maybe stop by the diner for a bite to eat. Just as she was about to stand up and say goodbye, Wanda spoke, looking intently at the space between her feet.

"The others can't see it, or maybe they won't see it. But . . . there's something very wrong happening in this town. Something *evil*, Staci. People go missing all the time, but up until now, it's been bums or dropouts, drunks or stoners, people that couldn't hold down a job or drifters. People that wouldn't be missed. Or wouldn't be missed much. But...it's like things have been escalating. First the couple of homeless people. Then it kind of worked up—the last ones that went missing were a guy whose wife had just left him and a kid who was a stoner but still lived with his parents. Now..." she gestured with one hand, helplessly. "Now it's three regular kids. So now...maybe whatever is doing this has decided no one is *ever* going to do anything about this, so it's gotten bold."

There was an itch at the back of Staci's mind, almost like a buzz just outside of the range of her hearing that she couldn't shake. It made her want to scream and stamp her feet and curl up into a ball and cry, all at the same time. "Stuff like that always happens even in small towns, though. In New York City, the same sort of things are going on all the time, too. It's just that people notice it more sometimes, and think that it's a pattern when it's just life." She couldn't put her finger on why, but her own words felt hollow, rehearsed in some way. She tried a weak smile. "If we just had a decent Internet connection, I could show you, I bet; show you the statistics of how many people go missing all the time. Probably the homeless people just took shelter someplace and died, and no one's noticed them because it's under a car on blocks, or under the dock. The guy whose wife left—well, what did he have to stick around *here* for anymore? And stoners are always wandering off and having bad things happen to them, it's not just *Reefer Madness* stories, they get dizzy and fall off docks or cliffs, or get lost in the woods..." It didn't sound convincing, not even to her.

"Staci...the Blackthornes have something to do

with all of this. You've got to see that. They run the town, practically. All of them might not be so bad. Mori is cool, if a bit creepy, even for me. But you've been around them more than any of us, hell, anyone in the town, probably. You must have seen something, *anything.*"

Staci shook her head, firmly. "Wanda, this is like—like stupid Internet conspiracy thinking, like black helicopters and secret societies and aliens abducting you every night. Seriously. I think this town is just driving you bonkers, a little. Sure, the Blackthornes are rich, but not even rich people get away with a dozen murders. And Sean is sweet, he's—he's actually really protective of people he likes. He kept me right by him during those freaky movies, and he makes sure even his cousin Finn isn't allowed to hardly look at me, much less hassle me. He was even in my room when I woke up a couple times because I was having nightmares and he heard me—he wanted to make sure I was all right, and when I woke up he was sitting in a chair across the room, just watching over me—"

"He was *what?!*" Wanda leaned forward in her chair, hands on her knees. "Staci . . . you do know that you pretty much just outlined the beginnings of an abusive or possessive relationship, right?"

"Uh—what?" She gave Wanda a startled look. "That's ridiculous. He's never touched me, he's barely kissed me, and he sure hasn't—"

But . . . she couldn't help but think of the—yes—*possessive* way he held her close to him when he was with his cousins. How he had monopolized her conversation except when the gang was around, and even then, how he'd kept her with *him,* making sure the others had things they could do, or other people who claimed their attention.

"Staci, all that stuff that you said that Sean was doing? That's called *grooming*; it's the same kind of thing kiddy diddlers do to get their victims used to being abused, to make them think that it's normal. To make them comfortable with it. He's been controlling you more and more. He compliments you a bunch, right? Like, that's the only thing he has to say to you, ever, pretty much?"

"But what's wrong with that?" she objected. "I say the same kind of things to him!"

Wanda started ticking off fingers on her other hand. "He gets jealous anytime someone else shows an interest in you. He gets angry quickly, over that, too, right? He tries to monopolize your time as much as he can; more and more, lately. And he picked when you could see your friends, even when you could leave his house. Hell, he was choosing what you could wear, just about."

Staci could feel herself getting cold, because...this was all hitting much too close to home. "But...most of the time I was wearing my own stuff," she said feebly. "You just didn't see it because it was cosplay nights...he doesn't tell me what to do, ever." *No, he doesn't tell me what to do, but...what else can I do up there except things he wants to...*

"Doesn't tell you what to do, but he's the one giving you the only options to choose from. It doesn't matter which one you pick, because he picked them all *first*; whatever you choose, he wins. Then there's the whole super creepy watching-you-while-you-sleep bit. Stalkers do that sort of crap." She sighed. "Staci," Wanda put her other hand on Staci's, her voice going quiet. "I'm not trying to rain on your parade. I'm really, really not. I'm scared for you. Because...because I—my sister went through this exact thing and I saw it all myself. I don't want to see it happen to you, too."

Wanda pulled her hand back, but the touch had... done something. Nothing *sexual*, it was more like a pail of cold water had hit her, waking her up. *What the hell was wrong with me?* Suddenly it all came rushing back. The kid in the maze—was he one of the ones missing? Sean talking to the Hunter. The cousins on their terrible horses, with those black hounds around them. The blood in the pool...

How could she have forgotten any of that? It was as if—

As if someone put a spell on me!

And something about being here, being in the bookstore, talking with Wanda, had somehow snapped her out of it.

She couldn't tell that to Wanda though. Good God, Wanda already had enough crazy ideas and conspiracy theories *without* being told that magic was real, and there were elves and—

And some of them tried to kill me...which means if Wanda knows...some of them might try to kill her, too.

So instead, she acted as if this was perfectly normal relationship advice, crinkled up her forehead, and said hesitantly, "You might be right...if nothing else, he's kind of overprotective...."

"Just be careful, okay? I know I've said it before, but I mean it, now more than ever after everything you told me. It'd be really easy to get blinded by all the money and everything, and not notice something going on right in front of you." Wanda stared at her for a few moments more, then seemed satisfied that Staci was taking her seriously. "I've got to get going, too. But I'll see you tomorrow, okay?"

"Definitely," Staci said, without getting up, clutching her coffee mug in both hands. "I think you might be the best friend I ever had, Wanda."

"Oh Goddess, don't say that," Wanda scoffed. "If nothing else, don't say that, 'cause in horror movies, the next thing that happens is that the *best friend* becomes *victim du jour*. Mm, 'kay?" They both laughed at that, and Staci couldn't help but marvel at how good it felt. Wanda gathered her bag, hugged Staci, and then left the bookstore, saying goodbye to Tim on her way out. Staci decided to stay for a few more minutes, though.

She felt as if she was completely awake for the first time in a week, and she probably *was*. She had the horrible feeling that Wanda was right. At the very least, Sean was manipulating her, and probably casting magic on her. Maybe it was to protect her, keep her from remembering things she saw and shouldn't have, because he didn't know that she wouldn't just blurt that stuff out. But... it was still manipulation. And she had the horrible feeling she was some kind of... trophy to him. Something he had that Finn couldn't get. And she was clearly something that Bradan approved of. No... no, there was some very creepy stuff going on, and she needed to talk to Dylan about it, and find out if he was actually on Sean's side, and what he really *knew* about the Blackthornes.

Staci picked up her shoulder bag, stood up and then set down her coffee mug by the sink next to the coffee machine. On her way out the door, she stopped in front of the register counter. Tim looked up from a heavy, leather-backed book.

"You look like you're doing better. Coffee that good, huh?"

"It's like magic," Staci replied, more than a little seriously. "Thanks, Tim. I think this bookstore is the best place in Silence."

He smiled broadly at that. "Thanks, Staci. I'm glad that you think so. You and your friends are always welcome here, of course."

With a final nod, Staci pushed the door open, walking out into the dim sunlight coming through the low cloud cover. There was plenty of time to talk to Dylan and get home before nightfall. Food could wait. She was determined not to be kept in the dark anymore.

CHAPTER SEVENTEEN

It was, as always, a long bike ride up the Hill to the spot where Staci usually met Dylan, and it was made longer by the fact that she kept looking over her shoulder for those psycho lawn gnomes or one of the leather-clad Hunters. Her call to Dylan just after she left the bookstore had been brief and tense; Dylan must have heard the fear in her voice, because he had only said "Usual spot," and hung up.

He was waiting for her on the Hill, instead of her arriving and having to wait around for him. He looked concerned, arms crossed and leaning against Metalhead; when she crested the Hill and came into view, he immediately started walking towards her.

The expression on his face at least gave her some comfort. He was clearly worried. "What's wrong? Are you okay?"

She closed her eyes for a moment to frame her reply. "I . . . found out about a lot of things. I'm just not sure where to start."

"Let's go from the beginning. You were up at the Blackthorne Estate for a full week; let's break this down, day by day." He waved his hand towards the tree, inviting her to come take a seat. She made a little face; it wasn't the most comfortable of places to sit . . . but at least they couldn't be spied on there. Unless there was something *in* the tree, but she figured Dylan would have seen and cleared out anything like that. She followed him over; they both made themselves as comfortable as they could, and she began. First with the mundane details, about the party, the guests, her friends. Then she dove into the rest of it; Dylan listened intently to her every word, but seemed to be particularly focused when it came to the magical parts she described.

He started when she described finding Sean in her room the first time. She felt very odd about that . . . it made her feel *really* stupid, that she had been so blasé about finding a stranger in her room, watching her. Wanda was right, that was way, way over-the-line stalker stuff, it wasn't romantic *at all,* and she felt like a complete idiot for not seeing that, right then and there. And she had let him get away with it, not once, but three times!

"Staci, you were bespelled," he said flatly, when she was done. "It's one of the lowest, most vile forms of magic, the way he was using it on you. It changes how you think, can make slaves of people. He was trying to draw you under his power, fully. If you had been there much longer . . ." He let his voice trail off, shaking his head before cursing himself. "It was stupid of me to send you into that. I should have seen it coming." He started again, looking to her. "How did you break out of it?"

"It . . . well, it just kind of wore off after a while. Maybe it was being away from him, being away from that place." She shrugged. "Maybe it's because Wanda made me actually think about it. Although..." She frowned. "It didn't really start to wear off until I got to Tim's bookstore. And then it kind of went all in an hour or so. So maybe it was because I was with my real friends again?"

He was silent for a moment, digesting the information. "Maybe." He looked at her strangely, like he usually did whenever she had surprised him. Was he just shocked, or did he feel protective about her? Dylan had been warming up to her for some time now, but for the most part it had been a bit detached, as if he was keeping her at a distance. "Still, it was stupid of me not to anticipate that you'd be in danger from something other than getting caught looking around. I'm sorry, Staci; I fucked up, and bad. I should have anticipated this. And I should have prepared you, or helped you with some sort of protection. It's my fault for dragging you into this crap." He stood up quickly, stalking away a few feet. She could tell that he was fuming, angry with himself.

And he hasn't heard the worst of it yet. She wondered how he was going to react to *that*. But at least he wasn't detached anymore. *Okay ... I guess he's got skin in the game now. He isn't just thinking of me as an ... ally? ... he's thinking of me as someone that he doesn't want to get hurt.* This wasn't that creepy possessive-protective shit that Sean was pulling. This was ... genuine. Like Wanda opening up about herself, only ... Dylan wasn't another girl. He *liked* her, maybe way more than just liked her ... and when she contrasted him with Sean ... Sean wasn't coming off too well.

She got up, and caught him on the turn by grabbing his elbow. "Hey," she said. "Stop. Look at me."

He did. His expression was full of doubt and he frowned, as if he was frowning at himself. "This is only going to get more dangerous from here on out, Staci. This isn't your fight—"

"Maybe it wasn't before, but it is now," she said firmly. "It really is. These are *horrible* people, Dylan! Or...whatever they are, they're horrible, and we can't let them keep getting away with it!" She filled him in rapidly on what else she had seen—the trip to whatever was on the other side of the gazebo, the kid who had been chased by the hounds, and the worst of all, when she had seen the Hunters and realized that they'd killed...something. Only now, she knew it was some*one*. And that she was pretty sure the three kids missing from the party were dead. "You said you came here to stop something, and I guess this is the sort of thing you're trying to stop."

"You're right. I know you're right." He sighed heavily, shaking his head. "What you saw was a Wild Hunt, or the aftermath of one. Dark elves riding down 'prey' for sport. The Hunters are like houndsmen; they scare the prey, get it to run. It's not so much about the killing, for them, as it is the chase, and the fear and despair of the prey. That's what feeds them. If they're doing Wild Hunts, out in the open like that, it means they're becoming more brazen. Something bad is coming, Staci."

She got a sinking feeling. "What do you mean, something bad?"

"If they're not bothering to hide their killings, it means that they're consolidating their power for something big. I don't know what, but whatever it is, it means a lot of people are probably going to die.

And not quickly." He gave a mirthless chuckle. "Not enough suffering, even from grieving families. I've seen this kind of thing happen before. It's exactly what I came here to stop."

"What . . . how could anything be worse than what they're doing?" she asked . . . not really wanting to hear the answer, but also knowing that she had to know. She sat down on a tree root.

"Ever been to Detroit? That's small-scale, long-term influence. Slow burn. There are plenty of ghost towns in this country that would still be alive if it weren't for the Unseleighe. The Rust Belt, poisoned rivers and streams that have been the lifeblood of towns for generations, places where people rarely make it past sixty years old . . . Silence is on the chopping block for that, and worse. Mass death, but slow, and painful, and less hope than even now. That gazebo—it's a kind of gateway to Underhill, which is where all the elves, Seleighe and Unseleighe, come from. There are more of them over there. That's probably where all those 'cousins' are actually living, when they aren't partying and hunting at the Blackthorne Estate. The Unseleighe get their power from misery, and that gazebo lets them funnel the misery back home. It's like a pipeline." He frowned. "I'm not sure how that kid got over there, whether he went through by accident, or they brought him through. It's more likely the latter; they might have wanted a Hunt on their own ground, where they could keep chasing him, hurting him without killing him, without a chance that he'd escape and somehow get the authorities looking for whoever had been hunting him. Those Gates—portals—generally have a lot of protections on them."

"So, if we destroy that, it's over, right? We win, they can't go home and can't use that power? Can we even destroy it?"

Dylan shook his head. "It's not quite that simple. Gateways like that aren't easy to take down; you couldn't just set it on fire, for instance. They're warded with devastatingly powerful magics, and it'll fight back if it comes under assault. Even if we can take it down—and that's a huge if—that might not stop the Blackthornes from doing whatever they're planning on doing to the town. Being cut off from Underhill will weaken them significantly, but"—He shook his head—"unless we can get rid of them permanently, or get them back on their own side and seal them off, well, I'm not sure what they can do. They still have Silence to feed off of. They might even be able to reopen the Gate."

"So—what do we *do?*" she asked. Because this sounded like a no-win situation...

"We need to find out what their big plan is for Silence. You've done great so far. If it weren't for you, I wouldn't know that they were ramping up for something really nasty. Once we figure out what they're planning, we can stop it by destroying the gateway. Any of them that we don't lock behind it..." He paused. "I'll think of something. But I won't leave them *here,* to start all over again."

She nodded. What else could she do? It was like they said, once you know something you can't un-know it. And now that she knew, she had to keep right on helping him. Partly, it was self-defense, because there was nowhere else for her to go. But right now, mostly it was because of Dylan. He'd convinced her this was the right thing to do.

And maybe she had some skin in the game too—if she was partly of elven blood, well, she needed to figure out how to make this all stop.

"Before I send you back into that viper's nest again, we need to make sure that you're prepared. When Sean," he said, spitting the name out, "was trying to bespell you, it's only luck that you were able to break free. I'm going to teach you how to do spellbreaking on your own; how to recognize casting, and what to do to stop it or negate the effects. That, and some more defensive magic; you've been progressing *way* faster than I had expected, so you're definitely ready for this."

He wasn't kidding either, as she found out for the rest of that afternoon. He worked her harder than she had ever worked before in her life. This wasn't just learning a couple of tricks; this was learning how magic worked, and why, and how to find the weak point in something that was being done and shove a stick in there and let the thing break up under its own momentum. Because, as he kept telling her, over and over again, "A spell is a *process*, and not a *thing*." And a process was something that kept going until it ran out of steam, or was stopped.

He was just showing her *how* to make it stop.

He also showed her how to make it stop in two ways—by just letting it break up, or by stopping it violently. Because when you did the latter, all the energy it was using snapped back in the caster's face, like a bungee cord stretched out as far as it could be and then breaking. And at that point, spellbreaking actually became a weapon.

He showed her several kinds of "shields" to make,

like the one he used; little ones you could hide behind, like the shields that riot cops used. Big ones, like hiding behind a wall. And dome-shaped shields that you could duck under and just let things rain down on you while you were protected.

She felt as if she was burning off energy, like running a marathon, and she actually must have been, because right after she'd gotten the hang of the little shields, her stomach growled. He looked at her as if she had suddenly turned into a Red Cap, then laughed.

"Yeah, I guess I forgot to warn you, spellcasting burns a lot of energy." He strolled over to his bike and came back with a plastic grocery bag. "I know this little gal, earth-mage, drinks so many Meals-In-A-Can she has to buy them by the pallet-load. Here. It's what I've got."

The bag turned out to be full of energy bars, and she tore into them as if she hadn't eaten in a week. So did he, actually; within fifteen minutes, there was nothing in the bag but empty wrappers. She finally looked at a wrapper when she had eaten the last bite of the last one. *Gammabars? That's not a brand I ever heard of.*

"I'll buy you a real meal later. Right now—back to work," he said, and began teaching her how to *see* magic, so she'd know when someone was trying to do something to her. Really see it, this time, and not just the effects, like the shimmer in the air she got when she put up a shield. Hard to describe, it was... like unfocusing your eyes for those weird hidden 3-D pictures that had been all the rage when she was little. When you did that, you could *see* the process, like colored threads weaving together, in constant motion.

By the time she got the hang of that, and everything else he'd been teaching her, it was after six. The energy bars had completely worn off. And she was not looking forward to biking all the way down the Hill and back to her house, only to have to clean up whatever mess her mother had left, and *then* cook.

Dylan laughed when he saw the hungry look in her eyes as she glanced at the empty Gammabar wrappers. "Told you, magic takes energy. Mind taking me up on that offer for some real food?"

"Oh God, yes," she said fervently. "Are you going to magic it up or something?"

"Magic takes energy, remember? I'd burn off more than I would get from the food I'd make. Actually, I figured we'd sample some local cuisine. The next town over has a roadside stand that serves some mean lobster rolls. And fries made from real cut-today potatoes."

"That sounds amazing." She thought for a moment, then looked over her shoulder at her bicycle.

"Don't worry, we'll leave it here. I can hide it so that no one will be able to find it, save for you. So, what do you say?" He grinned at her . . . and she realized that all this time, when he'd smiled and grinned at her before, it hadn't had the sort of nuances she was seeing now. *We're in this together,* and *you're special, and I am going to share things with you I wouldn't share with anyone else.*

"I say, I'm starving!" she said with enthusiasm. He turned to look at her bike; squinting a little, she could *see* the filaments of magic covering her bike, until it faded into the background and became invisible. They walked over to Metalhead, who revved with what sounded like happy pleasure. And at Dylan's gesture, she climbed aboard, putting on a helmet he took out of the bike's storage compartment.

"Ever been on a cycle in the daytime before?" he asked.

Because, of course, he'd given her one ride at night. She shook her head.

"You'll like it." She could hear the smile in his voice. "Just hang on and enjoy the ride."

Staci had expected the ride to be fast...but not *this* fast. Despite the helmet that Dylan had given her, the roar of the wind still filled her ears, with only Metalhead's...engine?...cutting through the noise. The trees and other vehicles were quickly passing blurs to either side, with the road as one long black river in front and behind. She held on as tightly as she could to Dylan, who seemed utterly unconcerned as he rode bent forward in the seat.

There was something strangely sexy about all of this: the speed, the wind, the smell of leather, the feel of Dylan's warm body under the arms she had wrapped around him. And yet...it was a sort of dispassionate sexiness, remote. He wasn't talking to her, he wasn't even facing her, he probably wasn't even *thinking* about her. All his attention was on his driving, or his and Metalhead's; she realized she had no idea of who was doing what. It was like watching an intensely romantic movie all alone. Lots of feeling, but no one to share it with.

It didn't take long for the pair—well, trio, actually—to arrive at the next town. Staci thought it was called Greenville something or other; the sign had been almost a complete blur as they sped past it.

They ended up on the other side, at a little white-painted shack called "Ray's Eats" with open shutters overhanging the service counter and a long line in front of it, and within shouting distance of some docks. But the weathered gray picnic tables over on the side were empty; it seemed as if everyone was grabbing their food and going straight to their cars. Dylan parked Metalhead by the tables and got in line, while she picked out a place on a picnic bench that wasn't too splintered.

The clouds that perpetually shaded Silence were nowhere to seen here. Or rather . . . you could see them, but they were lumped off in the distance to the north. It was sunny, hot; the boats at the dock rolled back and forth in gently moving, sparkling waves. Were they lobster boats? They certainly weren't pleasure boats; these were stubby, working, fishing boats and little seagoing motorboats that looked like they had crews of two to eight on them.

Well, it would make sense to put a lobster shack where the lobsters were coming in.

The line was moving pretty briskly, and it wasn't long before Dylan came back with two paper boats and two soda cups balanced in a carrier stuffed with napkins and a couple of plastic forks. He put the carrier down on the table between them and took a soda. The drinks were both clear, so they were probably ginger ale.

Each of the paper boats held a generous portion of fresh-cut french fries with little bits of skin still on them, a tiny styrofoam cup of cole slaw with a pickle on top, and two hot dog buns loaded with warm chunks of lobster meat. In one of the buns, it looked like the meat had been mixed with mayo. In the other, it was glistening with melted butter that had soaked into the bun. Dylan sat down across from her. "Got one of each for each of us; I thought that you could try both, and I know you've already worked off all the calories. They're both great."

She'd never had lobster rolls before Sean's beach party; they were way too expensive in New York City. "I like both kinds," she said, picking up the one with the mayo first and biting into it. The sandwich was perfectly sweet and juicy and there was the exact right amount of slightly spicy, homemade mayo, and she remembered exactly how hungry she was, eagerly taking another bite. The two of them sat there, eating quietly save for the occasional happy sigh from Staci around a mouthful of lobster or fries.

When she got to the second roll, she was ready to slow down a little. This seemed a good time to start asking Dylan some questions. He wasn't going to jump up in the middle of a meal and motor off, abandoning her here, after all.

"So, for the last couple of weeks, you've been teaching me all of these spells. I get it, magic exists. But...how? Where does it come from?" She picked up a couple of fries, nibbling on them as she waited expectantly for his answer.

"Everything that's alive makes it," he said. "The more intelligent something is, the more magic it makes. That's why humans are a good source. Also, the more emotional someone is, the more magic they make. I guess"—he scratched his head—"it must be a kind of by-product of intelligence. I dunno, you'd have to ask someone who does all the theoretical side. But that's why killing someone gets you magic; it releases it all at once. And why making people miserable gets you magic. Only, the magic you get is flavored by how you get it. If it's gotten by death and misery, it's ... nasty. At least it is to my people, the Unseleighe love it." He ate some fries, thoughtfully. "It's easier to use magic Underhill, but there's a lot more competition for it, too. That's partly why elves come here in the first place."

She nodded, taking in the information while sipping on her soda. "Why did you come here, in the beginning? How'd you get to be ... well, you know, doing what you're doing now?"

Dylan sat silently for a few moments, studying her before he finally spoke. "I told you that I was a kind of 'roving troubleshooter,' when we first *really* met ... the night that the Red Cap attacked you. It wasn't always like that for me." He sighed heavily, shaking his head. "What I'm about to tell you is something that I've never really told any other mortal before. I wasn't always hunting down Unseleighe enclaves. I used to be normal, by my people's and clan's standards. That changed in the late '80s—1980s, that is."

"Late '80s? You couldn't have been more than a young kid back then."

"Not quite. We don't age like humans, Staci. I'm actually almost three hundred and fifty-six years old; still pretty young for an elf, all told."

Staci felt her eyes bugging out of her skull at this revelation. *He's over three hundred years old? How is that even possible? Why doesn't he sound like someone in a Shakespeare play when he talks?*

Jeez, how old is Sean, *then?* Suddenly, that made the

idea of some three-hundred-year-or-older guy hovering over her in the bedroom *even creepier*. Like...would that be pedophilia to...*No. Not going there*. They both acted like they weren't all *that* much older than she was, and it just didn't seem as if you could, like *act*, act that way. So—*argh! This is too complicated!*

Questions swirled through her mind, about her feelings for him, what his feelings were for her, how they could even relate to each other as well as they did; it was all too much. She settled on sticking to the present.

"Three hundred years old, don't look a day over twenty-something. Got it." She shook her head once. "You were talking about the '80s. What happened then?"

Dylan looked down to the ground, his voice becoming softer and losing that carefree lightness that it always seemed to hold. "I...well, I lost someone, Staci."

"Lost someone?" She gulped, suddenly regretting her question; it was obvious that whoever it was, he was still hurting over it. "Listen, Dylan, we don't have to talk about this if you don't want to..."

"No, no, it's fine. It's just not easy, sometimes." He smiled at her sadly, then continued. "My cousin and I had come up topside for an R.E.M. concert in Savannah. I love music, or at least I did back then, and so did my cousin. Human creativity astounds my kind: the innovation, the emotion, and a lot of us flock to it. My cousin was older, and loved introducing me to new bands that he had just discovered. I used to count the days until we could both come up for another show. That was actually the last concert I've been to, now that I think about it." He sighed heavily. "We were on our way back from it, heading for the Fairgrove Gate just outside of Savannah, when we were stopped on the road. Ian was challenged to a race. That's—very traditional, although it *wasn't* traditional for an Unseleighe to do the challenging. I *knew* there was something wrong with it, but Ian was full of magic and music and laughed it off. He and the Unseleighe took off, and even though he told me not to, to go home, I followed. He lost the race. And ran right into an ambush."

Dylan stopped talking, brooding, looking down at his food for a long time. Staci decided that keeping quiet was probably the best idea, and just finished her food.

"I tried to help him; I think they must have thought I was dead, too, when they left us. The group at Fairgrove—not my clan, we're Emerald Thorn—knew we were due to use the Gate and came looking for us when we didn't turn up at the right time. Once I was in any state to do so, I went back to my clan and told them that I wanted revenge. They told me that Ian had lost a challenge, and that was that. They said that going after the other clan would start warfare Underhill, war we've been dancing around for centuries. Since it hadn't occurred in Underhill itself, they said that it wasn't worth pursuing the matter. I told them they could stick that where the sun didn't shine, I came up out of the Fairgrove Gate and I've been hunting Unseleighe ever since."

"That's . . . a really long time to do nothing but hunt. Have you ever gone back to Underhill, to your clan?"

He shook his head, and took a savage bite of his food. "No. Why would I want to associate with cowards who would watch idly as their own kin are slaughtered?

Sometimes I check in with Fairgrove; they, at least, know what to do about Unseleighe, although they concentrate on just keeping the area around their Gate free of infestation. I can't fault them for that."

Elven politics were a lot more complicated than she could have imagined. The careful balance that prevented all-out war, the internal struggles evident in the Blackthorne family...or was it clan?

"Couldn't we ask for help from them? This Fairgrove bunch? They helped you before, right?" Surely he'd thought of this already, but maybe not; sometimes guys just got all stupid about asking for help.

Dylan shrugged. "They've got enough on their plates. Besides, even though they know how to handle Unseleighe properly, there are other clans that don't. A big move by Fairgrove is a lot harder to ignore than a renegade biker elf. Wars get started when players like Fairgrove get involved."

The way he said it though...she sensed there might be something more. Maybe these Fairgrove people had warned him off, told him that they *weren't* going to get involved if he stirred something up. Or maybe he just didn't trust them. He usually worked alone, after all. She seemed to be the first person he had let in in a long time.

She shivered at the thought of what a fight waged with magic would look like; certainly nothing like in the movies or fantasy books. The little taste of deadly magic she had already been exposed to illustrated very clearly how horrible such a fight would be. But she saw Dylan's point, too. How could anyone sit by, and let murderers and torturers run loose in the world, so long as they played by the rules? At first, she had decided to help him out of self-preservation, but now she was committed to see this thing through because it was the right thing to do . . . and also self-preservation.

She watched Dylan for a few minutes. He kept his gaze towards his food, as if he were trying to stare a hole through the paper boat. From his clenched fists to his posture, it was obvious that he was both angry and still grieving. Staci's heart ached for him, in that moment. He had lost more than his cousin all those years ago; he had lost his home, and the only family he had known. He had lost his world; it reminded her of her own situation, being suddenly thrust into a hostile and harsh environment with seemingly little choice in the matter. She could also see little glimpses now and again of what he could have been like if things had been different; the nonchalant and confident way he talked and carried himself, the smile that would come easily if he would let it, and the light in his eyes that showed exactly how much he really did care.

"I'm sorry, Dylan," she said before the silence became awkward. "I can't imagine what losing your cousin, and then your clan in Underhill, must have been like for you. I wouldn't wish something like that on anyone." Carefully, she put one hand over one of his clenched fists. After a moment, he unclenched, squeezed her hand, and held it for a moment, before letting it go. Then he exhaled in a long sigh, and finished his meal.

"It was a long time ago," he said. "Thirty years. You get used to a lot of things in thirty years."

Staci decided to change the course of the conversation a little bit, to keep him from brooding too much more. "How do you find the Dark Elves? Why did you choose Silence, instead of any of the other places where the . . . Unseleighe must be? Also, did I pronounce that correctly?" she added quietly.

"Yeah, you got it right." He wiped his hands on his napkin, took a sip from his soda, and ran a hand through his hair. "I'm not a mage, actually, I'm just a fighter. I can only do the kinds of magic any of our kind can do." He finally looked at her, with a lopsided smile. "Kind of like everyone learns to read and write in your schools, but not everyone learns how to make a living writing. Anyway, what I can do is fairly limited, and it's not real good at tracking things down. So after I clean out a trouble spot, I just get out the map and do some dowsing, looking for the 'next dark place nearest me.' This time, it turned out to be Silence."

She nodded. "That makes sense." *But what about after?* Staci suddenly found herself afraid of what the answer to that would be. She realized that she didn't want Dylan to leave. Even though she had been in danger since she had met him, she felt safe when he was around. She had felt the same thing around Sean, but now she was wondering how much of that was real, how much of it was infatuation, and how much of it was dark magic? She didn't like the idea that what had felt so genuine had actually been nothing more than games and evil manipulations, that her emotions were playthings to be bent to someone's will. She didn't get that with Dylan; hell, he had even shown her how to defend against that very thing. She felt safe with him not just because he was strong, but because he was teaching her how to be strong. "So . . . after we're done with what's happening here in Silence, what will you do?" Staci was very careful in her choice of words; she didn't want to give him any suggestions to stay or to leave, not yet at least.

"Head to the next dark place nearest me," he replied. "There's always another one."

Staci's heart sank. That was exactly what she was afraid that he might say. Still, she hung onto a shred of hope, willing herself to meet his eyes. "Is there anything that might make you change your mind?"

He gave her a sharp glance. "I don't know. But if there's one thing I've learned in thirty years, it's never to say *never.*" He got up, and stretched, collecting the debris from their meal. "But right now, I'm concentrating *on* right now. And right now it's time to get you back to the Hill so you can get home before dark. I don't think it's a good idea for you to be out alone after dark anymore."

She nodded, dusting crumbs off of her lap and standing up. Dylan's answer was better than nothing. He had already opened up to her, admitting that it had been more than he had ever told another human.

There had to be a reason for that, didn't there?

CHAPTER EIGHTEEN

The ride back to the Hill with Dylan was as much of a blur to Staci as the ride to the lobster roll stand had been. Metalhead seemed to relish taking bends in the road at breakneck speed, passing other vehicles with ease. She was somewhat worried that they would get pulled over; Dylan had had enough trouble with the police in Silence hassling him. Whether that was due to the way he looked, or some sort of influence from the Blackthornes, she couldn't know. All the same, they didn't have any trouble during the trip, pulling up to their usual spot on the Hill as some of the last rays of the sunset came through the trees.

Maybe he'd put some sort of invisibility on himself and the bike. That would make sense, actually. Maybe the reason he didn't do that in Silence was to stay under the radar.

This was about the only time you actually *saw* the sun around Silence; at sunset, when it managed to drop below the clouds that perpetually covered the town.

Dylan stayed astride Metalhead while Staci climbed off, letting the elvensteed's engine idle. With a wave of his hand, the air shimmered and her bicycle appeared right where she had left it.

"That could be real handy, you know," Staci said, smiling as she looked from the bike to Dylan.

"In time, young Padawan. Let's focus on the task at hand, first." Dylan patted Metalhead's gas tank, and the elvensteed shut its engine off. "Even with you knowing some decent combat magic and spellbreaking, and all of my tricks, I'm not sure we're up to this one. There's still a lot of things we don't know about the Blackthornes; which of them, precisely, are in on whatever this plot is and *what* they're planning to do that's going to take this town to hell. A lot of unknowns means a lot of danger . . . maybe more than we can handle." He sighed. "Still, we got to give it a shot, right? That's what the good guys do."

"We're all right as long as they don't know we're snooping, right?" she asked, suddenly reminded again that this really wasn't a movie . . . and that what had happened to the missing kids could, all too easily, happen to her. "And if it looks like too much, can't you, you know, get some help? Maybe not from your clan, but from those other guys you talked about? I mean, if there's a whole town in danger?"

Dylan simply shrugged. "I can't say for sure. Again, the Fairgrovers mostly keep the dogs at bay in their own neck of the woods. We can't count on anyone coming to bail us out." He jutted his chin towards the setting sun. "You need to get home. I'll talk with you again tomorrow. We can figure out the next move then. Get some rest, Staci. You did good work today." Metalhead's engine revved to life with a throaty roar. With a wink, Dylan gunned the throttle, and the pair were off.

Well, if we can't get help from other elves... There *had* to be someone else around!

And then, like a flash, it came back to her. It seemed like ages ago! But it hadn't been more than a couple of weeks.

Tim *knew* Dylan, or at least knew what he was. Knew why he was there. And had warned him that he didn't want any part of it...which meant Tim knew about magic, heck, maybe he did magic himself! After all, if Staci could do magic, there had to be other humans who could! And maybe Tim had warned Dylan he didn't want to get involved before...but that was before they knew that the Blackthornes were going to do something horrible!

He can't just walk away now. And Staci was going to see to it that he didn't.

She got on her bike and started the long trip back to town.

It was full dark; really close to curfew, actually, although given that Staci was probably now known to be "Sean's girl" by the cops, she kind of doubted they were going to do more than give her a "fatherly warning" if they caught her. Still, she did her best to stay off of the main streets and out of view; no reason to get stopped if she could help it. She was lurking in the alley at the service door for the bookstore, next to what *had* to be Tim's car, a battered old blue Volkswagen Beetle that had seen much better days, just like everything else in this town. She'd never seen Tim come out the front door after he locked up, so she'd reasoned there had to be a back one, and here it was.

She took a few breaths to ready herself, tamping down last-minute doubts and hoping that she wasn't making a mistake. When she felt prepared, she very gingerly tried the door handle; it turned, thankfully without a squeak. Slowly, she pushed the door inwards, and it swung silently on its hinges. The aroma from the coffee maker, and the familiar smells of the books and leather seats all washed over her, the warm yellow light from the bank tellers' lamps still on and inviting. Moving slowly and quietly, she shut the door behind her, trying to keep her steps light as she moved into the bookstore.

"Staci, why are you sneaking in through the back just as I'm locking up?" Tim's voice seemed extra loud in the quiet of the bookstore. She half jumped out of her skin, and turned to see Tim to her left, coming out of the backroom with a leather backpack over one shoulder and a money box under his other arm. She had expected him to be up behind the counter, like he always seemed to be. *Damnit. Well, at least he didn't sound angry...just surprised.*

"I need to talk to you," she said. "And I didn't want anyone seeing me come in the front."

Tim set down the backpack on the ground, placing the money box on top of it. "It's late. Curfew soon, if it isn't already." He studied her for a moment. "But, I'm guessing that this is something that can't wait. Why don't you grab a couple of cups of coffee. We'll sit down and talk." He walked past her, finding his way to a couple of chairs in an alcove nearer to the front of the store than where her group usually sat. She complied, moving woodenly for a few moments from the shock of being caught in the act of breaking into the business of one of the few people she counted as a friend in Silence. But was it breaking in, if the door was unlocked? She filled up two large mugs from a pot of coffee that was still warm and didn't look or smell too old, then followed to where Tim had sat down. He was leaning forward in his chair, his elbows on his knees and his fingers woven together. He smiled as he accepted the mug she offered to him, blowing on the surface of the liquid before taking a sip.

"So, what's the emergency that needed you to come here in secrecy, when no one else is around? If you're a ninja assassin sent to kill me, I warn you, I'm a screamer and won't go quietly."

She pondered her next move. On the one hand, she just wanted to confront him and get it over with. On the other...well, he might laugh at her. And then what? He'd shove her out the back door and she might miss her chance at getting some help.

"You know Dylan," she said finally. "Or at least, you know what he is."

Tim's face betrayed nothing; he kept his voice even and his eyes on his coffee, blowing on it again and taking a sip before speaking. "Why would you say that?"

"Because I was there the day that he came in here and you two were talking. I overheard you. You told him that you knew what he was here for, and you didn't want any part of it." There. That was putting it out in the open without actually saying the "m" word.

"Guys like that are trouble, Staci. I'm not sure what he's told you, or what you *think* you overheard. I try to avoid trouble, as a rule; it's why I run a bookstore. Save for the occasional ninja assassin, it's nice and quiet."

She frowned. It sounded as if he was going to stonewall until she found a way to break through. And that he didn't think she had a way to break through without sounding ridiculous, easily brushed off and her statements rationalized away.

She dug into her purse for her phone and the cell charm on it. "You know, I *could* point out that my phone doesn't work here for anyone other than Dylan," she said. "But I'd rather *show* you this."

And she made the charm blaze up. This time it was brighter than any time she'd ever made it light up before; so bright that she let out an involuntary "Shit!" and cupped her hand over it, spots before her eyes.

Tim hadn't moved when she stopped shielding her eyes. He was still watching her, though now she could see the barest hint of a grin at the corner of his mouth. "Well. He's taught you a little bit of magic. You've got talent," he said, with some pride. "I could strangle that pointy-eared bastard for dragging you into this world." He took a very long pull of his coffee this time, setting the nearly empty mug down on the short table between the two of them. "No more games on my part. You know about magic, and clearly a little bit about elves. What do you want to talk about?"

She let out a sigh of relief. That was a start and more than she'd had a little bit ago. "The Blackthornes. They're elves, and they're bad, and Sean is going all possessive on me and I think that's probably a bad thing. He was messing with my head this weekend to make me think that lurking in my bedroom while I slept was sweet."

Tim's eyes narrowed slightly. "That's why you don't get involved with elves. You can't trust them." He looked her up and down quickly. "You seem to be doing better now."

"It started phasing out when I got inside the store, and then when I was talking with the gang it completely snapped," she said. "And Dylan showed me how to break it myself, so they can't put it on me again." The last was said a little defiantly, in response to *You can't trust elves.* "So...what's this store, anyway? Why did it help me break the spell?"

Tim sighed heavily, leaning back in his chair and crossing his arms. "It's a haven. For me, and any who seek it. The only place like it in all of Silence; at least, the only place *left* like it. Enchantments, hexes, bewitchings, curses...the magic etched into every board and nail of this place cancels it out. I'm honestly surprised it took as long as it did to work out whatever was put on you. Your friends definitely helped, though. Good energy there, something that people take for granted far too often." He waved his hands outward. "All of these words? They have power. Every little word you utter has a small measure of power in it. Cussing someone out, a word of encouragement, even a simple thing like saying 'thank you'; there is energy that's transferred. Talking with people that care about you helped to break the last link of the spell that was put on you."

"But why's it *here*, in Silence? Why are *you* here?" she asked. "I know the Blackthornes have been here and doing nasty stuff since before this store was here, because you aren't all that old."

"It's easier to hide in plain sight, sometimes. I don't bother with politics, especially with goddamned elves." Staci was shocked by the venom he put into the word *elves*; there was a lot of anger in Tim, and she was afraid to find out where it came from. "This place is a sanctuary, right in the lion's den. No one would think to look for it here, and it can do the most good for those that need it. The spells on this place are old, and powerful, feeding off of one of the few ley lines in the area that hasn't already been tapped. It's safety, and there's precious little of that in Silence."

She digested that for a bit. "Okay, so... if you don't bother with politics and elves, then why did you come here in the first place?"

He shrugged. "Had to settle down somewhere. Quiet town, cheap real estate. No one much bothers anyone around here, which is how I like it."

"Well, it's not going to be that way anymore," she said flatly. "The Blackthornes are killing people, Tim. They're hunting them with these dog things. And they're going to do worse. They're going to do something that hurts the whole town and everyone in it." She was starting to get exasperated. "I *saw* the Wild Hunt with my own eyes," she said stubbornly. "And I saw a guy they were hunting—one of the people that's missing now! And I overheard Sean talking. Plus they think I'm not paying attention, so they talk in front of me. They're planning something big, and that can't be good for Silence!" She glared at him. "That means you—and all this"—she waved her hand around, indicating the store—"are going to be right in the firing line whether you like it or not!"

This time Tim frowned. "And what makes you so sure? *Dylan* told you all of this, I'm guessing? And what makes him such a trustworthy advisor?" He shook his head, keeping his eyes locked to hers. "Staci, elves use people. Seleighe, Unseleighe, good, bad; it doesn't matter. They *use* humans for their own ends.

Whatever philosophy they try to wrap it up in, it's still not a dynamic where the human benefits, unless they can't help it or it's by happenstance. Why do you think this Dylan character came to me before he turned his eyes towards you?"

That gave her pause for a moment. *Was* Dylan using her? Well...

No. Oh maybe a little at first, but not now. He's been totally up-front about everything since I started using magic. He keeps trying to warn me off. Tim's wrong about him.

"I think he came to you because this is the fort in the wilderness," she said flatly. "He says he goes from 'one dark place to the next,' cleaning them up. He says Silence was the 'next place he could find' and I bet he was surprised to find the bookstore here and figured you'd help him. And I don't know why you *aren't*."

"It's not my problem, Staci. If your friend wants to carry on the good fight, I say let him. I know this," he said, pointing at her. "*You* need to get as far away from him as possible. Elves only leave wreckage behind them, especially when they start playing their games with each other. That wreckage all too often has names and families. Don't become part of it, Staci."

She frowned, fiercely. "It *is* your problem, because you live here," she pointed out. "And if crap starts flying, you're going to get spattered. Why are you acting like this, anyway? I mean, if what you *really, truly wanted* was to be left alone, you wouldn't have put this bookstore together right here. You'd have found some cheap house out in the middle of nowhere with no neighbors and ... I dunno ... started an Internet bookstore, if you *had* to run a bookstore. Or an organic herb farm, or something.

What you're saying doesn't make any sense with what you've made here! So...why are you saying it?"

"I don't have to justify myself to you, or anyone else for that matter, Staci. I have my own reasons for doing what I do, and that's no one's business but my own." Tim sounded almost...sad? She couldn't put her finger on what it was in his voice, but there was a sort of hollowness in what he was saying.

She crossed her arms over her chest and glared at him. "If you want me to go away, you're going to have to give me a good reason. Because otherwise, I'm not going to stop nagging you."

"You want a reason? You *will* get hurt doing this, Staci. It's amazing that you haven't been killed already, to be honest. Magic is dangerous; mixed with elves, it's deadly in ways that go beyond just having your body die." He looked at his coffee cup, avoiding her eyes. "I know."

She clenched her teeth. "I'm *stuck* in Silence, Tim. I'm a kid, I can't just move out or run away—well, I could run away, but chances are I'd be hooking for a pimp in Las Vegas before you could say 'crack addict.' My dad *won't* take me back for the good reasons of my mom being a lush, and her boyfriend's trying to molest me—you think he'd take me back if I started spouting off about dangerous elves? Besides, my friends are here, and I thought you liked them! Whether we fight or we don't, the answer is the same: we're either going to have to *do* something and maybe die trying, or we become collateral damage hiding in the cellar! So why aren't you *doing* something?"

"Because I've already done enough!" He slammed his fist down on the table, causing both of their coffee

mugs to jump. There were a tense few breaths where
Tim's eyes were fixed on hers, and she felt frozen by
his sudden outburst of rage. Then the moment passed,
and the anger faded from his face. "I'm sorry, I didn't
mean to shout at you like that, Staci." He sighed, leaning
back in his chair again and covering his face with his
hands for a moment. "But I know how this is all going
to play out. Whether the Blackthornes 'win,' or you and
Dylan 'win,' it's all going to be the same; the elves do
what they want, and damn everyone else." He was quiet,
lost in thought, and his eyes became unfocused as he
stared past her. "I was like your friend, a long time ago.
I even worked with his kind, on occasion. There was
always more to do; I was younger then. Stupid. There
were so many people that I lost, but I told myself that
so long as *the mission* was there, that it all wasn't for
nothing. I made the mistake of trusting an elf to have
my back. Then I was left twisting in the wind when I
needed help the most. And, like I said, there are worse
things than dying when you get involved with elves."

Staci was taken aback by the hurt in Tim's voice. It
sounded very much like Dylan, when he had been talking about his cousin. This was different, though; Tim
had been pushed too far, past the breaking point . . .
and then some. He *had been* broken. She shivered
involuntarily, not wanting to ponder on what could have
happened that had been so bad that it could have broken
someone like him. She had to say something to bring
him back to the present, to keep him from self-pity.

"Dylan isn't that other elf. *I'm* certainly not an
elf—well, mostly. I don't know what you went through,
Tim, but I'm sorry that you had to do it alone. I can't
just turn my back on this, though. Even if I wanted

to, I don't think it would do much good; this stuff with the Blackthornes...it's going to keep coming after me, even if I ignore it or run from it. So, my only option left is to fight; fight to survive, fight to help save this town and everyone in it. Even you. Even," she gulped, "if you won't fight to save yourself."

That got a response. There was another burst of anger, more contained now, but still smoldering behind Tim's eyes. For a second, it looked as if he was going to say something; maybe the spark would catch, and he would see reason and help her. But then it was gone again. "I'm tired, Staci. You should go home. It's not safe out after dark; you know that, now, better than anyone else in Silence."

"Tim—"

"Go home. I don't want to talk about this again." There was finality in his statement. She had tried to get through to him, and lost. Without another word, she angrily gathered up her shoulder bag and stormed towards the back door. As she was about to shove it open, she looked back to Tim, still hoping that he might change his mind.

"I meant what I said, Staci; you don't want to be in this fight. Run, or hide. Better yet, forget you have ever even heard of magic. And just hope that it forgets you right back."

She didn't have a response for that that wasn't laden with cussing, and she didn't have the energy to get into it with Tim again. So, she left, letting the door slam behind her.

It was...weird. On the one hand, now she was completely aware that she was in the middle of something really, really bad. Like being under siege or something. But on the other hand, everything looked and seemed completely normal. The missing three kids? Well, concern about them just faded away, and even the gang stopped talking about them after a day or two. It was business as usual in Silence, and even Wanda was keeping her lip buttoned about it.

She finally decided that it *had* to be part of whatever spells the Blackthornes had woven over the town. Sort of a "nothing to see here, move along" that made everyone forget things that were inconvenient to the Blackthornes.

And she—even while she felt as if she should be fighting something, or running, or trying to hide like Tim—had to act the same, if she didn't want to paint a great big target on herself. It was a strange week. If she was going to do what Tim thought she should do...she should have been figuring out how to hide from everyone. Instead, she was acting completely normally. Laundry, housecleaning, increasingly infrequent trips to the Hill to check her increasingly sparse messages, grocery shopping, breakfast at the diner, gaming with the gang...

And waiting for another invitation from Sean, which she didn't want to accept, and knew she had to. And yet, she wanted to accept it too, because Dylan had stressed how important it was that they find out *exactly* what the end game for the Blackthornes was; she was their best bet for that, since Sean was interested in her and kept bringing her back to the estate. It made her skin crawl, imagining him trying to break into her room to watch her sleep again.

And right on schedule, Thursday night, the call came

from Sean to come up to the estate for the weekend. There would be a new twist to the entertainment, this time. The cousins were going to play some polo games, a sort of tournament over Saturday and Sunday. Staci accepted, of course, faking the enthusiasm that she had felt before, working through her anxiety, and keeping her voice chipper and upbeat. She wasn't into sports all that much, so she hoped that the games would be enough of a distraction that she would be able to slip away while most of the cousins—and Sean—were otherwise occupied. She did her best to keep her mind off of it for the next day, dodging her mother and keeping to chores. She let the gang know where she was going to be, but avoided going back to the bookstore; she wasn't ready to face Tim again, and was still angry with him after their last conversation.

Friday afternoon came far too soon for Staci's liking. Her every instinct told her to run, or to use some of the defensive spells that Dylan had taught her when she saw Sean's car pull up to the curb in front of her house. She couldn't tip their hand now, though; she needed to just grit her teeth and bear through it, do what needed to be done...no matter how loathsome she found being around Sean, now. Even if he wasn't a part of all of the bad stuff willingly, he wasn't doing anything to stop it or warn anyone. That was just about as bad as pulling the trigger itself on whatever was going to happen to Silence, at least in her mind.

"You look wonderful as always, Staci," Sean was leaning against his car, arms crossed in front of his chest as he waited for her to make her way off of the porch and to the street. She had concentrated on everything being normal; that included taking as much care with her wardrobe as if she still *wanted* to be his girlfriend. She was wearing another New York summer outfit: mint-colored yoga pants and a matching crop-top. Given that there was going to be sports involved, she had khaki shorts and polo shirts in her bag, and her vintage jumpsuit and accessories in case they were having a formal dinner.

He was grinning, a sort of *lookie-at-something-that-I-own-coming-this-way* smirk that she wanted to wipe off of his face with a two by four. But instead...

He might not be in on this. And this is kind of how he was raised. What did I tell Wanda? You might not like the customs of another country but... you deal with them. So she smiled brightly, and then dropped her eyes as if she was a little shy so he wouldn't catch how much she wanted to grab him by the shoulders and shake the truth out of him. *Treat it like you're an actress in a play, girl. Just play the part of the happy-to-be-here ditz hopped up on hormones. Though, it doesn't hurt that he is still drop-dead gorgeous, when you set aside the creep factor.*

Fortunately, she was never required to actually make any conversation with Sean, only to supply him with an audience. So on the trip up, he chattered away about polo, and how much the cousins enjoyed it, and how this was the annual tournament between his mother's side of the family and his father's.

Well, that gave her the opening to make it sound as if she was interested. "Which side is Finn on?" she asked.

He snorted. "Father's, of course. Which is why he keeps sucking up. He's the captain of the team, in fact."

She made a little face. "Hold back my surprise. Do you play?"

"I'm captain of the team for mother's side," he replied, surprising her a little. "Father's idea. I don't mind; it gives me a chance to put Finn in his place. Anyway, this is how tournament weekend always goes. There's a formal dinner tonight, with Father in prominent attendance. Everybody goes to bed pretty early, and the first game is at ten A.M. Each match is eight chukkas—that's like an inning in a baseball game—and the whole match will last a little less than two hours. Then break for lunch, and two matches in the afternoon, break for dinner, and everyone goes to bed early, because polo matches are basically like battles. Same thing Sunday." As she looked at him a little incredulously, he smirked and shrugged. "Seriously, I promise you, everyone will be too tired Saturday and Sunday to stay up past . . . say . . . ten P.M. And *that* will be late. The cousins take this annual thing very seriously. It's like, whoever's side wins the match not only gets bragging rights for the year, but gets some kind of status boost."

"Let me guess," she said. "Finn won last year."

He nodded. "Very sharp of you. And I intend to win this year." There was that hint of something darker in his tone again . . . she had to wonder exactly what was *really* at stake with these games, what was going on behind the scenes. *Focus. Use the distraction.*

It took all of her will to muster a smile. She put her hand on Sean's arm, "I'm sure you will, Sean. I'd even put money on it."

Sean smiled warmly at the compliment. Staci had the simultaneous urges to retch and to swoon, though the latter was *much* more muted than it had been. She would have given anything to be able to peer inside of his head, and find out exactly how much of him was genuine, and how much was scum.

He pulled his sports car into the driveway, and got out. As usual there was a servant waiting to take it off to be garaged. She reflected that she had never seen the garage. She wondered how many dozens of cars it held, and if any of them were elvensteeds.

"Shall we?" He offered her his arm. Without missing a beat, Staci put her arm through his. Still smiling, he led her up the steps and into the mansion. She suspected that this would be the longest weekend she would have had to endure yet since she came to Silence, and that was saying something.

CHAPTER NINETEEN

This time she wore her black silk jumpsuit with an equally vintage black lace top with bell sleeves. She wished she had her grandmother's cocktail ring that Brenda had stolen. It was about the one thing she owned she thought would impress the Blackthornes.

Something that would impress them would presumably distract them from *her.* She wanted as many distractions as possible. She wasn't dazzled by the mansion or any of the other finery anymore; this was a mission, now, and if Tim and Dylan were right, it was literally life or death. Staci had never imagined herself being in a situation like this, but she was damned if she was going to back out now, even if she could.

In a way, it was a good thing that dinner was "formal." It kept conversation very formal as well, and gave her an excuse to be quiet. Bradan presided over the table like a monarch, with the cousins all attentive to his every word. After aperitifs and other refreshments were served along with the appetizers, Bradan struck a glass with his soup spoon for silence, bringing the hushed conversations around the table to a stop. He cleared his throat, smiling wanly to the assembled Blackthorne clan.

"Our family has always prided itself on excellence: excellence above all others, and excellence among ourselves. The tournament is an extension of our constant striving for greatness; though we all work together towards the elevation of our family name, we still seek singular fame and recognition. I know all of you will do our family proud during the next few days, your devotion being shown in your exertions and competition. With that, I propose a toast." He raised a wine glass; the full-bodied red wine uneasily reminded Staci of blood. She raised her own glass of ginger ale in response. "I believe I will paraphrase the . . . Olympic motto."

And Staci wondered about that pause. Had he been about to say "human" or "mortal" Olympic motto?

"Better. Smarter. Stronger."

Yeah, I'll drink to that. For us humans, you pointy-eared freak. She smiled and sipped her ginger ale.

The rest of the dinner proceeded a little differently than the last one she had been at. At the last one, Bradan had been preoccupied with his guests. At this one, he was preoccupied with the cousins, singling out Sean and Finn for admonitions and remarks designed to amp up their already intense rivalry. Bradan, behind his quiet reserve, seemed to enjoy goading the two of them. Given the sick enjoyment that she had been told Unseleighe took in suffering, she wasn't terribly surprised, but still disgusted. *These people make my stepmother seem like a Girl Scout in comparison.*

Meaghan—clearly Finn's girl—stayed completely out of it and completely silent, and Staci followed her example. There was . . . a *lot* of testosterone, or whatever the elven equivalent was, on display at the table. It wasn't just Sean and Finn, it was the males of both teams. Presumably, women were not on either team. Then again, now that Staci thought about it, pretty much all the males among the Blackthorne clan had exhibited varying degrees of belief in "masculine superiority."

Yet another reason to hate them.

Staci's attention was drawn to the very end of the table. She had noticed on one of her latest visits that the Blackthornes often seated people at the table in order of importance; Bradan at the head of the table, with people like his personal guests or Sean to his sides, and on down the line. At the very end tonight was Morrigan. While still reserved like the other women, she was clearly fidgeting, drawing a few sharp glances now and again. *She looks as uncomfortable as I feel with all of this sexist and macho crap.* Wanda's instincts had, in retrospect, been pretty good so far, with all of the weird and creepy stuff happening around the Blackthornes. Staci needed to remind herself to really apologize to that girl, and soon. Wanda'd been there for her, even when she didn't think she needed anyone. And her impression about Morrigan—"Mori"—was that she was one of the good ones. *I'll need to let Dylan know about her. Not all of them have to be bad, right?*

It was both a relief and a strain when the dinner broke up. A relief because of the high level of tension at that table. A strain because now Sean's attention would be centered on her.

But just as dessert was cleared away and Bradan

signaled dinner was at an end, a servant came hurrying up to him and whispered in his ear. After a few moments, he frowned, and crooked a finger at Sean, who whispered an excuse to her and joined his father. While she sat with hands and napkin folded in her lap like a good little serf, the two of them began what looked like an intense and urgent conversation.

It went on for about fifteen minutes by her watch, and when it was over, Sean arranged his face in an apologetic expression and returned to her while his father got up and hurried off, much to the confusion of the cousins.

Before speaking to her, Sean addressed those still at the table. "I'm afraid one of our current research projects has unexpectedly... shall we say, 'ripened'? Father and I will need to personally oversee it this weekend. The tournament is postponed."

She kind of expected disappointment and outrage. Instead there was... well, it looked like a flash of *greed* on most of their faces. And then, they began breaking up, talking among themselves, and leaving the table. In moments they were gone.

"I'm sorry to ruin your weekend, Staci," Sean said, as the last of them left. "But it can't be helped. I'll drive you down to Silence myself; I need to be there anyway. This really *is* urgent." Then he leaned down and whispered in a conspiratorial fashion, "This is what is going to put me ahead of Finn in Father's eyes in a way he will *never* be able to counter." There was that unhealthy twinkle of greed in his eyes, just like the others around the table.

"Well then, that's *way* more important than the tournament or anything else," she replied. "I'll run up and get my bag and meet you out front." Without waiting for an answer, she pushed away from the table, and headed at a fast walk for her room. *Whatever is going on, it's something that I need to learn about. This is exactly why I'm here. There's something going on with Bradan and Sean. And with the way Sean's talking, this might be the break that Dylan and I need.*

That thought gave her a little jolt. *Dylan and I.* She was starting to fall for him. He was rough around the edges, but now that she knew what his past was, what he had been doing before she was even born, well, that was to be expected. He had kept her at arm's length in the beginning, but that was changing. Even with that, he was still trying to do what was right, and that counted for a lot. Not only that, but he trusted her enough to include her; it was a partnership. He was even teaching her magic, ways for her to defend herself. Sure, it was scary as all hell, being opened up to an entirely new and terrifying world. But at least he wasn't hiding anything from her, like Sean. Even Tim, who was certainly her friend and who seemed to be trying to look out for her, wasn't telling her everything, and never had, even when he almost *certainly* had known there was something about her that wasn't like the other kids.

She pushed all thoughts of Dylan and Tim out of her mind, as hard as it was to do that where Dylan was concerned. She needed to play her part, like an actress on Broadway. She headed back downstairs with her things, smoothing out her clothing before she came into view of Sean. For the split second it took before he noticed her, she saw that he looked impatient, even upset. All of that vanished when he became aware of her. *He's good about putting his mask back on.*

She said nothing as he handed her into the car, then took the driver's seat. Only when they were on the way did she say anything.

"I'm not gonna ask you what this is all about, 'cause I know that has to be all kinds of trade secrets and everything," she said, putting a lot of simpering into her voice, and glad he couldn't see her face while he was concentrating on driving. Which he was. Very fast. "I'll just say I hope you have every bit of luck you deserve." *All of it bad.* She kept her head down, just in case, so it would be harder to see her expression. A thought occurred to her, and she cleared her throat. "Um, could you drop me off near the diner instead of my house? I'm still hungry, that was kind of a tense meal and I didn't eat much."

"You're a gem, Staci." He leaned over and kissed the top of her head. "I'm really sorry that we couldn't have the weekend together again. I was so looking forward to it. But this...development can't be put off, and needs my personal attention." He grinned, showing his teeth. "I knew you would understand, though." Their course changed, taking them away from the edge of town and down towards the docks. *A lot shorter of a run from the diner to whatever "business" he has in town than from my house. Maybe I can keep up with his car if I use the back alleys...*

They passed the warehouse district. And...to her glee as they passed, she spotted a limo. Granted, one limo looked pretty much like any other, but how many people in Silence could afford one, and how many were likely to be parked at a warehouse at this time of night? Okay, maybe a drug dealer, except in New York drug dealers generally drove SUVs or sports cars. She committed the location to memory; if she hurried, she might be able to run back to where she saw the limo before it left.

"And here we are." He pulled up in front of the diner. She wanted badly to jump out—but that would be out of character, now. So she waited for him to come around, open the door and hand her out again. But he was clearly in a hurry; he only gave her a peck on the cheek before getting into the car and speeding off. He didn't even wait to see if she went into the diner, he was in that much of a hurry.

She had changed back into jeans and a polo shirt before leaving, making sure that both of the garments were dark colors. But what to do with her bag? Finally, after a little dithering, she stashed it deep in the overgrown bushes around the bottom of the diner. *I really wish I had had time to learn that invisibility spell or whatever it was that Dylan had used for my bike.* It was really hard to push the bag down in there, and she hoped that would keep her stuff safe. It would be a drag to lose that vintage clothing. . . .

What am I thinking? This might be the key to keeping us all alive! *Why am I worrying about some outfits?*

She looked around again, trying to make sure that no one—and no Red Caps!—were lurking around, but the street seemed completely deserted, and the two people inside the diner were intent on whatever it was they were eating. She crossed the street and took to the alleys as the best way of staying out of sight.

She figured it took her about fifteen minutes to

get to the warehouses at the docks; she slowed down when she got close to where she had spotted the limo. It was funny, now, how well she knew the streets and alleys of Silence. She couldn't get lost now if she tried, and never again would anyone be able to run her into a dead end; she'd spent a lot of time with a real map of the town, and then with several walk-throughs, memorizing it all. Getting cornered once by people that wanted to kill her was more than enough for Staci. Still, she made sure to take note of the features of the alleys; no telling what she would have to throw in the way or jump over if she *did* get chased out by someone.

Finally, she was there: the warehouse was identical to nearly every other warehouse in the area. Rusted metal walls, painted over dozens of times in the same shade of beige. Slowly, she edged to the corner at the end of the alley she was in. Crouching low and only allowing the edge of her face to show, she peered around the corner. *The limo, it's still there! And there's Sean's car.* She didn't see Sean or Bradan anywhere, just a couple of guys in suits. They did *not* look like limo drivers; too big and heavily muscled. *Guards?* She had never seen anything like guards around the estate; just servants and cousins, really. Whatever was going on here, it had to be important. And with the two heavies at the front door, there was no way she was going to be able to get in by that route.

Staci slowly backed off from the corner, following the wall of the warehouse. She traced the route she had taken, making her way around the building. She walked, careful not to knock over bottles or otherwise disturb trash that might make some noise that would give her away; it made for slow going at certain points. *There's got to be another way to get in...jackpot!* There was a window about six feet off of the ground; the pane of glass was hung on a vertical pivot, and it was open. It only took her a few moments to find what she needed; a wooden pallet and an empty 55-gallon drum. She moved the pallet under the window, then stacked the drum on top. With a few grunts of effort, she was able to scramble over the top of the drum; it was stable enough that she could stand on it without needing to balance too much. It was hard for her to button down on her excitement and nervousness; she couldn't afford either right now, if she wanted to keep from getting caught. Standing to her full height on top of the barrel, she was able to see past the bottom windowsill and into the warehouse.

Luckily, there seemed to be a stack of crates right below the window on the other side; she wouldn't have to gather anything to get back out, just hop up on those and back out the way she had come.

She realized immediately that this place was a lot older than it looked on the outside. Instead of having steel I-beams holding up the roof and as roof construction, it had massive wooden beams holding up the wooden ceiling two stories above. She'd only seen something like that once, when she'd visited a school friend whose family lived in a converted warehouse loft in Dumbo. The friend said that the building dated to around 1900, maybe earlier, long before steel-framed buildings were the usual thing even in New York. There were cone-shaped light fixtures dangling on long wires coming down from the center of the roofline. From the dim, yellow light they cast, she guessed that they were old-fashioned incandescent bulbs, not fluorescent. The floor was poured cement, now cracked everywhere. An angle beam right next to her led up to overhead support beams. *Now, if I just had superpowers, I could climb right up there like a monkey and see everything...* Stupid thought, even if she *could* climb the slanting beam, she'd probably fall off if she tried to scramble around the upper structure.

There was no sign of overhead cranes, or machinery, just some industrial-sized air ducts and silent fans up there. *So I guess the place gets heat in the winter. Figures they don't care about summer, not that Silence ever gets warm. And whoever is hustling stuff into and out of this place is doing it all with forklifts.* Because there were plenty of boxes of something piled up in neat rows, and an old, rusting forklift parked right by her window.

At the end of the warehouse farthest from her, she saw what looked like a two-story office setup with lit-up windows. Whatever was going on, was probably going on there. She couldn't make out anything from here because of the big stacks of boxes between her and it. She stayed crouched after she climbed through and down from the window; the crates must have had something heavy in them, because they held her weight and didn't shift an inch. She thought that it was quiet in the warehouse, but it was hard to tell due to how large it was and how much stuff it had in it. She started towards the office, going slowly; even with the boxes in neat rows, they were piled high enough that she could get lost if she didn't pay attention.

As Staci got closer to what she thought was the

center of the warehouse, she began to hear talking...
and, quieter, whimpering. Crouching low behind a
couple of boxes at the end of her row, she noticed
that there was a break in the lines of crates. The talking and whimpering was growing louder. She licked
her lips; it wasn't any more dangerous now than it
had been, but she still felt like the stakes had been
raised. As she looked around the edge, she came to
the sickening realization that she was right.

The first thing she noticed were the four kids: two
boys, and two girls, all of them her age or maybe
a little bit older. They were huddled together, and
looked filthy; their clothing was torn, all of them were
bruised, and they had clearly been treated roughly.
They were all terrified, clinging to each other, but
daring not to move so much as a muscle, save for
the sag of their shoulders as they sobbed.

Past the group of teenagers were Sean and Bradan,
flanked by two "cousins" each. They were both apprais-
ing the huddled group of teens, talking with each
other. She strained to hear what they were saying.

"...procured earlier this morning. Hitchhikers who
are also runaways; all of them originating far away
from here, unlikely to be missed or reported any
time soon, since they are already deemed missing.
They'll just enter that enormous database of 'missing
children' that no one in this country seems to care
about. I was alerted only a short time ago that they
had been prepared and were waiting here, Father."

"Still, this is ahead of the projected schedule that
you had initially supplied to me. This is very good,
Sean. *If* the ritual works."

"It will. This is a small-scale, fast-acting test run;

an accelerated version to highlight the effects and
the resultant payoff. Once the Gate is prepared, we'll
be ready to begin the full-scale program. The police
are already integrated for our purposes, along with
the local media outlets; everything will be closed off
and contained within our borders, so we'll have full
control to draw it out as long as we wish. And this
is just the beginning, Father." With that, Sean waved
a hand towards the teens. The cousins on either side
stepped forward, surrounding the frightened group,
causing them to try to move closer to each other and
their moans to grow louder. They were past the point
of using words, they were so scared.

Bradan nodded. "Well, as the humans say, *show
me the money.*"

Sean laughed. He held his hands, spread above his
head; the two cousins on either side of him did the
same. Staci had expected some chanting or something,
but this was done in utter silence. First, a cold white
circle of light formed on the concrete around the
teens. Then, in the next second, a dome seemingly
made of cloudy white light sprang up, covering them.
One of the boys gave a high-pitched shout and ran at
the dome, only to bounce off it. Whatever that magic
was, it affected physical objects, too.

Sean lowered his hands to shoulder-height, and so
did the cousins; the milky color of the light of the
dome shifted to pink, then to red, as the teens inside
shouted or cursed or cried.

Whatever was happening, it was *bad*. Staci panicked
for a moment; she considered throwing her hands up,
screaming, throwing a rock, anything to make them
stop—*make them stop!* She reached into her pocket,

pulling out her cell phone and snatching at the charm. It was a focus, and it might help her with what she was about to try. She cleared her mind, then started to concentrate, building up the emotions and energy inside of her. Her urgency added to all of it, ramping the energy up. She focused her will on breaking the spell that was being cast; she didn't recognize it, but if she could put the right monkey wrench in the gears, maybe it would seize. Hell, maybe even spring back and hit Sean in his rotten face. She fed her disgust for him into the spell, and the energy built up until she felt that she couldn't stand it any longer. Silently, she released all of it.

The spell rebounded, fizzling out; she could see the pent-up magic sparking out into the air in front of her. Some of it kept coming back, though, and she didn't even have time to throw her hands up before it struck her. It felt like all of her nerve endings were on fire for a split second, and she was frozen with the shock and the pain of it. All of the hair on her arms and the back of her neck stood up on end, and she was thrown backwards to land hard on her rear. Her entire body felt drained of energy, vitality even, and her joints felt sore. It felt like she had been exercising for a couple of days straight with no water or rest breaks, and her vision was fuzzy.

She scrambled to her feet, just in time to see the dome turning a dark, old-blood red, and then there was a sudden flash of light inside that blinded her for a moment.

When she could see again, the dome was back to being milky white. But inside the dome, things were...horrifying.

The teens were clearly all suffering from the immediate onset of some sort of disease. Their bodies were rapidly being covered with boils, their eyes were bleeding and there was blood coming out of their ears. Their veins were dark, swollen.

And they were screaming in pain, dropping to the floor, curling up and writhing. Their hands contracted into fists, or they clawed at their faces, leaving bloody furrows. Blood was oozing from the corners of their mouths now, and when they opened the mouths to scream, their gums were bloody.

Staci clamped her hands over her ears, torn between wanting to rush at Sean and beat him until he reversed whatever it was he was doing, and wanting to run away, far away. Her stomach churned.

And she was completely terrified.

The screaming stopped…not because the kids were dead yet—they weren't; horribly they still kept writhing on the ground—but because all that could come out of their mouths was a bubbly, whispery rasping.

Just as quickly as it had began, the spell stopped. The dome was still in place around the dying teens. She immediately saw why; even the concrete around the teens was seemingly infused with corruption, the ground cracking and buckling in some places with a horrid-looking ooze. Sean looked back to Bradan; the older man was nodding approvingly.

"That was…magnificent. The pain…what is the prognosis for the final version?"

"Two months, with medical care. Three weeks without, after the onset of stage three symptoms. Stages one and two weren't properly displayed here, but should be equally…delectable, in the suffering produced.

The rate of infection will be carefully monitored and controlled, so that the population isn't reduced unnecessarily or too soon. With proper cultivation, we should be able to draw out the total harvest for a full year, maybe more depending on any influxes of population. Cleanup has already been established, as well; chemical spill, rendering the entirety of the town uninhabitable."

"And what are the prospects of repeatability?"

"If we apply this model to suitable candidate populations . . . I'd say the prospects are high. This will be enough to sustain us for generations, especially once the process has become more refined. No more piecemeal hunting—well, save for sport. The power that this will generate will ensure our position, and the elevation of our clan."

My god. They're not just planning on killing Silence. They're going to do this anywhere else that they can. Staci felt a wave of nausea at the thought of other small towns like Silence; there one moment, gone with hardly a whisper the next. From the sound of things, the Blackthornes had already planned out exactly how they were going to keep it all a secret, too. Like Dylan had said, how many Rust Belt counties, ghost towns, and other blips on the map had been ground under the heel of Unseleighe?

With a final gesture towards the dome, there was another flash. Staci had spots in her vision, and felt lightheaded. When she was finally able to see again, the area where the dying teens had been . . . was scorched clean. The dome had disappeared, and the concrete that it had been containing was blackened. There was nothing left; not the teens, not the evil-looking ooze, not even ashes. A fresh wave of nausea washed over her.

She put out a hand to steady herself. And moved a little too quickly, knocking over an empty soda can that was balanced on the nearest stack of boxes. It fell to the floor with a clatter that was horrifyingly loud in the silence. Staci felt as if her insides had turned to ice, and for a split second, she froze in place. She didn't bother to check to see if Sean and Bradan were looking in her direction; immediately, she started running, keeping low and thanking all the stars that her sneakers were nearly silent against the concrete. It was a good thing she had taken a moment to memorize the organization of the crates; it would have been far too easy to get confused in the rows and get lost. Before she knew it, she was at the rear wall again, scrambling up the stack of crates as quietly as she could and slipping out the window.

Staci nearly fell when she landed on top of the 55-gallon drum that she had stacked up under the window early, with the drum tipping wildly to one side before she caught her balance. She didn't even think as she climbed off of it, running as soon as her feet hit the ground. She must have run nearly the entire way back to the diner, weaving through alleys and side streets, before she realized that she hadn't heard any sounds of pursuit. No gang thugs, no guards in suits, nothing. She spent the next few minutes catching her breath, tamping down on her fear and the feeling that she was going to be sick. Watching those four kids... it had been like something out of a horror movie, but worse; worse because it was real and they were right there in front of her. Those weren't special effects, or anything like that; those kids were dead, and had died in agony. And there hadn't been anything she could do to stop it.

The guilt of that alone—having tried to save them, and failed—was almost enough to bring her to her knees on its own. *No. You did your best, even though you were scared to death. The thing you need to do now is make sure that it doesn't happen to anyone else.* The thought was hers, but she heard it in Dylan's voice. *That's the next step. Call Dylan, let him know what I saw. We have to stop it.* Every shred of doubt that she had had about Sean's intentions and involvement had disappeared the moment she saw him start casting the spell in the warehouse; all of her infatuation and soft feelings for him had been replaced with anger and resentment.

Confident that she was at least mostly composed, she brought up Dylan's contact page on her phone and hit "dial." He answered immediately, and she kept her words short, letting him know that she was okay, but that something really horrible had happened and they needed to talk in person immediately. After she hung up, she got a glass of water inside of the diner; Beth wasn't working, so that saved the need for any chitchat. Once she was done, she dug her bag out of the bushes and started straight for home; if she hurried, she could get back, get her bicycle, and get to the Hill by the time Dylan arrived.

CHAPTER TWENTY

It had been a matter of moments, not minutes, once she got to the house. Open the door, throw her bag inside, get a drink of water from the hose spigot outside and grab her bike. She hadn't wanted to have to confront Mom, but from the darkness and quiet in there, either Mom was passed out, or she was working a double shift.

The thought of Mom going through what those kids had gone through suddenly passed through her mind, and she found herself on her knees, throwing up everything that was in her stomach. All she could do was retch, and try and shove those images out of her mind. Maybe she didn't *like* Mom very much now, but . . . somewhere in the back of everything was the memory of the times Mom had dressed up like a fairy to surprise her and her friends, shower them with candy and gumball machine trinkets, and disappear again. Or when she'd taken Staci to the zoo, and showed her how to make the tigers come to the front of the cage by "puffing" at them. "That's how they say 'hello,'" Mom had told her, though Staci had no idea how Mom knew that. At that moment, she realized how very little she actually knew about Mom. Except she knew things only someone with a lot of education could... all those fairy tales Mom had told her as a kid had never come out of a Disney book. Some of them she'd never been able to find again when she'd looked in storybooks once she could read.

I can't let this happen to Mom... the gang. I don't know how... but I can't. Whatever it takes, I have to stop it.

But Dylan would know what to do! Surely, Dylan would know.

She wiped her mouth, rinsed it out from the spigot and drank again, then got on her bike before any more horrible thoughts made her sick. Once she was riding, she could concentrate only on that, on getting a little more speed out of the bike, on her burning legs and burning lungs. On making sure she avoided the cop beats, as she hurtled through the dark and damp air, keeping to the side streets until she got to the road up the Hill.

She just hoped Dylan was going to be there when she got there. Undoubtedly he'd understood the urgency in her voice and he and Metalhead had raced to beat her there!

Except... he wasn't.

When she put on the brakes and skidded to a halt at the usual spot on the Hill, there was no one there.

The Hill was silent, cold, and dark. It was so silent that all you could hear was the sound of the waves washing up on the beach far below. Despite being cold and damp, the atmosphere was so still it felt... airless. As if she couldn't get a full breath. Or as if the air itself was pushing on her, keeping her from breathing in.

She almost didn't hear the sound of someone moving behind her. She spun around, expecting Dylan, but the smile on her face died as soon as she saw the suit jackets. It was the guards from the warehouse. Both of them were smiling broadly at her, showing yellow and crooked teeth.

"Lost, miss? Maybe—"

"—we can be of some help."

They looked to each other, still smiling, before looking back to her. Then they separated, circling around her in opposite directions. Like dogs—like those *hounds*—circling their prey. There was something feral and not quite human about them that put the hair up on the back of her neck. Staci's breathing still felt strained, but this time she knew it was from adrenaline and panic. Surreptitiously, she reached into her shoulder bag and retrieved her cell phone, grasping the charm tightly. Her head snapped around constantly, trying to keep her eyes on both of the guards.

"I'm waiting for a friend! He'll be here any minute, so I don't need any help, thanks!" She sounded more shrill than she had wanted to, but she couldn't keep the fear out of her voice. *How did they get here so fast? There isn't a car anywhere; I would have seen it. Did they follow me? And if they did...how?* There had to be some sort of magic involved, and that made her even more scared. Both men looked extremely similar; they were both completely bald, so heavily muscled that their suits bulged, and had the same hollow, hungry look in their eyes.

"No, we don't think anyone is coming, girl. More's the pity, because you—"

"—don't look like more than a snack, does she, *nisayenah*?"

"No, she doesn't, *nishime*. The masters keep us pretty well-fed, granted. But it's so rare for us to get any live meat."

Something started to...happen, to both men. Their clothing stretched in certain places, and fell loose in others, as if they were losing and gaining mass in different places. Staci heard the fabric start to rip, and watched as their shoes burst at the seams, grotesquely long toes ending in yellow and cracked nails protruding through. Their wrists pushed past the ends of their shirt and jacket sleeves, the hands growing twice as big as frying pans with the same wicked nails at the end. Their elbows split through their jackets, and soon their shoulders did the same, shredding the clothing and causing it to fall to the ground. Where they had been previously well-muscled, they were now both sunken-chested, with protruding bellies. Their mouths, still smiling, each turned into a gigantic rictus, with the lips pulled back over their teeth and the jaws dislocating to hang open. The most unsettling thing was their eyes; the orbs had recessed into the sockets until two black pits remained...and then the sockets were lit up with what looked like red-hot coals.

Both of the men—the *monsters*—were fifteen feet tall.

One looked at the other—who kept his eyes on her. She felt like a tiny bird being watched by a tiger. "How should we divide her? Top and bottom?"

The watcher shook his head slowly. "No, the head,

heart, and liver are the best parts. Better that we pull her apart like a wishbone. Fair that way."

The first turned his head to look at her again, drool dripping from his lower jaw. "Right you are. Let's start; I'm hungry, and the masters will want to know about this."

Staci's first instinct was to run away. Do something, anything that might distract these monsters, and then run as hard and as fast as she could. But to where? She shut the idea from her mind. These things, whatever they were, had tracked her from the warehouse, all the way from down by the docks. They were like the Hunter; they *loved* the chase before they captured their prey. There wouldn't be any running or hiding from whatever these things were. She was going to have to fight if she wanted to leave the Hill alive.

The two monsters must have seen a hint of the mental calculation that she was doing; without so much as a shout or any other sort of telegraphing action, they sprang towards her, their ropey limbs propelling them unnaturally fast. Staci bit back a scream, then quickly cast one of the most powerful protective spells that Dylan had taught her.

Instantly, a milky white dome of energy sprung up around her, encompassing the ground ten feet on any side. She watched, as if in slow motion, as some of the energy passed from herself to the shield, empowering it and strengthening it. The monsters impacted with the shield simultaneously from opposite ends, both of them being thrown back a considerable distance by the rebound. This did nothing to change their expressions; they were both still smiling wide, the same hungry expression occupying what passed for their distorted faces.

Both creatures charged again, attacking the same spot, but not throwing themselves headlong into it. They only seemed slightly surprised to find that they were repulsed yet again, but this was quickly replaced with amusement. *Time to change that!* She focused her fear, frustration, and revulsion into the very center of her being, letting the energy grow and grow...then released it, crying out, *"Beura!"*

An overwhelming flash lit the entire top of the Hill, like a miniature sun being born. Again, time seemed to slow down for Staci. She watched the threads and cords of magic spread out from her, from the focus of the cell phone charm, washing over everything; it even seemed to strip some of the skin and strains of energy from the surface of the two creatures, causing both of them to stumble backwards and fall to their knees, shielding their eyes. The grass, while ruffled as if by a stiff breeze, bent down, and was generally unharmed. Even the trees bowed slightly. Staci felt a moment of elation. *That's got to send them packing!*

The feeling died immediately, as she saw both of the huge creatures rise to their feet. They weren't smiling anymore, at least. Now, they were snarling, and that was so much worse. Their maws—mouth was no longer an appropriate word to describe it—were dripping with bloody saliva, their prominent brows knit together. They were angry...and focusing all that anger solely on *her.*

The monsters began to beat against the shield, the impacts sending spiderwebs of energy across the surface of the dome. Both of them uttered guttural screams while pounding furiously at her protections. *Got to try something new.* Staci had only practiced the next spell under Dylan's supervision; she hadn't tried it solo before, so she was a little scared as she began. She watched as some of the energy she had been preparing fizzled in front of her, and cursed herself. *Stupid, stupid. Dylan always said, "Focus and calm, power comes from that."* She fought through her fear, and all of her other emotions this time, keeping her concentration on the desired outcome. She was sure of the mental picture of what she wanted to happen, sure of the effect it would have. Turning sharply to her left, she thrust both of her hands out in front of her; a blue-white ball of energy manifested a foot in front of her hands, and sped out to strike the chest of the monster that she was facing. Flesh and bone blasted away from the site of the impact, but the monster didn't falter. It continued to rage and beat against the protective shield. *I've got to be hurting it! Just got to hurt it* more.

Staci kept her counterassault up, switching between the two targets from blast to blast. Every time she fired, another heaping chunk of gore flew from the creatures, splashing against the ground and steaming. But no matter how much she shot at them, they didn't stop hammering away at the shield. She almost didn't realize how much this was taking out of her, when suddenly she stumbled, half-falling to a knee and putting a hand out to steady herself; the monsters realized it immediately, however. They were both smiling, again, and began pounding at the shield even more fiercely than before. This time, they circled around instead of hitting the same spot over and over again. Her shots became more erratic and wild as she continued to fire energy at them. *What is going on?* All too late, it dawned on her what had just happened. She had been overconfident, and expended too much of her energy trying to attack the monsters; her shield, still siphoning energy from her, was starting to fail. Patches were showing through the milky white dome, and wherever the creatures struck, the shield became more translucent.

They were breaking through.

Staci tried to refocus herself, redirecting her energy towards the shield. But she was too drained at this point; it felt like she was pouring water into a sieve. The monsters must have sensed this; they stepped up their assault, and more of the shield crumbled before her, the energy dissipating in the air.

With each blow against the shield, Staci felt the impact as if it was striking her body. Surely, it had to be muted somehow, but still she felt the physical damage. Light, at first, as if someone was shoving her around. Then the hits became more urgent, more painful, like punches, then powerful kicks. She fell to the ground, throwing her arms over her head, but it was no use; however much she tried to cover herself, she still took blows all over her body. She had never really been in a fight before, and the panic she had tried to negate earlier flowed through her freely now. Her vision began to go dark around the edges as she saw the last of the shield give way, the final threads of energy falling to the ground and sparking out among the grass.

I hope it doesn't hurt too much, was Staci's last thought before the monsters were upon her. Just when she thought that she would feel those horrible claws and teeth digging into her, there was a flash, and a cry. With the last ounce of strength that she could muster, Staci turned her head; one of the creatures had the end of a bright metallic arrow jutting from its chest. The other monster screamed, turning around just in time for an identical arrow to plant itself in its sternum. Both of the beings started scrabbling at the arrows, trying to dig them out; whenever they touched the shafts, their hands caught fire. Soon, there was smoke issuing from their mouths and eyes, and both fell to the ground, kicking and clawing at the dirt. With a final screech, both of the creatures were consumed in flame, finally still.

With a roar that sounded much more like something that should have come from the throat of a wild animal than the engine of a motorcycle, Metalhead screeched to a halt beside her, and Dylan spilled out of the bike's seat, throwing aside what looked like a bow to Staci's bleary eyes. Suddenly she was engulfed in a green glow, light so bright she couldn't see through it, and the pain began to fade.

She just closed her eyes in exhaustion and let whatever it was do its work. At this point she didn't even have any energy to spare to put two thoughts together at once, much less try and figure out what it was that Dylan was doing to her.

The light felt—well, it felt exactly like sunlight on her skin, like sunbathing on a perfect day, when the air wasn't too hot, and there was just a whisper of breeze. It felt *good,* deep down, as if it was sinking into her, slowly taking away all the pain of the blows she had taken. She didn't want to open her eyes, actually, didn't want to have to think about those monsters, and especially didn't want to have to think about what she had seen in the warehouse.

But she knew she had to do all those things. So, when the last of the ache had faded, she opened her eyes, and the glow around her vanished abruptly, leaving her pushing herself up off the ground as Dylan sat back on his heels. His skin had a sheen of sweat and looked paler than usual, and his eyes had dark bags underneath them.

"You need to start keeping better company than Wendigos, Staci. They're no good at parties, and they never bring enough dip." With that, Dylan fell back off of his heels, landing on his rear with a sigh. "I got your call. What happened?"

There wasn't any recrimination in his voice, but Staci still felt like she was shrunk down to the size of an insect by her own guilt. She just blurted out words without thinking about what she was saying.

"I was dumb. I couldn't do anything to help them, and then I let those monsters follow me here! They must've followed me to the diner, followed me home, too! My friend at the diner, my mother—"

"—are both fine. Wendigos don't really stray off of prey once they're locked in." He patted her hand reassuringly. "When they get hungry and start following something, they don't stop until they have it . . . or they're dead. Which, really, is hard as hell to make happen. I'm going to need to hitch a chain to both of the husks and get them somewhere where I can *really* make sure they're burnt. But not right now. Slow down, take a breath. You called me before you knew these baddies were on your trail. Let's get to *why* you called me. What did you find out?"

She forced herself to just *stop*. To take a deep breath, and organize her thoughts. *The best way to do this is to start from the beginning*, she decided, and started from when the servant had come to tell Bradan and Sean the news that had sent them to the warehouse.

"...and then I got here, and those *things* were waiting," she finished. "I tried using everything you showed me but it didn't seem to do much. I guess maybe I tried too many things at once, because the shield you showed me how to make started caving in, and then it went, just as you got here, I guess."

"I didn't expect you having to go up against something like Wendigos, that's for damn sure." He sighed heavily, shaking his head and looking at his feet. "You've got elven blood, sure, but overextending yourself *will* drain you, weaken your spells. From what you said about the spellbreaking you tried in the warehouse, the spell's energy rebound didn't do you any favors." He looked up, staring straight into her eyes. "That's one of the bravest things I've ever heard of."

"Uh—what?" she replied. "I didn't do anything brave—"

"Staci, you attempted to break the spell that five older, trained, and full-blooded elves were casting. It was a *major* spell. Everything I've showed you was just stuff any old elf can do. You should be dead, from all of the feedback that you got. If I had been there, I wouldn't have even tried to do what you did; it was that much of a stacked deck. Yet...here you are. Not only did you do everything that you could to save those kids, but you actually lived to do more than that. Now we know what the Blackthornes are planning on, we can save the *town*."

She bit her lip, her chest feeling tight. Some of the guilt eased a very little bit, not all by any means; she still felt as if she'd have been able to save those kids if she'd just done...something else. But at least Dylan had said *he* wouldn't have been able to break through, so, well, maybe no matter what she'd done, the hitchhikers would have been doomed. She didn't want to dwell on it, not right then.

"Okay. But how? There's so many of them, and only two of us. What about the other elves, the ones you were talking about?"

"Not an option," Dylan said, biting his lip. "The time it would take me to convince them that this is just a beginning, and that the same thing will be showing up on their doorstep soon enough...well, it'd be too late by then. We're on our own in Silence." He sat down, looking tired but determined; the healing he had done on her must have taken a lot out of him. "The Gate is the key. Without that, they won't have access to much of their power in Underhill. If we can take out the Gate, they won't be able to pull off the final version of that spell."

"But there's still the Blackthornes. They won't just let us waltz up to the Gate and take it out. How do we handle them?"

Dylan was silent for a moment, thinking. "Your friends. You mentioned at one point that one of them knew things were up with the town. Do you think you could convince the rest of them to help out?"

She stared at him, horrified. "Are you out of your mind? *I* can't handle their guard dogs with magic! What would they have? Hit them with Monster Manuals?"

"No. But steel or iron weapons and armor are pretty

effective against elves; it disrupts magic, weakens us. It's kind of like a life-threatening allergy." He made a face. "To use the terribly battered cliché, 'It's our one weakness,' and it's a doozy. Actually getting wounded with an iron or steel weapon is like—well—one of you mortals getting hit with something coated in curare. It's one of the reasons why we disappeared from human history once the Iron Age started, and are only coming back now, when you've got so many substitutes."

"And just where are we supposed to *get* armor and weapons?" she asked, pointedly. "I mean . . . seriously. This isn't medieval times. We don't have armor in the hall."

"Leave that up to me. If we have your friends helping us out, we might be able to pull this off. Humans coming after them with steel and iron weapons will probably panic more than a few of them: cultural memory and whatnot of bad things in the past. That'll give us an opportunity to get in there, and get to the Gate. So . . . do you think you can convince them to help us?"

She sighed. "I can try. God, this is insane. 'Hey guys, you know the Blackthornes? They're elves bent on killing the town with a horrible plague. Want to grab a pitchfork and some torches so we can storm the castle and burn down a gazebo?'"

"You *may* want to phrase it a little better than that, but yeah, that's the gist of it." He mock-punched her shoulder. "We're almost done with this. Just got to go the last mile here with me, okay?"

"I'll *ask* them, but I am sure as hell not going to try to *convince* them," she snapped, frowning fiercely at him. "If I have my way, I won't convince them to play cannon fodder, I'll convince them to find a ride and get the *hell* out of here and not come back until it's over!"

Oh my God. I sound like Tim. . . . And was that . . . so bad?

Dylan checked himself. "No, you're right. Sorry; I've just been doing this solo for so long, that I sometimes forget that not everyone is . . . invested the way that I am. This isn't their fight, and—"

"It's not that it *isn't* their fight, moron!" she snapped. "We're *kids*, for godsake! The only reason I'm doing this is because I don't have anyplace else to go! At least they have families that . . . that . . . that aren't worthless and didn't throw them to the wolves!"

"You've had a rough hand dealt to you, Staci. I don't think anyone could deny that. Did you ever stop to think how much of that might be due to Silence? Due to the Blackthornes? Was your mother always the way that she is now? How many other families are being destroyed by dark elven influence? How long until your friends' families end up the same way?" He shook his head, standing up. "We need all the help we can get. If you don't think we should ask your friends, then we won't. It's as simple as that. But either way, their asses *are* on the line, whether they know it or not. If it was me, I'd want a fighting chance, instead of having something nasty come from out of the blue and sink my whole town."

"Or at least enough warning to get out," she sighed. "All right. I'll lay it out for them. I have no idea if they are going to believe me or not. And I am going to let them make up their own minds." She grimaced. "Too bad *you* can't handle some of that iron and steel.

But I can. Maybe that'll make a difference." *Maybe if we just mess up their plans a little, they'll back off anyway. At least their old ways didn't kill too many people at once.* She never thought she'd be thinking anything like *that. . . .*

"We'll see. Let's get you home; it'll be safer than out in the open, and you need to rest some after the day you've had so far." He regarded her bike for a moment. "Tell you what, this time I'll ride escort for you, keep both of us under the Blackthorne radar. I'll come back for the husks later."

"Okay," Seth said after a very long moment of silence. "You have on a Very Serious Person face. And you didn't bring your game stuff. What the heck, Staci? Is this like, 'I just broke up with Sean so no more parties,' or is this like 'I'm moving back to New York,' or is this like 'I have to tell you the Zombie Apocalypse is next week'? Because I am totally down for the last one."

Kind of a mix between the first one and the last one, actually. Staci had made sure that she was the first one at the bookshop. She had breezed by Tim, only offering a half-hearted greeting before she camped out in the back, out of sight. This was going to be hard enough to do without Tim thinking something was up and interrupting her. The group arrived together not much later than she had, talking about the usual subjects. Wanda was the only one that seemed to immediately realize that something was up, and it was only after she quieted the group that the others noticed.

"What's going on, Staci?" Wanda had probably thought it was something like Sean being abusive physically, or something to do with her mother. If only it had been a simple, everyday problem like that. One without magic, or elves, or dead kids.

"This...is going to sound insane. And if I hadn't been living through it, I wouldn't believe it either," she said. "Just...don't interrupt me. And when I'm done, we'll slip out into the alley for a couple minutes and I'll show you something to prove I'm not in need of a padded room and an 'I love me' jacket. Okay?"

"Okaaay," Riley said, edging forward on her seat. "No interruptions. Especially from Seth," she finished, elbowing him lightly.

Okay. Here goes. Staci started, well, logically. From the beginning. So that it all unfolded for them the way it had for her. That took a while, obviously, but she knew if she blurted the important part out first, she'd never convince them even to come out to the alley with her. Wanda narrowed her eyes when she got to the part about seeing the kid from town in the maze, and bit her lip. The others, well...she was having trouble reading them.

Finally she got to the part in the warehouse. And the Blackthorne plans for Silence and beyond. She had to stop and sip water several times to keep from throwing up; even the *memory* of what had happened to those poor hitchhiking kids made her sick.

Seth was the first to speak. "Elves and magic are real. The Blackthornes are evil, and planning on killing the town. You're working with that biker guy to stop them, and a bunch of other monsters. Does all of that sound right?"

"Yes, that's about the sum of it."

"Right. Well...I mean, are you coming up with

your own RP setting? Because if so, I like it. But, you know, it's all just a game, Staci. It's not *really* real." Seth looked extremely uneasy. Jake was already brushing it off as nothing, even though Riley still looked concerned. Wanda spoke next.

"Staci is right. There *is* something bad going on with the Blackthornes." A little hope, there; with Wanda on her side, she might be able to convince the others. "But... magic? Like real fantasy stuff, not Wiccan spells with candles and athames and whatnot?" She felt that little bit of hope die. Even Wanda was still skeptical. Maybe she thought that Staci had lost it, that Sean or Dylan had messed her head up. And why shouldn't she? Staci felt so turned around sometimes by this entire godawful mess, she wondered if she really was going insane.

There was one thing left to do.

"Follow me outside. I told you I could show you some stuff that would convince you." She narrowed her eyes. "Unless you're scared to be convinced."

"C'mon, guys. I want to see what she's going to do." Jake stood up, gesturing towards the door. "Lead the way."

She got up and took the door into the back. The restroom was also back there, so with luck Tim would just think the coffee hit them all at the same moment. From there, she went into the alley, making sure the door was unlocked before letting it close behind them.

"Okay," she said, clutching the cell phone charm, as the others watched her with varying degrees of skepticism. "Here we go." She made her mental preparations—which, admittedly, were a whole *lot* easier since there were just her friends here and not two giant half-corpses discussing how they were going to turn her into a "make a wish" treat, and muttered the word that brought up the shield. The dome-shaped one, which was a little bigger than she had planned—maybe because she was nervous, and actually shoved Seth and Riley into the bookstore wall.

Both of them screamed.

Jake stood there, his mouth open, eyes fixed on the shield.

Wanda was the first one to speak. "Holy shit. You're using *magic* right now. For real, no playing around, *magic*." She walked forward; Staci had backed the shield off from Seth and Riley. Riley was definitely scared, while Seth was transfixed much the same way as Jake. Reaching out gingerly, Wanda touched the shield. Then she knocked on it. "You have *got* to teach me how to do that."

"Everything you said...it's all real, isn't it? Elves, the Blackthornes, what's going to happen to the town..." Riley looked as if she was about to break down crying. Staci felt for her.

"I wish it wasn't. Let's get back inside," she said, shutting off the shield. Jake and Seth both nodded their heads, with Jake putting his arm absently around Riley's shoulders. Wanda opened the door for everyone, and they all followed Staci back into the bookshop.

Now comes the really hard part. Figuring out what to do...

CHAPTER TWENTY-ONE

"There's a lot of heavy packages for you in the living room, Staci," her mom called as she left out the back door where her latest boyfriend was waiting to pick her up. For work, maybe, but whatever it was for, Staci was just glad she was going to be gone for this. "I'll be late, don't worry if you hear the door at 5 A.M."

Staci was just back from a food run, with five pizza boxes in the cart behind her bicycle on top of a bunch of two-liter bottles of soda. She didn't even bother to take them as far as the kitchen; the gang would be here any minute, and she was pretty sure they would all need fuel. After the "revelations" from earlier, she gave them all a little time to digest the information, and told them to meet at her house to talk more. Everyone seemed grateful for the chance to think a little, save for Wanda; she had wanted to stay with Staci and follow her home, but Seth and the others were able to convince her otherwise.

Dylan would be arriving soon as well, probably. So some of the soda was ginger ale. He'd explained, when she called him, that caffeine was also a poison for elves. Which explained why there was never any coffee or cola up at the Blackthorne Estate. She was wondering now if that could somehow be weaponized. Maybe Jake or Seth could come up with an idea.

Weaponized cola. There was a time I would have never even thought of the same words in a sentence. So much has changed.

Mom was right. There was a stack of boxes in the living room. They weren't *big*, but they were plenty heavy. And they all had overnight shipping labels on them. *Guess Dylan went ahead and got the weapons and armor; when you can magic up gold, express shipping costs must seem like nothing.* Amusingly, they were all from the same source. *I guess you can get everything online from there.* The return address, in teeny little type that Mom probably hadn't even bothered to squint at, was "Greenwood Armory; 'For All of Your Hack and Slash Needs.'" So at least some poor grunts in an overheated warehouse hadn't been forced to schlep the stuff at minimum wage.

She got a knife from the kitchen, and the pizza slicer and paper plates. She figured she was going to have to open the boxes if elves were so allergic to steel.

Staci checked her answering machine; the number of missed calls from Sean had piled up. It was a good thing Sean assumed her cell didn't work...well, it didn't except for Dylan's "elf tower" or however he worked it. Sean had no way of knowing whether or not she'd even picked up the answering machine messages yet. At least she hoped so; nothing much was certain when magic was involved. She decided not to listen to any of them. Not now. Maybe not ever. Instead she went to work opening the packages, and sorting out what was in them. Five chainmail shirts. Five sort of hoods made of chainmail. Five round steel things that looked like hubcaps but which turned out to be shields. Five short swords. Twenty knives that . . . kind of looked as if they had been made out of railroad spikes. Five heavy leather belts and five scabbards for the swords. Twenty scabbards for the knives.

I guess if you can make gold, it doesn't matter whether or not you think you can get people to actually use this stuff . . .

Then again, what did he have to lose? If the gang signed on, well, the stuff was here. If they didn't, oh well, there was something for her to wear anyway. *Better to have it and not use it than need it and not have it, I guess.*

And the heaviest box of all. What looked like *hundreds* of jacks—the little six-pointed things from kids' ball-and-jacks game—all made out of iron, with wickedly sharpened points. *What the hell? What are we going to use these things for?* She didn't have time to ponder the question; there was a knock at her door, and she could see it was the gang through one of the side windows at the front of the house. She ran to unlock the door and let them in.

"Whoa, 'za!" said Seth, immediately zeroing in on the stack of pizza boxes on the table in front of the couch. "I'm starving!"

"You would be," snarked Wanda, whose attention was drawn to those *other* boxes. She didn't say anything else, but her eyes narrowed as she examined Dylan's purchases.

Jake and Riley were less enthusiastic. Staci herded

them towards the food and drinks; it'd be better if everyone was fed before they started talking more. They might lose their appetite when the discussion got down to the details of what was going to happen at the Blackthorne Estate.

There was hardly any talking while everyone ate; none of the usual banter about games or movies, just an awkward silence until Seth belched. They all laughed at the break in the tension, but it was forced and short-lived. Wanda, ever the one to be impatient with formality, was the first one to speak once everyone finished eating.

"We're all here, Staci. Your turn: what's in the boxes?"

She wiped her hands on a napkin. "I'll get to that in a minute. First, I wanted to say I was sorry."

"Sorry? Why are you sorry?" Riley asked, and the rest looked just as puzzled.

"Because of what I told you. I kind of wish I had never found out, myself. It's a really big bomb to drop on someone. Well, a lot of big bombs, now that I think about it. Magic, elves, monsters, what the Blackthornes are doing to Silence . . . and what they're going to do . . ." Her voice trailed off. What else was there to say, really? She was sorry, and yet . . . she wasn't sorry, because at least she had warned them.

"Don't apologize," said Wanda. She threw a hard look at Staci. "I wish you had told us sooner. Everything you and I talked about, about how there was something bad going on in town, the weird feeling I had about everything . . . it's right that you told us. But you should have done it sooner; we're not in danger any less now than we were before. At least now we *know* about it." She paused a moment. "And at least now I know that I had a good reason to be the paranoid one around here."

"Then I'm sorry for that," Staci replied, a little bit annoyed. Wanda had a point, though. They were her friends, and she hadn't trusted them enough to tell them the truth. "Even knowing what I know, I still have a hard time believing it. I know what you mean, though. And that's why I asked all of you to come here. You *know* about this stuff now. And that *does* put you in more danger. The sort of things out there that are involved in this... they don't like normal people knowing about them. And with what's going to happen soon... I don't know. I don't think you guys should be here when it all goes down." She bit her lip. "Can you guys like... make up something to get you and your families out of town? A camping trip or something?"

There was a chorus of protests and questions, everyone talking at once. It took a minute before Staci was able to quiet everyone enough so that she could even hear herself think.

Again, it was Wanda that spoke first. "You want us to leave? What makes you think we even could? If the Blackthornes are going to pull off what you're talking about, and soon, who's to say that they already haven't sealed off the town? And, even if we get out, it might not be much better; what monsters are out there, waiting? Like you said, there are a *lot* of them in Silence."

"Plus," added Jake, "how would we? Just tell our folks, 'Hey, we're all leaving for whatever for a week'? Even if they would let us go, it's not like we could just *leave* them; they'd be facing all that bad shit on their own, and they wouldn't even know what it *really* was. There's no way they'd believe us if we tried to warn them, unless you're willing to put on another magic show for, like, twenty people. Even then, we'd all be more likely to get committed than anything."

Staci didn't have any good response to . . . well, any of that. They were right, and she didn't *want* them to be right. *She* wanted to run away, and she had magic on her side! She couldn't, she knew that, and it was only a part of her that wanted to run . . . but still! She would trade places with them if she could . . . wouldn't she?

There was another knock at the door. She held up her hands to forestall any other questions or recriminations, standing up and moving to the front of the house. *At least I don't have to answer them right now. Please let this be Dylan . . .*

She wasn't going to just open the door to anyone though. Not right now. Not when it could be . . . Sean. Or another one of those monsters. Or one of mom's boyfriends, though that seemed remote. Grabbing her cell phone charm tightly, she peeked through the glass in the entry door, cautiously, and saw the top of a shaggy head of hair with the tip of a pointed ear poking through it. Standing on tiptoes, she made sure that the hair and ear belonged to Dylan before she opened the door for him.

"Whoa—" he said, immediately skirting to the side of the room away from the boxes full of iron and steel stuff. He smelled like fresh sweat, warm leather, and—was that fresh-cut hay?—as he brushed past her, his hand lightly touching her shoulder. She felt a thrill run through her from being in such close proximity to him, and then scolded herself for even *thinking* about anything other than the horrible situation they were facing. But being around him made her feel safer, if not completely safe. He was self-assured, but not in the arrogant way that Sean was. "I see the party favors arrived. I could feel them from thirty feet away."

"Let me introduce you to the gang. They're . . . still taking everything in."

Staci's friends all watched Dylan as she led him forward; he stayed on the far side of her from the boxes, she noticed. *Even just being near that much steel and iron makes elves uncomfortable. Filing that tidbit away for later.*

"Guys, this is Dylan. He's the one that's been help-ing me with . . . everything. He's trying to help save the town. Dylan, meet the gang." She introduced each person in turn. Riley and Jake were both polite and cautious, Seth couldn't stop looking at Dylan's pointed ears (perhaps the iron was affecting his glam-our? Or—maybe he just wasn't wearing a glamour?), and Wanda was mostly reserved, watching Dylan as if she was calculating just how much of a threat he might be. Once that was done, he took the empty seat next to Staci.

Dylan cleared his throat, sitting up straight. "I wanted to thank all of you for being here. I know that it couldn't have been easy, for you to learn about the way things are in your town. About magic. I figure you all deserve to know a little bit about me before we go any further." He then told them about what he did: hunting down enclaves of dark elves, monsters, and other things that went bump in the night. Staci observed that he was a bit more circumspect when it came to details about *why* he had started; it seemed he was only willing to share that with her. The others, especially Wanda and Seth (though for different reasons and in different ways), asked him questions, and he answered thoughtfully and completely. That relieved Staci, somewhat; he wasn't trying to lead them on or sway them, as she had been afraid that he might. He was just stating facts, and letting them draw their own conclusions.

But what are those going to be? On the one hand, she wanted them all to run screaming for the hills, and get the hell out of town while they still could. They were her only friends, aside from Tim and Beth; she never even heard from anyone in New York City anymore, save for her father, and even that was getting rarer. She cared about them, and didn't want to see them get hurt. On the other hand . . . she didn't want to face this alone. She had Dylan, and there was definitely something there between them. She hated thinking about it when there were so many more important things to worry about, but that didn't stop her from getting butterflies in her stomach when he smiled at her, or goosebumps from going up her arms when he would accidentally touch her. Even with that . . . she wanted her normal friends to be there with her when she faced what was waiting for her at the estate. Maybe just to help her fight against her own fear; if they could do it, then so could she, with their help. It wasn't fair of her to ask that of them, though. They had to make that decision on their own; she was firmly set on that.

There was a break in the conversation, and all eyes

turned toward her. The Q-and-A session was done, and she had been lost in thought for a moment.

"You never answered my question from earlier, Staci. About the boxes," said Wanda. She sipped on her cola, watching Staci from behind the rim of the plastic cup.

She waved her hand vaguely at the pile of boxes. "They're weapons and armor; made from steel and iron, which elves are fatally allergic to. It disrupts magic, and even just nicking one with something made of it can seriously mess them up, even kill them. It's the sort of thing that can give normal people a fighting chance against elves. Dylan bought them...because he and I are going to go to the Blackthornes, and try to stop them from casting that spell. He can't wear or use the stuff, but a human like me can. It might give us an edge."

"So, wait a second, you're going to attack the Blackthornes?" Seth was wide-eyed, looking from the weapons, to Staci, to Dylan's ears, and back again.

"It's either that or let them kill more people," she said harshly. "Let them kill Silence, everyone in it. Look, I'm stuck here; I don't have anywhere to go and no one to turn to, even if I did. So I don't have any other options. Except maybe let Sean Blackthorne have me as his playtoy until he gets tired of me, and then let him..." Well, she couldn't finish that, because she didn't know what he would do. "And how could I sit up there like a princess in a tower and let him murder everyone, anyway?" *Well, easy, I could let him put that spell back on me and I wouldn't even think about what was going on. Of course, that would be wrong on so many levels I can't even count them... and if I let him do that, I wouldn't be me anymore.*

"Like we *do* have options?" said Wanda, incredulous. "This was our town first, Staci. We have our families here, our whole lives here. Yeah, it's crappy, and run-down, and has been getting worse. But we can't just pack up and leave, either. Even if we could run...what kind of people would that make us? Even if we could take our families, what about the rest of the people in town? They'd be doomed to that horrible...I don't know, Insta-Plague you were talking about. You all are my only friends, here or anywhere, but I wouldn't wish that stuff on my worst enemy in town. I'm staying. Judging from the boxes, you've got enough stuff so that there's enough for me, too."

Staci bit her lip, and her eyes stung a little. "Wanda... I'm not asking you to help. This isn't a freakin' game, where if someone dies they just roll up a new character sheet. This is *serious*, and we could all get hurt or worse—"

"—which isn't different from any other day," interrupted Jake. "We could get run over, struck by lightning, fall off the dock and drown, break our necks, our houses could burn down, there could be a tragic weedwhacker accident. We could already have been puppy chow for the Blackthorne hellhounds. You're our friend, too. We can't let you do this alone and still call ourselves friends. I'm with Wanda; I'm staying, and I'm going to help," he finished with a gulp. Riley looked shocked, tugging on his elbow, but it was clear that he was determined.

Riley shook her head. "This is insane...monsters and elves, magic and plagues? There's got to be somebody else that we can get to help, get to take care of this. The cops—"

Jake interrupted her, "—are in on it! You heard Staci. They're under the thumb of the Blackthornes. And it makes sense. The curfew, the little-shit gangs, the drugs; they've been doing what the Blackthornes wanted for a long time, and have been getting worse. Dark elves feed on . . . misery, right? Sounds like the police are playing right into that. Besides, who else would believe this stuff? 'Hello, Mr. President? Yeah, you're never going to guess what, but I need you to call in the National Guard and the Ghostbusters because . . .' You see? We're alone, here."

Riley looked deflated by that. Jake put his arm around her shoulder. "If we stick together, we can do this. It's our only shot, baby. I won't let anything happen to you, okay?" She seemed to take a little heart in that, but still looked scared to death.

"Seth? Where do you fall on this? You don't have to feel pressured; whatever you decide, it'll be okay." Staci almost wished Seth would refuse; maybe that would get the others to back out, if he did.

"I . . . um . . ." He looked at his feet, then stole a glance towards Wanda; only Staci seemed to notice. "I'm staying. I'm going to help. There aren't any other options that make sense, or at least good sense. Hiding won't work; plague will get us, or some other horrible monster. Running won't work—we probably can't at this point; we'd never get our families to come along—and anyway, if what you overheard is what they're really planning, this thing will eventually be everywhere. There's no one else that can save us, so . . ." He sucked in a long breath, then let it out in a heavy sigh. "So, we have to save ourselves."

Staci sighed, looking to Dylan. He didn't look

like he was pleased with himself, or triumphant. He
actually looked like he sympathized with her, a little
sadness in his eyes. *Glad he's not rubbing my nose
in it. Maybe there's more to him than meets the eye.*
"Is there anything at all I can say to get any of you
to change your minds about this?"

"You . . . cooould say that there is a hidden camera
crew, and that we're all on television as part of a
practical joke show," said Seth, looking around the
room with an exaggerated mask of suspicion on his
face. "But, I don't think you will. So, I guess we're still
with you on this. Guys?" Everyone nodded at that, with
Riley chuckling half-heartedly at Seth's attempt at a
joke. Jake and Wanda looked dead serious. Wanda still
had that odd air of vindication. Staci had to wonder,
now, just what sorts of conspiracy theories she'd had
going in her head until now—what had she *thought*
was happening in Silence? *Maybe compared to what
she'd been thinking of, elves and black magic are . . .
not as bad as what she'd been afraid of?*

"Well, if you're all set on helping us, it's best that
we give you every advantage that we can," Dylan said.
"We've got mail and bucklers for protection; just about
any magic that hits you on those ought to dissipate
and leave you relatively unharmed."

"Relatively?" Riley spoke up, looking skeptical.

"Nothing is one hundred percent, but it's better than
going up against dark elves in jeans and a T-shirt."
The gang all traded glances. "Moving on. We've also
got short swords; you can use them one-handed, but
they don't have much reach. There are also a lot of
hand-to-hand and throwing knives; you don't want
to use them as a primary weapon if you can help

it, since chucking your main weapon is generally poor form when it comes to fighting. But, any elves you're fighting won't pick it up to use against you, so you have that going for you. And lastly are some caltrops; pure iron, a specialty order that a friend of mine fabricated. If you start spreading those around, it's going to seriously mess up any magic for a good distance. Think of them like signal interference. We probably can't count on anyone actually stepping on one, but if it happens, it's going to pretty much take whoever does right out of the picture."

"Besides iron and steel, what weaknesses do dark elves have?" Wanda was listening very closely to everything that Dylan had to say about the weapons, and was equally intent on hearing his response.

"Other than that, not much, really. We're susceptible to all the regular stuff that humans are; stab us, shoot us, whatever, and we get hurt and can die just like regular people. Oh, we're also allergic to caffeine. It's like a super-potent drug; gets us high, and not in a good way. Enough of it can kill."

"Caffeine? So, like this cola..." Seth said, holding up his plastic cup.

"There's enough in there to really mess someone like me up."

"You know, that gives me an idea." Everyone turned to look at Seth.

"Well, are you going to share with the class, or do we have to beat it out of you, genius?" Wanda punched him lightly in the thigh, raising her eyebrows expectantly.

"Ow. Well, I was thinking...caffeine in cola and coffee is kind of diluted. At the health and wellness store in town, they sell all sorts of supplements. Like concentrated caffeine powders. Even a little bit of that stuff would dwarf what you find in cola." He looked at Dylan. "Do elves have to drink or otherwise ingest caffeine for it to affect them?"

"For the most part, yes." He thought for a moment. "But, if you could get a dose into their bloodstream some other way...say, through their eyes, or having them breathe it in..."

"Got it!" Seth pumped a fist up in the air. "Caffeine powder, maybe in a solution of...I dunno, an energy drink or something. Load it all up into a water gun. I know a mod that can boost the pressure up pretty high. Eh, long story. But anyways, you get that powder into a solution like that, blast someone in the face...no way they can stop some from getting in their eyes, in their nose, in their mouth. Super-concentrated anti-elf juice."

"Remind me not to give you a reason to be pissed off at me, Seth," said Dylan. This time everyone did laugh genuinely. It felt good, like they were making progress and could actually *do* this. Staci still had a bad feeling in the pit of her stomach, that they were all in way over their heads...which they were. But, having everyone working together somehow abated that, at least a little bit. "Also, I wish I didn't have to, but I've got to say this; it'd probably be best if all of you didn't really spread this knowledge around. Any of it, really. Elves don't like being known about, by and large. They don't like having their weaknesses known even more. Just a polite thing to keep it under your hat, okay?"

"Like we'd tell anyone about this," Jake snorted. "The first time we said the word 'elf,' our folks would have us committed. They already think we're border-line for playing games and LARPing, one hint that we thought any of it was real and we'd be looking at the world from inside an institution. In my case," he added thoughtfully, "probably a military academy for *troubled teens.*"

Dylan blinked a little, as the others nodded. "Brenda would love it if she could send me to a drug rehab place," Staci said bitterly. "Why do you think I haven't called my father? Why do you think I keep saying I've got nowhere else to go?"

Dylan scratched his head, with a peculiar expression on his face. "Huh," he said finally. "Keighvin might be—" Then he just shook his head.

"Who's Kevin?" Jake asked, sharply.

Dylan shrugged. "Ask me when this is over," he replied cryptically. "So, we've got the tools. Seth, do you think you can rig up a couple of water guns the way you were talking about?"

Seth grinned, as if this was some sort of prank they were planning, and not an assault on a den of killers. "Sure. Me and Jake can buy the powdered caffeine—it'll be less suspicious if we split the purchase between the two of us—and I already have a selection of water guns at my house. Also, enough energy drinks to keep a football team going for a week." He glanced over at the others, thrusting his chin towards the boxes. "Bet you guys never thought all that LARPing was going to come in handy, didja?"

Wanda just rolled her eyes. Jake grinned back a little. Riley bit her lip. "What's LARPing?" Staci asked, now thoroughly confused. This was the second time it had been mentioned.

"Live Action Role-Playing," Seth said, just a little smugly. "We stopped doing it just before you got to town because we lost our ride when Greyhound stopped serving Silence. But you're looking at the Shattered Shield Survivors. Three-time champions, to boot."

"Which means what, exactly?" Staci asked, with just a touch of impatience.

"It means," Jake replied, when Seth looked crestfallen that Staci wasn't impressed, "that the four of us actually *do* know how to swing a sword."

Staci closed the door behind Jake and Riley and put her back against it, staring at Dylan, who was contemplating a slice of reheated pizza in his hand. "This is insane," she said. "There's only six of us! How can we even *think* we have a chance?"

"I've gone through worse odds, and while alone. You ought to give your friends more credit; they're a brave bunch, and they all seem to have good heads on their shoulders. None of this is ideal, but we've got a damn good bit going for us." He walked over to her after setting the pizza back on a plate. "For one, the Blackthornes don't know that we're onto their plan. They know I'm in town, and they know that I'm snooping around, that's certain. But what they *don't* know is that you're helping me. I'm pretty sure they don't know that you've got magic. And they certainly don't know that your friends are going to be helping us, with iron and steel. That's a lot of surprises, and my kind doesn't always do that well with reacting on the fly. We love human innovation for a reason; it's something we can't easily grasp and do ourselves." He turned to lean his shoulder against the door, right next to her. "We've stacked the deck in our hand as much as we can. If it were just you and me...we might have been able to do it. But I would've had serious doubts; doesn't mean we wouldn't have tried, though. It's the right thing to do. With your friends, our chances of success have gone up, big time. It still won't be easy; I'm not *that* much of an optimist. I sure as hell like our chances a lot better now, though."

She couldn't help herself. Tears started leaking out of her eyes. "Dylan, I don't care *what* you thought of that crap that Seth and Jake were telling you, they *don't* know anything about really fighting. I doubt either of them has ever gotten so much as a broken bone doing that LARP stuff, or had anything worse than a papercut! It's all just"—she waved her hands helplessly—"video game fights to them! And if the bad guy cuts off your head, you just go back to the last savepoint!" She started to sob, because after having seen those hitchhikers die right in front of her, having seen the hounds with bloody muzzles, she could all too easily imagine what would happen if Seth went charging at one of the Blackthornes.

He stopped leaning on the door, stepping to the side and in front of her. "Hey," he said, taking her lightly by the shoulders. "It's okay, Staci. This is too much for just about anyone to have to shoulder. You've done better than I could have ever imagined; plenty of people would have cut and run way before now. I've seen it more times than I would care to admit. The fact that you care so much for your friends, and that you're putting their well-being first...that says a hell of a lot about you. Your friends are good people, Staci. I'm going to do my best to make sure they don't get hurt. I promise that, and that we'll do what we can and together we *will* save the town. We're almost there, if you're willing to go the last mile with me." He moved his hands from her shoulders to her face, cradling it firmly but softly at the same time. She felt like his hands were the whole world for a moment.

Could she believe him? He might have kept some things from her, but... *He's never lied to me. And he's been doing this for a long time.* "If something happens to them, I'll never forgive myself," she said, looking up into his eyes. "It's all my fault they're involved."

"It's your fault that they know what they're facing now," he corrected gently. "But they aren't three-year-olds. You laid it all out for them, how dangerous it is. Despite what Seth said, they *did* have a choice. They could have chosen to ignore it, or to run and hide. Those choices wouldn't have helped, but that doesn't mean they couldn't have gone those routes; most people do, when confronted with something like this. They're involved out of their own free will, Staci. You can't control them. You *don't* control them, and you wouldn't want to, would you?"

She shook her head. He was right. She was—maybe—giving them the only shot they had at doing something about the steamroller that was *definitely* going to roll over her, them, and everyone in the town. Wasn't going down fighting better than going down as a victim, if it came to that? But she couldn't help crying anyway. Because it wasn't any of it fair. "Okay," she said, sniffling. "I guess you're right."

"We'll get through this, Staci. Together." She looked up into his eyes, then. The warmth there, so unlike what was in Sean's eyes, flooded into her. Dylan cared, had been fighting alone for so long...but now he had her help. With her help, they could survive, they could win.

And now she was sure of it, as she had never entirely been sure of Sean without his magic working on her. Dylan cared about her. For her. Entirely outside of what she could do *for* him, she meant something to him, something important. Maybe she was the first person he had ever been able to care about in a long, long time.

Still cradling her face in his hands, he wiped her tears away with his thumbs. His eyes became everything for her, right then. Slowly, but deliberately, he leaned in. Their lips met, and all of Staci's fears and worries were forgotten, even if only for a moment. She felt as if she were preparing a spell, all of her emotion and energy rushing into the kiss, giving it a sense of urgency and strength. Dylan's hands fell from her face, and his arms circled around her back. It was the most beautiful and tragic moment that Staci had ever experienced.

CHAPTER TWENTY-TWO

Staci didn't sleep well that night, and woke up feeling anxious and groggy. She thought she had had nightmares; images of fire and screaming and crying all faded into mist as she clawed her way back to consciousness, leaving her with a general feeling of unease. She didn't think it was any sort of spell; she'd been through *that*. Probably just stress and anxiety about what was going to happen crowding her subconscious.

Once the gang had left, Staci and Dylan had some time to themselves. Remembering the kisses that they shared helped a little bit to calm her down; Dylan had been tender, and understanding, and had stayed with her for a few more hours. They didn't talk much after the beginning; he seemed to have understood that she just needed to be held, more than anything, and did just that for her. She didn't have a lot of time to reminisce, unfortunately; there was a long list of things she had to get ready before...

Just say it. The Battle. The Showdown. The Gunfight at the OK Corral. The Big I-Hope-Me-And-My-Friends-Don't-All-Die. This was going to be real, as real as those hitchhikers dying in front of her. It had to be done, everyone agreed on that—however reluctantly—but that didn't change the awfulness of it all, the horror that she was going to have to fight against people that wanted to subjugate and kill her. She wasn't a soldier; she didn't have years of training or anything like that, just a few weeks of practicing magic and almost getting killed, and she had been scared to death through it all. Sometimes anger or something else cut through that fear, but that didn't change the fact that it was there. Dylan had told her that brave people felt fear, and kept going despite it; if that was true, then she and her friends must have been crazy-stupid brave, with how she was feeling.

She couldn't dwell on it. She had to get her own gear ready; Dylan had showed her how to don the armor and adjusted it to fit last night, but she still had to practice getting it off in a hurry. The metal didn't completely negate her magic like it would for Dylan or any other full-blooded elf, but it still severely weakened what she could do. In the beginning of the fight, the hope was that it would keep her a bit more hidden and protected from the Blackthornes, while she and Dylan tried for the Gate. It moved well with her, but it was very heavy, and she wasn't used to wearing it or doffing it. You kind of had to bend over and let its own weight slide it off you because there was no way you could pull it off over your head like a T-shirt. Seconds would likely count when things got hot and heavy. She also had to check in on the others, and make sure everything was going okay with them. The water guns and their special caffeine powder and cola mixture needed to be modified and prepared, which would take time. Plus, the entire group was going to practice using sword, shield, and daggers with Dylan. The absurdity of how they all would probably look struck Staci. *Like a scene out of* Monster Squad *or something.*

But finally, she had done all the prep she could, and there were still hours to go before the group would meet to practice here. And she couldn't put it off any longer. She had to go tell Tim.

Because if everything blew up, she figured he at least deserved a shot at getting out of town before the Blackthornes turned the plague loose. *Cutting and running is probably his speed anyway,* she thought a little bitterly.

She locked the door behind herself—but rather than taking her bike, she decided to walk to the bookstore, trying to work out exactly what she was going to tell him. He was a mage, apparently an experienced one; he *could* help them, maybe. He'd already helped the gang with his bookstore; the protections and magic there had kept them safe—relatively—and helped her to break some of the spell that she had been under. Maybe, if nothing else, they could use the bookstore as a fallback retreat; if they couldn't close the Gate, they could run there and regroup, figure out what to do or how to get as many people as possible out of town. She knew Tim had been hurt, badly; was still hurting. But sometimes there were more important things than what was going on with any one person. She hoped that she could make him see that.

Staci was so immersed in her own thoughts that she almost ran into Wanda just on the other side of the diner. They both yelped in surprise, catching themselves after a moment.

"You scared the hell out of me. I almost peed," said Wanda, holding a hand to the middle of her chest.

"Sorry! I didn't mean to. I guess tonight has all of us on edge." Beth was inside the diner, working; Staci caught her eye and waved to her, the waitress waving back before getting yelled at by her boss. There were actually a good number of customers inside; a shift must have finished at the cannery or something like that. *Gotta remember to get some word to Beth, in case things don't go well tonight. She's one of the good ones.*

"What are you doing down in town?"

Staci looked back to Wanda, then debated with herself for half a moment on telling her. Maybe she could help, since Wanda had known Tim and been coming into his bookstore longer.

"I was going to talk with Tim. Try and see if he would help us with what's going on tonight."

A police cruiser rolled down the road, the officer in the driver's seat eyeing the teens. Both of them looked away, clamming up. *Ears really are everywhere in this town, for the Blackthornes.* Once it was clear that the cop wasn't going to circle back and give them trouble, Staci met Wanda's eyes and the questioning look on her face again.

"Why do you think he could help? I mean, Tim's cool and all, and I'm sure he'd care, but—"

"But he's a mage. He can do magic. His store is protected because of it, even from the bad juju that the Blackthornes can put on people."

"*What?*"

It took a couple of minutes, but Staci explained everything that she knew about Tim, the talk that she had with him at the bookstore that one night, and how she had been bespelled and the way she had shaken it off. Wanda listened with rapt attention, asking very few questions. When it was over, she only had one final thing to ask.

"Can I come with you? Help talk to him? He's a good guy... I can't see him leaving us to the sharks." Wanda looked both eager and determined, and it occurred to Staci that she had been "with" the Bookstore Gang for a *lot* longer than Staci had. Maybe Tim would listen to her when he wouldn't listen to Staci.

"It sure can't hurt," she replied. "Safety in numbers or something."

"Or something," Wanda agreed, and fell into step with her.

The bookstore had no customers when they got there. Tim was at his usual spot on a stool behind the cash register, exactly as if there *wasn't* Impending Doom hanging over the entire town. He seemed utterly immersed in his book, but looked up quickly when the bell over the door jingled.

Wanda reached behind herself and flipped the lock. Then flipped the sign to CLOSED without asking permission. Tim's only reaction was arching an eyebrow after he looked up, putting down the book he was reading and closing it.

"We gotta talk, Tim. Serious stuff. Well, Staci's gotta talk to you." She looked over to Staci, thrusting her chin at her. "Batter up."

Staci took a deep breath, then blew it out in one long gust. "Okay." She spilled it all to Tim; the plan that the Blackthornes had, what she had seen in the warehouse, what she, Dylan, and the gang were planning on doing about it. Then she got to her pitch.

"I need your help. No, *we* need your help. This isn't like before; this is worse, this is urgent. We *know* what they're up to, now. And it's not something that we can hide from. Hell, we don't think that it's possible to run from this; at least not in the long term, when they start doing this same thing franchise-style." Finally, now, she looked at him, really *looked* at him. He was doing his best statue impression. But there was something there, just under the surface . . . She wished there was some magic spell she could do to figure out what he was really thinking; maybe there was, but she just didn't know it yet. Something was . . . roiling inside of him. She seized upon that faint hint of emotion beneath the stony facade. "None of us know what we're doing, besides Dylan. Not really. A day of swinging swords around, a few weeks of practicing baby-elf spells . . . this is life and death, and it might not be enough." She didn't want to dispirit Wanda, but at the same time she wanted to drive home the point that they were in over their heads. "With you helping us out . . ." Staci left the words hanging there.

With you helping us out, maybe we won't be slaughtered. Maybe the town and everyone in it won't die.

Everyone was quiet for a moment. Staci could see Tim working his jaw, as if he was grinding his teeth, the muscles standing out in turn. Finally, he looked at her. She saw that his eyes were shrink-wrapped in tears that wouldn't fall, and that he was gripping the leather-bound book so hard that the cover warped underneath his fingertips. *No. Oh, no, please no . . .*

"You had to drag them into this, didn't you?" It was an accusation, and it was made all the worse by the fact that he never took his eyes off of hers. He was barely in control, now; all the pain, all the shame and rage that she had felt and seen in him before; it was right under the surface, and the slightest thing would bring it bursting forth. This was not how she wanted things to go. "This isn't going to solve anything. Don't you understand that? What you're going to try to do...it'll keep happening, and happening, and then what? Who wins? It's not us. The elves play their games and...we're...*goddamned* game pieces!" The indents in the cover of the book had grown deeper, his fingers burrowing in. Tim was shaking, as if there was something inside of him that had lost a bearing and was vibrating out of synch with the rest of the machine. It looked like he was going to shake himself apart. Then, without another word or outward indication, he regained control. The shaking stopped, he released his grip on the book, and sighed heavily.

"Tim..." Wanda said, reaching out for a second and then thinking better of it. He was back, but this was still dangerous. Neither of them had ever seen him like this.

"It's for nothing. One way, the other. It's nothing. None of you can see that, because you haven't *lived* it yet. And you shouldn't. No one should. Damn that elf for ever coming here. Damn him for ever talking to any of you. He's just as culpable as his cousins, the entire god-awful lot of them."

Tim looked surly, and beaten down. Like he had lost a final battle, and didn't have the strength to do anything but spit at his enemies. He didn't meet their eyes. Until he did, and he locked his eyes on Staci's. "They could have been safe. For a little while longer, at least. But *you* brought them into this. You didn't have a choice. You were in it because of that...*fae*. But you brought them in, too. And now they're right there with you, because of it. No choice, anymore." Every word was spat out like it was acid, cutting to Staci's core. She felt shame, and anger, and a deep want to explain, to exonerate herself.

Wanda tried to do it for her.

"Tim! You don't understand! Staci, she—she tried to tell us off, get us out of it! Yeah, sure, she told us about the whole mess first. She showed us magic," Tim sneered at that, baring his teeth and shaking his head in disgust, but Wanda plowed on. "It was the only way she could get us to see, get us to believe. This is a whole shit sandwich, and even if we didn't know about it, we'd have to take a bite. Surely you can see that, right?"

Tim was silent. He dropped his eyes to the counter, and seemed to be doing his level best to chew the inside of his lips off in consternation.

"Tim..." Staci stepped forward; it was risky, but she felt that she had to, had to break through to him somehow. "Please. We need your help."

He didn't look up to them when he replied. "Sign on the door says that the store is closed. You two should leave. Now."

"Well...do we practice with the armor, or without it?" Staci asked. She had tried to put the confrontation with Tim out of her mind. It was hard...but it wouldn't do any good to dwell on it and, well, that bridge was burned. At least now he knew enough to get himself out of town, and maybe anyone else he could persuade into his car.

The gang had arrived, and now they all stood looking at the pile of heavy, heavy boxes behind the couch.

"With. You'll move differently with it on; best to get as much time in it as possible, get used to it before the main event," Dylan said. After the disastrous meeting with Tim, Staci and Wanda had both retreated back to Staci's house. The rest of the gang showed up a couple of hours later; Jake and Seth had managed to rig up two large water guns, and also brought along enough water pistols—modified to put out a stream at higher pressure, like the big ones—for everyone.

"Okay then," Staci said. "I guess the chainmail is one-size fits most..." She had already picked hers out, and it seemed to be all right. The shirts had shortish sleeves. Hers came to just a little past the elbow. "It's just going to be easier if we unpack the stuff here and take our own down into the basement." They'd all agreed the basement was the place to practice. No chance of being spotted, the ceiling was high enough to swing a sword. Her mother, despite usually keeping the rest of the house in disarray, seemed to have left the basement vaguely organized; what few boxes were in it were stacked neatly along the walls. *Probably doesn't come down here much at all; no wonder it's semi-clean.*

Once everyone had finished moving all of the equipment—except for the jacks—downstairs, Dylan started them on drills. Practicing how to properly hold and position their swords, angle their cuts so that they wouldn't be hitting with the flat of the blade (even though, since the swords were steel, *any* hit would still do a number on elves), and use their bucklers for defense as well as offense. Since they were going to be paired up—Jake and Riley, Wanda and Seth, Dylan and Staci—Jake had the idea that Wanda and Riley ought to be carrying the large water guns. That way, each team would have a good ranged option besides the throwing knives, while whichever team member wasn't carrying one of the larger water guns could help defend their "shooter." Seth must have had a real brainstorm when he'd been working on the guns; each one came with a huge "backpack" that looked like a scuba diver's rig and must have held a total of five or six gallons of his potent caffeine mix.

"My own personal concoction: a pound of concentrated caffeine powder, a bunch of cola, and an energy drink that *normally* is banned here in the States." At the last he just shrugged his shoulders. "Gaming marathons, man; gotta haves me spinach to keep going." Whatever it was, the smell of it was enough to make Staci dizzy; Dylan kept his distance while they were working with the potent witch's brew of anti-elf juice.

Since she and Dylan were going to go straight for the Gate while the others kept the Blackthornes distracted and off balance, Staci only had a water pistol full of the stuff. She and Dylan would need to move fast, which meant they couldn't be weighted down any more than they already were. Staci just hoped that she and Dylan would be able to take out the Gate quickly; every moment that the others were fighting was another chance for them to get hurt. If the Gate could be shut down fast, maybe the Blackthornes would lose their taste for fighting, and just leave. Was that so much to hope for? She just wasn't thinking past that moment. Dylan had sworn that shutting it would weaken them a *lot*. Maybe the shock of suddenly finding themselves with about as much power as Staci had would make them cut and run.

So long as Dylan is there with me, I'll be brave.

She watched him as he took the rest of the group through the ad-hoc training. He never scolded or talked down to them, only gently correcting when necessary and always praising whenever someone did something well. He didn't even get angry when Seth almost clocked him with a wildly swung buckler; just laughed and cracked a light-hearted joke about Seth's "enthusiasm to bash things." The entire gang seemed to have become emboldened since they all first decided to fight. They were visibly determined; only Riley stood out as being subdued during the practice, but it was clearly not that she was less determined than the others, but more that she was still afraid. Staci figured that it was Dylan; his confidence in himself and in them transferred over, gave them energy and enthusiasm. Or at least...willpower.

Clearly, all of them must have gone insane. She most of all. Who would have thought that the fate of an entire town, maybe of the world, rested on the shoulders of a group of geeks and outcasts? In the movies, it would be the well-toned and handsome jocks, along with their drop-dead gorgeous girlfriends, that took out the bad guys and only got a cosmetic and oh-so-manly cut on the cheek for their trouble. Maybe a flesh wound to the arm. But this was real life. A bunch of teenagers that got most of their kicks from playing pen-and-paper role-playing games—or at best, had run around in the woods playing some LARP or another—were now practicing to storm a fortified mansion filled with evil beings bent on murder and suffering.

It's not as if we have any choice, she thought, a little numbly. Numb, because as crazy as it seemed, she was getting inured to the whole situation. *Wanda's right. I'm not the only one who has no choice here. None of us can leave. Or at least, none of us is* willing *to leave.* Because really, what would happen if they actually gave up on their friends and family and tried to make a run for it? Within a day, they'd probably all get picked up by the cops and brought home... or at least, back to Silence. *And then we'd become the next "test batch." Or maybe a set of matching Patient Zeros. Or as lunch for those hounds and Hunters.* She couldn't tell which would be worse. That didn't stop the whole situation from being tragically absurd. Tim's words came back to her, but she quickly dismissed them. She still hurt from that last talk, and didn't want to think about it. She couldn't afford to get angry, or feel anything about Tim right then.

They planned their attack to take place while the Blackthornes were at dinner. Staci knew from her weekend visits that the time never varied by as much as a minute, and Dylan had affirmed that elves tended to be creatures of habit. Wanda had borrowed the family van; by a small miracle that Staci had decided to treat as a good omen, she'd easily gotten permission to take it for the evening. Wanda herself had been shocked; she said she'd only ever gotten the van a handful of times in the past, and only by dint of a lot of begging. They planned to leave the vehicle out of sight, but within running distance. With that in mind, they figured to be in place about fifteen minutes after dinner had started.

But as they gathered up their things and prepared to head upstairs to pack up the vehicle and move out, an unexpected, literal "roadblock" presented itself.

Staci's mom was sitting on the top of the basement stairs, where she had been hidden in the shadows. Her eyes gleamed down at them from the darkness. There was a half-empty liquor bottle at her feet.

"Ma'am—" Seth began, but was silenced by a wave of her hand.

"I need to talk with my daughter. The rest of you can wait outside."

After exchanging a few looks, and getting a nod of assent from Staci, the gang started shuffling up the stairs and past Staci's mother.

"You stay," she said, pointing at Dylan. He stopped walking, coming to a stop next to Staci where he stood firm. Once she heard the front door close, she picked up the bottle that had been at her feet, and walked-stumbled down the stairs. It was very clear, from her state and that of the bottle, that she had been tying one on not long ago. "It's all true, isn't it? Everything you have been talking about?"

There wasn't any recrimination in her voice, which surprised Staci. Just a quiet, almost sad wonder. Staci glanced at Dylan, then looked back to her mother. "All of it. Every word."

Her mother sat down, hard, and began crying quietly. "For so long, I thought I was crazy. I thought that I was going to turn out like my mother, locked up in some loony bin. It was easier when I was drinking; I didn't have to remember, didn't have to see." She looked up at her daughter with eyes shrink-wrapped in tears. "I didn't want to. I lost your father, and he couldn't understand.

I lost you, too. I didn't want you to end up like me, and...and I..." Her sobs grew deeper, wracking her entire body. Staci had never seen her mother like this; she was always the "party girl," always blissfully ignorant or blissfully drunk. The memories of the early years when her mother had been the bright and whimsical woman who had been so wonderful to her flooded back, and she found herself crying, too. She moved to her mother's side, kneeling down and wrapping her arms around the other woman's shoulders.

"Mom, it's okay. You don't have to be sorry. It's okay." She finally understood who her mother was. It was heartbreakingly tragic, and she felt guilty for all of her past feelings of indifference or disgust with her mother. "It'll be okay, I promise."

"Be careful, my precious girl. Please be careful." Slowly, the sobs subsided, and when Staci looked down, she saw that her mother had fallen asleep in her arms. Dylan walked up to the other side of her mother, kneeling down opposite of Staci.

"Let's get her into bed," he whispered. Staci nodded, wiping away some of her tears with her shoulder. Gently, Dylan looped his arms under her mother's knees and arms, then picked her up as if she weighed nothing. They took her upstairs to her room, where Dylan set her on her bed on her side while Staci pulled the covers over her. She had begun snoring ever so lightly, and Staci couldn't help but laugh a little, if only to break the tension and to stop crying. Dylan waited until they were back downstairs in the living room before he spoke.

"She's got elven blood, like you. Not as much, and not...in quite the same way. She can't do magic, for instance. But she has seen things that normal people can't. That's what she was talking about, down there."

"I know," Staci replied, sniffling and wiping her face with the back of her hand. There was more that she wanted to say; she wanted to go back upstairs, lie down in bed with her mother, and talk with her when she woke up. Help her get through it all and let her know that, *really*, it would be okay. That they would make it okay together. But she couldn't, and she knew it and hated that. So instead, she joined Dylan in the living room, where the others were taking the last of the stuff out to Wanda's van. It was down to the jacks actually. They came in small boxes that weighed about five or ten pounds each, and that meant a lot of boxes. The gang was going to take the van as far as the start of the Blackthornes' driveway where it met the road, then wait for Dylan and Staci to come. Dylan was going to scout for the closest spot to safely—if that term could actually be used in this situation—leave the van within sprinting distance of the mansion. Then he'd come back and guide them in.

Seth had just gotten the last of the boxes and was carrying it out while Jake held the door open for him as Dylan and Staci got to the living room. "Everything okay?" Jake asked, uncertainly.

Staci grimaced. "Is *anything* okay?" she replied, rhetorically. "It's as okay as it's going to get," she qualified. "I'll...explain more, later." *If there is a later...*

"Right. See you up there, then," Jake said, and let the door fall closed.

After the van had sped away, Staci turned to Dylan. "So, we're totally doomed, right?"

He regarded her for a moment before grinning. "It's either that, or we kick serious ass. No other way we can go about it. We'll win, or we'll lose. We've prepared as much as we can in this short time, and now it's up to us to do the deed."

"You're way too calm for all of this crap, you know," she said, putting a hand on his chest. "It's annoying."

"I've been told that before." He put his hand over hers, squeezing it lightly. "Truth be told, I'm just as scared as the rest of you. But it doesn't help to show *them* that. We can only do our best, and hope it's good enough to see us through. When you think of it like that, things tend to simplify. It'll be what it'll be, one way or another."

She sighed heavily. "It's even more annoying when you're right. Especially when I don't want you to be."

"We've got to get moving." Metalhead, parked a few yards away, rumbled his agreement with a throaty roar from his engine. "People to see, things to do, catastrophes to avert. Average day." Staci nodded, and they both walked to the elvensteed-motorcycle. They both pulled on helmets—the last thing they needed was to get pulled over for violating helmet laws at this stage. She waited until Dylan was astride the bike, then climbed on the back, hugging him tightly around the waist.

He turned his helmeted head around; she couldn't see his face. But she could hear his voice.

"Okay, babe. Ready to light this candle?" And without waiting for her answer, Metalhead gunned his engine, and they were off.

And all she could think of was . . . *Babe. He called me "babe."*

CHAPTER TWENTY-THREE

The van was waiting just a little way from the gate to the Blackthorne Estate, half hidden by bushes, as Dylan and Staci pulled up. They had made the ride in uncanny silence; without the need to counterfeit that he was a "real" motorcycle, and with *every* need for stealth, Metalhead had made the entire journey with no more noise than the rush of the wind past their helmets.

Staci got off first, followed by Dylan. And as soon as she had...there wasn't a motorcycle there anymore. There was a horse. A gold and black, metallic-looking horse, which nodded once to Dylan, and ran off soundlessly through the gate, fading into nothing as it did so. "Metalhead is going to scout the perimeter," Dylan explained, as Staci stared. "I'm going to look for a good way in." By this time they'd been joined by the rest of the gang, looking...odd...in their chainmail shirts and hoods. "Do you think if you had to, you could sprint from the Blackthorne manor to here?"

"If it gets to the point where that is an option I have to consider, I don't think I'll have a problem with it. Getting chased is great motivation." She knew that from personal experience. Remembering that night in the maze, and the hounds...she wasn't quite getting cold feet, but all of her surety about their chances drained from her.

"All right then. The first thing I want you to do is put a good barrier of those caltrops around the van." Dylan indicated with his hands how wide he wanted the barrier to be. "The last thing we need is for the thing you retreat to turned into a trap."

The gravity of the situation seemed to have settled in on the gang, as well. No one was joking or smiling now; most of them were gripping their weapons and shields with white-knuckled fists. They were all scared, but none of them were backing out, so she supposed that was a good sign. Each of the would-be warriors grabbed a sack of caltrops, and started spreading them out as Dylan had prescribed, leaving space for the tires of the van in the direction that it would have to go if they were forced to run. They would be using some of the caltrops inside of the manor, too, to confuse and hopefully hurt anyone that got near them.

"Will there be some sort of signal when you guys take down the gazebo thingy?" Riley was shifting from foot to foot, staying close to Jake.

"If we take it down, you'll definitely know. It'll be immediately noticeable, both in the bad guys and the entire manor." Staci picked up on the fact that Dylan had said *if*, not *when*. She appreciated that he wasn't feeding the rest of them any bull, but still... not helping with her confidence.

But he looked them over without any hesitation or

doubt in his expression. "All right, wait here. I won't be more than fifteen minutes. I'm going to clear a path for you to get to the mansion, and once we're there, you know what to do."

There was no warning, at least so far as the gang was concerned. One moment Dylan was there, the next—he wasn't. Except Staci could see a sort of shadow-Dylan sprinting towards the wall, leaping for the top, and pulling himself over, to disappear on the other side.

The silence was spooky. Seth startled everyone when he cleared his throat. "Anyone else get the *Return of the Jedi* vibe? Like, on Endor, when they're trying to take out the shield generator?"

"Yeah, except we don't have any muppet cavalry to come save us if we screw the pooch," Wanda responded. Her normal sarcasm wasn't evident; her heart didn't seem into the retort.

"Hey, if we stick to the plan, we'll be okay," Jake said. He nudged Riley with his shoulder, smiling. "Dylan looks like he knows what he's doing. Like Staci said, he's been doing this sort of thing for a long time. And besides . . . it's not like we can back out now."

"Well, we *could*, but then what? We'd end up as hellhound chew toys, or Patient Zero," Seth pointed out before Staci could. He shook his head. "The only way out, is through."

They all fell silent, then. It was already dusk (the Blackthornes ate late) and there should have been lightning bugs and the sounds of crickets. But there was nothing but silence and growing darkness, as if even the insects had taken alarm and hidden. Each passing moment seemed to drag on forever, heightening the tension all of them were feeling. Staci wished they could just get on with it already, before they freaked themselves out too much.

They were all so keyed up that they *all* heard the soft "thud" next to the wall, and all turned as one, weapons raised defensively, as Dylan faded into view again. "Got a corridor in," he said shortly. "First thing, we go over the wall. I'll boost you on this side. Everyone wait right there until we're all over. Follow me." Dylan set off at a trot; with his long stride, the rest of them had to hustle to keep up. It didn't take long for them to reach the wall. "Jake, help me get the others over. I can't touch your armor or weapons, so...be careful." They both began boosting the rest of the gang over the wall, one at a time. Staci was one of the first, so she didn't see how Dylan managed to boost Jake without getting near his armor. Maybe he didn't; all she saw was Jake pulling himself on top of the wall, then letting himself down on the other side, with Dylan following.

"All right. We're going to give you guys three minutes once we hear the festivities. They should be freaked out enough by the steel that they'll be all over the place, at least the more craven of them. That'll keep them spread out, and will give us the best chance to get to the Gate. Spread caltrops if you get cornered. Remember to watch each other's backs when you get in there; don't take any dumb risks, and don't get backed into a corner. Good luck. I would shake on it, but I'm a little allergic to your accessories." A short chuckle rippled through the group, save for Staci. She kept wondering if this was going to be the last time she was going to see any of them.

"You heard the man. Elf. Whatever. Let's get this over with." Wanda, to the surprise of everyone there, was the first to start running. Seth had to double-time it to catch up with her, lugging around his water pistol and the backpack with the feeder line. With a final hug, Jake and Riley trailed behind them.

Staci and Dylan hung back, as was the plan, but it still felt wrong for her to watch her friends run into danger. Especially since it was danger that she had dragged them into. "God, I hope they don't get hurt."

Dylan said nothing. They waited in silence until they heard faint screams and shouts coming from the mansion. Dylan didn't meet her eyes, or otherwise signal her. He just started running. Staci was forced to sprint after him. The front door of the mansion was wide open, and light streamed out of it, but the gang was nowhere in sight.

The armor was heavy, even heavier than it had seemed when she had been practicing in it. She was lagging behind Dylan as he charged in through the front door. He must have magicked up his sword and shield as he ran, because he hadn't had them when he'd begun running, but when he hit the cone of light from the door, he had both. And, incongruously, he was still wearing his motorcycle helmet.

"Stay close to me and keep your head on a swivel," he growled. He was constantly scanning around, sword and shield at the ready. Staci moved closer to him. She could hear shouting and the sound of break- ing glass, things being toppled over, and a couple of high-pitched screams. From the back terrace she saw bright flashes that threw everything into jagged shadows. *Magic. They're fighting back.*

"We've got to hurry! They're outside—"

"Quiet!" Dylan said in a harsh whisper. "Not alone."

They hadn't taken more than three steps when there was a shout from their right. One of the Blackthornes came running at them, swinging two short curved swords above his head. Dylan brought his shield up in time to catch one of the blows, but the second sword cleaved into his helmet. Staci's heart stopped; she thought he must have been dead, until he broke contact with the other elf, shoving him backward with his shield and striking him in the shoulder with its edge. Dylan's helmet fell to the floor as he shook his head; there was a gash on his forehead, but he was otherwise intact. The dark elf smiled at the sight of the blood, and charged in again. They began trading blows, sword against sword, sword against shield. Dylan was staying on the defensive, probing with his sword with back cuts whenever the dark elf attacked; the dark elf was all rage and a flurry of strikes, overextending himself and cutting too far with each swing.

Staci wanted to help, but didn't dare try to enter the melee; she'd probably just get in the way, and get herself or Dylan killed. She was so preoccupied with Dylan's fight that she almost didn't notice the shadow that was creeping towards her from her left. She turned at the last instant to see a female Blackthorne raise a long and ornate dagger, readying it to plunge down into Staci's chest. In one of those surreal moments she had read about when someone was faced with life or death, she pondered the little details; like how she remembered this particular Blackthorne cousin. She was prissy with her table manners at the family dinners, and seemed to be perpetually scowling.

She screamed, throwing up her hands and dropping her own short sword. In that instant, she felt her emotions well up inside of her, a single word—a resounding *NO*. Her hands exploded into light; it wasn't like the other times she had used the flash, though. The light burst in a fireworks spread that kept on looping back from her hands to her armor as fast as a strobe light. It scattered off of her chainmail like a spotlight off of a disco ball, and sent the female elf reeling backwards. Staci knelt down quickly, scrabbling for her sword. The dark elf shook her head as if trying to clear it, then came at Staci again; she was weaving slightly, as if she was drunk or stunned. Staci's fingers finally found the hilt of her sword, and with a shout that sounded suspiciously like a squeak, she brought the sword up just as the dark elf reached her, snarling and wielding her dagger.

The murder left the dark elf's eyes as Staci's sword scored a line of blood across her forearm. Where the sword had touched her, the skin peeled back and blackened, as if she had been touched with a white-hot burning rod. The dark elf fell to the floor screaming and clutching her wounded arm, kicking at the ground to try to push herself away from Staci. *It's like I have an anti-elf light saber.* It was pretty clear to Staci that the female elf wasn't a threat any longer. She looked like she was in utter agony, her only rational thought being "Get away from the pain." She turned to see Dylan pulling his own sword from the chest of the other Blackthorne, the body falling to the floor. He glanced over at her, then the female dark elf, and nodded. There was something very, very different about him since they had arrived. Maybe this was just him with his game face on? He was all business, which made sense, but Staci still felt a jolt, as if she was seeing him without a mask for the first time, and what had been under that mask was...something she didn't, couldn't, understand.

But he was waving at her to follow, and turned to go forward without seeing if she was coming along. Following him a few steps behind, they burst into the living room.

Or rather, what had been the living room.

The windows were shattered, furniture overturned, art smashed. Strangely, three of Blackthornes were staggering around like drunks, oblivious to what was going on around them. The fronts of their shirts were soaked, and their faces were dripping with what was undoubtedly Seth's super-caffeine concoction.

Without missing a beat, Dylan walked calmly forward. Staci caught a glimpse of his eyes for the barest moment; he was emotionless, fixated on the three dark elves. Before she could even say anything, he swung his sword in three, quick slashes. All three of the elves fell, their throats opened by Dylan's sword. Staci was struck speechless by the brutality of it all. It still paled compared to the cold and calculating murders she had witnessed at the hands of the Blackthornes, with the homeless kids and the plague...but even with that horrible act to hold up against, this was awful. She knew, on some level, that maybe it had to be done. That didn't change the fact that she felt sick watching it, now. Once the last of the elves had finished kicking against the floor and lay still, Dylan was about to continue marching toward the back of the house, when there was a rustling sound in a sort of nook off of the living room. There were four of these, bigger than window seats, big enough to hold a sofa and a couple of tables and lamps, and when Staci had last been here, the cousins had used them as places to get a little bit away from the crowds watching movies or playing the video games. This one was just out of sight—and it looked as if someone had overturned the sofa to provide some semblance of a barricade. Dylan was already raising his sword when Staci heard talking from behind the sofa, and recognized the voice.

"Wait! Stop!"

Dylan pulled back at the last moment, his shield hand still on the couch and ready to flip it over and strike. Staci rushed forward, pushing him out of the way; he winced, falling backwards a step from the proximity of her chainmail. She roughly shoved the overturned couch to the side, grunting with the effort. Behind it, she found the person she had heard: Wanda, kneeling next to an unconscious and bleeding Seth. He was still breathing. His chainmail shirt was gone. She was cradling his head in her lap while holding a makeshift bandage against his chest. *Why didn't we make sure all of us had first aid kits of some kind?* Wanda kept on talking to him, telling him to be okay, and how she would hate him forever if he died. It took Staci a moment to realize that there was a third person behind the couch. Tucked against the wall to her left was one of the Blackthorne cousins: Morrigan, the Goth one that had latched onto Wanda during the gang's first visit to the estate. Morrigan was holding some sort of elaborate bow, with an arrow nocked to it. From the look of things, she had been protecting Wanda and Seth with it. Her gaze was riveted on Dylan.

"Dylan ap Gwynnerian ap Griffud," she said calmly, although her voice sounded strained. "Why am I not in the least surprised? I claim sanctuary—"

"Not of—" Dylan began harshly.

"No, I'm not insane. I claim sanctuary of Elfhame Fairgrove and Keighvin Silverhair." Her hands twitched a little, but she didn't raise her bow. "Last I heard, which was only a fortnight ago, you were still allies."

Wanda looked up from Seth, and immediately broke in. "She helped us. Seth got hurt, and I ran out of stuff for my water gun. He wouldn't get back up, and...she dragged us both over here when I got his shirt off. He's gotta wake up..." She didn't cry, but she couldn't look at anyone but Seth after that.

"Dylan, if she's helping us..." Staci reached out, lightly touching Dylan's arm. He didn't quite recoil from her touch, but it was clearly unwelcome, right then. He looked from Staci, to Wanda, and back to Morrigan. After what seemed like an eternity, he slowly lowered his sword.

"If they live, then so do you. Otherwise, you'll share whatever fate becomes of them. Understood, *twp slebog*? You know me, which means you know I'll keep my promises." He thrust his chin towards Wanda and Seth. "Protect them, and you'll have sanctuary."

"Then give us protection for a moment," Morrigan demanded. "If you really want this human boy to live."

"Make it quick. We have a job to do."

Morrigan didn't reply; instead, she put down the bow and arrows, and knelt next to Seth, avoiding Wanda's chainmail. She put one hand over Wanda's, hissing a little, and whispered something Staci couldn't quite make out.

Then there was a whining sound that ramped up in pitch, and a crystal pendant that had been around Morrigan's neck exploded. Wanda and Staci both jumped and yelped, but it seemed that Morrigan had been expecting something of the sort. She stood up, bow and arrow at the ready again. "It's a good thing I like you, humans," she said. "That talisman cost me the better part of a week to make. If it weren't for all the blasted iron all over the place, that spell would have been more powerful."

Staci glanced down at Seth. He was still unconscious, and when Wanda pulled up the wad of fabric she'd been pressing against his chest, there was still a wound there. But it wasn't bleeding anymore, and looked half-healed.

"I hope that's surety for you, Dylan ap Griffud," Morrigan said, putting the arrow back on the string and taking a ready stance. "The boy won't die of that, at least."

"There's still more night to go, Morrigan. And I don't have any more of it to waste on you, for now. Keep them breathing." Reluctantly, Dylan turned and started towards the back of the house. Staci lingered a moment, facing the—former?—Blackthorne cousin.

"Please . . . make sure nothing happens to them."

"Many things I have done, but I am no murderer of children," Morrigan replied. Then she softened a moment. "All that besides, you and Wanda have been better friends to me than my own kin. A change of coat is in order, methinks. The Silverhair is not so harsh in judgment as some others . . . and not so quick to abandon his allies when they are no longer immediately useful." She glanced from Dylan to Staci, then back down again. Staci thought there was something—a warning?—in Morrigan's expression when she said that last. "Go now. I'll keep these two safe. Do the same for yourself."

Staci started to move away, then saw Seth's chainmail shirt discarded a little way away, along with a smear of blood on the carpet. Next to it was one of the leather bags they'd used to hold the jacks. She sprinted over to grab it, then spread out the jacks on the carpet between the alcove that held her friends and the rest of the room. Morrigan flashed her a thumb's-up, as Staci threw the pouch aside and dashed after Dylan, who was heading for the dining room and the patio entrance—and from there, the outside and the maze.

There was a flurry of activity outside. There were easily a dozen Blackthorne cousins, along with servants, running all over the place, most looking like they were confused or terrified or both. Almost none of them paid any mind to Staci and Dylan; any that ventured too close were greeted with Dylan's sword, either the menace of it or an actual slash. A lot of them were staggering rather than running, not as bad as the three inside that Dylan had killed, but looking very confused. Was this the result of the caffeine-saturated stuff from the water guns?

Staci spun around as she heard a crash to their left, followed by more shouting. This wasn't the same panicked sort that she had been hearing since they got close enough to the mansion. This was *fierce*. Dylan had noticed the sound as well, and was moving purposely towards it, clearing the way for her. Through the gaps in the rushing bodies, she saw that there were two figures, their backs against the

swimming pool, being harried by several others. They
were fighting back ferociously.

It took her a moment before she realized it was
Jake and Riley. They were standing side by side, both
staying in the low fighting stances that Dylan had
showed them. Jake was hacking and slashing with his
sword, dancing in and out as he sliced at the nearest
dark elves. Any that he struck fell back, only to be
replaced by more, though the replacements were less
and less bold with every encounter they had with his
sword. Riley, on the other hand, was something else
entirely to behold. She was constantly moving, her
lips pulled back in a snarl, occasionally screaming at
the dark elves. She switched between using her water
gun and throwing knives, first blasting a dark elf with
the super-caffeine mix, then throwing a blade at the
now-staggered Blackthorne. Most of her knives were
landing home, though a few hit at the wrong angle
and did little more than a surface burn where they
hit. Staci's heart skipped when a single, stockily built
Blackthorne bulled through the ranks of his cousins,
raising a war axe high above his head and bringing
it down at Riley. She threw up her water gun at the
last instant, catching the axe blade; a pressurized blast
of the mixture sprayed outwards from the impact
point, mostly splattering the dark elf bruiser. Before
he could even react to that, Riley had dropped the
cracked remains of her water gun and reached into
the pouch at her side. With another scream, she
chucked a handful of the iron caltrops directly at the
dark elf's face; more than a few of them stuck there,
sending the elf screaming to the ground, unable to
even clutch his face in pain. Before any of the others

could press the advantage, she had her backup water pistol up and out of her belt, spraying away.

"We've got to help them! They're—"

"Doing what they're supposed to do. They're distracting most of the trouble, so that we can get to the Gate. Think of *Return of the Jedi*; they're the fleet, we're the strike team. Sooner we do our job, sooner they're safe. If we get bogged down here, we're *all* dead. Let's move."

She felt utterly torn. She knew he was right. It was the plan. It was what they had talked about, practiced for. But that still didn't help her feeling helpless, watching her friends fighting for their lives and having to leave them. Even if it was ultimately to help them, she still felt a wrongness about leaving. They were her friends, and she had made a promise, to herself at least, that they would be safe!

In the end, she found herself following Dylan. He was the voice of experience. Even though he was in some zone of his own, he still made sense; they had to get this over with. The sooner the better, for everyone; especially for her friends. Jake and Riley were doing all right at the moment, but that could change any second. The same went for Wanda and Seth, hiding in the house; even with Morrigan protecting them, there could only be so much that one formerly dark elf could do against several attackers.

He cut—sometimes literally—a path for them to the entrance of the hedge maze. They had to make their way through the injured, the dead and the dying to get to the Gate, and she was dreading that moment when they reached the maze more than anything. Memories bombarded her, memories of that night she had fled through it, terrified. Seeing the Fae drinking blood from the cauldron, the night she had gone through the Gate and been chased by the Hunter's hounds. She pushed all of that down to a deep and dark place inside of her; she could cry and shake and be scared later. She had to control all her emotions, she had to be brave and calm, if she wanted any chance to save her friends.

Staci almost ran into Dylan, he had stopped so suddenly. She immediately saw why he had stopped. Five Blackthornes stood in front of them, weapons drawn and ready...and they were blocking the entrance to the hedge maze. Dylan was good—better than good, he was *phenomenal*—but even with her trying to help, the odds were against them. She didn't have reliable magic while she was wearing her chainmail shirt and carrying the sword and daggers, and it would affect Dylan's magic, too. Sword for sword...they were outmatched. She sensed that Dylan knew this...but just didn't care. *He's going to take them all out... or die trying.* She felt equal parts admiration and horror for him.

Five against two at the entrance to the maze. Both sides seemed to tense, about to spring forward and attack, when both were interrupted by something unexpected. There was a sound in the distance, something carrying over the din of the fighting and assorted chaos on the grounds...and it was growing louder. Something like a growl, guttural and primal, but also...mechanical? Staci realized what it was at the last moment. Everyone's gaze, even the fighters near the swimming pool, was drawn towards the second story of the mansion. There was a light coming from one of the balcony doors. For a split second it became brilliantly bright, a solid rectangle of light. A futuristic motorcycle—all chrome, brushed aluminum, and metallic light blue coloring made it look like some sort of scifi missile on wheels—burst through the balcony door, then the stone railing in a shower of glass and rubble before sailing into the night air. Staci, transfixed, watched as the motorcycle...suddenly wasn't a motorcycle any longer, but a gigantic warhorse, still possessing the same coloring, and now wearing the spiked armor and bridle that she remembered from the first time she had seen the elvensteed. Metalhead touched down just before the line of Blackthornes, kicking up great clods of dirt before he bowled into the dark elves. They barely had time to throw their hands up before they were trampled underfoot or turned into rag dolls after being dashed against the elvensteed's shoulder armor. The clamor immediately resumed now that the spectacle was over. Staci was aware that her jaw had dropped, and closed her mouth quick enough to make her teeth click. Metalhead pawed the dirt for a moment, snorting.

Staci swallowed hard. "Uh, good boy. Good boy, Metalhead." She took a step forward, petting Metalhead's muzzle. Metalhead bent his head and accepted the caress graciously, before backing a few steps and rearing up on his hind hooves. He pawed the air, then dropped to all four feet again and snorted, tossing his head in the direction of the now-open entrance to the maze. Then he was off, charging forward into another crowd of dark elves, the ones converging on the last place Staci had seen Riley and Jake.

She hesitated, but Dylan waved her on to the maze.

"He's going to go help your friends. Don't worry about him; this is *fun* for him." A rush of relief hit her; at least *someone* was going to help her friends! She turned and followed Dylan into the maze.

Staci and Dylan had memorized the layout of the maze prior to getting to the mansion, at least enough so that they could get to the Gate quickly; every second counted, after all. Seth had asked during their planning sessions, "Why not just cut through it?" According to Dylan, it wasn't that easy. Apparently, like everything to do with elves, the maze wasn't just rows of hedges; magic infused into the maze from the Gate kept it from simply being slashed through. He stayed in front, his shield and sword swinging with his arms as they ran. They were almost done with this entire awful ordeal. They just had to get to the Gate, so that she and Dylan could shut it down. She wanted to cry with relief. She was so caught up in concentrating on *getting to the Gate*, that she had run ahead enough that she was abreast of Dylan. She turned her head to look at him, and it probably saved her life. A chilling whisper of wind that was all wrong for the direction they were running brushed through her hair and against her face; Dylan cried out, and she saw that a gigantic spear was actually sticking *through* his manifested shield. They both skidded to a halt; for Staci, it was more like skidding, stumbling, and almost falling flat on her face. Somehow she managed to stay on her feet. They both turned to the direction the spear had come from: a deep shadow in a dead end of the maze.

And then, the assailant stepped out into the light. He was tall, at least eight feet tall, and muscled like a weightlifter. He was dressed in crude clothing made of rough leather hides and furs; a sort of sleeveless tunic that revealed arms crossed with scars and corded with muscle, and some sort of pants wrapped with narrow leather straps to hold them tightly to his legs, and crude leather boots. One hand held a spear with a small shield no bigger than a dinner plate strapped to the back of his hand. The other held a club. His face was hidden in the shadows of a hood. He moved his head back and forth, and she got a glimpse of his face. Just a flash, but the expression on it chilled her to the bone. He looked like a blood-crazed Viking.

She recognized him with a start, though she had only ever seen him at a distance. It was the thing that had been talking with Sean, the night she had gone into the maze. The creature she had mentally tagged as a "Hunter."

"Okay, we're totally running, right?" she said, keeping her eyes on the Hunter.

"No. That's what things like him enjoy; chasing prey." Dylan was also keeping his eyes on the Hunter. "Instead, we'll do *this*—"

Without any other warning, Dylan charged the Hunter, sword in front and cutting at the monster's massive wrists. For his trouble, he had a spear thrust at his chest; due to his forward momentum, he was barely able to knock it to the side and side-step the follow-up blow from the club. He whirled his left arm over his head; his shield dissipated, sending the spear that had been stuck in it flying away—specifically out of reach of the Hunter—before another shield manifested in its place. The two opponents had taken each other's measure. The Hunter was hungry, clearly

savoring the dance to come before the final blow.
Dylan was cold and calculating, circling his opponent
and waiting for his moment to exploit any weakness.
Both of them seemed to have forgotten about Staci.

I am not *the useless girlfriend sidekick, goddamnit!*

Staci stuck her sword in the ground, pulling out
three of the throwing daggers that she was carrying;
she kept two in her off hand, while she sized up her
target and readied the last in her strong hand. She
judged the distance, then wound up and flicked her
wrist at the end of the throw. She hadn't been as good
as Riley in practice, but she wasn't bad, either. The
knife sailed end over end, and landed just about where
she had wanted it to go; she had been intending to
hit the Hunter dead center in its chest, but instead
the dagger lodged in the side of its throat. The fabric
of its hood, pinned to its flesh, grew dark with blood.

"Take that, you bastard!"

She had expected the Hunter to react like the dark
elves; frantic to distance themselves from iron and
steel, the materials burning and charring their flesh
wherever it touched. Surely a wound like that would
have been a death sentence for a normal person, and
especially an elf. The Hunter, however, casually reached
up and pulled the dagger from its neck with its huge
thumb and forefingers, letting it drop to the ground.
Without missing a beat, the Hunter swung and stabbed
at Dylan with his spear. She could see as the hood
flapped back that the wound in the Hunter's neck was
already closing and healing. She gulped and stumbled
back a couple of paces, suddenly grateful he was too
focused on Dylan to have noticed—or cared—where
the knife had come from. What could she do?

Dylan and the Hunter went back to circling each other, probing each others' defenses with strikes and parries. *Think, girl! This thing can heal. It's not weak against iron and steel like elves are. What can you do without getting squashed by that friggin' tree it's swinging around?* The Hunter pressed forward, using the longer reach of its arms and spear to keep Dylan back and on the defensive; anytime he would try to get close—inside of the spear's reach, and thus safe to attack—the Hunter would use its massive club to drive him back, and Dylan had to retreat lest he get crushed. Although they were in a small clearing in the hedge maze, there still wasn't very much room, especially with how large the Hunter was. Dylan was going to have his back pressed against a wall soon enough, and his options would fall away if that happened; he had taught her that much during their fighting practice.

In desperation she tried something...new to her, anyway. One of the new tricks Dylan had tried to teach her, a *levin-bolt*. He'd called it both that and *elfshot*. Seth (was Seth still all right?) had laughed when Dylan had described it and said, "Oh, you mean a magic missile," and Dylan had given him this disgusted snort, before gently correcting him...

She still couldn't pull it off consistently, but what other choice did she have? She stuck out her hand as if her index finger was a magic wand, pointed it at the Hunter's face and *willed* like crazy, whispering, *"Tân!"* because she didn't want to get the Hunter's attention if it didn't work.

But it did, though it was disappointingly small—
The tiny fireball sped towards the Hunter, then

suddenly deflected downward, hit the dagger still lying on the ground, and then bounced up, moving twice as fast as it hit the Hunter in the back of his bicep.

For the first time, the Hunter made a sound. He uttered a brief curse, and spun in place, as if looking for what had struck him from behind. Dylan seized the opportunity, slashing deeply into the Hunter's lower back, then its calves just below the knee, and stabbing once into where a normal man's right kidney would have been. The Hunter spun around, clipping Dylan's shoulder with a backhanded swipe of his club, sending him to the ground in a sprawl. Staci's heart jumped as the Hunter slowly turned around. It knew that the game was over, and was ready to deliver the finishing move. Not just ready, but relishing the moment.

The adrenaline dump helped, but it seemed as if time slowed down for her. She remembered when she had tried magic against the Blackthorne cousin in the mansion. The underpowered *levin-bolt* she had willed into being and shot at the Hunter was here in the maze. In that drawn-out second, her mind screamed to make a connection between the two . . . and then it all snapped into place.

Iron.

Without hesitation, she dropped all of her weapons and then shrugged out of her chainmail shirt, stripping it off despite some of her hair being caught in the links and being ripped out painfully. She swung it over her head for momentum, then flung it as hard as she could. The chainmail shirt landed at the Hunter's feet. It was still distracted, readying its club to crush Dylan. She let her emotion and her inborn magic build up inside of her, focusing her intent on the outcome that she was envisioning. When it felt like she couldn't hold it anymore for fear of bursting, she released all of the energy into what she had come to call her whammy; the spell that Dylan had taught her for knocking anything attacking her for a loop. A magical kick to the *cojones*.

When Staci released all of that pent-up energy, she didn't aim it at the Hunter. Instead, she focused it on the chainmail shirt. The magic struck the metal with lightning speed, and looped back in on itself in faster and faster iterations; each time it looped, it also hit the Hunter. First it was a crackle, like an ice block breaking. The crackle soon became an electrical roar as the looping magic ramped up, feeding back upon itself against the iron and the Hunter. The effects upon the Hunter were immediate; wherever the magic struck, dark furrows were carved out. And though they healed quickly, they were still enough, and piling up fast enough, to drive the Hunter to its knees. No longer was it confident, about to savor a kill. There was fear in its body language, and a muted roar emerged from its throat. There was no doubt; the magic feedback was *hurting* it, and badly. It couldn't even get back to its feet, so strong was the obvious pain it was in.

Dylan recovered with a start. His head jerked up, took in the situation, and then he acted. He pushed himself up from the ground, stood up halfway, then dove forward into a roll that brought him behind the kneeling Hunter. In one smooth stroke, he brought his sword down between the knobby vertebrae at the back of the Hunter's neck, separating its head from its shoulders. Even as the head hit the ground with a meaty thud, the body was still reaching up to grasp the stump of its neck. The Hunter's upper body toppled forward onto the chainmail, the magic still looping back between the Hunter and the iron. Dylan's eyes grew wide, and he threw himself to the side; a moment later, the Hunter's body exploded in a shower of light, steaming bits of gore shooting up into the air. Thankfully, none of it seemed to land on Staci; she had cowered down to the ground just in time.

CHAPTER TWENTY-FOUR

She shrieked and then punched when she felt a hand on her shoulder.

"Ow!" She looked up and saw Dylan rubbing his shoulder with his shield hand. "You throw a mean right, even if you're not looking."

"Sorry! I'm just a little jumpy. You know, with the killer elves and exploding monsters." She grinned sheepishly as he extended a hand to help pull her up.

"About that last part; that was good thinking. Fast thinking, too. I've never seen anyone use iron and magic like that," he said as she settled onto her feet.

"It was a Hail Mary," she responded. "I'm just glad it worked."

Dylan glanced over his shoulder at the smoldering remains of the Hunter before turning back to favor her with a lopsided grin. "Me, too." She felt her cheeks flush slightly; it was the first time since they had started this mission that Dylan had shown her any warmth. Despite the circumstances—the fighting, the death, the dire stakes involved—she couldn't help but respond to any signs of affection she could get from him. She shivered, not altogether unpleasantly, and then decided to think about something else, to keep focused.

"I think the chainmail shirt is a loss," she said. What few pieces she could see glinting in the moonlight were scattered and covered with filth from the dead Hunter. She still had her daggers and sword, however. Now, at least she would have the option to do magic on the fly without it going haywire.

"We need to move," Dylan said, suiting action to words, moving off at a trot without a backward glance. "Unless we get that Gate down, no matter how many wins we get, we'll lose. That's where all the power to make the plague happen is coming from, and if we can't close it, they'll just move up their timetable."

She gulped, ice threading her spine at the reminder of what was at stake. As he sped up, she followed. Though it seemed like hours, it took them less than a minute to reach the center of the maze. The Gate was there, just as she remembered it; it should have looked beautiful, the silvery wood all carved into sinuous and delicate shapes, like lace, with that clear, hard coating over it, making it shiny in the moonlight. But it wasn't beautiful. It glowed with a baleful, sickly blue power, and instead of looking like lacework, the entwined carvings made her think of a nest of snakes made of bone. Poisonous ones, just waiting for you to get close enough to kill you.

It was pretty obvious that *something* had made the Gate get all powered up. Was it the fight? Or—

Then she saw him.

It was Sean . . . Sean in a suit of elaborate, black armor that was out of a fantasy artist's hallucinations.

It just *couldn't* be practical, with all the flares, spikes, demon heads, and other ornaments plastered all over it. And yet she had no doubt it would protect him as well or better than Dylan's streamlined armament.

He was leaning against one of the Gate's four supports, twirling an enormous sword with an upswept crossguard that was stuck point-down into one of the gazebo steps. The sword was as fancy as the armor was, and at least as tall as he was. *Compensating, Sean?* she thought maliciously. He looked up slowly, almost casually, an easy smile spreading on his face as he took the pair in.

"Staci! I didn't know that you'd be bringing company. I think you've missed my calls, lately. I haven't heard from you in so long, and I was getting worried." The only things that moved were his lips and his hand as he spun the sword on its point, his eyes fixed on her and Dylan. It looked almost unreal, how still he was. "Still hobnobbing with the dirt-eaters, Dylan? At least your tastes have improved a little; this one's a mongrel rather than a cavegirl." He slowly raised his off hand, inspecting his nails. "Then again, I've dipped into *that* particular pool a few times, myself. The water isn't quite pristine anymore, if you catch my drift."

Dylan kept his eyes on Sean, but Staci's eyes were drawn to his hands; with his shield hand, Dylan surreptitiously waggled a few of his fingers, motioning for her to move to the left. In their planning, he had taught her that signal, in case it would be inopportune for them to communicate aloud. She started sidestepping left, moving forward a little bit each time; Dylan mirrored her, only moving right.

"Really?" Dylan drawled. "I thought all you ever did

was watch." He was careful in his movements, matching Sean's practiced casual manner; his sword and shield both dipped to his sides, and he walked—albeit slowly, with precisely placed footfalls—as if he were just taking a normal stroll, rather than approaching a deadly enemy.

"I placate my inner voyeur when it suits me. But I *really* enjoy getting down and dirty. Servants, underlings...it gets boring having people do everything for you. For example, right now. I'm going to kill you with my own two hands, in front of your girlfriend. To put it mildly, what happens to her afterwards will be...far less pleasant."

"You ought to be more worried about how badly she'd mess you up, rich kid. One thing your kind always does is overestimate their own...*abilities*, and underestimates their opposition. From what I've seen so far from your *cousins*—the ones that are being mowed down as we stand here—your clan is no exception." Dylan curled his lip into what could only be a sneer. Staci and Dylan were now nearly opposite each other on either side of Sean. That last quip definitely got a reaction from him, however. His head snapped up towards Dylan.

"You *filthy*—"

Sean didn't get a chance to finish his curse. Dylan, quick as a cat and just as silent, charged Sean; his shield out front, his sword tucked behind it in a high guard. Sean was momentarily caught off guard, barely bringing his two-handed sword up in time to block an overhand strike. What struck Staci was how *quickly* he had been able to bring the massive sword up, even with its point stuck into the Gate's step and only one hand on it initially. Now it was time for Dylan to be taken by surprise; just as quickly, Sean slashed and thrust with his sword, driving Dylan back with each blow. He moved with preternatural speed, so fast Staci had trouble following him. The cuts must have been powerful, too; she knew how strong Dylan was, and every time he blocked with his shield or his sword, his arms shook and he yielded with the impacts, sometimes almost enough to drive him to the ground. Even circling around and sidestepping attacks, there was no way that Dylan could keep this up for much longer; every counter he tried was easily swatted away by Sean.

He's a rich kid elf... how is he beating *Dylan, who has been doing this for decades?*

On instinct, Staci unfocused her eyes and stretched her senses out. First, she saw the threads of magic coming through her clothing where her magical cell phone charm was. Then she saw Dylan; streamers of magic coursed off of his sword and his manifested shield, as well as the bright glow of his inborn magic that came from just under the surface of his skin. Finally, her eyes fell on Sean.

It was like staring into a sun made of darkness; that was the only way she could describe it. Thick, black rivers of magical energy flowed from every surface of the Gate to coil around and *through* Sean. Every time he swung his two-handed sword and connected, there was a pulse in the energy.

He's getting magic through the Gate! she realized. And that's when it flashed into her mind... if she could just distract him for a moment, he might lose control of that magic power long enough for Dylan to take him. To kill him.

She pulled her short sword from her belt, readying it in front of her the way Dylan had showed her. She could feel the iron pulling at her magic, distorting it. But could she *use* that? The iron in the blade was trying to pull her magic into it—could she just let it, charge it up as if it was some sort of battery?

Why the hell not?

Staci relaxed; instead of resisting the pull, she fed into it. The sword began to vibrate in her hand; it didn't seem to know what to do with the energy, but was still ready to accept more. She kept going, putting more and more magic into the sword, until she started to see cracks of light appear in the blade, tendrils of magic leaking out. *Now!*

Sean's back was turned. He was pressing his advantage on Dylan, trying to beat him down and finish the fight. She charged as fast as she could, the point of her sword readied in front of her, ready to plunge into the small of Sean's back, where there was a small gap in the armor. When her sword tip was less than a foot away, Sean seemed to sense something; instantly he pivoted and swatted at her blade.

The sword exploded in her hands, the magic released in a blinding shower of sparks and fragments. She felt the hot-needle stings of the shards of sword biting into the skin of her arms and face; luckily, she had closed her eyes a split second before the sword had been destroyed. When she opened her eyes, Sean was staring at her, bewildered, as if he didn't understand what had just happened. The look of confusion became one of unmitigated rage, and he kicked at her. Staci barely got her arms up in time before the hit came.

His foot hit her left forearm. She could hear the

bones break in her arm, but it happened so fast that she didn't have time to register pain as she was sailing through the air. The pain did come, however, when she landed on the ground, all of the air driven from her lungs. She couldn't breathe! No matter how hard she tried to suck in air, nothing was happening and her lungs as well as her left arm were on fire. It felt as if she was dying, and panic swept through her for a moment.

Then, just as her vision started to get dark around the edges, suddenly, she was able to gasp in a breath. She cradled her left arm in her right, kneeling, crouched over, just concentrating on breathing.

It couldn't have taken longer than ten seconds, from being kicked to being able to breathe again; it had felt like an eternity. Still forcing air in and out of her lungs one gulp at a time, she looked up. Sean was still watching her, his sneer of disgust and puzzlement marring his face so that he looked like some sort of medieval gargoyle. Dylan chose that moment to act.

The light within him just amped up over the course of a few seconds until Staci could scarcely look at him. Then he thrust out his right hand, palm facing Sean, as if he was shoving at Sean's chest. And even though Sean was several feet away from him, at that moment, it looked as if he had been hit by a hurricane-force wind. He staggered back a pace or two, his pupils dilating then contracting again. He looked shocked, then his face set into a fierce glare as he tried to fight against whatever it was that Dylan was throwing at him.

But even though he set his feet, he was pushed back, his feet plowing two furrows in the earth. Dylan's power began to pulse, and with each pulsation, Sean was forced back a little more.

And then, as Dylan let loose with a final pulse of power; his "light" cut off abruptly. Sean staggered back a few more paces, then stumbled forward as the force cut off.

Sean was far enough away from Dylan, now. Reaching into a jacket pocket first, Dylan threw something at the gazebo.

It looked like a gilded starfish, or some type of ninja throwing star encrusted with jewels. Even though Dylan had thrown the object with deadly accuracy and speed, it changed constantly, or so it seemed to her vision. It was made specifically to not just close the Gate, but destroy it, *permanently*. She held her breath as it sailed end over end, changing constantly—

—and then exploded to pieces as the edge of Sean's sword cleft through it, releasing the magic within in a small pyrotechnic display.

Sean leaned on his sword, panting a little, but grinning nastily. "That was *it*? That was your big play? A black market *relic*? How anticlimactic. It's even going to be disappointing to kill you."

Dylan, clearly deflated from his failure, regained some of his composure. He settled into a defensive stance, sword and shield up and at the ready. She saw something in his eyes, a kind of surety and resolve. *Oh, no. No, no, no. He's ready to die fighting.* Her mind scrambled for some solution, any way she could prevent the inevitable. Sean stalked towards Dylan, his sword raised high above his head; there was no fear or hesitation there, as if the coming strike was a foregone conclusion. And it probably was; with all of the power that Sean was drawing from the Gate, he was more than a match for the more experienced Dylan. She couldn't attack him again; she probably *would* die if she attempted that again, with how hurt she already was—and she already knew she wouldn't succeed in doing anything but distract him briefly. She innately knew that if she tried to hit him with magic, the result would be the same; he was too supercharged.

Supercharged. Like my sword was. Like my chain-mail shirt.

Every little movement pained her, but she pulled one of her last daggers from her belt. Biting down on the blade, she undid the leather belt and threw it, along with the rest of her iron weaponry, to the side. Her left arm was tucked against her breast; it seemed to throb with her every heartbeat, but she ignored the intense pain. She readied her dagger in her one good hand, awkwardly shuffling the grip around until she was holding it in a reverse grip, with the point down. She moved as quickly as she could towards the Gate, her whole body aching.

As she neared the Gate, she was met by a wall of crackling, blue-white energy that rose up around her, as if she was on the inside of one of those lightning globes her mom had had until a stoned boyfriend broke it. The tendrils of lightning converged on her, making her eyes water with pain where they hit her and danced across the surface of her skin. Her hair stood out all over her head as if she was holding an electrode, and she whimpered as the crackling tendrils continued to lash her. But she pushed forward anyway.

Every step was agony, and it felt as if she was barely in control of her own body. Through the haze of pain, she saw that she was close to the Gate. The same dark magical energy that was flowing to Sean trickled from the Gate and licked at her in dark eddies of current, caressing her skin. With a fierce yell, she raised the dagger above her head, bringing it down as hard as she could into the post nearest her.

Whatever sort of energy field she had stepped into immediately faded away. Her dagger, however, had taken on the same sort of look that her sword had. This time the energy seeping through the cracks was dark. Instinctively, Staci knew she had to add energy to it, otherwise the dagger would be destroyed. She knew that she couldn't suffer through trying to get another piece of iron stuck into the Gate. She focused everything she had felt and experienced since she had come to Silence—all of the fear, the anger, the acceptance, even the love—into the blade, pouring her own magical energy into it. In starts, the energy coming through the blade started to turn light, then golden, until it blazed through, banishing the dark energy in the surrounding area.

It's working!

Staci was almost startled enough to let go of the knife when she felt not just the energy she was pouring into it pass through her, but also even more energy being drawn from her. The Gate and the iron of the dagger were sucking her energy, even her very life-force, away from her. Everything was going dark for her. She was aware of Dylan and Sean, still fighting, in the periphery of her vision. Dylan's shield was completely gone, and he was clearly injured. Sean was readying a final downward thrust that Dylan couldn't possibly defend against.

Staci screamed. The last of her energy, all of her emotion and magic bundled up into one final exclamation, thrust into the blade, and then the Gate, in a burst. There was a shock wave that threw all three of them to the ground. Staci tumbled backwards bonelessly before landing on her back. The angle she had landed at allowed her to see the Gate, her head lolling to the side. The dark energy had been completely dispelled, and the entire structure of the Gate looked as her sword had; great seams and cracks ran along its structure, with golden light pouring out of it, illuminating the entire clearing. With a deafening roar, the Gate exploded, gold and black flames dancing out in all directions. Her dagger and the post that she had stabbed it into were the only parts left standing of the Gate. Both had turned charcoal black, carbonized and smoking in place.

Slowly, her gaze tracked to Sean and Dylan. Sean was on his knees; his sword was in pieces; he was still grasping the hilt, the barest sliver of the blade planted in the grass. His armor was ruined; it was cracked in much the same way her sword and the Gate had been, with smoke seeping through the cracks. His once perfect hair and skin were burnt and smudged, and his eyes were vacant and unseeing. He looked hollow.

Dylan, who had been laid out facedown, raised himself up. He took in the scene for a moment as he came to his feet. Deliberately, he bent down, retrieving his sword. Without uttering a word, he limped up to Sean, placing his left hand on the dark elf's shoulder. Then, while looking him in the eyes, Dylan slowly pushed his sword through Sean's breastbone and out his back. Sean could only offer a single gasp before he slid off of the sword and onto the ground, dead.

Staci couldn't move; she was fighting for every breath. Everything hurt, and what didn't hurt, felt as if it didn't work anymore. Dylan sheathed his sword, and limped over to her, looking down at her impassively. "Well," he said finally. "You did it. You really did it. Damn. Well, time for me to go." He started to turn to leave.

Staci fought for breath, fought to say something, and couldn't get anything out. What did he mean, *Time for him to go?* "But—why?" she choked out.

He turned back. And for the first time she saw something other than anger or a devil-may-care expression on his face. It looked as if he was fighting with a myriad of emotions. He opened his mouth to speak, then shut it quickly. Finally, his shoulders sagged; something had changed, and he had made a decision. "I was just going to keep walking. To leave you and let it break like that, hard and clean. But...I owed you more than that. I'm leaving because what you want out of me will never work. It never has, and it never will. Elves and humans...you live and die in less than a couple years, so far as we are concerned. I'll look like this when you're a wrinkled old woman. And then what? And what about the years in between, when first people think I'm your boytoy, and then I'm your son, and then your grandson? I already know how you'd take that, because I've seen it before. Before it was over, you'd hate me, loathe me, blame me for bringing all this on you. So hey, now I'm just part of Staci's Big Adventure. Leave it that way, kid. We're both better off. You don't want to follow me where I'm going; there's still more Unseleighe. And I'm not through with them."

In that moment, Metalhead pulled up next to him. He threw his leg over the motorcycle...and roared off.

Staci felt her heart break in that moment. She had saved her friends—she couldn't hear any more fighting or screaming in the distance—and saved the town. Even saved Dylan from being killed by Sean. In the end...he had deserted her, as if everything they had shared had meant nothing to him. She wanted to curl up into a ball and sob, but she didn't have the energy to do even that. Instead, she stayed on her back, tears streaming down the side of her face in silence save for the labored breaths she was barely able to manage.

She didn't know how long she was there, lying on her back in the clearing. She had closed her eyes for a moment, and when she opened them...Finn was staring back at her. He was standing over her, grinning horribly. There was a manic look in his eyes, as if he was on the verge of hysteria. The rest of him looked like it had been put through the wringer; half of his face was smeared with blood, his hair matted down by it. There were cuts and burns on the rest of his body, and his right arm hung limp at his side.

"I *knew* that Sean wanted you as more than a plaything, you little *bitch*. I was going to steal you at one point and use all that tasty power of yours for myself, or maim you in ways that would make him not want you anymore, and then claim you anyway. But, no. You shacked up with *him*"—he huffed out the word, looking up in the direction that Dylan had gone—"and ruined everything. The Gate is closed, Bradan locked in Underhill and no way to open it. The clan is sundered. You helped kill Sean, which I must thank you for...but you have *destroyed* what was rightfully *mine*! I'm going to kill you, now. I must say, I've been waiting a long time to do this—"

She sobbed in terror; but then the sobs stuck in her throat, as movement in the air above Finn's head made her wonder what new horror was coming. The air seemed to solidify into a mesh, like a—net?

Then, without warning, even as Finn slowly pulled a dagger from his belt, relishing the fear in her face, the mesh fell on him. Before she could blink, it had covered him from head to toe, contracting instantly and holding him imprisoned, with a wider stretch plastered across his mouth like duct tape.

Somehow, he didn't fall, but he twitched in place as he struggled against his prison, his movements growing more frantic as the meshes of the net started to glow with power.

She smelled...burning. Burning hair, burning fabric. And burning flesh. The net was *burning* Finn, and he first whimpered, then tried to scream, as the burning mesh ate into him, flesh and fabric charring as if the net was made of white-hot strands of metal. And as it burned, it contracted, and the fabric of his clothing began to catch fire.

A heartbeat later, and where Finn had been standing was a man-shaped tower of flame, still writhing, still trying to scream.

Then the tower stopped moving and fell over, but it continued burning, burning with the terrible, sweet smell of cooking flesh, until finally there was nothing on the grass but a smear of greasy char.

Staci's vision was starting to contract, going dark at the edges. Whatever was coming, it was powerful;

even without the benefit of her vision, she could *feel* the magic emanating from it. She almost wanted to give up, just let whatever had killed Finn kill her, too. She wouldn't have to think about Dylan, think about him leaving her. The betrayal. But . . . there was a tiny voice inside of her that still told her *Fight.* Feebly, she tried to roll onto her side, the pain in her shattered arm screaming through her all the while; maybe if she could reach a dagger, she would be able to do something.

She was aware that someone was kneeling next to her. Still she tried to move, do anything, even though her body barely responded. Finally, she was able to bring her right arm up; a final gesture, she thought, before the end came. The figure next to her didn't kill her, however; instead, it gently took her hand into its hands. There was a pause, and then she felt . . . light flowing into her through her hand. Not just light, but *life.* It took her body a moment, but it recognized the energy, and she started when the darkness pushed back from the edges of her vision. The figure was still blurry, but dropped one of its hands to cradle her shoulders, lifting her up.

"Take it easy, kiddo. You've had a rough night."

That voice . . . she knew it, and her mind struggled through memory and the haze of pain to attach meaning to it. Then her vision cleared. The leather jacket. The pale skin from spending too much time indoors. The full beard, full of salt and pepper, surrounding the same understanding smile. The leather jacket. And finally the gray eyes.

It was Tim.

❖   ❖   ❖

"Bye, Staci; 'Night, Tim!"

"Don't forget we're starting the Steampunk game Thursday."

The gang filed out of the bookstore, making their farewells as if the fight up at the Blackthorne Estate hadn't happened, as if Seth wasn't still favoring his right side, Riley wasn't limping, as if Staci herself wasn't walking gingerly with her left arm in a cast and sling, with the cuts and burns on her face and arms.

Impossible as it seemed, the entire town had accepted the explanation that "multiple propane tanks" on the Blackthorne Estate had exploded, causing a "tragic fire" that had killed everyone there. Certainly, the buildings had burned down; in fact, as Tim had collected Staci and carried her to Wanda's van where he'd managed to herd up the others, the fires had already started. From the satisfied look on Tim's face, she suspected he might have personally helped those fires along.

Tim had taken Staci to the ER himself, once they all got back to town. The doctors had simply taken his word for it that he'd found her at the side of the road when he'd gone up to see if he could help with the fires. "Don't say anything," he'd told her. "You're in shock. You don't remember anything."

That part had been easy enough for her; she genuinely had felt like she was in shock, and not remembering felt much better than remembering. So, she played dumb. The cops that interviewed her, while initially skeptical, soon caved in and took her statement at face value. Besides, there was no one left to argue the point. And it wasn't as if they were going to think she was some kind of cross between MacGyver and the Girlfriend from Hell and had gone ballistic over something "her boyfriend" Sean had said or done and blown up the place herself. She was the Dumb Chick from New York City, who just happened to be dating the Silence version of Richie Rich. That suited her fine, even though that hadn't been the truth for a good long while.

The last couple of weeks had taken on the same surreal feeling she had had when she first started out in Silence. Meeting Sean, meeting Dylan, learning about Red Caps and Hunters and all sorts of other horrors that go bump in the night . . . and sometimes the day. Her mother was doing better, tapering off on the booze and bad boyfriends, though nowhere near fully recovered. The whole town was much the same way, as if her mother was some sort of barometer; ragged, broken in all sorts of ways, but slowly rebuilding itself, hopefully. Time would tell. All of the industries and businesses involved with the Blackthornes were in legal turmoil, but the general consensus was that it would be sorted out, one way or the other. There was talk of a company from back East that had eyes on Silence—Fairgrove Industries. Tim had cautiously mentioned them, and the name was familiar to her from something Dylan had said. It seemed they didn't completely fall under his umbrella of "all elves are crap." And so life marched on, returning to a new sort of normal for Silence.

Tim came over to her with a steaming cup of coffee; from the smell and the look of it, it was fixed just the way that she liked it, with a liberal dollop of real cream and a spoon of sugar. He set it down in front of her, and she accepted it with a smile; he sat across from her, cradling his own mug in his hands.

"They seem to be doing well," he said, throwing his head back slightly towards the door.

Staci cooled her coffee before taking a sip, smiling and nodding as she swallowed. "I think they are. They will be. It's weird, but even with all of the awful crap we all went through, all the death, the killing, the sheer screwed-upness of it all, it's brought them—us— together even more. Not quite like a shared secret, but just... something we've gone through *together*, and that makes it better, somehow."

"Burdens and joys shared are lessened and magnified, in turn. In other words, it's good to have friends."

"It is." Then, after another sip of coffee, she spoke again, with more conviction. "It really is." She had learned so much about herself, more than she had even thought that she had before the assault on the Blackthorne Estate. And she knew that she couldn't have done it without the help of the gang, and, at the end, without the help of Tim, whom she had almost written off as a coward. Yet, when she had been abandoned by the one person she thought that she could finally love, it was Tim who had come to help her. From what she had heard from the rest of the gang, he had singlehandedly destroyed over a dozen dark elves and other creatures, all on his own. She had witnessed what she had done to Finn, whom she had feared for so long. It surprised her; not only what he was capable of, but that he had actually committed to a decision that she had thought he was opposed to entirely.

"I guess the question is, what do you plan to do now? School should be starting up again pretty soon. Are you going to stay in Silence?"

"Well," she said slowly, "I'm still in the same situation I was before. I've got nowhere else to go. But honestly, even if I did, I'd still rather be here. I've got real friends, not fake ones that only care about shopping and that shit. Even if my mom isn't capable of finding a decent boyfriend with a map to the clue machine, as long as she stays sober enough to keep her job, we can probably keep getting by." She grimaced. "Plus, there's always blackmail power with Dad if we need something, and you know, I don't think it's wrong to use it. And there are still things I can do here. Things I can learn."

That earned her an arched eyebrow from Tim. "Oh?"

She leveled a straight gaze at him. "You *are* going to teach me about magic. Right?"

He regarded her for a moment, swirling his coffee around in his mug before setting it down on the table between them. "Yes. If that's what you want, I will teach you about magic. Everything that I know. But, I'll warn you now, Staci. It's not an easy path. And it's not safe, even discarding external threats. Magic is knowledge. Knowledge is power. And power is very dangerous, even in the right hands. Are you sure that that is what you want?"

"So? Having it and not knowing how to use it didn't work out all that well either," she pointed out.

"I think we're in agreement on that point. Power without control isn't effective. What I'll be teaching you will take monumental control, intense concentration and indomitable willpower. I just want to make sure that you feel ready; once we get started, it's not going to be so easy to turn back." She could tell that there was something else behind Tim's words. Expectation. Even a hint of a smile at the corners of his mouth.

"Just one thing," Staci said. "Something I want out of *you*."

"I promise nothing, but will allow for damn near anything. Shoot."

She grinned. "If I'm gonna have all this stuff to learn, so should you. So, you have to join Seth's game."

It was Tim's turn to grin, wide enough to show his teeth. "Poor boy won't know what hit him. My pen and paper, dice and rule table pedigree is quite good, I assure you. I accept, if you do, *mageling*." He reached down for his mug of coffee, bringing it up for a toast.

She clinked mugs with him. "It's a deal."

"I'm going to warn you, we've got our hands full. Even besides dealing with your education. Not all of the Blackthornes were accounted for; a fair number escaped. Though they won't be able to achieve the same level of power they had through their connection to the Gate, they'll still be dangerous. There are other avenues of power, after all. Not to mention all of the...creatures they summoned to themselves. Red Caps and Hunters are but a fraction of what they drew to Silence, and many of those same things are lurking nearby. Without the Blackthorne clan to cow them into submission, things could be getting awfully interesting soon, and not in a good way. That'll fall on us to deal with."

"So we deal with it," she replied. "With the help of our friends. Right?"

"I think—no, I *know*—that you're right. I lost sight of it for a long time. Too long, in all honesty. But I think that you and I are of the same mind on this. Then it's settled? I'll teach you, you'll learn, and we'll fight the good fight with the help of our friends, against all challengers?"

She nodded, and felt as if her life had suddenly *settled* into something she wanted it to be. Not drifting back and forth, without any true direction. This was something she felt to her bones. Something righteous, and not just that, but *Right*. "It's a deal."